Susan White is a doctor and a writer living on Wurundjeri land in Northcote, Melbourne. As a clinical geneticist, Susan hunts for answers to undiagnosed genetic conditions in children. Her young adult novel, *Take the Shot*, was published in 2019 and nominated for several literary awards. Shortlisted for the *Kill Your Darlings* Unpublished Manuscript Award in 2017, *Cut* is her first work of adult fiction.

C
U
T

Susan White

affirm press

affirm press

First published by Affirm Press in 2022
Boon Wurrung Country
28 Thistlethwaite Street
South Melbourne VIC 3205
affirmpress.com.au

10 9 8 7 6 5 4 3 2 1

Text copyright © Susan White, 2022
All rights reserved. No part of this publication may be reproduced without prior written permission from the publisher.

A catalogue record for this book is available from the National Library of Australia

ISBN: 9781922806383 (paperback)

Cover design by Sandy Cull © Affirm Press
Cover image by Ildiko Neer/Trevillion Images
Typeset in Garamond Premier Pro 12/17 by J&M Typesetting
Proudly printed and bound in Australia by McPherson's Printing Group

MIX
Paper | Supporting responsible forestry
FSC® C001695

Content note: This book contains depictions of sexual harassment and sexual assault.

For all sisters who seek to heal

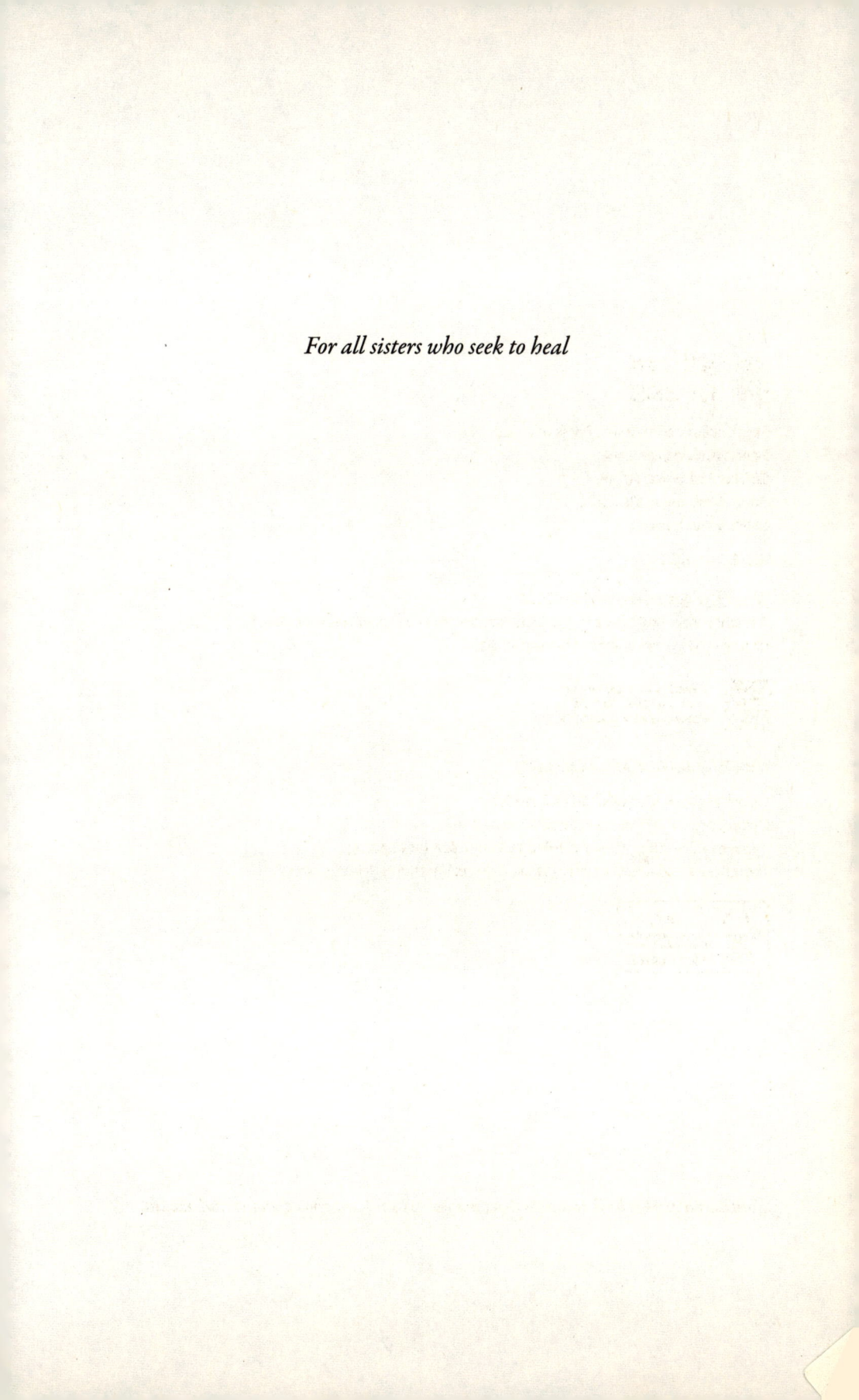

AFTER

I can only tell it sideways. The memory constantly shifts its shape.

I find a set of scrubs scrunched into a ball in the bottom of my wardrobe. In the pocket, a souvenired scalpel, the blade still wrapped in plastic.

I peel back the packaging and connect the blade to the holder, the metal cool and smooth in my hand.

What my hand remembers – an incision on virgin skin, the exhilarating excision of malignancy, the satisfying draining of a tense, pointed abscess.

The scalpel might remember a surgeon waving the bloodied tip at a nurse when he wasn't happy with the lighting or the diathermy or how much sex he was not getting.

The scalpel would recognise the rhythm of Verdi's Requiem and the tremor in my grip after Liv's first surgery. I wouldn't need to explain the whole messy picture – the scalpel *knew*.

In the mirror, I catch a glimpse of myself, holding the scalpel. I remember hearing its voice as we stood over Liv's paralysed body: *cut with care.*

I know the way.

It's through the darkness.

~

It is the night of the gala, 9 July. The ceiling is low, the walls lean in. I need light, I want light, but darkness surrounds me, pressing into my back and arms and legs, pinning me here to the floor. I become aware of a word pulsing in my head, *run, run, run*, but my legs won't move, and when I open my mouth to scream, my voice is a hoarse, empty nothing.

The hospital carpet smells of disinfectant and ambition. I want to get away from that smell. I scrabble on all fours, this way and that. I don't know where I am.

My fingers find a wall, and on the wall is a switch, and flicking the switch brings light. I sit, back against the wall, breathing hard. Fluorescent light buzzes above me, and I glance around, gaining my bearings. I'm in the hallway outside Prof's office on the sixth floor of Prince Charles Hospital.

How did I get here?

The hall is empty, but its shadows hold secrets, and I can't move but I can't stay. My breath comes in shallow gasps, and I try to slow it.

They are long gone, I tell myself.

I stand on shaky legs. My body feels stunned; my brain refuses to process. Ignoring the stairwell, I take stuttering steps towards the glinting steel doors of the lift, crossing another empty hallway, my heart pounding at the shadows.

I'm a surgeon, who can't operate. I'm a victim, of possibly the oldest crime.

This must be told, and I must say it.

Only then, perhaps, will I find a way through.

BEFORE
Infusion

the introduction of a solution into a vein, artery or tissue

November 2014

Early on the first Monday in November, I jogged up the path by the zoo. Against the dull thud of my feet on the asphalt, everything felt sharp – the scent of eucalyptus mixed with elephant shit, the alarm-bell piping of bell miners, the whine of a tram straining up the hill.

At first, the hospital was a tiny red blob beneath a massive cloudless sky, a buoy on the horizon. But as I ascended the hill, it grew larger, engulfing land and sky, its main building tall and straight like a pointed finger, the others herniating from it higgledy-piggledy. When I reached the rise, the gum trees and zoo fell away behind me, and the hospital was all I could see.

And then, as I skipped up the steps, past the gowned patients sucking the life out of their first cigarette, I could *feel* it – wisdom and authority cemented in the red bricks and cream mortar.

Blood thrummed in my temple. Thoughts circled and whispered and wondered –

Is *this* the day?

I showered in the change rooms and dressed in my work clothes, checking myself in the mirror, liking the way my skirt skimmed over my hips. That morning, I'd considered the row of neatly hung pencil skirts in my wardrobe. Charcoal? Olive?

Olive, for the rich colour. And for the way this skirt turns heads. Nothing wrong with putting your best foot forward, right? Especially when you're summonsed by your boss.

I climbed the stairs to six, walked the hall, knocked on his door.

The olive skirt made a statement. A bold one.

Maybe charcoal would have been better?

He called me in.

Prof sat at his desk, writing, his head of wavy silver hair bent over the page. I took a seat opposite him, sitting on my hands.

The run had woken me up, but as soon as I sat, fatigue bit at my eyes. I had snatched only a few hours' sleep between cases on the weekend – five, max. Through the window I watched dog-walkers, cyclists and joggers cross the park on paths fringed by opalescent gums and Moreton Bay figs, and my armpits prickled with sweat.

I sat, while he wrote – God knows what – aware of the way his presence filled the room. I both craved and dreaded the moment he would fix his gaze on me. I'd seen it drill holes in residents and medical students, his gravelly voice stripping bare defences and excuses, revealing weaknesses as soft as skin that had never seen the sun.

Among the junior doctors, he was feared and revered. The word *bully* sometimes fell from surly lips, but though he could be tough, I didn't see it. He was the one the other doctors called on when they were sick, and if I needed a surgeon, I'd want *him*, hands down.

Maybe what filled the room was power. His word could make or break careers. When I was with him, I sometimes caught myself searching for a sign of approval – a tilt of his head, or a smoothing of his frown.

A smile?

No, too much.

He kept writing as if I weren't there, and I wondered how he saw me – how he judged *my* ability to impact a room. It's harder to command a room from a height of five foot two. I worked with what I had, choosing well-cut clothes that flattered my small frame, but my olive skin, almost-black hair, and di Pieta nose stood out in this sea of navy suits and alabaster complexions like a European handbag at the football. That's before we even got to my sex. My impact on a room was: what is *she* doing here?

The boys' club had Prince Charles Hospital firmly in its grip.

Eventually he put down his silver pen and the furrows in his forehead softened as he looked at me. 'I've heard good things,' he said, and his deep voice took *good things* from hearsay and made it so.

Good things. My breath turned shallow, waiting on his words.

'The laparotomy you did with Phil. He was impressed.' He leant back in his chair. 'I'd like to see you step up, take responsibility. We need to know you can handle that.'

I was up for it, no doubt, but – did they issue the same challenge to Toby? I pushed the thought away. *Good things*, he'd said. Hearing those words brought forth *the* question, the one I'd cocooned inside me every time I assisted him in theatre, every late night and each weekend on-call, the one I'd carried this morning up the hill and into the hospital and up the stairs and into this room.

'Prof, is there any progress – on a consultant post?'

His tight smile conveyed I'd overstepped. 'Nothing yet.'

My hopes deflated like a punctured tyre. He never liked to be rushed, I should have known that! But when – when would I know? I'd been working towards this job for ten years. Goddamn Benson, would he ever retire?

'Rest assured, when there is a job, I expect you will apply.'

Over the Moreton Bay figs, I glimpsed a pale morning moon. 'I will.'

'Good. Now, I'm due in theatre next Tuesday but I have a competing commitment. Will you start for me? Should be straightforward, mastectomy, I believe. I'll join you by nine or so.'

This was a sign, Prof delegating to me. I nodded and made a note in my calendar, feeling every bit the swotty schoolkid chosen to collect the lunch orders.

'Toby will be assisting.'

Gold. Pure gold. I smiled on the inside.

'And could you check on Mrs Greenidge today? An intern called, something about her platelets dropping.'

He was entrusting me with his most precious long-stayer, who painted her brave smile in coral lipstick while bacteria ate away her pelvis.

'I'll see her this morning.'

I'd postpone my teaching session. Sleep would have to wait.

I'd do anything.

~

By Thursday a blustery cool change had blown through, and I wore a light trench coat over my pencil skirt – classic black today – when I met Toby, Will and Hamish for breakfast on Errol Street.

Our cafe was a converted warehouse with exposed beams and tattooed waiters. We stood out in our suits, but we liked the feel of the place and the coffee was the best in North Melbourne.

I slid into the seat next to Hamish. His bald head caught the light as he hunched over his Blackberry, mouthing as he typed. Across the table, Will greeted me with a smile and then mimicked the oblivious Hamish's moving lips and fast fingers, drawing a grin from Toby.

I stole a glance at Toby. Thighs splayed, he sat on the edge of his chair like he had somewhere he needed to be. His shirt was the colour of an early spring sky, and I had the urge to lean close and smell the money in his aftershave, and brush my fingers along the angle of his clean-shaven jaw –

And kiss him, slow, on the mouth.

Instead, I ordered an espresso.

Will asked if anyone had news. 'How about consultant jobs – any updates?'

I shrugged. As a consultant, wouldn't Will know any news before me and Toby? I searched Will's face and then Toby's for secrets but found none.

'Rumour is Benson will finish this year,' Will said. 'He must be at least sixty-five. I went to his sixtieth at the club years back.'

Hamish glanced up. 'Sixty-three, I believe,' he said, and no one argued.

'Surely it'll be soon, then,' Will said.

Toby snorted. 'Benson will go on forever. He'll probably cark it at the table.'

'Doing the world's slowest colectomy while he flirts with the nurses,' Will added, laughing at his own joke.

An oily queasiness filled my pelvis.

Will looked from me to Toby. 'When it actually happens, I take it you'll both apply?'

I sat up tall, met his eye and said of course.

'You bet,' Toby added.

'Excellent,' Will said, raising an eyebrow. 'Fun and games.' His voice was loaded with innuendo, and I froze. Could he possibly know? How, when we were so careful?

I watched Will's face.

'Could mean the end of our breakfasts,' he said, smiling, and I breathed again. *Fun and games.*

'Breakfast will never end,' Toby said. 'Seven years we've been going. Survived exams –'

'One in four on-call –'

'Three kids!' Will said.

'Not to mention Evel Knievel,' Toby said.

Evel Knievel. I wouldn't forget him. Our first breakfast, seven years earlier, followed Will and me pulling an all-nighter, trying to save a teenage biker who had mashed up his abdominal organs. By seven a.m. we had to stand back from the table. I'd lost patients before, but they were mostly old and usually sick. Afterwards, we both loitered in the tearoom, Will looking as bewildered as I felt. I wasn't ready to be alone, so I asked him if he wanted to go and get breakfast and we'd decamped to Errol Street, downing coffee and reassuring each other we'd done everything we could.

The next week, Toby joined us for breakfast and presented us with two tiny figurines of Evel Knievel on a motorbike, and I was about to pay out on him for hitting us when we were down when Will guffawed – maybe a little too loud – and so I accepted the Evel Knievel and tried to laugh, pushing from my mind the image of the white-faced, pulseless biker and the tormented keening from his mother.

We were all trainees back then – Will a fellow, Toby and me six years out of med school but several years his junior. We met every week, unless we were rostered for theatre, and we kept it up even after Will got his consultant post. The jokes intensified when Hamish joined. He was the newest urologist at PCH and an old schoolmate of Will's – if being someone's whipping boy sat within the realm of friendship.

I'm not sure why Hamish fronted up every week, but for me, initially, it was to spend time with Will. Breakfast gave me a chance to be near Toby and I'd always say yes to that, but Will was someone I wanted to impress. He was the youngest consultant in our team, and he played golf with Prof. He had a say in which trainees got the accredited jobs, and I was sure I got on the program at least in part because I laughed at his pranks.

Yes, the banter was sometimes puerile and often boring, but this was my *tribe*. I wanted to belong.

Will turned to Hamish. 'Got anything for us this week, Seacombe?'

As if by reflex, Toby added, 'Caecum. One great big shit heap.'

Hamish ignored the familiar pun on his name and put down his Blackberry. He pulled a journal article from his bag and gave it to Will. I wondered if Hamish had had old-man eyes when he was swaddled in his mother's arms, and I thought the answer was likely yes.

As Will read the paper, his cheeks turned as scarlet as his tie and his shirt buttons strained against his paunch.

'Take a look at this – they got couples to do the deed in the MRI and took scans while they were at it!' Will rocked back and forth in his chair. 'This is a beauty, H – you really are the man.'

Hamish permitted himself a small smile that almost reached his eyes.

'Got this one in the spreadsheet already?'

Hamish didn't see the joke. 'Indeed.'

Will waved the paper around. 'You've unearthed some quirky stuff in your time, H, but this could be the best yet.'

Hamish frowned. 'The design is not as elegant as the teaspoon study.'

Toby screwed up his face. 'Who gives a shit about spoons disappearing from tearooms?'

'Right – this is infinitely more interesting,' Will said. 'Though they do liken the old fella to a boomerang – not sure what I think about that!' His eyebrows danced up and down as he passed me the paper.

'I was merely pointing out the superior design of the teaspoon study,' Hamish said. 'And it is relevant, when you're making a cup of tea –'

'They're *fucking in the MRI*,' Toby said, tapping the table with each word. 'Who gives a shit about tea?'

I threw Hamish a sympathetic look and flicked through the paper, my eyes drawn to the black-and-white image of a man and woman intertwined, the two pubic bones angled towards each other like elders leaning their heads close to share a secret. Aside from a thin black line separating skin from skin, it was hard to tell where one body started and the other stopped. Strangely beautiful, how they fitted together.

I became aware of Toby, sitting next to me.

I knew how it was when our bodies fitted together.

Toby felt it too. 'It's like porn.' His cheeks flushed.

'I don't believe that was their intention,' Hamish said.

'Who cares?' Toby glanced at me, and I knew what he was thinking: want to do it in the MRI?

He had no limits.

Toby had no limits.

The thought excited and terrified me.

The waiter brought our breakfasts. I sliced into my poached egg, the yolk glistening as it ran over the buttered toast. While we ate, Will and Toby argued about whether the bent penis moulded against the vaginal wall most resembled a banana or a boomerang or the letter S.

Will grinned at Toby. 'All of this is reminding me, you know, of the strap-on! That nearly sent Carla right off. The look on her face!'

I rolled my eyes. Ate another mouthful.

'It was a harsh joke, that one,' Toby said, shooting me a protective look.

'No, not so!' Will glanced at me. 'You're one of the boys, Carla. I wanted you to know.'

'We should remember that it has not been easy for Carla to get where she is,' Hamish said. 'Credit to her.'

'Exactly!' Will said. 'Hence the strap-on. You *are* one of us.'

Only Will could think that gifting me a strap-on when I made it onto the surgical program was some kind of perverse compliment. The pink plastic penis and black leather harness had made me seethe, but, then and now, I knew the unspoken rule: *go with the joke*. 'Turned out to be a very practical gift. Came in handy just last night.'

'Fabulous!' Will said. 'Get some any way you can, my dear.'

'Only way I can,' I said, deadpan, and it was then that I saw Toby flinch, eyes fresh with hurt, and I wanted to take back my words, only –

You're the one who wanted this a secret.

An alarm sounded on Hamish's Blackberry. He turned it off and stood. 'Eleven minutes until clinic.'

'I take it you don't want to talk about the old boy, then?' Will asked him.

'Bet he's still sitting on your mantlepiece at home,' Toby said.

Blotches appeared on Hamish's neck and, knowing where this was going, I signalled for the bill. Months back, Will had given Hamish an engorged testis he'd somehow souvenired during a visit to Timor from some poor guy whose testis had spun like a mirror ball and cut off its own blood supply. To Will and Toby, it seemed like the perfect gift for a urologist, but rule-abiding Hamish had stared nonplussed at the testis in the specimen jar, whispering, almost to himself, 'But what do I *do* with it?' His reaction sent Will and Toby into hysterics, and made me want to protect him from every joke he didn't understand.

A wave of humiliation crossed Hamish's face, and Will sensed he'd gone too far and handed his credit card to the waiter. I wanted to tell him that paying the bill didn't make up for jokes the wrong side of mean, but that was Will – tone-deaf and generous, in equal measure.

Hamish accepted Will's gesture with a nod, and Toby slapped Hamish's back. I felt a strange fondness for them. I raised my espresso cup. 'Here's to breakfast. Long may it continue.'

'And to the job, if we can ever roll Benny on,' Toby said. 'May the best man win.'

We clinked coffee cups and Toby and I locked eyes.

Game on.

~

'How will you handle it?' Fleur asked as we stood on our terrace balcony looking over the plane tree canopy to the sun sinking behind Rathdowne Street rooftops.

I took a closer look at the starfish-shaped leaves of the plane trees. Some were plump and rudely green, but others drooped brown-edged from their branches.

'Look at these leaves. Do you think these trees are getting enough water?'

Fleur nudged me, repeating her question.

I shrugged. 'It's not a big deal. We're adults, our personal life is separate.'

Fleur tied her long red hair into a topknot and sank into a wicker easy chair, her legs curled under her. I felt her gaze on me. 'So, if he gets the job –'

Secretly, I didn't think that was going to happen. 'I'd be fine. Take it on the chin.'

'And if you get it?'

I pictured the parched tree roots, tunnelling downwards deep under the Rathdowne Street bitumen, licking at the dust. 'He'll cope.'

'Have you ever, in all the years you've known Toby, seen him in a situation where he didn't get what he wanted?'

I wasn't going to answer that. A breeze rustled through the plane trees like a stranger making their way through a crowd.

Fleur sighed. 'Okay. I'll leave it. You could bring him to my birthday, if you want?'

'It'll just be me.' I knew better than to lie to her. 'We're ... keeping it on the down low.' I stood. 'You want a drink? I bought rosé.' I went into the kitchen and returned with two glasses of wine and handed one to Fleur.

She sipped at the clear pink wine. 'So, you're really into him – and he doesn't want to tell anyone.' Her words were clipped and certain.

I screwed up my mouth. Fleur might be out of the hospital system, ensconced in her cosy community unit, but she knew the risks – the gossip and innuendo, the rumour mill running all the way to our bosses. A good reason for keeping quiet.

She caught a glimpse of my expression, and when she spoke again, her voice was softer. 'He must mean a lot to you.'

We'd both known Toby since uni, but back then he'd hung with a different crowd. Our group always had one eye on the next exam and took the idea of doctoring seriously, while he was in the boozy circle who left lectures early for the pub. He was on–off with Phoebe for years, and in between there was a stream of other girls, so I'd always viewed him as out of reach, like the curvy ceramic figures Nonna had positioned on the highest shelf in her lounge room, away from the smudgy, clumsy fingers of her grandchildren.

But Toby was a living, breathing version of my dream man – beautiful, clever and with a sureness about him that I wanted a piece of. I heard his exasperated voice as I prevaricated over the menu at Chin Chin. *No second-guessing, Carla.* That was how he lived, and I wanted it, too. I tried to find the words.

'It's like he has this – aura, this certainty that I want to be around.'

'Narcissism?'

'No! He's not like that, not when you get to know him. He's actually very generous.'

'What, then? Is it power?'

I rolled my eyes.

'I'm not trying to judge ... I want to understand.'

I thought about Toby, walking through the hospital hallways with shoulders free and arms swinging. The image of the intertwined bodies in the MRI floated into my mind.

'Do you ever think it would be easier if the world was black and white?'

'You're drawn to his dichotomous way of thinking. Very surgical, I guess.' Her eyes narrowed. 'You do know that's a fantasy, right?'

I shrugged. Maybe Toby could make it so.

'Listen, I ... only ask this because I want to make sure he's good to you. Is he kind?'

I grimaced. *Kind* was a great-aunt knitting bedsocks for the homeless, or earnest greenies trying to nudge a beached whale back to water. Not what I looked for in a man. 'He's – well, for starters, he's an amazing cook. And so romantic, you know, he's always thinking of ways to surprise me.'

Fleur nodded, her frown staying put.

'Listen, don't overthink it – we've never liked the same type of guy.'

'You mean, you only date surgeons.'

'Not true! There was, what was his name? Bernie.'

Her frown furrows deepened. 'Who?'

'A boy I kissed in year five.'

She laughed.

'Anyway, you have your own type. Intense, tortured, that's your go –'

Fleur chewed at a fingernail. 'Richard is driving me insane. You'd think, after fifteen years, that it was time to get on with our lives, but no. In his head, he's still nineteen and confused about what he wants. And I've realised – don't judge – I'm ready.' She winced at my confused face. 'To start a family. Before I'm completely ancient. I see Rose and Emily making those choices, and – I want that to be me.'

Ever since I'd met Fleur in first-year uni, she'd made life decisions through the prism of becoming a mother. Psychiatry would be a good career to combine with a family. *I don't want to defer a year to travel, not with my body-clock.* So I shouldn't have been surprised. But Fleur's sisters, Rose and Emily, were neck-deep in nappies and had stepped sideways in their careers to do that. Is that what Fleur wanted?

'Thirty-five is not too old.'

Fleur sighed. 'I'm ready. Don't you get that feeling?'

I had thought about it – not much choice, with Gina's relentless questioning: *when am I going to be a Nonna, why are you so obsessed with work, why did you choose such a busy job?* It felt like a decision for tomorrow – I didn't know how I'd make it work with surgery, and there was no way I was going to be a stay-at-home mum.

'I guess I've been caught up with the job ...' I said.

Fleur cast her eyes skywards. 'It's not enough. Not for me.'

I hesitated, and then asked her what Richard wanted.

'He's scared.' The sun disappeared behind rooftops, leaving fingers of pink strewn across the darkening sky. 'You will come to the party, won't you? It's important.'

Something about her voice made me suspicious. 'You're not springing a wedding on us, are you?'

She squeezed her eyes shut and scrunched up her nose.

'You are! Spill.'

One eye opened, looked at me sideways. 'Not a wedding. An announcement, maybe.'

'Engagement?'

'Maybe. I've called him on it. He'd better get his frickin' act together.'

It was a risky move, giving Richard an ultimatum, but now wasn't the time to go there. I jumped up and hugged her, tight. She smelt of frangipani and longing. 'I hope – I hope it all goes exactly how you want.' Her body trembled and I silently vowed that if Richard let her down this time, I would triple the testicle collection on Hamish's mantlepiece.

She pulled away from the hug and thanked me. 'Oh, and one last piece of advice from your therapist – don't let Toby sell you short. He should be shouting your name from the rooftops.'

Trying not to sound defensive, I told her he needed time. 'It's not that long since he split with Phoebe.'

She tilted her head. 'It's you I'm thinking about.'

'Yeah, well, be glad for me. The job's coming, I'm seeing a fantastic man.' I smiled at her worried face. 'Trust me, I know what I'm doing.'

Exsanguination

death caused by loss of blood

I arrived super early on Tuesday. I loved starting the day in the empty whiteness of theatre, before the circus arrived with gowns and gloves and people flurrying and machines beeping. Today, standing in for Prof, I thought the quiet would calm my nerves.

But when the lift doors opened on the ground floor, Toby was standing there. I got in beside him. We stood in front of a cleaner with a mop and bucket and next to Lachlan, one of the registrars who, from his bleary eyes and crumpled shirt, must have been finishing up a night shift, and I didn't know how but the air felt charged with everything Toby was thinking. He was mouth-breathing shallow, anticipatory breaths and I wondered if Lachlan and the cleaner noticed.

The lift stopped at two, we edged closer to make space for people to enter, and his fingers brushed my skirt.

Lachlan addressed me. 'Theatre today?'

I looked up at him and nodded.

'She's standing in for Prof,' Toby said. 'Big boss man today, aren't you, Carla?'

'Wow.' Lachlan flashed me an easy smile. 'Enjoy.'

We exited the lift and Lachlan walked away towards the nurses' station.

Toby spoke. 'Do you have a minute?'

Five innocent words.

I reminded him we had to go to theatre.

'Won't take long,' he said, walking towards the quiet room at the end of the ward. 'It's about the first patient.'

I hesitated. What if someone saw? He was already opening the door, sure I would follow. Glancing around, I saw empty corridors.

At high school, there was a boy I liked who'd barely even spoken to me until the day he asked me to skip maths and go to the park with him. Even though I was a study nerd, I knew what happened in the shadows behind the scrubby banksia and I so wanted to say yes – only, it was the last class before our semester test.

I'd gone to maths, and a few days later I saw him with another girl from our year.

I stood now in the hospital hallway. Taking a deep breath, I followed Toby into the quiet room.

I sat down on the cheap pine couch with the salmon-coloured vinyl. On the wall opposite was a pastel painting of an impossibly pretty sunset. That was what families would see as they listened to us tell them the game was up for their loved one. They would search the sunset for a glimmer of hope and find only hues of pink and apricot.

Toby shut the door behind me and locked it, leaving the lights off, and drew me to standing, kissing me, and even with the sad ghosts in this room, my body was primed to respond. He pulled a small, wrapped box from his pocket and gave it to me. 'Reminded me of you.'

I took the box, my heart skipping a beat. Could it be a ring? Don't be ridiculous, I told myself, we'd only just started seeing each other. I unwrapped the paper and opened it. Inside was a silver necklace with one impossibly large diamond.

The stone sparkled. It brought me undone, that he had bought this, for *me*. A small voice inside me said, *you don't wear jewellery like that*, but I pushed the thought away. I had never owned anything so expensive.

'Toby, it's too much. Thank you.'

He fastened it around my neck and pulled me close, kissing me long and hard. As he began to unbutton my shirt, I reminded him again of theatre. 'I want to check the file, make sure everything's ready.'

'It's all sorted. Come on, Carla – live a little.'

I wanted to, I really did. Before I could say anything, his mouth was on my neck, and my body warmed to him. His pager went off, and he unclipped it from his belt, flinging it to the floor, and with it went my self-control. I pressed my body against him and put my arms under his shirt, my hands passing over his abdomen and back and chest, thrilling at his smooth skin. I touched his erect nipples, felt the defined muscle bodies of his rectus abdominis and the hollow beneath his clavicles where the skin was soft. I ran my fingers down his spine. I wanted to touch every centimetre of skin. I was a dog, pissing for territory.

He kissed his way down my chest.

I unzipped his trousers.

His pager beeped again, and then a third time, insistent. It broke the spell, and I remembered. *Theatre. Mastectomy. Prof.*

Summoning all my self-control, I pushed him away from my breast so I could meet his eye. 'We can't. Let's meet up after work, tonight.'

He groaned, shook his head and tried to kiss me, and then I heard something, outside the door. Footsteps, and voices.

Someone tried the handle of the door.

Fuck!

I panicked, fumbling at my shirt buttons.

'Anyone in there?' a voice called. Irish accent. *Maggie.*

Getting sprung by the nurse unit manager with a king-size doctor complex was the worst of all possibilities. Last week, I'd overheard Maggie dressing down a resident on the ward for ignoring a page from one of her nurses, which seemed less about the situation and more about the truth that in a hierarchy dominated by doctors, Maggie would always be a nurse.

Fingers trembling, I re-tucked my shirt. We were screwed.

'Maggie, it's me, Toby,' he said, his voice falsely cheery. 'Can you give me five minutes? I'm in the middle of a phone call. To my mum.'

There was a minute's silence, and then Maggie's clipped voice. 'I have twelve nursing students here for a tutorial. I have the room booked, you know.'

Of course she did.

'And I think Thao was looking for you,' Maggie said. 'She wanted the mastectomy for this morning reviewed.'

'No worries. Why don't you all grab a coffee – tell Amir it's on me – and I'll come and get you when I'm done.'

Maggie grumbled something I couldn't catch, and we heard footsteps peak and fade.

I exhaled relief. I had to give it to him, that was one hell of an escape.

Once it was quiet, Toby looked a question at me, and I shook my head. He was impossible. No way. Not now.

I straightened my clothes. 'See you in theatre.'

~

At eight seventeen, I put scalpel to skin, making a neat incision across Olivia Lai's chest, through skin and fat to muscle and bone.

Meeting Toby in the quiet room had left me distracted and short of time, and the anaesthetist wasn't in the mood. While I had scoured the file a few minutes earlier, searching for the bone-scan result, he said, 'Can we get on with it? What are you doing over there, anyway – painting your nails?'

My cheeks burnt. I shut the file.

As we gowned and gloved, I asked Toby if he'd checked the bone scan.

'Benson saw her pre-op,' he replied. 'It's all good.'

'Did you go and see her this morning?'

'I said, it's all good.'

It wasn't an answer, but it was all I was going to get, so I began, Toby holding the retractor so I could dissect away the left breast.

'The big cheese today,' he said. 'How does it feel, Miss di Pieta?'

I ignored the teasing in his voice and told him I could get used to it.

'You're going to have to fight me for it, you know that.'

In gown and gloves and mask and head covering, all I saw were his eyes, taunting me, and I returned the look with interest. 'Can't wait.'

'Nah, you're a shoo-in, Carla,' he said. 'One of the best surgeons I've seen.'

My cheeks flushed, remembering what he'd seen.

'Want some suction? Carla?' The scrub nurse asked. I startled and looked down. My incision was slowly filling with blood.

Toby applied the suction catheter. 'She's a bit of a bleeder, young Olivia.'

'Too young to have breast cancer,' the nurse said. 'What is she, thirty-five?'

Same age as me. I asked for suction, my voice sharp. I had no time or space to think about how young Olivia was. Flecks of gritty white tissue dotted the chest wall.

While we operated, someone put on classical music, and Toby chatted with the nurse about her daughter in year twelve and her son with the horse obsession. I had no idea how he remembered that stuff, but now was not the time. I blocked out the noise and stared at the white flecks. Why were we operating on a patient with disseminated cancer? Shouldn't she be having chemo and getting her affairs in order?

I made a separate incision in the axilla and found two matted and calcified lymph nodes. Cancer. Dissecting around the primary, I searched for clear margins, but tumour extended as far as I could see. And blood filled the new incision.

An alarm began its slow, dull thud, and the anaesthetist and his tech spoke in low voices.

The anaesthetist appeared over the drape. 'Her CO_2 is low and she's bloody hard to oxygenate. I'm getting a gas.'

'Think we might have hit something.' Toby drew back flaps of tissue so I could see, but blood oozed into the space.

'Have you noticed the mets in her chest wall? Or were you too busy chatting?' My voice was tight, and I tasted acid in my mouth.

In the background, the music swelled, and I recognised it – Verdi's majestic Agnus Dei. Prof's favourite.

Prof. He could be here any minute. I had to get control of this before he arrived. I remembered my elation at being asked to stand in. I was so sure this was his way of telling me I was next in line. This train wreck of a mastectomy could jeopardise my job, even my career.

I caught myself. Jesus. Something bad was going on with this patient, and I was thinking about my job?

'Sats are dropping,' the anaesthetist said. 'And she's hypotensive. I need adrenaline. Can we get nitric in here? Set up for an art line.'

The pool of blood grew in front of me. 'I need suction.'

'Diathermy,' Toby said.

'Get me two more packs.'

While I snapped orders, Toby cauterised a few blood vessels with diathermy, leaving a lingering smell of burning flesh. My rising pulse pounded my head, jumbling my thoughts. Could Liv have a clotting disease? Why was she so unstable? And the most burning question: what the hell do I do now?

Blood. It made its own stream in the wound now. We shoved in packs that filled in minutes like sponges.

'Would you like Prof paged?' The nurse asked me quietly.

I shook my head. There had to be a reason for all this. I thought back to Maggie, saying the nurse wanted Liv reviewed pre-op. 'Toby, why did they want her seen this morning?'

He shrugged. 'Sore leg, or something.'

Sore leg, in a patient with breast cancer. I racked my brain, remembering an oncology presentation on complications in metastatic cancer. Perverse processes like Disseminated Intravascular Coagulation, when the cancer caused clots, and those clots consumed and depleted the body's platelets and clotting factors, meaning that a patient who clotted too much was also prone to bleeding.

'Could have been a DVT,' I said. 'She could have DIC.'

Toby frowned. 'She didn't sound *that* sick.'

'Her platelets were low normal,' the anaesthetist said. 'It's possible. Get me the ultrasound, I can scan for a PE. And set up some Heparin.'

'But she's bleeding everywhere,' I said, startled. 'Heparin will make that worse.'

He shook his head. 'No good choices here, right? If it is DIC, she's clotting off her lungs as we speak, same time as bleeding out on the table. You're going to need to close her up. And who's the consultant on for this list? We need them here.'

'Let me get control of the bleeding, then we'll call Prof –'

'No. We need him now.'

Fuck. The incision filled with blood again. I called for more suction, and asked for someone to get Prof on the phone. 'And turn off that music. Suction! I can't see.' My voice sounded like it belonged to someone else. 'More traction. More suction.'

Beep, beep, beep. The heart rate monitor sounded, fast and insistent.

'More traction, I can't see.'

The white packs in the wound turned crimson. A second alarm

began a grating drone. Toby fumbled the retractor and it clanged on the floor.

The heart rate alarm grew faster, louder.

This could not be happening.

The alarm squealed its protest.

Not to a patient so young.

The monitors whined and moaned.

Who should never have had surgery.

The heart rate alarm ceased its fast, angry chime. For a moment there was a pause like the monitor was drawing breath, and then the thready knell of a perilously slow heart rate rang out across the theatre.

AFTER

There's a saying in medicine: *when you arrive at a cardiac arrest, first take your own pulse.*

Standing over the mess we'd made of Liv's body, I didn't have the presence of mind to follow that advice. It may have been better if I had.

Distance. Before everything happened, I had no issue finding it, finding comfort in the numbness. It's probably the only way to do this job – taking a scalpel to unblemished skin and excising tissue, opening body cavities, plunging yourself up to your elbows in blood. When a patient threatens to bleed out and the only obstacle is your steady hand, there is no time to care that this is a person, with a partner, and a sister, and a phobia of caterpillars.

The system relies on you detaching and, as Prof would say, *doing the needful*. It's more difficult, though, when the buck stops with you, and harder still when your own fate is tied to the human on the table. Hardest of all when your emotions can no longer be trusted, which is me since the hospital gala.

A memory surfaces, from when I am about four years old.

I am at my grandparents' home, where Nonno keeps a jar of lollies on the coffee table for Luca and me. Nonno is minding me while Nonna is out on one of her many errands, maybe to the shops or to set her sister's hair. I am watching TV and sucking on an orange lolly that is wedged into the hollow of my palate, my tongue working away at the hard, sweet casing, and I am about to steal an extra lolly when a noise comes from the bathroom, a groaning, choking – not like anything I've heard before.

I run towards the noise and find Nonno standing at the sink, clutching at his arm. Although he is a joker, I know from his contorted, purple face that this isn't a prank.

He slumps to the floor, not exactly a fall, more that he loses his grip on being vertical. The bathroom is tiny, and he is wedged against the bath, so I clamber over and huddle beside him with my knobbly knees up against my chin. He smells of musty oregano and the sweet, sharp alcohol from the shot of Centerba he added to his morning espresso.

I sit there between the bath and the toilet and suck my orange lolly until I can feel with my tongue that it is now a thin disc and eventually I crunch it with my teeth, and after it is gone I regret doing that, and I think about going and getting another one, but I don't want to leave Nonno. The only noise is my breathing.

When Mum arrives, her shrieking fills the silence, and in the days that follow, the more she wails, the quieter I become. She tries to get me to talk about what happened, but I can't.

Distance served me then, with Nonno, though I carry with me a dislike of small spaces. And as I've travelled through med school and into surgery, I've returned to that numbness with increasing frequency and ease.

Somehow, though, standing over Liv, I couldn't find that safe, detached space from where I could work. I couldn't stop myself feeling the situation – Liv's paralysed vulnerability as we worked on her lifeless body, the stony weight of responsibility that our carelessness contributed to this mess, and my sheer panic at my career bleeding out along with her.

And now, months on from the gala dinner, distance is one of the many things I can't rely on at all, because at any time, memories of that night surface like flotsam on waves of panic I can't ignore and can't control.

Maybe that day with Liv was the beginning of the breaking down of that persona, dismantling the surgeon that I was.

The shattering of a mirror, glass shards falling about me.

BEFORE
Resuscitate

to revive a person from apparent death

I stood motionless over Liv's body. Around me, people hustled, grabbing fluid and drugs and defibrillators.

The anaesthetist shouted over the noise. 'Her scan shows a massive PE. Start cardiac compressions. Get haematology on the line. Are cardiothoracics around?'

'They're in Theatre Two.'

'Okay, get them too. She needs embolectomy, fast.' He looked at me. 'Where the hell is Prof?'

The question startled me into action, and I began cardiac massage, ignoring the blood now pouring from the wound. The anaesthetist pumped adrenaline and units of blood into the IV while a nurse put pressure on the axillary wound where the bleeding was at its worst. Toby stuffed in more packs.

Come on, Liv. I put all my force into the next sternal compression, *come on, Liv,* and I felt the chest wall give way before I heard the splintering crack, like the snap of lamb bones under my father's blade.

I looked down. Liv's rib cage now had a V-shaped deformity.

I blinked and resumed CPR. A fracture would heal.

I kept going with compressions until my arms burnt. Instructing Toby to take over, I found a bleeder in the axilla and compressed it with every force I could summon. And I was in this position when Prof arrived.

He scrubbed in and surveyed the scene, his face grim surprise. I couldn't meet his eye. The anaesthetist updated him, and we continued CPR until cardiothoracics came in and took over, and then Toby and I were relegated to spectators while they got to work, Prof alongside them at the table.

We stood in the corner and waited. My tongue found its place of worry against the inside of my lower incisor, and I pressed hard until I tasted blood. They murmured to each other, but I couldn't make out what they were saying and I couldn't see what was happening. I wanted to find out how long she'd been down for, but the nurses were frantic. I was desperate to help in some way, but what?

After what felt like a very long time, I heard one of the cardiothoracic surgeons say, 'We've got it,' and I guessed he meant the clot, but I wasn't sure. When I heard the slow, quiet chime of the heart rate monitor, I exhaled a long-held breath and nearly keeled over.

'We've got an output,' the anaesthetist said. 'But sats are low.'

'Let's close her up and get her to ICU,' the cardiothoracic surgeon said.

Toby turned to me. 'How come she had mets?'

I frowned, and remembered the anaesthetist sniping at me pre-op. *What are you doing over there, filing your nails?* Sweat built on my forehead. My pulse thudded in my ears as I told him to check the bone scan.

'I'm sure it was okay –' he began.

'Just do it.'

He moved to the computer, made a phone call and returned a few minutes later.

'Carla.' His voice was low. 'Benson ordered it, and I was sure I checked it, but – it was done in private, so maybe I didn't see it. She has multiple hot spots.'

I stared at the mess that was Liv on the table, the bloodied packs, open wounds, a rib cage full of tumour.

The nerve in my cheek twitched an irregular beat.

~

It wasn't until the evening, when all other demands on me were met, that I made it to ICU, where Liv lay, paralysed and ventilated, alarms calling out *low blood pressure, hypoxia, tachycardia*. They'd filled her with fluid, and her face was disappearing into the bloat.

One of the registrars saw me and came over. 'This is a bit of a shit-show,' he said in a low voice, gesturing at Liv. 'What happened?'

Sideswiping colleagues in another specialty was standard practice, especially in ICU, so I smiled and took the hit.

My phone rang – Nino. He wouldn't usually interrupt me at work. It was then I remembered missed calls from my mother, earlier in the day. I stepped outside and took the call. He apologised for bothering me, but Silvia's rosary was tomorrow night, and it was important I was there.

I remembered Zia Silvia pinching my much younger cheeks with her knobbly fingers and telling my mother *brutto naso*, and I had covered my nose with my palm while she laughed.

Nino was talking.

'I know, Silvia was difficult, but she was your Nonno's sister. Your mother wants you there. Please, Carla. Work is important, but – this is *family*.'

I heard disappointment in his voice.

Through the glass doors, I watched as the nurses suctioned Liv's endotracheal tube. I took a shallow breath. 'I'll try, Dad. I promise.' I ended the call.

When I returned to the room, the ICU team had ramped up her ventilation pressure and given a bolus of fluid, and the alarms quietened, and soon the ICU doctors were called away to the next unstable patient.

That's when I became aware of a tall woman sitting in the corner wearing jeans and a vigilant expression. Her neck swivelled left and right as she surveyed the room like a sentinel meerkat. I tried not to meet her eye, but she saw me and strode over, holding out her hand. 'Anthea Hooper. I'm Liv's partner.'

In our grim conversation after theatre, Prof had told me there was a girlfriend, a lawyer. *Do not under any circumstances engage with her*, he'd said.

'Carla, Carla di Pieta. One of the surgical doctors.' I tried for a neutral facial expression.

'No one is telling me anything.' Anthea's voice had a brassy edge.

'I'm sure – didn't Prof meet with you today?'

'Someone should tell him not to try legalese on a lawyer. Look, I need to know the facts here – what is going on?' She ran a hand through her hair. 'Is she going to survive?'

I looked across at the nurse adjusting Liv's IV.

The nurse spoke, her face wary. 'She seems a bit more stable,' she said.

'For God's sake, enough with the platitudes!' Anthea snapped, and the nurse jumped. When she spoke again, her voice was softer. 'I'm sorry, please – I've got to know.'

The saturation alarm sounded anew, and all eyes turned to Liv, paralysed and hypoxic. The nurse dialled up the oxygen and shot me a glance.

'We're doing everything we can,' I told Anthea, 'but we don't know.'

Anthea stood still and I wondered if she'd heard me. Then the nurse gently wiped drool from Liv's chin and Anthea's face crumpled.

'Oh, Jesus,' she said. 'I don't know – what will I do? She's all I have. If I lose her – I don't know what I'd do.'

The nurse comforted her, the monitors resumed their screeching and wailing, and I stared at Liv's body and wondered the same.

DURING

Anthea.

I'm in the lift at PCH – 9 July. The gala dinner. My mouth tastes of vomit and there is something wet on my cheek – dribble? I wipe it away. The doors are closed but we're not moving. I stand there confused: what do I do now?

After a minute, I remember: press the button.

Down, down, down, from six to five to four.

Where am I going?

Did I bring my car to work, or did I walk in? I search my mind and find I don't know.

I'm not sure my legs can walk home. I'm tired, so tired. So much wine, too much – I'm flooded with wine regret.

And then, I'm no longer alone. A tall woman stands next to me, texting on her phone. Where did she come from? I'm struck by how long her text is. What is she writing, a novel?

She glances across, and I know her face.

Carla, she says, and I search and scrabble, but my brain refuses to retrieve her name.

She talks in that brassy voice, staccato words I don't remember, and it's clear we know each other. I listen, feeling like I'm underwater and trying to follow a conversation on land. I don't grasp the meaning.

The lift stops and the doors open. She waves her arms in front of the sensor to keep the door open and peers at me. Are you okay? Have you been crying?

I wipe at my cheeks. I'm a professional. Can't be seen like this. I tell her I'm fine.

She says okay, if you're sure, and backs out of the lift, scanning the hall left and right.

BEFORE

Balm

an aromatic salve or oil

Thirty-six hours after Liv's surgery, I slipped into the back pew at St Jude's, patron saint of lost causes. I stared dry-eyed as the priest wafted incense over the coffin, alternating prayers in Italian and English. Zia Silvia was a battleaxe, and most people here knew it, including those dabbing away tears with a tissue.

What was I doing here? My body was wrung taut with the effort of holding everything together. My thoughts jumped from Liv to Prof to the job, which had surely slipped through my hands.

But Nino's comment – *work is important, but this is family* – stayed with me.

As if he could hear my thoughts, Nino turned from the second pew, and when he saw me, a smile deepened the lines on his face. I smiled back, breathing easier. Others in the congregation noticed me as well and looked pleased and surprised. *Fair enough*, I thought. It had been a while. I eased back on the seat, trying to loosen the knot between my shoulder blades. No one here knew about a botched surgery sending a young woman to ICU. They were just glad I'd shown up.

I murmured along with the congregation, *Santa Maria, Madre di*

Dio, prega per noi peccatori, adesso e nell'ora della nostra morte, and the rhythm of the prayer soothed me. I'd always dissed the saintly Mary, mother of God, thinking that Mary Magdalene saw way more action. Now here I was, comforted by praying to her.

Snap!

A loud, cracking noise came from my left.

I gasped, hearing Liv's rib, snapping under the force of my cardiac compressions.

Down the pew from me, someone giggled. One of my cousins, fastening her purse shut.

Liv's bloated face stuck in my mind. Would she survive? Would Prof ever trust me again?

We stood and prayed: *Glory be the Father –*

I saw Prof's dark face when I met with him after the surgery. I had bowed my head as I apologised, explaining that I thought Benson or Toby would have checked the scan. He had lectured me that any surgeon worth their merit must take responsibility for their patient, that of course we rely on our team, but I should have satisfied myself that everything was in order.

And the son –

What he didn't say was that most surgeons left the checking of pre-op investigations to the junior staff, and that Prof himself was no different.

And the Holy Spirit –

The only conclusion he could draw was that I wasn't ready. Or that responsibility had gone to my head somewhat. Even consultants have to do menial tasks at times, he reminded me, and I bristled. I'd worked harder than any man to get this far.

As it was in the beginning –

His lips set in a line as he said, 'Let this be a lesson. And let it be the only time.'

Is now, and ever shall be –

Then the killer blow. 'Make sure you have a presentation ready for next Thursday.'

World without end –

I wanted to say no. I couldn't face an M&M, where every stuff-up was pored over, searching for a scapegoat.

'Yes,' I had croaked.

Amen.

With the congregation, I sank to my knees, and prayed for mercy from a God I didn't believe in, an all-seeing God who knew about my pre-op detour to the quiet room. I pleaded, *forgive us our trespasses* – let Liv survive, get her out of ICU, get me back to theatre.

Don't let this be the end.

As the rosary finished, my phone buzzed, and I fumbled for it. I'd been away an hour; anything could have happened.

It was Toby, wanting to hook up.

I ignored the message and gathered my things. I needed to get back there, to know she was still alive.

After the priest left the church, my parents walked down the aisle and found me, and I kissed them hello.

'Good that you came,' Gina said, and in those four words she conveyed her pleasure to see me and disappointment for every other time. Master of the backhander, my mother.

Weary of the battle, I asked her if she was okay.

She sniffed. 'She was eighty-eight. What can you do?'

We stood to one side of the crowd lined up to give condolences. Luca joined us and Gina's face lit up to see him, and I saw him as she did – beautiful even with bloodshot eyes and a five o'clock shadow. He had a radiance that drew warmth from people – even sometimes from me.

Based on his track record, I guessed those red eyes were not from inconsolable grief. What would Gina think if she knew her son had turned up stoned to a rosary?

Gina pointed at my neck. 'Look at the size of that diamond!'

I clutched at the necklace. 'It was a gift.'

Luca's eyes grew wide. 'Have you got an *admirer*?'

I drilled him with my best big-sister *cut it out* look.

Nino asked me about the consultant job, and I shrugged. My impatience about the job had evaporated now that I needed time to win back Prof's trust.

'This new job,' Gina said. 'Will you still have to work day and night? Easter, Christmas, all that?'

'We thought once you finished with all the training, you would have more time,' Nino said.

'People get sick on public holidays,' I said, feeling cornered. My parents had been proud of my achievements in surgery, but lately they'd lost patience with the hours I had to work. Now that I was in my thirties, Gina made it clear they expected me to focus on family, possibly start making one of my own, which was the last thing on my mind. And it wasn't lost on me that Nino's seventy-hour weeks at the butcher were no different to mine at the hospital.

'Carla di Pieta, saving the world, one appendix at a time,' Luca said, grinning, but his words stung. *Liv*.

'Yes, well,' Gina said, turning her gaze on Luca. 'You should be working yourself.'

'I am! Did a catalogue just yesterday. Target, jocks. Think you'll be able to spot me, Mum? I'm the one –'

'Enough,' Gina said. 'I get the idea.'

'It was wild, actually, the shoot – they put us in this old warehouse, and it must have been minus five in there. And everyone knows what happens to the Crown Jewels in the cold – whole lotta guys with nuts the size of sultanas. So, we're shoving socks down there, to make up for what nature provided. Anyway, if you're looking for me, I'm the best hung one.' He nudged me and whispered, too loud, 'Explorer socks.'

'*Basta!* Come with me,' Gina said, and she dragged Luca to pay respects to Silvia's children.

I stayed alongside Nino. Dark settled in the sky and my mind drifted back to the hospital. Maybe ECMO had done the trick; ICU seemed to think it brought patients back from the brink. And if it hadn't, I needed to know.

'Carla,' Nino said in a low voice. 'Come, have a bowl of pasta with us after. She cooked the sauce, in case.'

A panicky feeling rose in my chest. 'I can't, Dad.'

He looked disappointed, and then nodded, kissed my forehead and folded me into a hug, and for a moment I rested there, breathing in the smell of soap and coffee, his chest rising and falling against me.

Afterwards, I drove back to the hospital under a cloudless, velvet sky. Toby texted twice, *where r u*, and I didn't answer – I couldn't face him.

I needed to see Liv.

Climbing the stairs to ICU, I hoped for a miracle.

~

Toby downed his espresso. 'Been there all night?' His voice was measured, but there was a barb behind it. He'd been trying to get me in person for days now.

I stared at him through a haze of fatigue. 'I'm trying to keep her alive. Is that okay with you?'

'Keep next weekend free,' he said, ignoring my tone.

I checked my calendar and confirmed what I feared: I was on-call.

'Jesus, Carla. Swap out.' He'd never used that harsh tone with me before, and part of me wanted to retreat. Only, I sensed that this was his way of trying to connect. Uncertainly, I reached for his hand under the table, and he interlocked our fingers.

'Are you okay?' I ventured, stroking my thumb on his skin.

He exhaled. 'Been a big week. I could do with some downtime.'

The touch seemed to soothe him, and now I ran my fingers over his hand, relieved to see the clench in his jaw slacken. 'I'll try to swap.'

As Will and Hamish arrived and took a seat, Toby held my hand under the table. 'It'll be worth it, I promise you that.'

'What'll be worth it?' Will asked.

Toby grinned at Will and gave him nothing. He squeezed my hand and then gently released it, and immediately my skin missed his touch.

'Well, I have something for you,' Will said. 'First – have I shown you Hugo's latest?'

Dutifully, we watched a video on Will's phone of his son playing a violin wedged under his pudgy chin. The sound reminded me of a wailing possum.

'Lovely,' I said when it was done. '"Frère Jacques"?'

Will frowned. 'Pachelbel's Canon. He's studying Suzuki method. Turns out he's gifted.'

'Sure is.' Toby handed back the phone and turned to Hamish. 'What's happening with your kids?'

A look of pain crossed Hamish's face. 'Arabella, same as ever. Ballet four nights a week and it's all she ever talks about. James – well. We're trying a new intensive therapy. Eight hours a day. The literature on it is somewhat speculative, but Ursula thinks we're making inroads.'

No one knew what to say. After a minute, the quiet grew uncomfortable.

'Perhaps he'll turn the corner,' Will said. 'He could turn out like you, with all your spreadsheets ...'

Hamish's shoulders hunched inwards, and Toby saw it. He held up his palm in Will's direction. 'Steady on, Will.'

'James is seven and can't communicate his needs,' Hamish said in a low voice. 'When he's frustrated, he bangs his head on the wall. It's a long way from spreadsheets.'

'It must be so tough,' I said. I shot a quick look at Will, whose face had fallen as he saw his mistake.

'H, shit, I'm sorry,' Will said. 'I didn't realise ... and, you know, we love your – special quirks.'

Around us, waiters bustled, customers collected takeaway lattes, and a ghost of a smile graced Hamish's face.

Will turned to Toby and me. 'Well, I have something more for you. For the both of you.'

Please God, not more violin videos.

'A job?' Toby asked.

'Two jobs?' I added.

'Not quite,' Will said, reaching into his bag and pulling out a rib bone. 'Which one of you gets the honour? Want to show us how it's done?' He laughed at his own joke.

Toby held up both palms. 'I had nothing to do with that.'

'Of course, Tobes,' Will said easily. 'You're always missing in action when it comes time to take responsibility.'

Toby screwed up his face and looked away.

Will handed me the rib, and I traced a finger along its slender edge, from where it once articulated with a vertebra, arcing around to where it would have met the sternum.

'C'mon, C! Show us how it's done!' Will guffawed and Toby grinned, and in my head, Liv's rib splintered.

'I sacrificed this baby from my old anatomy skeleton at home, just for you, C.' He raised his coffee. 'To the bone crusher.'

'Will – the patient's still in ICU,' Toby said quietly.

Will's grin slid a little. 'Too soon? Okay, poor form on my part. Sorry, Carla.'

'She'll get out of ICU,' Toby said. 'But she's got mets, so ...'

'Onc said the histology was favourable,' I said, a defensive edge to my voice. 'There's a trial she's eligible for. And for some of these patients with metastatic disease, it's become more of a chronic disease than a death sentence.'

'Carla's got a bit involved,' Toby said.

'Shut *up*!' I said, louder than I meant. 'It was a king-size fuck-up and, well ... just don't.' I handed the rib back to Will.

Hamish turned to me. 'I believe your comments are accurate. I read a recent review suggesting quite a paradigm shift in the management of breast cancer. That could be important to raise at the M&M.'

The M&M: my public reckoning. I would need all the help I could get to survive that. I nodded thanks to Hamish and took a knife to my fruit toast. The cafe music changed to some kind of traditional jazz, and Will came to life, telling us how he loved Miles Davis and demonstrating his best chair-dancing, one shoulder forwards and then the other, his gut wobbling in time with the beat.

With the rib resting on the table like a failed one-liner, he began a story from his days in ortho.

'I call in this patient, a woman needing a new knee. She limps into the room, followed by a man and a woman, and I presume they're all family, right, here to help her given she can barely walk. Anyway, they all sit down together, and I'm going through the consent, and the second woman is staring at me, like, "What are *you* doing here?" I press on, but it's a bit unnerving.' He laughed at the memory.

'Then, we're about to sign the forms, when the second woman stands up and says, "I don't know what I'm doing here." She turns to the woman with the sore knee and wishes her luck with her operation and then she leaves!'

'Psych ward?' Toby asks.

'I have no idea. Neither did the patient! She said to me, "I thought she was with you!" So much for patient confidentiality.'

Toby laughed. 'I can beat that. I nearly stuck a chest tube in the wrong patient once!'

Despite my simmering anger, I had to smile. Only Toby would compete over stuff-up stories.

'Go on, Tobes,' Will said. 'Tell us your worst.'

'Well, the reg called and asked me to put a tube in a Mr Tan, okay, fluid up to his neck, apparently. So, I arrive on the ward, but there's no interpreter and I can't find a bloody nurse anywhere. Anyway, I waltz into the first room and there's this Chinese guy sitting up in bed, and I said to him, "You need a chest tube?" And he says, "Yes, Doctor," so I get on with it. I've prepped the chest and injected the local when a nurse rushes in and says, "What are you doing? This is Mr Lam. Mr Tan is in bed five down the hall!"'

'Priceless,' Will said in a dry voice. 'Oh, and you'll love this: I have a new item for the Rectum Collection. It's a beauty. You have to guess.' He looked around the table. 'Take your time.'

We thought for a minute.

'Tick, tick, tick.'

'Not a clock?' Toby said.

'Sixty-year-old, married guy. Driven to ED by his wife with a clock up his arse.'

Hamish asked the dimensions, and Will told him to use his imagination, and Hamish's cheeks coloured pink.

'Imagine if the alarm went off!' Toby said, and we laughed, and I let my anger go. In their own weird way, they were trying to cheer me up, one foreign body up a rectum at a time.

DURING

Will, and jazz.

Jazz, and Will.

They play jazz, 9 July, an organised chaos of trumpet and trombone and silky piano, the bass and the clip of the tin hat keeping the beat, but I listen for that moment when the trombone and the trumpet cease their furious competition for boldest and brightest, leaving the swish of a brush on a snare.

These quiet moments are a reprieve. Couples slow their moves on the dance floor, and I can draw breath, steady my balance – Goddamn this spinning room – and appreciate the silence. As I drink it in, it occurs to me that in the pauses lies the music.

Watching the band, I don't see him coming.

Just as the band shifts gear and ramps it up, I feel a hand, behind my knees, unlocking them, so I buckle like a camp-table.

Then I'm spinning.

Not the room, now – *me*.

Someone's arms are around me, and now I'm upside down, legs in the air and my head tips close to the floor, and I'm totally in the control of the person holding me.

My dress rides up.

I hear laughter.

I'm totally fucking furious.

I'm swung around, doll-like, until I'm upright, and Will's flushed, grinning face comes into focus.

He yells over the music, 'Don't you love Miles Davis?' Before I can answer, he grabs my hand and spins me.

Blurry, leery faces whiz past and, incredibly, I hear cheering.

I'm too shocked and slow and too damn compliant to do anything except be thrown around, stomach lurching, dress awry, hair dishevelled, as he picks me up again and I brace myself for another upside-down move but mercifully this is a low dip. I'm flung to one side and then the other, his hands under my armpits.

Applause now, for the guy and his plaything.

Enough.

I don't want his hands on me.

I right myself and draw away, even as the music continues.

'I'm not a fucking doll!'

He reels back. I see the whites of his eyes.

He tells me it was just a bit of fun and shakes his head at what a bad sport I am. He holds out his hand for another dance. *Peace offering? No stunts this time.*

I back away, mouthing 'no', and the crowd parts as I leave the dance floor.

I'm done, even then.

I long for home, for my bed, for the music found in silence.

BEFORE
Complication

an unfavourable consequence of a disease, health condition or treatment

Liv held on. I visited at the start and end of each day, and grew to know her small hands, smudged with bruises, the mole on her neck near her central line, and the fine features disappearing into her swollen face.

But Anthea was falling apart. She kept a vigil by the bed, picking at the fluff on her clothes, scrutinising any health professional who visited. I dodged her questions and tried not to meet her eye.

One morning, I was checking Liv's charts when Tess, one of the surgical registrars, messaged asking to meet for a coffee. She would be needing an accredited job next year and I presumed she wanted advice about that.

Avoiding Anthea's gaze, I scurried from Liv's room and met Tess at Bea's. I looked her over as she sat across the table from me. She was a tall girl who wore a floral dress and a lot of jewellery – a brooch pinned to her jacket, dangling earrings and a necklace with an amber pendant. She had long, blonde hair that spiralled into ringlets, which she wore in a complicated, messy bun.

I didn't dislike the look – it would work just fine for a bookseller or street artist – but it wasn't going to wash for a surgeon. She'd take longer to tie up her hair and remove her jewellery than it took a patient to bleed out.

She sipped her almond latte and clasped her hands together. 'I'm so glad we have a chance to catch up ... it's so cool.'

Hyperbole. Did everything have to be the coolest, most awesome, amazing? How would she describe, say, a mediocre day?

Maybe it was the way of Tess's generation, this desire to paint the world in extremes.

I stifled my irritation and asked how her rotation was going.

'Oh. My. God. I love surgery so much. I mean, I've learnt heaps already, and the other day Phil let me finish an appendicectomy, and I had this feeling' – she placed her palm on her chest – 'like it is such a privilege, to do what we do. If I could get on the program, that would be the best.'

I wished her luck.

'So, I wanted to propose something,' Tess said. 'Ooh, I'm nervous! Never mind. We're starting this group at PCH, okay, and we thought you might come? It would be so great if you did. So far, it's me, Isobel, Yasmin and Liane. We're hoping all the female trainees will come. The idea is, we talk about what it's like, navigating the world of surgery, and support each other, share ideas of what has worked. That kind of thing.'

She glanced at me, and I became aware of my face screwed up into a grimace. From my earliest days in surgery, I had sensed a push for trainees to associate by gender. The men would play golf and bond over their shared school tie. The women were no part of that. Did we want to form our own circle and cement ourselves as outcasts, when what we really wanted was genuine inclusion?

'I suppose I'm wondering – is this the best approach, isolating yourselves like that? And, being honest, is there any risk to your career, starting something before you're accepted onto the program?'

Tess looked uncertain. 'I – hadn't thought of it like that. We can still be part of the fraternity, you know. It's not like we're excluding ourselves from anything. It's more a recognition that it can be hard, right – and maybe we can help each other. We've been talking about it for a while.'

I nodded, unconvinced. Fact was that it was a male world, and the best thing we could do was recognise it and work within it.

'Do you ever find any of the consultants – overstep the mark?' Her words came out in a rush.

I kept my face neutral. 'In what way?'

Her cheeks flushed. 'A couple of times, Benson has made me feel ... uncomfortable, I guess.' She rotated the ring on her thumb. 'I don't mean to be ungrateful or anything, he's been so kind to me, but – the way he stares at my chest.'

When I had started at PCH, I'd taken my cue from how the theatre nurses dealt with Benson, their weary acceptance of his clumsy flirting demonstrating that, in their eyes, he was just an ageing surgeon, increasingly irrelevant and no threat to anyone.

I wondered how old Tess was. Twenty-eight, twenty-nine? Surely old enough to cope with a dirty glance or two.

I shook my head.

'Oh, well, I'm glad he hasn't bothered you,' Tess said, and I cringed at her generosity in the face of my lie.

My pager buzzed with a message from ICU. *Please review Olivia Lai.*

I stood and told her I had to go.

'Okay ... the first meeting is in a couple of weeks, and Edwina Storer is coming, isn't that incredible? She's run a similar group at Spotswood.'

Edwina was a surgeon on the make, working her way up the college ladder. She was an impressive speaker and didn't come across as though she'd ever asked for or needed a handout. 'That's great,' I said.

'So, you'll come?' Tess asked, her earrings jangling.

'I – I'm not sure it's my thing,' I said, trying not to sound too evasive.

Tess winced. 'Oh, but – it won't be the same without you there. Would you at least think about it?'

'Okay. I'll think about it.'

'Great! Awesome! That's the best!'

I hoped speaking in superlatives wasn't contagious.

~

At week's end, I walked home from work on weary legs. Liv was stable, and I told myself I could do nothing for her now, and that was fortunate because I had nothing left. I craved wine, a bath. Maybe together.

Under the branches of the Moreton Bay figs, I put one foot after the other, through the park, enduring the mockery from a pair of sulphur-crested cockatoos whose screeching chided me for my detour before Liv's surgery. Alongside the snarl of peak hour, I walked down Alexandra Parade and onto Rathdowne.

Key in the front door, the bath calling me now – limp limbs floating in searingly hot water, letting everything slide –

Through the open door, I heard voices and laughter. Damn! Maybe it was just Richard, and I could plead fatigue. But as I walked down the hall to the kitchen, there was another male voice, which I recognised but couldn't place.

Fleur greeted me as I entered the living room.

'Look what the surf washed up!'

I surveyed the scene. Next to the couch, two surfboards rested against the wall, Richard stood in the kitchen putting a pot on to boil, and on the couch, one leg nestled under the other, was Xander Arlen.

I blinked. Tried to smile and failed. I was immediately conscious of my dishevelled hair. After the week I'd had, I was sure I'd have bags under my eyes. I shot Fleur a look: *you could have warned me*.

It must have been ten years, maybe more. His hair was rockstar long.

A smile stole darkness from his face. 'You look like you've seen a ghost.'

'It's been a while.'

Richard walked into the living room wearing an apron and holding a wooden spoon. 'What a day. This has made my week, man – gotta tell you.'

My week. Standing over Liv's bloodied body, not knowing what to do. Realising the bone scan was not checked. And watching her in ICU, waiting and hoping she would make it out.

I rubbed at the knot in my shoulder.

'Who runs into an old friend in a three-metre swell?' Richard turned to me. 'I'm out the back at Gunnamatta, freezing my balls off, shitting myself that I'm going to die out here. And this one' – he gestured to Xander – 'comes past on his board, on an absolute mother of a wave, like he's cruising on the back of a giant bird or something. Crazy, man.'

Richard grabbed his board and laid it on the floor and jumped on, wobbling a little. 'Like this. The waves were huge, right?' He began to sway as if riding a wave, and the euphoric look on his face coupled with the apron and the wooden spoon made me laugh despite my grumpiness.

Fleur passed me a glass of wine and in a low voice I asked her if Richard was drinking again.

She shook her head. 'Just excited.' She turned to him. 'Richard, stop. You're being ridiculous.'

'I'm like an old man out there compared to him. But, jeez, it felt good.'

'You know you're alive,' Xander said.

'Hell yes!' Richard said. 'You should try it some time, Carla.'

Fleur started counting on her fingers. 'It must be fifteen years since we've all been together.'

She made it sound like we were long-lost family. 'I don't think the four of us ever hung out.'

'Well, you know, since we were all at uni.' Fleur's face was flushed. I didn't understand why she got such a kick from connections with the past. If Xander had wanted to stay in touch, he would have.

I remembered standing outside a pub in Prahran, a kiss in the darkness – cold air on my cheeks, the only warmth from his lips.

Fleur jumped up and put on some music, and of course it was Xander's, one of those songs whose chorus stays in your head. She bounced around the room singing. Everyone wanted to know a celebrity, apparently, but not me. I longed for that bath, plunging my head under, my hair swirling like seaweed, thoughts deadening.

Fleur declared the next song her favourite. I listened to the laid-back rhythm with a touch of melancholy, and I had to admit, it was good. I remembered it had been the backing music for a Peugeot ad.

'"Angels Tripping on Cobblestones",' Xander said. 'Been dining off that one for years. Sometimes, I can hardly believe it's mine. 'Specially since the writing dried up.'

Fleur laid cutlery on the table. 'You've stopped writing?'

'Nothing. For over two years.'

'That's too bad.'

'I – my dad died, a couple of years ago, and since then – I just can't.'

'I'm sorry,' Fleur said. 'About your dad. I didn't know.'

'Fifteen years is a long time,' Xander said. 'Stuff happens.'

'Well, selfishly, I hope you get your writing bug back, because I love your songs.' She smiled at him, then sniffed at the air. 'Excuse me, smells like something's –' She went into the kitchen. 'Richard,' she called, 'you've completely burnt the rice!'

'No way,' Richard said, following her. 'That's not burnt, just – crispy.'

'Who ever ate crispy rice?'

The argument grew louder, and I grimaced at Xander, who asked if I'd show him around the house. We took our wine with us, and I gave him the tour, telling him how the house had been my grandparents' first home when they arrived by boat after the war. I pointed out the pressed metal ceilings in the bedrooms. Xander paused to admire the soft coloured light drifting through the stained-glass window in the stairwell, which had always reminded me of church.

'This house has great bones. I can see why you love it,' he said.

I was pleased, and annoyed with myself for caring.

We climbed the stairs, and I remembered sitting on the creaky third step, sulking over a comment from Zia Silvia – *you have your father's nose, such a shame!* – and then becoming distracted from my bad mood by the noisy arguments at the dinner table between the men while the women cooked and fussed and fetched. Even then, I didn't know who I would be, but I knew I wouldn't be one of *those* women.

Upstairs, I unlocked the balcony doors and we stepped out into the night, under a fat yellow moon. I drank my wine, and the quiet soothed my jagged thoughts.

Xander leant his forearms against the balcony and inclined his head back towards the stairs. 'They always like that?'

'Fleur and Richard? Yeah, pretty much.'

'That's intense.'

I smiled, because intense was the word I would have used for him. I turned towards him, noticing the golden skin on his forearms.

'So ... you're this famous muso now.'

'B-grade celeb. The worst kind of fame, enough so that you can't have a latte in peace, not enough to pay the bills.'

'You must like it a bit.'

He drank his wine. 'Some parts, sure. When I'm on stage, and the crowd's into the song, that's cool. Bit of a power kick, actually.' He looked sideways at me. 'Surgery would be like that too, right?'

I saw Liv's bloated face in ICU.

'No.'

He raised an eyebrow. 'People hand their bodies over to you to be fixed. There's power in that.'

'I don't think of it like that. It's more a – a privilege.' I caught myself recycling Tess's words. 'Almost an act of intimacy, kind of. That people would give you that trust.'

He nodded. 'I can see that. Would you be out on a limb, with an attitude like that? In surgery, I mean.'

I frowned. 'I think every doctor –' Okay, maybe not Toby, and possibly not Will. 'Lots of surgeons think that way.' I hoped he wouldn't ask for a list.

'Maybe it was just my experience. I did my surg term at PCH, and I didn't meet a single one ...' He saw me roll my eyes and smacked his forehead. 'You're kidding me. That's not where you work?!'

'It's the best unit in Melbourne.'

'Sorry – it was such a male hunting ground, when I was there, I didn't think any woman would want –'

'What's that supposed to mean?'

He startled. 'Hey, I'm sorry – I mean – it's serious establishment territory, right? Boys' club, private schools. No women consultants, at least back then.'

'Things have changed.'

'How?'

It had always irritated me, how doggedly Xander followed a line of questioning – no getting away with half-truths.

'They just have.'

'Is Hargreaves still the head?'

I nodded.

'Surgery was my last term. No coincidence there.'

I took a good look at Xander – shoulder-length hair, black linen shirt, a thick silver ring on one thumb – getting more annoyed by the moment. There was nothing about his looks and charisma that entitled him to take pot shots at Prof.

'He's a great surgeon.'

'I'm sure.'

'What are you trying to say?'

Xander paused. 'That surgery term for me was –' He shook his head. 'That was when I knew I had to leave. The way they went about it – their culture – was all part of it.'

I bristled. 'I thought you dropped out because you failed. One too many surfing trips, wasn't it?'

He smiled. 'True. And hey, it's your world, I'm not trying to diss it. Just saying – the hypocrisy, I couldn't hack it. It was the right call. Should be grateful to them, actually.'

I gulped down my wine.

'I've offended you,' he said. 'I'm sorry.'

I shrugged. 'It's okay. I've had a bad week, that's all.'

He looked a question at me, and I wanted to tell someone, but he'd just insulted my tribe. 'I – something went wrong with a patient. A stuff-up, I guess.'

'Are you okay?'

It was the first time anyone had asked. 'I will be.'

'Sounds like it was hard going.'

'Yeah, well, that's medicine. Why are you in Melbourne, anyway?'

He laughed. 'You ready for me to leave?' I didn't answer, and he laughed more. 'Well, your wish is just about granted. I'm only here for a few gigs. That, and chasing the swell.'

That pretty much summed up Xander.

My phone buzzed in my pocket.

> I am outside ur place

I startled and looked out onto the street, where Toby's Audi was parked. What was he doing here? Then I remembered the conversation at breakfast, and the weekend away. Jesus.

The car horn beeped, and Xander looked down.

'Um – that's for me.'

Xander stared at Toby's numberplate, illuminated by a streetlight. 'Tenner,' he read. 'Complete wanker –' He stopped, colour draining from his face. 'No – not Toby Tennyson?'

It wasn't enough that he'd badmouthed PCH, now he had to start in on Toby? 'Yes, actually. What's it to you, anyway?'

He drew breath, ran a hand through his hair. 'Nothing. Just – Carla, that guy –' He shook his head.

'Thanks for the advice. Not needed.'

As the car horn beeped again, I said goodbye.

~

'Thought you were going to stand me up,' Toby said as I threw my overnight bag into the back seat and got into the car.

'Some friends dropped by. I couldn't just leave. *You* could have come in.'

'Nice necklace.'

My fingers went to the diamond around my neck. I tried to smile.

He turned onto the freeway and put a hand on my thigh. 'You haven't been taking my calls.'

'I've been busy – with our patient, among other things. Remember her?'

'Oh, yeah. How's she doing?'

'Better.'

'Good to hear.'

I couldn't believe his distant tone, like we were discussing lawn bowls. 'Aren't you – shaken up? I mean, her surgery was a complete disaster. And we're going to have to front the M&M.'

'I know, right?'

How did Toby manage to stuff up an operation and move on like nothing had happened?

'We'll work it out. Will reckons Benson could be in the firing line.'

'Benson?'

'He saw her in clinic, right? But Prof and Benson – they go way back. So depends if Prof is ready to knife his right-hand man.'

I leant back in my seat, smelling its leather. Through the window, I watched as we sped past blurred shadows of trees. The murkiness of scapegoating Benson sat uneasy with me, but it would bring about the job. Maybe one good thing could come from this shitstorm.

After a while, he spoke.

'I'm sorry if I've been – distant over all of this. I *am* shaken up. Dad's been giving me a really hard time. Loves bringing me down, pointing out my flaws. It's the way he is, but – it takes its toll.'

I'd only spoken once or twice to Geoffrey Tennyson, never having rotated through plastics, and all I'd seen was a successful Chief of Surgery who was polite and respectful to me, silver-fox handsome, maybe even a bit charming. I'd assumed that having your father on staff would be a huge advantage, but if I believed Toby's take on things, maybe not?

I put my hand on his forearm, and he put his right hand over mine and I drew comfort from the warmth of his touch.

We stayed that way as we passed through the township of Yarra Glen and arrived at a cottage, its entrance framed by a weeping willow. Inside it was cool and dark. I lingered at the photos in the hall, family snaps of waterskiing and Christmas. An attractive family with confident smiles and well-constructed photos. There was a sister, older than Toby, I guessed. I felt an ache that I was here in their holiday home and yet I knew almost nothing about them, and they didn't even know I existed.

Toby had unpacked the food in the kitchen and was marinating prawns in garlic and chilli. As I poured us wine, I asked about his family and said I'd like to meet them.

'You sure about that?'

'Yes. Yes, I am. They're part of you. I want to know them.'

'Not much to know. Miranda is a Daddy's-girl lawyer at Minter-Ellison who hangs out with a crowd of semi-famous arty wankers, Mum is a stay-at-home wife who you'd have nothing in common with, and Dad is God's gift to plastic surgery, which you already knew.'

'The thing is – I don't want us to be a secret anymore.'

He shrugged and picked up a prawn from the frypan with his fingers. 'Try this.'

I took a bite of the prawn. It was tender and spicy, and juice dribbled on my chin. He watched as I ate, and then fed me another one, and it was like some kind of foreplay with our eyes locked on each other, only something niggled. This house was full of his family, almost like they were sitting at the kitchen table watching us.

Slowly, keeping him at arm's length, I unbuttoned my shirt. He grinned and reached for me, but I held his hand away from my bare chest.

'Turn off the frypan.'

He turned a dial on the stove. 'Done.'

I stood there, topless and terrified. 'Promise me you'll introduce me to your parents.'

'Really?' he said with a groan. 'We're going to play this game?'

I waited. He wouldn't leave me hanging, would he?

Eventually he grumbled, *okay, I promise*, and only then did I reach for him. He lifted me onto the kitchen table, where I came once with his touch, and again with him inside me. In a thick-throated voice, he called my name.

Afterwards, we cooked and ate the rest of the prawns and around midnight, under a moonlit sky, he took me to the jetty over the river. The water was still and dark and the sky enormous.

He sat on a bench overlooking the water and gestured to the buttons on my shirt. 'Do it again.'

'Here?' I laughed.

He nodded. Biting my lip, eyes on him, I unbuttoned my shirt and straddled him. The cold air goose-bumped my skin. I tilted my head back and laughed up at the sky and its tiny stars, scared and excited.

His hands ran over my body and when he gripped my back, I knew I'd never felt anything like this. Once he was inside me, I was past caring who might see. Every part of my skin tingled.

If anyone ever asked me, *how did love feel*, I would answer –

It felt like this.

Tourniquet

any device for arresting bleeding by forcibly compressing a blood vessel, such as a bandage tightened by twisting

Morbidity and mortality meetings were held the third Thursday of the month and I hurtled towards it, feeling as unprepared as a hungover registrar facing a morning list without caffeine.

Liv was out of ICU. I visited her on the ward, but she was mostly sleeping, still on oxygen, in quite a bit of pain. Anthea was a barricade by the bed, and I did my best to avoid her and her unanswerable questions.

My anxiety eased with Liv's improvement, but still the M&M loomed. Standing in front of my peers, defending our decision to operate? I'd rather volunteer for a month of assisting Benson and his tremor.

On the day prior to the M&M, Will and Toby had a morning list, so it was only Hamish and me at breakfast. I was glad for the reprieve from Will and his jokes. I couldn't laugh about what had happened to Liv, or deal with another stunt.

I ate my poached eggs and watched Hamish use the edge of his spoon to divide his porridge into four quadrants and then delicately bisect two halves of a poached pear and place one pear slice in each porridge quadrant. He began eating in a clockwise direction. I'd first seen him eat like this on a shared country rotation. 'You and me ... like old Traralgon times.'

He nodded. 'Minus the tandoori pizza.'

'And the shit coffee.' I grimaced at the memory. 'That pizza was the worst!'

'Once eaten, never forgotten,' Hamish said. 'Actually, I have quite intense memories of it.'

'Six months in the Latrobe Valley will do that,' I said lightly, but I guessed he meant something else. The night he had driven to the pizza shop to collect our Napoletana and returned with chicken tandoori pizza was the night that Ursula had called. I remembered opening the pizza box while he spoke to her, and, as I surveyed the fuchsia chicken topping, I could hear her crying down the phone.

Once off the phone, Hamish looked bemused at the pizza and bravely ate a mouthful. His expression didn't change but he placed the rest of the slice in the bin. It was then he told me that James had been diagnosed with autism.

I remembered all of this as I asked him how James was doing.

After a mouthful from the porridge at three o'clock, he ate the first piece of pear. 'It's his birthday tomorrow.'

'Are you celebrating?'

He sighed. 'Ursula has invited everyone she knows. She does this every year, even though crowds usually bring on a spectacular meltdown for James and he spends the rest of the party in his room watching The Wiggles.' He bowed his head. 'It's not how I imagined it would be.'

'How did you imagine it?' I ask gently.

'If I'm honest, I find it excruciating. All the children from school, doing things he will never do. Until he got diagnosed, I'd assumed he would have all the opportunities I had. But the behavioural therapy is barely stopping him from biting the skin off his hand and head-banging the wall.'

'I'm sorry.' Hamish didn't usually talk about James. Knowing Will's sense of humour, I didn't blame him for keeping it inside.

'Have you spoken with anyone?' I asked. 'My friend Richard, he's a paed, he talked about a kind of mourning, for the child you hoped for, when your child is diagnosed with developmental issues. A sort of living grief.'

He squeezed his eyes shut tight, and then opened them. 'Grief of the worst kind, trussed up with guilt, because he is still here. And secrecy, because Ursula – she won't even countenance that a parent could feel that way. She thinks it's shameful.'

'You care, though – I mean, you do so much for him –'

'Oh, I feel the tug of parental responsibility, no doubt. But the affection I feel for Arabella, when she hugs me –' His voice cracked.

Was he saying he didn't love James? I didn't know how to ask, or how to respond, or even whether I wanted to know the answer.

'I love my son,' he said. 'But I don't know how to show it.'

I put my hand on his arm. 'Don't be too hard on yourself, Hamish.'

He inhaled a jagged breath. 'Thank you, Carla. I've not talked to anyone about this. I'm truly grateful to have someone who understands.'

I wasn't sure that I did understand, but I nodded. He ate his way to eight o'clock, and then pulled a wad of journal articles from his bag. 'I collected these for you.'

The first paper was another of Hamish's quirky finds. It described the speed-hump sign, where patients with appendicitis experienced increased pain when they were driven over a speed hump. I pictured Hamish standing at the end of a cubicle bed in ED, dispassionately asking patients writhing with abdominal pain how they felt travelling over a speed hump.

While I read, I was aware of him, gripping a pen between his teeth the way a dog holds a bone, and then taking it out of his mouth and rolling it under his nose. He saw me grimace and put the pen down, gesturing to the paper.

'I rather thought that you could approach the M&M in the same way.'

I looked down at the paper and then back at him. 'Short-term pain for long-term gain ... is that what you mean?'

He nodded. 'There will be something to learn from this.'

I admired Hamish's belief in the learning opportunities afforded by scrutinising medical errors, but I was more focused on survival. 'Here's hoping it's not a six-car pile-up.'

'Indeed. The other papers cover surgery for patients with metastatic breast cancer. On that topic, you may wish to invite one of the oncologists to the M&M.'

I thanked him. 'I don't know how to approach the meeting. Toby has prepared some slides, but they don't say what actually happened.'

Hamish drank his long black. 'Every error will have a series of moments or decisions that led to the ultimate outcome. It is almost never just one action. Or one person.'

My thoughts clouded as I digested this. Me, in the quiet room with Toby. Me, in theatre, starting the surgery without checking the bone scan. I shook my head.

Hamish cleared his throat. 'I can see that you care for this patient, and that could leave you vulnerable to taking the blame. While you don't want to hang anyone – that would be bad form – you don't want to take the entire rap yourself. Did the patient enquire about her bone-scan result?'

I didn't know.

'And forgive me for asking, but why were you unsupervised in theatre in the first place?'

'Prof had a meeting, or something.'

He ate the last quadrant of porridge and the remaining segment of pear and laid his spoon at twelve o'clock. 'Well. Not only your responsibility, then.'

Maybe. 'Thanks, Hamish.'

'Best of luck for tomorrow. These days M&Ms are meant to be a no-blame investigation, remember.'

Somehow, I didn't think Prof had read that memo.

~

I spent the night at Toby's. I told myself we could handle the M&M and it would be best if we did so together.

When I arrived at his apartment, he pulled me inside, and we were at it before I had even shut the door behind me, his hands running under clothes and over skin, searching, hungry.

I pushed away all thoughts of tomorrow and went with it. With my shirt off and Toby's mouth on my breast, I reached over and slammed the door, and he pushed me up against it.

We fucked, our ragged breath in time with the door rattle. After he came, his head sank onto my shoulder, and I felt his warm, shallow exhalations on my skin.

After, we lay on the hallway floor, my ear to his chest, and I listened as his heart rate returned to resting. This urgency we felt for each other, it was real, unstoppable. We had to get through the M&M and whatever happened with the job, and then we could get on with our life together.

After a restless sleep, I woke at almost light. Toby was asleep next to me, his palm cupping his serene face, his other arm draped over me. I leant up on my elbow and drank him in.

I could not have wanted him more. I loved every millimetre of him.

We just had to get through today.

~

The room was full of surgeons and trainees. They came to watch blood spill.

I made my way to the front row, where Toby was already seated, legs splayed, scrolling on his phone.

My thoughts drifted to last night, him pressing me up against the door –

I wrenched myself away from the memory.

Today was about survival, and I would do what it took.

Prof arrived and took his customary seat at the end of the second row, part participant, part observer, all power. Geoffrey Tennyson joined him and smiled encouragement at me when he met my eye. I wondered how Toby would feel about his being here.

Directly in front of me was a portrait of William Casterton, the founding surgeon at Prince Charles. His large hands clasped his belly, fingertips touching at the midline. His blue eyes asked me a question and I didn't have the answer.

A fragment of the 'Our Father' prayer came to me, words I had muttered as a child, kneeling outside the confessional after the priest had decided the penance for my sins was ten Hail Marys and an Our Father.

Forgive us our trespasses, as we forgive those who trespass against us.

A registrar stood and presented the first case and his words washed over me: *alcoholic, difficult historian, late diagnosis, ruptured bowel.* Here, the surgeons were the cavalry, getting involved when the die was already cast. The stuff-up belonged squarely to the physician who had treated her for five days for constipation before noticing the air under the diaphragm on her chest X-ray. Prof surmised that missing this cardinal sign of bowel rupture cost the patient her life.

With no physicians in the room, no bullets hit their mark.

The next case was a diabetic smoker who died during an aortic aneurysm repair. We and vascular had been involved, but the patient was crumbly, and Geoffrey judged that the surgeons had done the needful. I felt the room exhale relief. No one liked to lose a patient on the table.

Then Toby stood, and I drew my arms around my rib cage as he presented Liv's history, his eyes steadily on his notes. He glossed over the calls he'd received from the nursing staff asking him to review Liv pre-operatively, and I marvelled at his rewriting of events. Apart from me, did anyone else in the room know the truth? It would only take a flicking through of Liv's hospital file to find out.

Toby carried on, recounting the surgery, Liv's decline into hypoxia and hypotension, the moment when we realised she had a huge pulmonary embolus blocking the blood flow to the lungs.

Then he paused, and Prof spoke. 'If I am correct, a nurse asked for this patient to be reviewed that morning. Regarding a sore leg.'

The room fell silent.

Toby scratched at his eyebrow. 'That is true, but unfortunately I was busy.'

My fingers reached for the diamond nestling in the hollow between my collarbones. What was he going to say?

'Mrs Greenidge was quite unstable that morning, and I had my hands full keeping her alive.'

'And you, Carla?' Prof asked.

I swallowed against a dry throat. 'I – I ... wasn't aware.'

Behind me, people murmured disapproval.

Toby continued the presentation, describing the undiagnosed metastases. When someone asked about the bone scan, Toby opened his mouth to speak, and then closed it.

The room was quiet, waiting.

Benson spoke. 'I saw this patient pre-op. Lovely young girl. She wanted to have the scan done closer to home, so she had it done privately, I believe.'

'And no one thought to check it?'

Benson fixed his rheumy eyes on Prof. 'It seems not. Of course, it wasn't *my* list.'

I'd never seen Benson and Prof disagree before, and in the mildest of ways, Benson had thrown a hand grenade at Prof, who drew himself tall and looked at me. 'Carla?'

I pressed one thumbnail into the other until it hurt. 'Clearly if we'd known, we wouldn't have operated. I – it – I don't know why it wasn't checked.'

'It was in her file?'

'Yes,' I whispered.

'But no one thought to look at it, the morning of the surgery. Better things to do, perhaps.'

Forgive us our trespasses.

I heard a snorting noise from behind me, and I turned to see Will and Lachlan, one of the registrars, stifling laughter.

Toby caught my eye and gave me a sympathetic look.

'Um, excuse me.' It was Tess speaking up, a little hesitantly. I turned to see her sitting down the row from Lachlan and Will. 'There's a very sick patient at the heart of this, and I – I don't think we should lose sight of that.' Her lips trembled a smile at me, and I returned with a nervous one of my own.

I cleared my throat. 'There is also the recent literature out of Boston, suggesting you should excise the primary even when it has spread, to reduce tumour burden.'

'Excellent point, Carla,' said a voice on the other side of the room. I swivelled to see Prof Herath from oncology. 'Clearly, this patient needed to be stabilised first, particularly with respect to her coagulation, but we may well have suggested surgery, once we had her clotting under control.'

I exhaled a lungful of air. Was he giving me an out?

'Interesting observations, Mohan,' said Prof. 'It would represent something of a change in practice for these patients. Although, as this case demonstrates, their surgical risk might be somewhat greater than a patient without metastases.'

'Nothing you can't handle, Alister,' Prof Herath said.

They debated the point some more, and then Toby completed the presentation, summarising the cardiac arrest, CPR and embolectomy in a monotone that made them sound as mundane as a weather forecast.

'And where was the consultant, exactly?' someone asked, and there was a silence while I waited for Prof to reply.

'Carla?' someone prompted.

'Um ... ah ... Prof?'

He looked at me over his glasses and I knew that I had done wrong naming him, but I was bewildered – what was I meant to say?

He cleared his throat. 'If I had not been called away to an emergency, perhaps things might have been different.'

I felt the wind knocked out of me. *Emergency?*

'Well, then,' Prof continued. 'Undiagnosed metastases and a massive PE. Quite a lot to learn from this case, I would think. Notwithstanding Mohan's comments, it prevails on us as surgeons to be sure – or as sure as we can be – that our patients are fit candidates for surgery. Which this woman' – he tapped his pen on Liv's file – 'clearly was not.'

Bill Casterton stared down at me from the portrait on the wall. Prof delivered the rest of his sermon, talking about communication and teamwork. A nerve throbbed on my cheekbone.

Then I realised the room was quiet and Prof was looking at me. 'An update on the patient, please?'

'She is out of ICU. There are plans for chemo, I believe.'

'And a mastectomy,' Prof Herath said, and there was a titter.

'We shall look forward to a better outcome next time,' Prof said, his eyes roaming from Toby to Benson, and coming to rest on me. Fat chance I would have of being anywhere near that surgery.

With that, we were done. I fixed my gaze on the exit sign at the end of the hall and forced one step in front of the other. In the stairwell, the tremor in my legs took over, and I stopped and leant my forehead on the cool concrete.

Above me, the door opened, and Will smiled down at me. 'Here you are. Come on, bone crusher, I'll buy you a coffee.'

I shook my head. He didn't get it.

'Come on, you'll feel better. Lachlan showed me the funniest meme – have you seen the one where the guy falls into the pool trying to rescue his cat from the tree?'

If I spoke, I would cry.

I held up my palm, shook my head, and fled.

AFTER

Anger isn't a comfortable emotion for me. I don't like its storming and thumping, the slamming drawers and stomping feet. I don't like how it surges out of me like blood pulsing from a severed artery. No: stem that flow, clamp that vessel, bring the system into haemostasis.

That's not to say I don't know it, anger – oh, I know it – blinding hot, plundering, blundering, hands trembling, thoughts blurring. I know it well enough to be frightened of how hopeless it renders me – a tremulous, head-spinning surgeon is no use to any patient – and fearful of what I might be capable of, when in its frenzy.

After the M&M, it only takes an hour for humiliation to morph to fury. It's Toby's text, suggesting a hook-up, that does it. After he dumped me in a shitstorm with his fabricated Mrs G alibi!

Humiliation chafes like sand in my bathers. Fools don't get consultant jobs, not at PCH. I should have known they would all play the same game. I should have come up with my own set of lies and snookered Toby, Benson and Prof, while I was at it.

But Liv is my patient, and I let her down. I cannot lie about that, even if I want to.

After pacing the house for a while, caged with a feeling I don't know what to do with, I go for a run, thudding my feet onto asphalt and gravel. At least in telling the truth, I had stood by Liv, and I am proud of that. My anger is that this truth-telling has landed me in a huge pile of shit.

BEFORE
Poor historian

a patient who is unable to present a coherent medical history

I was glad to be busy the weekend after the M&M. Between sick ward patients and ED presentations, some of whom we admitted and took to theatre, there wasn't time for stewing – though I was rostered on with Lachlan, and each time he spoke, I remembered him sitting with Will, stifling laughter while my cheeks burnt.

Around three, we took ten minutes for lunch and wolfed down sandwiches at Bea's. Outside the internal window, Christmas lights flickered on a large plastic tree in the hospital foyer.

Lachlan had the look. His lilac shirt was brushed cotton with a buttoned-down collar. He was toned, like he worked out, but he had the full, soft cheeks of a toddler. He opened the bread of his sandwich, sniffed at the processed chicken and soggy lettuce, and made a face.

'You know, I work more than any of my friends – a lot of them are in banking and stuff, and they're out every weekend partying while I'm slogging away here and eating this shit,' he griped. 'And still, it doesn't feel like a sure thing that I'll get on the program. Five perfect score references, who even gets that?'

I remembered the feeling, but it was hard to have much sympathy for him.

'You're in with a damn good chance if you put in the work.'

'You think so?' He raised his eyebrows. 'Got any tips?'

I gave him my standard lines: take every opportunity to learn; keep on Prof's right side; don't piss off the nurses. Then I added one extra. 'Treat every team member – *everyone* – like you would want to be treated.'

He nodded, saying, *sure, sure,* trying one of his easy smiles on me, expecting me to smile back, but instead I shot him a death stare. I knew his quiet confidence and straight-toothed smile would unlock plenty of doors, but not with me.

I held the glare until slowly, slowly, the corners of his mouth turned down. 'You don't think I do that?'

Between us on the blue Laminex tabletop were salt and pepper shakers, small clear glass containers with silver perforated lids. Lachlan picked up the salt container and drummed it lightly on the table, and the salt within it did not move, one large amalgamated, useless crystal.

I felt the grime of Bea's, the autotuned, formulaic pop songs from some generic radio station on low from a speaker, the strangely yellow hash browns and fried dim sims under constant light in the bain-marie.

'I think laughing at a colleague is cruel.'

He frowned at me, and then looked away as he remembered. His mouth made an O shape, and he bowed his head.

'Right, yeah. That was –' He checked himself. 'I was going to say it was only a joke, but I can see now how that might have felt to you. I'm sorry.' Blotches appeared on his neck. 'I can explain – you know how Will loves a laugh ...'

Now it was me smiling, grimly, shaking my head. I didn't want him to open that wound; I had a whole weekend to work. 'Do better next time.'

We were interrupted by a message on Lachlan's pager about Iain, one of the post-ops from Friday, complaining about pain from his wound.

'He just had his butt sliced open and a cupful of pus drained out,' Lachlan said. 'What does he expect?'

Iain was a freckle-faced, slab-a-day, pack-a-day guy whose ischiorectal abscess drainage was possibly inducing an unplanned withdrawal from nicotine and alcohol.

'A beer?'

Lachlan shook his head. 'He's a geezer.'

'Yeah, well – right now, he's *your* geezer.'

Lachlan sighed. 'Yes, he is. Iain, my geezer, my man.' He looked at me. 'You don't want to go see him, by any chance?'

I exhaled an incredulous laugh.

'Okay, that's a no. The guy – he keeps asking for a *real* doctor, you know? Seriously, what am I?'

'Welcome to my world, Lachlan,' I said, trying to stifle my frustration. '"Excuse me, nurse? Oh, are you the cleaner? Could you let me know when the surgeon is coming?" It's fucking tedious.'

His jaw dropped and his cheeks flamed pink. 'I – right. I didn't think ... I didn't realise. People seem pretty used to women doctors these days.'

'Yes, but when they picture a surgeon, they see a man.'

He listened. 'You know, Carla – I hadn't thought about it ... but it's impressive, how you take everything in your stride. I guess you've been through a lot, to get where you are now – practically a consultant. I hope one day I'll be half the doctor you are.'

I took the compliment warily, half expecting he was bullshitting, but his face was sincere. 'Why do you want to be a surgeon?' I asked.

He picked up the saltshaker and bounced it now, in his hand, as if weighing its contents. The salt mass stayed stubbornly immobile.

'Well, I've never told anyone this, but when I was a kid – the sight of blood made me vomit, like actually throw up. And my brothers – I have two older brothers – they thought it was hilarious. You know that fake blood you can buy? They'd do shit like put it in my bed, smear it on their face to freak me out. So when I got into med, they were all like, "No way he'll do surgery." And here I am, and you know something? *I love it.* Fixing stuff, it's the best.'

I nodded. 'It's an amazing job.' I drank my espresso and stood up.

'Hey, about the blood thing ... you won't tell anyone, will you? I mean, blood doesn't bother me anymore.'

Imagine the fun Will would have with a fact like that. 'I won't tell anyone. Listen, back on Iain, I get that he's annoying, but he's just a lonely old guy who doesn't want to be stuck in hospital for Christmas.'

'Yeah, okay. My geezer, right?'

Now I smiled. 'Your geezer.'

I told him I needed to get back to ED, and to call me once he'd seen Iain. Striding the corridor in my scrubs, I was glad I'd called Lachlan on his behaviour. He had no clue what the M&M was like for me – he was a self-absorbed kid trying to prove his brothers wrong.

I walked down the stairs and into ED, where staff hustled around me. On the weekends, I was the most senior surgical doctor in the hospital. Whatever anyone said in the M&M, I knew how to do this job. I liked arriving in ED and knowing I was the one who would work out whether the emaciated young woman in front of me with unwashed hair and track marks really did have an acute abdomen or was just hunting for a fix.

The look in her eyes was a little too hungry, so I offered her Panadol and exploratory surgery, and she swore at me and took off.

I guessed right, then.

Standing in ED, watching her go, my resolve strengthened. I knew I could do this job. I would make up the ground with Prof, whatever it took. I would get Benson's job when it came up.

I pulled the curtain around the cubicle of the next patient. 'Hi, I'm Dr di Pieta, from surgery. Let's get you sorted out.'

~

On Sunday at four a.m., I was at home when I was woken by a call. I answered, my voice soft with sleep. Lachlan was on the line, mumbling about a breathless patient on the ward. My brain startled to alertness when I heard *metastatic cancer* and *rib fracture* and *pulmonary emboli*, and I realised his voice was shaking.

'The partner is threatening to take her home. They asked for you, it's a bit – volatile.'

I began dressing. 'Up her oxygen. I'll be there in fifteen.'

The hospital hallways glowed night-light yellow as my footsteps clipped the laminated floor. When I was night registrar, I walked these halls listening to snores and sighs, soothed by the quiet murmurings of sleeping patients, but tonight I hustled.

As I passed the nurses' station, one of them saw me.

'Carla! Is she that sick? I didn't realise he'd called you in.'

'I was in the hospital anyway.' I couldn't explain why Liv could not be left to Lachlan.

'Right. Hey, when you're done, can you check in on Iain? He's asking for more analgesia.'

I promised her we would sort it out and made my way down to Liv's room, where Lachlan was listening to her chest, a nurse took her blood pressure and another adjusted her IV, while in the corner, Anthea threw Liv's belongings into an overnight bag – orange and white dotted pyjamas, a dressing-gown, two thumbed-through novels and a pair of fluffy yellow slippers with duckbills at the toes.

Liv gasped for breath, the sheet pulled up under her chin. Her eyes darted around the room, searching –

And fixing on me.

Her hands gripped the bedsheet, tight.

Anthea dropped the bag and rushed over.

'Look at her. She's suffering. What the hell is going on? No one will tell us anything! And, they had the gall to shove this under her nose,' she said, waving a piece of paper at me, 'like it's just another day, another mastectomy. She nearly died and you expect us to just go back there – you people are mad!'

I took the piece of paper. It was a surgical consent form. I looked at Lachlan, who winced.

'We're trying to get her stable,' said one of the nurses. 'If you'd let us give her some painkillers –'

'You're trying to bloody kill her!' Anthea's neck veins bulged.

'We need to get her settled.'

'Liv, listen to me,' Anthea said. 'It's time to get a second opinion. I want to take you home. They stuffed up the first time and now they want to do it again! You're not safe here.' She went to the bedside. 'C'mon, Liv. Do you think you can stand up?'

Liv's eyes grew wide, and she shook her head. Lachlan looked at me, pleading for help.

The situation felt like a lit firecracker.

'Anthea,' I said. 'Let's make a plan here. I will assess Liv and then we'll talk.'

'Talk? Really talk?'

I blinked. *She is my patient, and I let her down. I will not lie about that.* 'I'll answer anything you want.'

Anthea exhaled and sat down in the corner of the room.

I checked Liv's obs and listened to her chest. Her hand trembled as I took her pulse. Tachycardic. 'Bad night?'

She nodded, the whites of her eyes showing.

Lachlan joined me to check her chest X-ray.

'She woke breathless and in pain. I can't find a cause.' He tapped his pen on his notebook. 'Sats are fine, but CO_2 is down. My differentials include another PE, sepsis or a pneumothorax but her chest sounds okay, a bit dull in the bases is all I could find. I can't work out what is going on.'

In a woman who had already had one massive PE, there was always the worry of a recurrence, but haematology had kept a watchful eye on her coagulation, and this presentation was different. I felt as though the entire room was having a panic attack.

It was a big call, and a bad one if I was wrong, but it was four-thirty in the morning and there was nothing to do but trust my gut. If I could take the heat out of the situation, maybe Liv's symptoms would settle.

I sat down next to her. 'Your X-ray shows some minor lung collapse, which happens a lot after surgery. It can make it hard to breathe, but it will get better.' I turned to Lachlan and the nurses. 'Good job, everyone. I'm going to have a talk with Liv and Anthea now. Lachlan, I need you to go and review the man in bed sixteen.'

Lachlan may have rolled his eyes. 'Okay.'

Once everyone was gone, I removed Liv's blood pressure cuff and the sat probe from her finger. I'd be able to tell from her respiratory rate if I was wrong and she was going off. I rearranged her pillows, so she was propped up and comfortable. These were not normal surgeon activities, but there was no normal here.

Anthea stood beside me. 'Are you sure it's not another PE? The other doctor said –'

'Anthea, how about you sit down? It's been a long night.'

She hesitated, and then slumped into a chair. 'I've been so worried, I've got so many questions, and no one will tell us anything...'

I bit at the inside of my cheek. What was I going to tell them, and what if Prof found out? My shoulders tightened. I remembered a pre-exam breathing technique a psychologist taught us as med students.

I'd never tried it myself, let alone used it with a patient, but I got Liv to count to four on her inhalation, hold for four, exhale for four, hold for four. As I did the breathing exercise with Liv, I noticed Anthea was doing it too.

Liv spoke. 'When I woke up, I couldn't breathe. I was – I thought –' She stopped. 'Sleep isn't a safe place for me anymore.' She exhaled. 'I had this dream, it was awful. I was outside, in the cold, so cold it was snowing, snowflakes falling on me and I can't move, the snow comes down hard and I'm disappearing into it, until I'm gone, I can't see me anymore.' Her voice caught. 'At the end of the dream, I don't exist. I'm just snow.'

Snowflakes. The flecks of white, tiny nodes of cancer cells growing into Liv's chest wall. I swallowed, hard.

'Don't think about it,' Anthea said. 'Forget it.'

'I can't! Each time I close my eyes, everything turns to white.'

Richard once explained to me how when his paediatric patients drew their dreams, he learnt their darkest fears. There was no way Liv could know that her cancer looked like white flecks, but a snowstorm was the perfect metaphor. And I was out in the storm with her, soft white flecks falling on me.

'Liv ... what have they told you, about your cancer?'

'That it's bad.' Liv's voice was flat. 'It's in my liver, my ribs ...'

'The oncologists told us yesterday that eventually they want her to go back for another mastectomy,' Anthea said. 'Again! And we don't even know what went wrong in the first one. And when we asked, they told us to speak to the surgeons, only the surgeons don't want to answer anything about anything.'

Do not under any circumstances engage with the family.

'I don't know if I can do it again,' Liv said. 'If I go to sleep, I'm scared I – I'm scared I won't wake up.' Her breathing quickened.

'This is what I think,' I said. 'You're frightened, and I get that. But there is a point to all of this. The mastectomy is so we have less cancer in your body to treat, so the chemo can be more effective. We can't get rid of it all, but you can live with this thing.'

'I don't want to die!' Liv's face contorted as she choked out the words.

'Don't talk like that,' Anthea said. 'It's not good to think those things.'

'How can I think anything else? I nearly died the first time. Prof said that's why they had to cut through my breastbone.'

The weight of what happened in theatre sat heavy on my chest. If I didn't tell Liv and Anthea the truth, she wouldn't agree to have the operation, and Anthea might just flip her lid and make good on her threat to take her home. But if I did tell them, they might sue, or lodge a complaint, or refuse the surgery anyway. And if Prof found out, would that be the end of my job prospects?

I breathed in for four, held it for four, out for four. *She is my patient, and I let her down. I will not lie about that.*

Into the dark night, I sent a silent prayer: *forgive us our trespasses*, and then I went from the start and told them almost everything, skipping the part about me and Toby in the quiet room, but laying out the ugly truth about the missed bone scan. I explained the sternotomy, needed to remove the clot, and the fractured rib, a common sequela of cardiac compressions. It wasn't easy, to admit, in essence – *your doctors fucked up*. I had trouble meeting Liv's gaze.

'I want you to know, even though things went badly, and if I had my time again, I'd do things differently – we were doing our best.' I hesitated, and then I said, 'I'm sorry.'

Eventually Anthea spoke. 'So, if you'd known about the bone scan, or the DVT, the surgery wouldn't have happened.'

'That's true,' I said. 'At least, not when it did.'

'Okay,' Anthea said. 'Okay.' She got up and walked to the window, looking out into the inky night. Then she turned back to me. 'Finally, someone actually fronts up. All the way along, I've known that there were things people were not telling us. So now we know. Tell me this: in your opinion, is another mastectomy safe?'

I nodded. 'I would recommend it.'

Liv held herself very still. 'Are you scared to die?'

I sat back in my chair. A personal question like that would usually be my cue to shut down the conversation, but Liv and I had shared the most awful day. It meant I couldn't duck and weave.

'I don't like to think about it too much.'

'So you are. Afraid.'

I felt it again, the paralysing terror, standing over Liv's body as she tried to die on the table. I didn't know how to respond, so I said the only thing I could think of, and something I wouldn't normally say to a patient, or even to myself.

'I think it's okay to be afraid.'

'I am, I can't help it. I don't want to be brave.' She exhaled a stuttering breath. 'I'm not one of those stoic people, it's not me. I don't want to be something I'm not.'

Her words unstitched something inside me.

She looked at her bruised hands, and then at me. 'I – can't commit to the surgery right now. I don't know what I want. But you've told me the truth, and … that counts for a lot.' She let go of her grip on the bedsheet, panic falling away like a shed snakeskin. After a few minutes, her breathing deepened and her jaw slackened, and I was sure she was asleep.

Anthea's eyes were trained on Liv, her face one of deep concentration.

What was she going to do with what I just told her?

I said goodbye, and told myself no matter what happened, I'd done the right thing.

My footsteps in the hall felt lighter.

~

We started Tuesday's ward round in ICU, as was Prof's habit – the opposite of most surgeons, who preferred to convene on the home turf of Four North and work their way down. A few minutes before eleven, we met in ICU, dawdling in the hallway until everyone arrived and the registrars led the way to the first patient. Only Lachlan was late.

Prof huffed as he checked his watch and glanced repeatedly at the glass doors, waiting for Lachlan to materialise. Toby caught my eye and raised his eyebrows, and I shrugged back. We hadn't spoken since the M&M, and I had no idea what I would say to him. I messaged Lachlan, *we're in ICU, u better run*. Toby engaged Prof in some discussion about Prof's dwindling golf handicap, and one of the residents lamented that the stores weren't open late on Christmas Eve as they hadn't finished their shopping, and Prof tapped his toe.

When an out-of-breath Lachlan arrived a few minutes later, Prof peeled back his jacket sleeve to check the time. I felt as though he were making a note in Lachlan's file, the force of his stainless-steel pen indenting the paper: *kept me waiting for eight minutes.*

'Sorry,' Lachlan said breathlessly, 'I thought we were meeting on four.' Prof was already striding away from him, into the ICU.

Another note in his file: *imagines I am the same as every other consultant.*

We covered off our sickest patients and then returned to Four North, where Maggie greeted us with a steely smile and folded arms. In her thirty years at PCH, she would have seen tardy residents come and go. I imagined her dirt file bulging with everything she knew.

'Your nurses keeping out of mischief here, Maggie?' Prof asked.

'Doing our best, Prof,' she replied.

She followed the ward round a few steps behind the doctors, and it was intended as an act of deference, but there was something defiant about the way she kept her distance. She knew more than anyone about the care of surgical patients, especially the nitty-gritty of what it took to nurse a patient to the point of being ready for discharge: it must have galled her to have to defer to the likes of Lachlan, and me. I imagined her aiming knives at our backs.

'I have an adrenalectomy I need to bring in next week,' Prof said to Maggie as we walked towards Mrs Greenidge's room.

'Between Christmas and New Year?'

'It's necessary, unfortunately. The patient is a cardiologist from Spotswood. I'd rather them be here than HDU. Will you be here?'

'I will make it so,' Maggie said, bowing. It was bizarre, how they rolled: a passive-aggressive rumba, with the nimble Maggie always keeping her feet out of the way of Prof's steps.

Mrs Greenidge was sitting up in bed, her coral lipstick bright against the white of the hospital sheets. Her fine grey hair was neatly brushed, and I wondered if our twice-weekly ward rounds were the closest thing she had right now to a social event. She had talked to me about her nieces, but we didn't see them visit her often.

She greeted the team members by name, and while Prof examined her wound, she nudged the nine-letter puzzle from the newspaper towards me with a conspiratorial smile.

In the base of Mrs Greenidge's substantial wound, new tissue the colour of calamine had grown, which Prof told her was most encouraging. He suggested a stint at home with nursing support, and Mrs Greenidge was delighted. If anyone could shake Prof from his bad mood, it was Mrs Greenidge.

I stared at the nine-letter puzzle, lingering so that I was the last to leave the room. 'Atonement,' I whispered, and she nodded, pleased.

I caught up with the rest of the round in the final room, where Iain was, and as soon as I drew back the yellow curtains, I knew that something was wrong. Iain was lying semi-prone, his head turned to one side, his white buttocks covered in fair, curly hairs, his abscess wound open. He had the drawn, stuttering breathing of a man in pain.

Iain's lunch tray was delivered, a bowl of bright orange pumpkin soup, and a small round bread roll on a side plate.

'Ooh,' Iain said, looking at the food.

The salty smell wafted over me, mixed with the unpleasant sweetness of packet bread. I could taste the processed tang of the soup and feel the too-smooth white bread texture of the dinner roll in my mouth. I felt queasy.

Prof's face was suffused purple, and he faced the ward round, towering over us.

'Who did this?'

I stared at Iain's buttock, trying to understand what had gone on. The wound had been left open and looked clean. Then I realised there was something missing.

'Maggie, what happened to the drain?' Prof said.

Maggie frowned. 'Last I heard, the nurses reported that Iain was finding it uncomfortable –'

'The thing was a bloody nuisance,' Iain interrupted. 'Better out than in.'

Toby grinned, and mouthed words at me, and I read his lips: *when in doubt, drain.* Prof used drains more than any other surgeon, and he hated having them removed early.

'When did this happen?' Prof asked.

'Very early yesterday, I believe,' Maggie said.

The tips of Lachlan's ears flamed pink.

'And you let your nurses do this on your ward? When it was still draining exudate the day prior?'

Maggie held her hands up in surrender, and then lowered them to her sides. 'I – was not present, Prof. And I'd ask you not to assume this is the fault of the nurses.'

'Well, who was responsible? Anyone?'

Maggie's voice was low. 'I believe Carla was on.'

Prof turned to me. 'Carla?'

It was doubly humiliating, being hauled over the coals, and in front of a patient. I could only imagine that while I had been talking Anthea down from the ledge, Lachlan must have removed the tube. How did he not know the rules about drains?

Despite his pain, Iain was clearly enjoying the drama. 'I'm not sad they took it out. Hated the damn thing. Couldn't get outside for a ciggie.'

'I'd prefer you didn't smoke so soon after your surgery, Mr Macadam.' Prof gazed at the ceiling, and then back at me. 'I'm struggling to comprehend what went on here. Please assess the wound.'

I approached the bedside, where the unshaven Iain grimaced a jumble-toothed grin at me. As he wheezed, I smelt cigarette smoke and hospital food. I palpated his hairy buttock, starting some distance from his wound, where the muscle was covered by a decent layer of fat, until I got closer to the margins of the incision –

'Jesus, girl! What are you doing to me?'

I ignored him and finished palpation.

Part of me wanted Prof to know it wasn't me. We all had our square of reputation to protect, our white handkerchief that we hoped was pristine, and mine was grey and grimy after the M&M. It wouldn't help to add more dirt.

But Lachlan's hand was trembling as he wrote notes in Iain's file, and he was already in Prof's bad books. I thought of his brothers, laughing at him hating the sight of blood.

I knew then that I wouldn't bury a junior doctor with Prof.

I faced Prof. 'I believe – Mr Macadam was in quite some distress, and it was felt the drain was a contributing factor and removed. Unfortunately, it appears his collection has re-accumulated.'

With one hand, Prof cupped the back of his skull, his eyes wide and incredulous. Maggie picked up the lunch tray and quietly returned it to the trolley.

'I will organise drainage this afternoon,' I said, my voice small.

'No pumpkin soup for you, young man,' Toby said, enjoying this a little too much.

'Oh, Doc, again?' Iain said. 'You gotta get your act together, you people. Am I even going to be out of here by Christmas?'

No one answered him.

Prof walked stiff-shouldered away from the bed, and the round fell into step behind him. As Lachlan cast me a grateful look, I drilled a glare at Maggie, who didn't sidestep or even blink as she returned it with interest.

Contraindication

a specific situation in which a drug, procedure or surgery should not be used because it may be harmful to the person

Late in the afternoon, Prof requested we review Iain. I showed him the re-sited drain, which was to his satisfaction, although Iain was already muttering complaints. As we climbed the stairs to return to the surgical offices, Prof said, 'I have altered the upcoming roster. You will have more operating sessions than before, with Emmett. Just a precautionary step, to make sure you're ready.'

Probation? This was clearly a punishment for Liv's surgery. Was Toby getting the same treatment? I didn't think so.

I trudged a few steps before speaking. 'Prof, do you think one of those sessions could be the adrenalectomy you're doing next week? They don't come along very often ...' My voice trailed off. He was already shaking his head.

'Toby is rostered for that list.'

Of course he was. Did they make that deal on the eighteenth hole?

'There will be other opportunities.'

I walked on, stewing on the inside.

'It's good to see Olivia Lai improving.'

What did he know of my late-night talk with Liv and Anthea? Did he understand that I stopped them from leaving the hospital? Or had he already been served with papers from Anthea and her legal team, now that they knew the truth?

'She's – doing better, yes.'

'Oncology have raised the prospect of re-operating with her. I understand she's somewhat ambivalent.'

I nodded. Liv's snowstorm of cancer, the white flecks submerging her body.

'It would be best for her care if the surgery proceeded in a timely manner.'

'I have raised that with her. I think – I *hope* – she will come around.'

'Excellent. That would be a good outcome. For everyone.' He turned and locked eyes with me. I knew that we were not just talking about Liv.

'Now, that drain.'

I opened my mouth and closed it. 'Prof, it wasn't my fault –'

He held up his palm. 'I understand that patient is something of a difficult personality, but I would caution you: take a great deal of care with your day-to-day work. One must walk before one can run.' He raised an eyebrow. 'And that includes drains.'

There were so many things I could say, and I said none.

This was the man who had inspired me to go into surgery.

~

I first met Prof fifteen years earlier, in a seven-a.m. dissection class, where sixty medical students assembled in a rotunda with stairs so steep that from any seat in the room you could view the dismembered body part on the stainless-steel bench below. Yellow lights illuminated the bench, casting the rest of the theatre into darkness. Each week the tutor would call down a student to assist with dissection and analyse what they could see: pus within an undrained abscess, kidneys puce and shrivelled by uncontrolled hypertension, a fibrosed alcoholic liver.

I loved it. All of it. The lurid yellow of fat, the milky white of a cholesterol deposit, the avocado green of pus. I revised my anatomy and memorised the paths of nerves and vessels so that when my turn came, I could dissect confidently, and avoid the mocking tone the tutor reserved for students who cut crucial vessels and did more damage, if such a thing were possible, to the body part of an already-dead patient.

Fleur hated it. 'It's a piece of a person, lumped on the bench like a leg of lamb. It's inhumane. *And* it's before breakfast.'

Prof had just started his term as guest tutor, and when he called my name in a deep, sonorous voice, I made my way to the bench, donned gown and gloves, and stood beside him. He was a head and a half taller than me, and his hair swept back in a rolling wave from a widow's peak. Under his gown, I noticed a beautifully cut grey suit.

'Describe what you can see.'

I looked at the oval, scarlet-coloured muscle on the bench. Large vessels coursed over its surface and met at its apex. 'It's a heart.'

'Yes. Go on.'

I prodded the muscle with my fingers. 'The left ventricle seems flabby.'

Prof inclined his head. 'Can you think of a more precise, perhaps scientific, description?'

A couple of students laughed but I wasn't deterred. I picked up the heart and held it in my palm and even that act thrilled me. 'Enlarged? Dilated?'

'Very good. Now dissect the coronary vessels.'

I took the scalpel and cut through to the lumen of one of the surface vessels. It was small and slippery under my blade, and I struggled to keep my hand steady. After a moment Prof took the scalpel and elegantly divided the muscle to expose the vessel in its entirety, and then he showed me how to slit it open. I was mesmerised by the beauty of his dissection.

Inside the vessel, the lumen was occluded by a purple clot lodged on a yellow plaque.

'Atheroma,' I said, animated. 'With secondary thrombosis.'

Prof's hazel eyes sparkled. 'Excellent, Carla. Now, if we had diagnosed that before this man's myocardial infarction, you could have operated and saved his life.'

I doffed gown and gloves and returned to my seat, listening as he described the curative surgery a cardiothoracic surgeon would have performed. His silver hair caught the light. My leg jiggled under the seat; I could barely sit still.

I had found what I wanted to do.

~

As the clock ticked over towards nine, I gazed out the window at the city, the car lights winking red and the concrete mass of buildings twinkling with squares of gold, and I wondered why the buildings were routinely left lit up, even on Christmas Day.

Cast against the inky night, the fluorescent hospital lights seemed harsh. Above me hung a droopy trail of chintzy gold tinsel that the nurses pulled from a box in the storeroom each December, and I thought about Luca, Gina and Nino, opening presents without me, and Toby, who had sent a Happy Christmas text that gave me no clue as to when we might see each other, the shroud of the M&M hanging over us.

Tess and I had waited all day for a theatre to become available, and I was sure the appendix we were to remove would have been less close to perforation when we'd assessed the patient at eleven, but the number of open theatres was dictated by the availability of nursing staff, and a ruptured aortic aneurysm took priority, and took all afternoon.

I guided Tess through the surgery, showing her how to insert the ports and manipulate the camera to identify the curved edge of the caecum and follow the muscular bands of the taenae coli to where they converged at the appendix. In this young male patient, the appendix was an inflamed purple finger of tissue. Tess manoeuvred the equipment with a mix of caution and ease. She had strong, sensible hands. For the first time, I could see her as a surgeon.

Afterwards, while she wrote up her notes, I told her she'd done a great job, and she beamed.

'Oh, it felt so good! Most of the other fellows like to stay in charge. Thank you, Carla. You really are the best.'

'It was nothing.'

'No, it was everything! And I see it now, you know – the rush it gives you, to be able to master skills like that. I mean, that appendix – it was about to burst! You know, it makes everything worth it.' She lowered her eyes. 'I – I broke up with my boyfriend last week. It's a sad time of year to be single.'

'I'm sorry. Are you okay?'

'Yeah. He – I think he was jealous, actually. Of the job. He couldn't understand why I had to give so much of myself ... you know, not only the hours I work, but the study for the exam, writing papers, all that. So it's ... it's for the best.'

I scratched at my chin.

'Tess ... there's something I've been meaning to raise. You remember, in the M&M ... when you spoke up?'

She grazed her front teeth over her lower lip. 'I hope ... I wasn't out of line, was I?'

'No – I wanted to thank you, for doing it. I felt really – it was difficult. And it meant a lot to me that you said something.'

'Well, I'm glad I could be there for you,' she said. 'I didn't like how they treated you.'

'No big deal,' I said, turning away from the question in her eyes. I was about to leave the room when she spoke again, her voice hesitant.

'Hey, while I think of it – no pressure, but the Women in Surgery Dinner is next week, in case you've changed your mind?'

Was it a fleeting dose of Christmas cheer that made me agree? Tess squealed and clapped her hands together, her cheeks pink with excitement. She peeled off to the ward, where we were still struggling with Iain, whose alcohol withdrawal made him cantankerous and unpredictable. I told her to ask the kitchen to serve him a Christmas beer and up his dose of benzos – anything to make sure he didn't whip that drain tube out.

I was checking her operation notes, smiling despite myself at her loops-and-swirls handwriting, when Luca messaged me.

> U coming? Crostoli on the table
> Make it snappy
> Mum has started the dance of the slamming drawer fairy
> Driving Dad and me to drink
> If u don't hurry, we will finish the bottle

In my dry mouth I tasted the coffee I'd gulped down at four. My hunger had passed, but coffee and the sweet fried dough dipped in cinnamon sugar of Gina's crostoli would have been a perfect way to celebrate Christmas and buy momentary redemption from my parents.

I was about to respond to the text when I heard someone call my name.

'Carla. It is Carla, isn't it?'

I looked up to see Toby's father, Geoffrey. He was still a good-looking man in middle age, silver sideburns visible under his royal blue theatre cap, his body trim in his scrubs. His walk was slightly wide legged, and he led with his shoulders, square, with the same swagger as Toby.

I held out my hand. 'Hi, Mr Tennyson.'

'Geoffrey, please. I'm glad I found you – Maggie thought you might still be here. Aren't we the lucky ones, on for Christmas?' He smiled. 'I have a complex case I'm about to start, and my registrar is already doing a burns case. I could do with another pair of hands, if you're willing. It's an upper limb de-gloving in a woman who gave her partner a pit bull terrier for Christmas.'

I winced and he smiled. 'Bad choice of gift.'

My phone buzzed and I glanced down at a message from Toby.

> Up for a late-night Christmas present?

I swallowed a smile as Geoffrey continued. 'Have you seen a de-gloving before? Alister tells me you're technically very sound.'

A chance to assist the Chair of Surgery? I wasn't going to say no, even if his son wanted to hook up, or my mother's crostoli would go uneaten. I put my phone in my pocket. 'Sounds great.'

'Excellent. We have a few minutes to get coffee while they're setting up.'

I messaged Luca and apologised that I wasn't coming, adding the pit-bull detail to make the excuse sound suitably dramatic. I went to the tearoom and made myself a tea, trying not to think about Nino's disappointed face.

Geoffrey sat down on the couch in front of a TV screen and glanced across at me. 'I wanted to let you know – I thought you carried yourself well at the M&M. I admired your integrity.'

I scalded my mouth on the hot black tea. His own son had screwed me over and Geoffrey thought I'd handled things well?

'It was obviously a difficult case, and one thing I know, there's always a lot more to the story than gets presented at these meetings.'

'Thank you. That means a lot.'

'You're welcome. It can be – tough, trying to make it in our field. If you need any advice, or support – I'm here.'

I nodded, digesting this. 'I mean – you know I'd be competing against Toby, if a job comes up.'

'I want success for *all* our trainees, Carla.' He smiled at me again. 'I'm ambitious like that.'

Like me.

He rinsed his cup and set it on the sink. 'Now, let's go and see what damage this pit bull has done. You ever applied a skin graft before?'

Happy Christmas, Carla, I whispered, as we went to scrub for theatre.

~

Lachlan and I stood around the bed, staring at Iain's pale, hairy bum, while with efficient movements Maggie disconnected his IV line from the bag of saline. Lachlan squatted down and checked the drainage bag. 'Nothing since yesterday.'

Usually twenty-four hours with no drainage signalled that it was time to remove the drain, but after the events on the ward round, it was hard to know.

Iain grimaced at us. 'For the love of God, will you take it out?' He'd been more settled since Tess and Maggie had engineered a beer for him each night with dinner, with strict instructions not to tell Prof, but he was over being in hospital, and the feeling was mutual.

Maggie straightened the bedsheets. 'Up to you, Doctor.'

I would have loved Maggie's blessing here, given her experience, but she wasn't going to oblige, so I gave Lachlan the go-ahead.

Iain thanked us. He looked up at me. 'You're going to make a fine nurse one day, you know that?'

Maggie swallowed a smile, and I pressed my lips tight and nodded in response.

Lachlan drew me to one side in the hall.

'Carla? Thank you for taking the blame on the round. Iain really got the best of me. He demanded I take it out, and I didn't realise it was too early for that. I should have said something, you know, owned my mistake with Prof, I just – the job for next year felt like it was on the line, you know?'

I knew.

Maggie was close enough to hear our conversation. Her eyebrows raised, and her greying ginger hair rose from her forehead in a vertical sweep that accentuated her surprised look. 'Was it not you, then, Carla?'

In a voice that I hoped was professional, I told her no, it was not me.

'I'm sorry, then,' she said. 'I shouldn't have assumed.'

Part of me wanted to stay angry with Maggie. It was easier then; we both knew the rules. But her apology sounded genuine. 'It's okay. I'm in Prof's bad books anyway right now. Can't get much worse.'

'Oh, don't *I* know that feeling,' Maggie said, her Irish lilt sounding bitter. 'It isn't easy, what we have to endure some days.' She tilted her head back towards Iain's room.

'Lachlan,' I said. 'Want to get Maggie and me a coffee, so we can mark the end of Tube-gate?'

For a split second Lachlan looked startled, then he smiled his easy smile and nodded, ambling away down the corridor.

It felt like Maggie and I might be writing new rules of engagement.

DURING

The Irish lilt.

I hear it, echoing in the stairwell, saying my name, *Car-la*, like the sing-song notes of a doorbell, calling down to me.

I have fled the dining room and almost escaped. Two more floors to climb, following the small black line marking the edge of each step, then I will gather my things ...

The walls of the stairwell swoon and sway. How did I let myself get this wasted? There was so much riding on tonight, and initially the wine helped soothe my nerves. And then with Will tossing me around the dance floor, I felt I deserved another drink, and somewhere among the topped-up glasses pressed into my hand I lost count.

Is that you, Car-la?

Maggie's beady eyes narrow in on me as she descends the stairs I'm climbing. *We're both of us done for the night, aren't we?*

The lilt in her voice raises any sentence to poetry.

Yes, I tell her. I'm done. No lilt in my voice.

Are you all right, then? She asks. *You're a little wobbly on your feet –*

Fine, I say. I break one of my hospital rules and hold on to the black handrail to steady myself, and, yes, it is vaguely sticky and probably covered in multi-drug resistant Staph aureus.

You're a good woman, taking the stairs, on a night like tonight.

A good woman. Something about her words makes me want to cry.

Carla, could I – would you like me to run you home? It's no trouble.

No, I – I need to go now. I glance behind me, at the stairs I've climbed, and they dance and sway below, and my centre of gravity is lost, and Maggie reaches for me, and her small hands hold me tight. I smell her floral perfume and feel the tickle of her faux fur coat under my chin.

BEFORE
Pseudo-obstruction

dilatation of the colon due to an adynamic bowel, in the absence of mechanical obstruction

At the wall of glass at Vue de Monde, the sheer drop down fifty-five floors made my head spin. Or maybe it was the Prosecco on an empty stomach – or the thought of what I had to do.

I didn't want to have this conversation tonight. But when Toby smiled at me, saying, 'Our kind of place. Am I right?' I couldn't smile back, I couldn't pretend, even though he *was* right. I loved the quirky opulence of the glad-wrap chandelier over the bar, and the dark velvet wallpaper. Sitting here in the last of the daylight made everything seem more decadent.

He raised his martini, wished me a Happy New Year and said, 'Here's to surviving the M&M.' Melancholy and unease washed over me as our glasses clinked.

The chef came to the table, his long hair wrangled into a scruffy ponytail. He made small talk with Toby for a few minutes and then left.

'You know him?'

He shrugged. 'Dad holds all the plastics dinners here.'

'Maybe we could get Prof to do the same with ours.'

'Think he'd rather be on the golf course.'

I felt a prickle of paranoia. 'How often do you play? With Prof?'

'Once a month, maybe? Will likes a hit. You should come sometime.'

I downed my Prosecco. I didn't play, and he knew it.

A waiter brought us polenta chips arranged in an ochre lattice on a charcoal plate, topped with pearls of glistening caviar. The polenta was crisp and light, the caviar salty on my tongue. I needed to say it, now, before I was swept away by the grandiosity of everything.

'Toby, I need to ask you –'

'Wait. I have something for you.' He reached into his pocket and passed me a gift wrapped in lime-coloured tissue paper.

'Thank you, but I need to talk to you –'

He told me to open it, and it felt ungrateful not to. I unwrapped the paper to find a hot pink satin G-string.

Hooker-wear.

My heart plummeted fifty-five floors. 'Thank you, it's – lovely.'

He leant forward. 'I want to see you in it.' He glanced around the bar, which was filling fast. 'Come with me. There's somewhere I want to show you.'

I read the flush of his cheeks. I couldn't let sex waylay what I needed to say, not this time. 'I need to talk first.'

'We will, just – wait.' He stood up. 'Coming?'

I shook my head.

He sighed. 'Okay, let me paint you a picture. You're going to love this. A wall of glass, looking out on the best view of Melbourne. You and me – love in the air. Incredible, right?'

'Where are we, staring at this view?'

'The men's.'

I laughed. 'You want us to screw in the toilets?'

He winced, like I'd lowered the tone. 'If someone comes, we can go for a cubicle.'

He made it sound like a hotel room.

'No.'

Toby's face turned sullen. I forced myself to ask what I needed to know. 'Why did you say you were with Mrs Greenidge?'

He looked away and then back at me. 'You mean the M&M? Well, I was in survival mode. You know how it is.'

'I know you dumped me in it.'

'Oh, C – it wasn't like that at all. I – well, I couldn't tell him where I really was, now could I? I mean, if I'd told him the truth, I would have landed us both in it. Right?'

'Yes, but –'

'And I reckon Prof would've been jealous. He has a thing for you, you gotta admit –'

'Don't be insane.'

'C'mon, I mean it. You're like his project. Have you seen the way he looks at you? Can't take his eyes off that arse –'

'Toby, stop!'

'Neither can I.' He looked down and eyed me where I was sitting. 'Anyway, we're both in the shit, far as I can tell.'

'Seems like you've weaselled your way out of it quite nicely to me.'

'We're *both* in the shit,' he repeated. 'I just came up with an excuse for me. If you'd asked, I would have come up with one for you too.'

He sat back down and reached for my hand. 'I'm sorry you felt dumped in it. There was shit flying everywhere that day, looking for somewhere to land.'

My anger eased as he massaged my thumb, and I held on to his fingers, thrilling at the touch, wanting more.

'I don't want us to be secret anymore. And you promised that I would meet your family.'

He gave a little bob of his head. 'Well, let's see – you free this Friday? Family dinner, which I was going to bail on, but we could go together.'

'Okay.' I exhaled.

'I'll message Mum now.' He tapped a text on his phone and got a prompt reply. 'All sorted.' He tilted his head towards the bathrooms. 'You coming?'

My stomach churned. We'd made progress, but it wasn't enough. 'I want to talk about the job. When do you think Benson will move on?'

He gave a short laugh. 'No idea.'

'How are we going to survive competing for the same job?'

He frowned. 'We both apply and see how the cards fall. Look, you gotta trust me on this stuff. Like how we survived the mastectomy – we get through it, the fuss dies down. I was right, wasn't I?'

'You mean you lied, and I took the fall.'

He shook his head. 'Seriously, Carla? We went over this. Don't worry about it. Once the job is sorted, we'll be good.'

'How? How will *we* be good?'

We locked eyes, and for a moment I glimpsed the future as he saw it. He wasn't worried about us because he fully expected that he would get the role. I would be disappointed, but I'd cop it like the good sport that I was and keep putting out, which was what he cared about.

He wasn't thinking about me, not for one second. I only existed for him when I came into his view, like a moon orbiting his planet.

'You don't care. What happens to me.'

He clasped my hand now with both of his. 'Of course I do.'

'You only care if it affects you. Or the bits of me you want. My cunt. My tits.'

He grinned, despite himself.

'But not *me*.'

'Carla, where is this coming from? I love you –'

My breath caught. *Those words.*

'I love you as much as I've ever loved anyone.'

And there was the whole truth. The love I got from Toby was as much as he could give, only – it wasn't enough. I steeled myself. 'Except yourself.'

He screwed up his face in baffled disgust. 'What do you want from me?'

'If you loved me, *really* loved me, you would understand how hard the M&M was for me. You would have stood up for me, or at least wished you had. You would care – not just about your job, but mine too.'

His face grew red. 'What the hell? Of course I care. You don't see it because you're so damn focused on your career. There are more things in life, you know, than your bloody ambition.'

I had a moment of clarity as a fog lifted. I stood, half-filled glass in hand, thinking for a moment, before deciding *yes*.

Prosecco landed in a spray on his face.

~

I had a killer Friday-morning theatre list that ran late, and then a sick trauma patient who needed ICU but there were no beds. At four, I stopped to pee, my urine dark and concentrated. I'd had nothing to drink since breakfast.

I grabbed a bottle of water at Bea's and cleaned up the ward as best I could. When I met Toby at his car, his face was dark.

'We were meant to leave half an hour ago.'

I mumbled an apology and got into the car, straightening my charcoal pencil skirt.

'So. You going to throw another drink at me tonight?'

'Depends. You going to throw me under the bus again?'

'Depends.'

I had thought about bailing on the family dinner, but I'd fought hard to get my foot in the door, and I wasn't ready to give up on it, or Toby. I had messaged him to ask if he wanted to cancel, and he'd replied,

> Mum has already planned the menu

After a minute he added,

> Family dinners are the worst
> I'll go if you go

I felt sad for him and said okay.

We drove in silence across the city to Toorak. It was opulence from the moment Toby drove his Audi down a sloping driveway into a five-car garage, parking next to a Mercedes. It made me nervous.

Inside, we walked on plush cream carpet past massive original tapestries hung on the walls. In the living room, on white leather lounges, two women were sitting upright, like mannequins, martinis in their hands.

I straightened my shoulders as Toby introduced his mother, Judith, and his sister, Miranda. I felt short, stumpy and very aware of my nose.

Toby handed me a martini, and I took it, although I hated them. We made small talk about the recent heatwave, and Miranda complained that the olives in the martinis were too salty, and Judith protested that her regular supplier had sold out.

Judith asked me if I grew up in Melbourne, with a smile that lifted the corners of her mouth but didn't reach her eyes.

'Yes, in Carlton.'

'I do love Carlton. Some wonderful shops there.'

'Oh, please,' Miranda said, slipping off her shoes and curling her long limbs under her on the sofa. 'You never cross the river.'

I'd heard of ultra-wealthy people who never left Toorak, but had never actually met one.

Judith pursed her lips. 'I *have* been to Carlton. There's that wonderful little cinema there they use for the film festival.'

The hallway door opened, and Geoffrey walked in. He came over and we shook hands, and then he kissed his wife and daughter. With Toby, he launched into a sparring discussion about golf. Geoffrey asked me if I played, and I said no.

'Maybe I need to take some lessons,' I suggested.

'Not from Toby,' Geoffrey said, and Toby's cheeks coloured.

At the dining table, Judith served us individual spatchcocks with roasted parsnip, pumpkin and celeriac. We ate in silence, and I wondered if that was due to my presence or the norm here. The best part of a meal with my family – apart from the pasta – was the talk. A lot of it, and loud.

Sitting between Toby and Geoffrey, I became conscious of the clunk of my heavy silver cutlery on my plate, and of keeping my elbows tucked into my sides as I dissected the spatchcock, which proved challenging. Luca would have given us all permission to go at it with our hands, if he were here. My napkin slid from my lap to the floor.

'Carla, how did you get interested in surgery?' Judith asked.

'I like fixing things,' I said, wondering how much my answer really conveyed. 'And I think – it's the kind of job I'm good at.'

Geoffrey said, 'She did a marvellous job assisting me on Christmas night with a very nasty de-gloving –'

Toby swivelled his neck and cast a surprised look at me. *You kept me in bed waiting so you could assist my father?* I grimaced in apology.

'Geoffrey! Not at the table, please.' Judith turned to me. 'All that blood ... it must be ghastly.'

I rested my fork carefully on my plate. 'It doesn't bother me, to be honest. I grew up in my father's butcher shop. Perhaps that's why.'

'Oh, how interesting.' Her smile revealed two prominent front teeth. 'Is your father still in business?'

I nodded. 'Off Rathdowne Street. Nino's.'

'I know it! My friend Titia won't buy meat from anywhere else. She says the chipolata are divine.'

I smiled. Nino hadn't wanted to make chipolata – 'stupid excuse for a sausage' – but his junior butcher persuaded him that they would sell to people who didn't know any better.

'Still ... it must be gory, right?' Miranda asked. 'Cutting people up?'

'No more for me than the boys.'

She laughed. 'That is a very good point.'

'Miranda here is our crusader, did you know?' Geoffrey said. 'Human rights lawyer extraordinaire.' He raised his glass in her direction and she rolled her eyes, smiling.

'We all know how you feel about my job, Dad.'

'Oh, but you're still Daddy's girl, aren't you?' Toby said, swirling wine in his glass.

Judith raised her hand. 'Toby –'

Miranda turned to me. 'Is there affirmative action in surgery? I'd bet you'd need it.'

I could feel her trying to shift the conversation and was glad to oblige. 'There are lots of females in junior positions, but no consultants. At least at PCH.'

'What about other hospitals?'

'Other places do. PCH is – traditional.'

'Then it's all the more amazing, to have come as far as you have.'

I smiled at her in silent thanks.

'Well, it's not for want of trying, this lack of women as consultants,' Geoffrey said. 'You have to wait for a suitable trainee to come along.'

Suitable. What did that mean? I twirled the diamond between my clavicles.

'Anyway, from what I understand, your future looks bright,' Geoffrey said. 'Alister is quite enamoured of you, Carla.'

Toby grinned a sarcastic smile. 'Don't we know it.'

My cheeks burnt.

'You must have had to work very hard to get where you are,' Judith said. She meant well, and it was rare for anyone to recognise how hard it had been, but it felt patronising somehow. Next to me, Toby clenched his fists into his thighs.

'Surgery's a hard slog, no doubt about it,' I said.

'No argument from this corner,' Geoffrey said, filling up my glass.

'Easier when you have Daddy on the scene to smooth the way,' Miranda said, looking deliberately at her spatchcock.

'Don't be fucking ridiculous,' Toby said, and she frowned.

'We're just celebrating what Carla has managed to achieve.' She leant towards me across the table. 'What is it you see in my darling brother, exactly?'

Toby stood, pushed his chair back and left the table.

'We're only winding you up, Tobes,' Miranda called after him.

I sat at the table, wondering if I should follow him.

Judith brought a fruit and cheese platter to the table. 'You do torture him, Miranda.'

Miranda shrugged. 'He can take it.'

Geoffrey picked a bunch of grapes and popped one into his mouth. 'Toby has always found the easy way.'

'In fairness, Dad – you've played your part in that.'

Geoffrey thought for a minute. 'I only wanted to give him opportunities.'

I put some fruit on a plate. 'I might take this out to him.' I rose from the table, glad to get away from a tangle of family relationships that I didn't understand.

'Watch out,' Miranda said. 'He's got a temper.'

~

I walked past garden beds of cream roses whose perfume filled the evening air, towards the thwacking noise coming from the floodlit tennis court, where Toby served ball after ball. He saw me coming and hit the next ball flush into the net.

I unlatched the gate and offered him the fruit, which he declined. I slipped off my heels. 'Got another racquet?'

He fetched one from the cupboard to the side of the court. 'You going to play in that?'

I looked down at my skirt. 'I can have a hit.'

He hit a forehand at me, hard and low, and I swung too late.

'Or a miss.'

He went back to the service line and served at me, the ball hitting me in the thigh. It stung.

'Toby!'

'You're the reason,' he said, serving another ball, which I swerved away from, 'the reason we're here, listening to Miranda and Dad take turns putting me down.'

I stood behind the baseline, dodging balls, feeling small.

'If you keep trying to hit me, I'm going to leave.'

He relented and batted the ball over the net. I returned it, and we began to rally, Toby trying to hit the cover off the ball and me trying to keep it in play. After the tension at the dinner table, it was a relief to chase a ball, for success to be a shot that made it into the court.

Toby smacked a forehand winner. 'My family's always like that. Talk down to me, play up to a new audience. And you lapped it up.'

'I'm sorry. I guess I – wanted them to like me.'

'They're tossers. Forget about them.'

We found a rhythm with a rally of volleys. I liked scampering after balls and Toby liked winning. Watching him hit a fluent backhand, I felt a wave of tenderness mixed with desire.

He told me to bend my knees on my backhand, and I aimed a ball at his head. 'Did I ask for coaching?'

He sliced a forehand past me. 'I was thinking about what you said, the M&M, and everything. I'm sorry. I should have thought about you. When Prof gets all judgey like that, it reminds me of Dad.'

Low in the west sky, a full, yellow moon rose above the horizon. We met at the net, and I kissed him on the mouth, slipping my hands onto his taut shoulders.

'Let's get out of here.'

~

Once we were in the car, I said, 'Let's not go home.'

'Okay,' he said. 'Where to?'

I put my hand on his thigh and suggested the river.

He parked near Fairfield Boathouse. As we walked down the path, a strip of moonlight glistened on the water. The Boathouse was on our left, partly camouflaged by trees, its verandas dark and empty. Rowboats were lined up on the riverbank and a bat careened over the massive sky.

We were alone.

Toby pointed to the moon. 'Perfect.'

I knew what he was thinking, and I was up for it. We took the bluestone-lined path that sloped towards the pipe bridge, whose mustard-painted steel was covered in graffiti.

Once on the bridge, our footsteps echoed like a drumbeat, like my beating heart. And even in the dark, there was birdsong. Did birds ever sleep? I stopped in the middle of the bridge, near a rusted sign that said 'Danger'.

I breathed in the night air and stretched my arms above my head. I looked right and left, a last check for onlookers.

I unbuttoned my shirt, drew his hands to my breasts, unzipped my skirt, letting it fall to the ground. He tried to turn me around so he could enter me from behind, but I shook my head and straddled him, and I could tell he was surprised as he held me between his body and the railing.

I knew what I wanted. I felt as if all the tension of the evening had built to this.

We could be together and go for the same job. Who said we couldn't? Fuck the rest of them.

The cold air on my bare skin aroused me, and I wanted for Toby to touch me, but his radar was off and I grew impatient, so while Toby watched, I brought myself to climax, quickly, the reverberations shuddering through us and beyond, into the railing, and I imagined them shaking the very foundations of the bridge. Afterwards, I leant back and took in the enormous sky.

And then I let myself down, knelt on the cold, hard bridge, took him in my mouth and finished him off, just how he liked it.

DURING

Geoffrey, the night of the gala.

Standing in the office in his beautifully cut suit, the slightest clench of his jaw hardening his smile.

Why Carla, he says. *What are you doing up here so late?*

I stammer a response, I'm ... I'm looking for Prof, and he laughs. *Oh, I don't think you want to seek him out right now. Give him time to calm down first.*

I falter, my bravado evaporating. Is he angry with me? I ask Geoffrey.

You – could say that. Nothing you can't handle, of course.

But he is wrong, and my body knows it, as a tremor shudders through me and the events of the night threaten to overwhelm me.

Geoffrey sits against the edge of the desk, his kind eyes on me. *Well, perhaps I can help you,* he says.

BEFORE
Satellite lesion

lesions located in the skin or subcutaneous tissue in close proximity to the primary tumour, but discontinuous with it

In the empty wasteland that was outpatients in January, Liv and Anthea sat opposite me in a consulting room.

We talked about Christmas. Liv had seen her mother for the first time in years. She updated me on her symptoms, and I examined her wounds – her battle-scarred chest would always carry an honest and ugly record of that day, the lines running over her skin like pink rivers of history.

We did this to her, Toby and me.

'Healing up well,' I said.

Liv got dressed and sat back down on the chair. 'We've been talking, a lot, about next steps.'

I waited, trying to read her face.

'We don't agree,' Anthea said. 'My view is – with no disrespect to you, Carla – we should pursue the legal path now.'

Unable to speak, I unwrapped my stethoscope from around my neck and set it on the desk. They were going to sue? Jesus. Prof would lay the blame for that at my feet, and how could I argue?

'Whereas I think the opposite,' Liv said. 'You were honest enough to tell us what went on, and no doubt it's upsetting, but I'm grateful that you did that.'

Anthea turned to Liv. 'I only want the best for you. If you need care, a court case could help us pay for that.'

'We've been over this,' Liv said. 'I want to choose carefully, now, what I prioritise. I don't want to focus on getting even, or getting cash out of the hospital. I can't believe you're so obsessed with money, when – we should be living in the present.'

I listened, my thoughts spinning.

'I – I don't know what to say, to be honest.'

'Just to make it clear. If we sued the hospital, that wouldn't be good for you, would it?' Liv said.

I shook my head. A court case would pretty much kill my job chances. But could I blame them? I saw the flecks of tumour in Liv's chest wall, and the bloodied mess we'd made of her chest. I remembered my reason for bringing them in today, and I decided to address that.

'I can see both of your points of view ... but I think that caring for Liv is the most important thing right now. I'm hoping you've thought about the repeat surgery?'

Above Liv was a wall clock, its minute hand trying and repeatedly failing to tick over to midday. Each time it failed, it clunked back to eleven fifty-nine. Anthea startled at the noise and frowned as she checked the time on her phone. Nine-thirty. Never set your watch to a hospital clock, every doctor knew that.

Liv turned to Anthea and took her hand. 'I need you to come with me on this. I need to focus on healing right now.'

Anthea looked from Liv to me, and back again. 'Okay ... okay, babe. But one thing's for sure – I'm not going quietly, as far as this hospital is concerned. Somewhere, sometime – I'm going to let them know what I think of the way they communicated.' She glanced at me. 'Of course, I'm excluding you from that, Carla.'

Liv turned back to me. 'I'm ready to have that surgery, so long as – will you be there?'

I exhaled a long-held breath and promised I would make that happen. Liv having the surgery was the most important thing. I told myself I'd deal with Anthea's complaints another day.

The minute hand lurched forward and finally ticked over, both hands pointing proudly to twelve.

~

That evening, I stood in warm, mizzling rain outside the entrance to Matteo's, wishing to hell I'd said no.

A women's group. Seriously. What if Prof saw us together, having a good old whinge?

My scalp tightened against my skull and I felt the beginnings of a migraine. I reached into my bag for my phone. Tess wouldn't mind if I bailed; she already had enough people to make the meeting worthwhile.

I was writing the text when I became aware of someone behind me.

'Carla!'

I turned to see Tess, in a floral dress with a camellia behind her ear, her blonde curls tumbling on her shoulders.

'I'm so glad you came. I thought maybe you wouldn't.'

I shoved my phone back into my bag and forced a smile.

'Of course I came.'

Inside, we were escorted past an expansive floral arrangement of white lilies to a private dining room. A group of women were already seated, including Edwina Storer, her auburn hair set in an immaculate, regal bob.

I recognised most of the faces here and wondered why I felt so uncomfortable. I'd had plenty of female friends at medical school – why did my discomfort here match the rising pitch of the voices as they greeted each other? I liked some of these women, and even the ones I didn't like I respected. I just didn't belong here. I wanted membership of another club altogether.

An oaky chardonnay the colour of autumn sunshine was poured into my glass. We ordered meals, and I surprised myself by ordering a steak. I made small talk with the woman next to me. Yasmin was a small-framed, brown-skinned woman with a ready smile who was training in ortho, I learnt, and as my mind immediately pictured her wrestling with an orthopod's drill, she told me she boxed in her spare time, which, given the demands of both the drill and her teammates, seemed a wise choice.

She asked how it was for women in general surgery, and I muttered something noncommittal and was saved by Tess clinking her fork on her glass.

'Welcome to our first meeting of Women in Surgery!' She beamed, and tucked a curl behind her ear. 'We have nearly all the female surgical trainees at PCH from all specialties, which is fantastic. No consultants, of course – not yet, at least.'

I rubbed my palms on my skirt.

'But we do have Professor Edwina Storer, from Spotswood, to talk about her experience.'

Edwina spoke then. 'I'm not going to tell you about when I started in surgery, how I was called a lesbian because I wore trousers. How I was told to lower my voice and speak slowly to sound more authoritarian – more like a man. Although all those things are true, I'm not going to do that. Because that might make you think that things are so much better now, there's no problems to solve anymore. I'm here to tell you otherwise: our challenges are real, only they're insidious.'

She talked about sexism, as she saw it: mostly unconscious, but no less real. How women were judged according to different rules than men. Around me, women murmured agreement, and I grew more and more uncomfortable. If this unwanted behaviour was subtle, were we absolutely sure it existed? How could anyone prove it? It felt like trying to eat custard with a fork.

The waiters arrived with our meals. I cut into the hefty steak on my plate, through the charred fat rind into the meat, which was a deep pink tinged blue. Blood seeped onto my plate.

'We need to ask ourselves,' Edwina said. 'Are we part of the problem?' She looked around the table. 'Do we conform to stereotypes to fit in? Do we try to be one of the boys? Or do we try to be attractive, to please them? Or go the helpless act to make them feel important?'

The waiter poured me a glass of shiraz. I swirled it in my mouth, tasting mulberry and charcoal.

'If I'm honest,' Edwina said, 'I can think of a time when I've done each of those things.'

What? Did she really believe that? And anyway, how was trying to fit in a crime?

'Every time we do, we give ground. We tell them that their view of the world, where women are seen and understood only in reference to men, is the *right* one, the only one. We have to see ourselves differently before we can ask them – no, *tell* them – to do the same.'

Edwina sat down to raucous applause, and I looked down at my half-eaten steak. At PCH, I'd always thought about how I was judged by the men in surgery, but for the first time I wondered how the women here viewed my attempts to fit in. I saw it as what I needed to do to survive, but when I ignored and tolerated and tried to conform, was I letting them down?

While these thoughts swirled, around me came a flurry of confessional statements, women owning up to all the behaviours Edwina saw as part of the problem.

'Don't beat yourselves up, it's normal behaviour,' she said. 'Next time you catch yourself doing that, ask – would I behave the same if I were in a room full of women?'

'But ... that's not how it is,' I said, my voice red-wine raspy. 'We have to live in the real world. Surgery is full of men, and we need to get along with them.'

Edwina's gaze on me was fierce, but warm. 'That's true. But getting along with people does not necessarily entail fitting in with their world view. We can get along, be respectful, but stand our ground. Don't get me wrong: if being one of the boys is how you live every aspect of your life, and it's working for you, then knock yourself out. But if you turn it on to fit in, ask yourself why, and if that's who you are, and who you want to be.'

I skewered my steak with my knife.

'How would you deal with behaviour that ... crosses the line to offensive?' Tess asked.

'You have to call it out. It will never stop if you don't.'

Yasmin spoke then. 'I don't want to be the behaviour police. I'd rather ignore it.'

'That is one strategy,' Edwina said. 'But there's one thing I know for sure: it won't go away. It recurs. Like herpes.'

Everyone laughed.

'Remember what happened to Simone Gillies,' Liane said. A few of the younger doctors looked blank. 'She was the ortho resident, maybe six years ago.'

'Eight,' I said.

'Right. She spoke up about the culture. You know, the yelling in theatre, consultants abusing staff when things were not the way they liked.'

'And?' Tess asked. 'What happened to her?'

'So, first, HR dismissed her complaint, said there was insufficient evidence. And then, she didn't get a job the following year.'

The room fell silent. We could talk all we liked about standing up, but this – *this* was our reality.

'What about really inappropriate behaviour?' someone asked. 'Like, hands-on stuff?'

'Well, now,' Edwina said. 'No one should touch your body at work, in a sexual way.'

I felt the energy shift, saw the flushed cheeks and knowing eyes. I pressed my thumbnail into my fingertip, hard.

'You need support, from the top, to call it out. Tell me something: it does interest me, this phenomenon of no female consultants at PCH. What drives that, do you think?'

'We're hoping Carla might be the first,' Tess said. 'Just waiting on an opening.'

'All strength to you,' Edwina said to me. Glasses were raised, and I felt the support of the women at the table. Tess beamed.

Yasmin cleared her throat. 'I know this isn't why we're here, but – it's not only sexism.' Her voice shook.

Tess's face fell and the table was quiet. 'Can you tell me a bit about what you mean?' she asked.

'Well ... do *you* ever get asked if you're going home when you finish your training?'

Tess startled and shook her head.

Yasmin continued. 'It comes from all angles – the surgeons, the nurses ... even the patients. "Will you be allowed to operate in your own country?"' Her face filled with disgust. 'I was *born* here.'

'I can't imagine what that would be like,' Tess said. 'Thank you, for raising it.'

Edwina nodded. 'The intersection of prejudice. It makes sense, that misogyny is not alone.'

Liane spoke then, of the homophobic jokes she'd endured when she brought her partner Angie to the neurosurgery Christmas dinner, and I bowed my head over my plate. I'd always felt keenly my difference at PCH, not being male or Anglo, but it hadn't occurred to me what it might be like to stand out even more. Had I stood by and watched racial or homophobic put-downs?

It was uncomfortable to admit that I didn't know.

Later in the evening, we were drinking coffee when Tess came and sat beside me. 'I'm so glad how this has turned out,' she said. 'I was panicking no one would come.'

I looked around the room at Yasmin and Liane chatting to Edwina. 'It's been good – a lot to think about. I didn't realise what Yasmin had faced. Or Liane.'

'I know! That was brave of them, to speak up.'

I nodded. We drank our coffee. 'On the topic of sexism, I don't agree with everything that was said, but –'

'Oh, you don't need to tell me that. I knew from your face.'

She smiled at me, her eyes a clear light blue. It was impossible not to like her, Goddammit!

She hesitated. 'Do you ever think they give more opportunities to the boys? Lachlan is in theatre all the time, and I get double outpatients.'

I screwed my mouth to one side and thought about it. 'Maybe? Only – it doesn't help to get too fixated on that kind of thing. Just take every chance you can get, that would be my advice.' I gathered my bag.

'I will,' Tess said, her voice solemn. 'I mean, I have to get more experience to have any chance of an accredited job next year. Oh, and – do you play golf? Lachlan was telling me that he and Benson played at Hawthorn Dales with Prof –'

'What?!'

'Yeah, he dropped it into conversation over coffee the other day. It kind of annoyed me, because Prof has never invited me. So, I was thinking ... maybe we should play, sometime.'

I could not believe that they had asked Lachlan, a junior registrar who could barely tell his appendix from his anus, when in the ten years I had worked on this unit, I'd never once been issued an invitation.

'Apparently, they're both members there, or something like that.'

I put my bag down, called the waiter over and ordered more coffee.

'Show me your roster. We can look for more opportunities for you in theatre. I can let you know if I have cases you could do.'

'That would be wonderful!' She took out her phone.

'Have you got any of your references confirmed yet?'

She looked sheepish. 'Not exactly.'

'Well, you need to get onto it, because what do you think they're talking about on the fairways?'

Her eyes grew wide.

'And let's find an afternoon when we can play golf.'

Tess looked as shocked-surprised as I felt.

~

It was hard to sleep that night. I pictured Lachlan and his easy smile strolling the fairways with Prof – the same person whose arse I saved with his dumb decision to take out that drain. I told myself not to get hung up on it, this was a workplace, not a game of favourites. I needed to get Liv to her next surgery, that should be my sole focus.

I remembered her furrowed and pale face in outpatients this morning. I was grateful she had convinced Anthea to shelve her litigious plans. Now, I had to make good on my promise to be in theatre with her. Her surgery had to be carefully timed around her chemo, and she would be on Prof's list. I knew he would insist on that.

I reached for my phone and logged onto the hospital website, and found Liv's booking: 9 February, with Prof. Then I checked the fellows' roster for that week. Will had rostered me to Benson, and assisting Prof was Toby.

Leaving aside a gnawing feeling that Will was rostering Toby the best opportunities to impress Prof, leaving me with doddery, handsy

Benson, now I was going to have to call in a favour with Toby to meet my promise to Liv.

I would do it. Whatever it took, I was going to get Liv to that second operation.

DURING

The slab of meat in front of me is charred at the edges. From the kitchen, waiters swarm the room armed with plates, one beef, one chicken. Standard gala dinner fare.

Will, sitting next to me, stares forlornly at the white meat swimming in a creamy sauce.

He looks sideways at me and tops up my glass. 'Any chance?'

This is a choreographed dance we both know well, but tonight I baulk at my role. I want the steak.

Hamish calls for more wine, and my glass is full again, and I attack my steak with the gusto of one who has stared down a moment.

The room starts to spin, and I think it is possible that my small but significant triumph over the steak has gone to my head.

BEFORE
Comorbidities

coexistent disorders

Fleur set two glasses of champagne on the table and handed a mineral water to Richard. We sat on bar stools near an arched window, and outside wind whipped through plane trees. Fleur had talked me into coming, and now I was regretting it.

I had a morning list with Benson tomorrow, and I needed to have the conversation with Toby about swapping theatre lists. He might not like it, but keeping my promise to Liv was a must. I imagined Liv's surgery would be some kind of closure. Isn't that what Fleur called it?

For Liv and for me.

The houselights dimmed, and Xander came on stage, and it amazed and annoyed me how chill he was. His banter was smooth and funny and self-deprecating as he moved between keyboard and laptop, layering bass over drums and acoustic guitar, singing loops that he recorded and then sang over. The effect was like an entire band of Xander, and it was impressive.

Mid-set he changed the mood and sang 'Angels Tripping on Cobblestones' as a pared-back folk song. In my head, I was outside that pub at the end of fourth year, kissing him. The night of the kiss, I'd agreed to come to his gig the following week, but then Prof had offered me the chance to assist him operating in Timor, and no surgery-bound medical student was going to pass that up. Maybe I was here tonight to make amends for my no-show?

As Xander played chords on the keyboard, I noticed the curl of his bicep under his tee-shirt. What might have happened if I hadn't gone to Timor? Watching him play felt like sitting by a campfire and wanting to put your fingers in the flames.

Ridiculous. He was a man-child who chased waves and younger women. I couldn't see how our lives would fit together. Anyway, I was seeing Toby. My fingers felt for the diamond hanging from my neck, but I wasn't wearing it.

It could be so good, so exciting, when it was just me and Toby. Like at Fairfield Boathouse – I felt like I was just beginning to let loose. And we'd survived meeting his family. I was hungry for more, sick of us being a secret to our friends and at work. I'd invited him to Fleur's birthday party, so that might be the next step.

But if it came to a choice between the relationship and the job, I didn't know what either of us would do.

I shook the thought away. Why couldn't I have both? I wanted the relationship to be official, and the job, when it came up, to be mine. There would be other jobs for him – eventually. I decided I would settle for nothing less, and he would have to step up.

Xander finished the set with a bunch of songs he sang with a girl called Iona, who wore a kilt and hiking boots, and who flirted more and more overtly with him as the gig went on. It was like watching foreplay. Man-child.

At the first chance, I pleaded an early start, left Fleur and Richard bickering, and got the hell out of there.

~

Benson was late.

I stood in theatre, gowned and gloved and fuming, when he eventually walked in, holding his wet, freshly scrubbed hands in the air in front of his face as he navigated the door. Once he had gowned, he said to the scrub nurse, 'It's my birthday. Give me a little kiss, will ya, huh?'

She rolled her eyes and pulled down her mask and planted a peck on his tilted cheek. I got the feeling they had done this before.

'Get on with it, Benny,' muttered the anaesthetist, and that saved me from having to decide if I would let him repeat the ritual on me.

Once he made his way to the table, I presented a summary of the patient, an obese man with gallstones. Removing a gall bladder laparoscopically might be challenging.

Benson listened. Then, with a nod of his head, he let me take the lead. I made the three small port incisions, inserted the trochar and passed the camera and instruments, and we began. We operated in silence, the screen showing a dense, yellow fog of fat obstructing our progress. I wouldn't want Benson's ponderously slow surgery in any emergency, but I had to admit that his painstaking manipulation of the instruments showed me a way through the fat to identify the gall bladder and safely remove it.

Afterwards, we doffed our gowns and went to the tearoom, where Benson fetched china teacups and saucers from one of the cupboards above the sink.

'Assam or Darjeeling?'

'Assam,' I said, and he chose two delicate pyramid-shaped tea bags from the tin.

'One needs these small comforts, I find,' he said, passing me my tea. I held the hot cup, wondering at the contradictions that were Benson. None of the other consultants made me tea.

'How is your patient, after her mastectomy?'

'Okay,' I said, remembering I needed to speak to Toby. I sent a brief message: *need to swap sessions with you next week.*

Benson gestured at my phone. 'Your generation is addicted to those devices, aren't they?'

I put my phone in my pocket.

'But you can't learn a lap chole on an iPhone.'

'No. Thanks for your help in there.'

He bowed. 'And how are you? After the M&M? They can be dogfights, in my experience. Always at least one scapegoat.'

I sipped my tea. 'I'm fine.'

'All strength to you. In my career, I've noticed that doctors who care the most for their patients and try to do the right thing – they can be the most maligned, especially when everyone is defending their own turf.'

We finished our tea, and I took the cups to the sink and washed them. I didn't know which was worse: Benson seeing my mistreatment in the M&M and ignoring it, or Toby barely believing that it had happened.

I felt Benson come to stand behind me at the sink.

'Last piece of advice: take care of yourself because no one else will.'

He put his hands on my back and tucked the top of my scrubs into the pants, leaving his hands there, his fingers reaching past the fabric to my skin.

His musky Darjeeling breath was hot on my neck. 'Must make sure you're presentable, Dr di Pieta,' he said. 'We keep having to have this conversation, it's almost as if you want me to tuck you in.'

Underneath my scrubs, he moved his hands from the midline around to the sides of my waist, ostensibly tucking my top in. And yes, he had done this before, but he'd never put his hands *inside* my scrubs. I tucked my scrubs in every time I was in theatre with him, to try to prevent this very moment, but even the smallest scrubs hung off me so that I looked like a child in her dad's pyjamas, and they never stayed tucked.

Move, my brain hollered, but my feet were glued to the floor. My stomach lurched and my glutes clenched tight.

I wanted to tell him to get his hands off me, but this old, pathetic pervert was in charge of my probation. I could not make a fuss.

I dropped the teacup I was washing, and it clanged in the sink.

'Careful,' he said, frowning, looking over my shoulder to check if the cup had chipped. His hands moved around towards the front of my scrubs.

I leant my torso forwards, so I was pressed against the bench. I could not have his hands in my underwear, I could not –

A voice from the doorway startled both of us. 'Um, Mr Benson?'

One of the junior nurses stood there, her cheeks red.

He sprang away from me. 'Yes?'

'Your next case is ready.'

DURING

My glutes clenched beneath his hands.

The mossy smell of Darjeeling tea on his breath.

His tremulous voice.

And the gobsmacking disconnect, between the voice in my head – *get me out of here* – and my paralysis.

I am at the gala, standing next to Benson and Prof. There are words batted from one to the other, *look at this next generation of surgery, what excellent hands our future is in.*

Benson's eyes feast on my chest.

Prof agrees. They talk about me like I am not there.

And then we are searching for a seat, and we find a table with two vacant chairs, and I hesitate, wanting to escape, but Benson is already searching for another chair.

I stand there feeling stupid – I could have fetched my own seat, and what am I doing anyway, I want to get out of here – until he returns, sliding a chair in behind me and it's then that I feel his hand on my butt, between me and the seat.

He speaks into my ear, while his fingers feel the curve of skin where my butt meets my thigh.

My body freezes, my face burns. Is there anyone here who can help me? Two seats away, Prof has started a conversation with the person next to him. Across the room, Hamish sits at our table, staring at an empty bottle.

Wine muddies my thoughts. I will the moment on. When I can't bear it any longer, I shift my weight forwards and pull the chair in behind me, towards the table.

He leans close and I smell Darjeeling tea as he tells me, *you have the loveliest behind. Just as I remembered.*

Obturate

to obstruct a body passage, usually by impaction of a foreign body, thickened secretions or hard faeces

It was my idea to bring Tess to breakfast. Call it the closest I had to a golf course.

'This place is awesome!' Her silver teardrop earrings caught the light as she looked around the cafe.

Toby began by describing the latest addition to the Rectum Collection, this time a teddy bear, apparently furry and brown with a soft button nose.

'Went in head-first,' Toby said. 'I pulled him out by his toes.'

Tess's eyebrows raised at Will's loud laugh.

Hamish tapped into his Blackberry. 'Consider it added.' He caught sight of Tess's face. 'Please understand, they're always like this.'

Tess's laugh in response was musical and nervous.

While I ate my chilli scrambled eggs, Tess spooned fried kale and broccolini from her buddha bowl into her mouth and we listened to Hamish present a Christmas BMJ article comparing IQ and grip strength in orthopaedic surgeons and anaesthetists. Tess and I read the abstract, and then she put down the paper, pursing her lips. 'They only studied males.'

I hadn't noticed that. I mean, of course... right? Orthopaedic surgeons, say no more.

Hamish pursed his lips. 'I presume the concern related to the impossibility of comparing the two genders, particularly in orthopaedics.'

Silence, while we considered this, and then Will burst out laughing. 'Do you need a shovel, H?'

I sensed Tess was becoming uncomfortable, and I wanted to keep the peace. 'So, the grip strength would likely have been different in males and females ... and then they would have had a problem comparing the two groups, given there would be more female anaesthetists than female orthopaedic surgeons. Is that what you meant, Hamish?'

Hamish exhaled, 'Yes. That is right. Thank you for explaining.' He turned to Tess. 'Please forgive me, if I've offended you?'

'Not at all.' Tess smiled at Hamish, flecks of coriander between her teeth. 'I just think – if the article is only about males, they should qualify that in the title.'

'Indeed they should, yes,' Hamish said.

'And I wouldn't assume anything about any female who makes it in ortho.'

'Another point well made,' Hamish said.

Tess smiled. 'If you like this kind of thing, have you seen GomerBlog?'

Hamish had not.

'It's medical satire. You can find it on Twitter, or wherever. I particularly like the one about the female cardiologist who changed her name to Doctor.'

There was quiet for a minute, and then Toby said, 'What? I don't get it.'

'I am going to go out on a limb here. Is the subtext that because of her gender, she is never addressed as a doctor?' Hamish said.

'Yes!' Tess said.

Toby looked sceptical. 'Come on ... that's not an issue anymore.'

I eyeballed Toby. 'Happened to me just the other day. The patient addressed me as Carla, and Lachlan as Doctor.'

Toby laughed and then stopped. 'But I've heard you use your first name with patients. Do you want them to call you Doctor?'

'What I want is to be treated the same as men.'

Silence, then Tess spoke. 'To me, it's a subtle put-down, to use Carla's first name while giving Lachlan a title.'

'Exactly,' I said.

Will opened his mouth and then closed it.

Meanwhile, Hamish tapped away at his Blackberry. 'GomerBlog, was it?'

I had to smile at him. 'Like Christmas BMJ for millennials, Hamish,' I teased.

~

'You look incredible, birthday girl.'

In the mirror, Fleur applied a dark red lipstick to her lips, which curled into a tight smile at my compliment. Against her pale skin and auburn hair, her blue-black velvet dress shimmered.

She turned from the mirror and hugged me, exhaling a shuddering breath.

'Is he coming?'

'I don't know. Honestly, I can't believe it's come to this. He was sober for fourteen years, and now he goes on a bender with Xander? This was supposed to be a celebration, and okay – maybe I should've been more patient, but he's a paediatrician, for fuck's sake! What kind of paediatrician doesn't want kids?' She pressed her lips into a dark red line. 'The only conclusion I can draw is that it's *me* he doesn't want, and he doesn't have the guts to tell me.'

I didn't know what to say, but I did know that in half an hour, fifty or more people plus or minus Richard would be arriving at our house to celebrate Fleur's birthday. Somehow, I had to help her through this.

'I'm a psychiatrist, people tell me their secrets. But no, he'd rather pickle his pancreas than be honest.' She blew out a furious exhale. 'I am not going to do this. Not tonight.'

'Then don't. If he comes, then great. If he doesn't – his loss.'

She looked miserable at my words, but set her shoulders and murmured, *yes*.

We finished getting ready. I'd bought a new black dress that Toby had not seen before, and I knew I looked good in it. I had the feeling that Toby coming tonight was the start of our next phase, but I kept my excitement to myself – Fleur didn't need her nose rubbed in it.

We'd decorated the house with gardenias and tea candles, so that people followed a trail of warm scented light down the hall and up the stairs. At around eight, when most people were here, I got a text from Toby saying,

>sore back, not going to make it tonite

Furious, I messaged back.

>Did you play golf today

>Yes I did actually. Is there an issue

I paused before replying.

>No. Hope your back is better soon

I retreated from the party, shutting the door of my bedroom to keep out the noise, and sat on the edge of the bed, the hurt hitting me in waves. He might have told me he loved me, but it was lazy and careless, bailing on a date by text.

I told myself, *I can't deal.* And tonight was about Fleur. I kicked off my heels, exchanging them for flats, and returned to the party in host mode, taking around platters of finger-food.

As the night wore on, Richard didn't show. Fleur was surrounded by friends, but it wasn't the celebration she had planned. After midnight, Richard walked in, Xander and Iona behind him. Iona had her hand on the small of Xander's back as they moved through the crowd, and they had the unfocused gaze of the seriously wasted. Fleur marched Richard upstairs and the whole party heard her strident voice over the music as she gave it to him.

I was furious with Richard and there was no one here I could tell. I cleared some glasses, thumping them down on the kitchen bench.

'Ouch,' said a voice behind me.

I turned to see Xander, with a bottle of red in his hand. His light grey linen shirt was crumpled in the sleeves and his hair fell messy on his shoulders. His shabby chic was so perfect, it infuriated me.

'You want to join us for a drink?'

I shook my head. I had no desire to witness Iona climbing all over him.

He frowned. 'You okay?'

I filled the sink with scalding water and plunged a wine glass under the surface. 'Seriously, I cannot believe you people.'

'Us – people?'

'Richard – where does he get off, treating Fleur like that? It's her birthday, and he turns up now, off his tree? And you could've done something to prevent it.'

'He showed up at our gig,' Xander said carefully. 'He was cut by the time I saw him. I think he's doing it tough right now –'

'He's not the only one!' I flung a tea towel at him.

He picked up the tea towel and began drying a glass. 'I'm sorry. If I'd realised, I'd have tried to get him here earlier. He was pretty intent on getting hammered.'

I stared at him. What kind of a friend was he, to sit back and watch Richard self-destruct? Then something occurred to me.

'You do know he's an alcoholic?'

He swallowed, hard. 'I – I didn't.'

'At the end of fourth year, he went on a massive bender that landed him in ICU with pancreatitis. He nearly died. I thought you two were friends.'

'Once I dropped out, I – lost contact. With a lot of people. I was living overseas –'

Iona came into the kitchen. 'Where's our wine?'

Upstairs, a door slammed, and I heard Fleur's voice, yelling.

'As you were,' I said to Xander and Iona, casting him a look of disgust on my way out of the kitchen.

~

The next morning, I made coffee, serving Fleur's milky latte with a glass of water and paracetamol, and we sat on the balcony with our feet up on spare chairs as the morning light gathered intensity and drew colour into the day. The air smelt sharp with citrus from our neighbour's lemon-scented gum.

'He says ... he doesn't want kids.' Fleur's voice shook. 'He has all these reasons – overpopulation, food shortages, and I'm like, you're over-thinking this! I'm thirty-five, I can't wait for the world to sort out its population crisis. I've put my life on hold for him and now he's freaking out. I can't do this anymore. I love him, but it's not enough.'

I hugged her, sunshine seeping onto our shoulders.

'You know where he's gone? Up the coast with Xander.'

'What?'

'Apparently Xander got some last-minute gigs in Sydney, so they're driving up today. We both took time off, so we could' – her voice choked – 'start planning. The wedding, house-hunting, all that.' She let out a shaky sigh. 'I'm going to have a shower, try to clear my head.'

After she left, I stewed a minute. Was I willing to sit back while Richard fried his last remaining pancreatic cells? No, I was not.

I found Xander's number in Fleur's phone.

He answered after the call almost rang out. 'Hello.' His voice was a red-wine croak.

'It's Carla. Is Richard there?'

He took two quick breaths. Was he *panting*?

'Mmh? Carla?'

'If Richard is making this trip with you, you need to look out for him. It's on you.'

In the background, I heard a voice. 'Who is it, babe?'

Iona.

Mid-morning panting with Iona. I did not want to think about it.

'On you,' I repeated. 'He needs a friend who will look after him.'

He was silent for a moment. 'Do you always have to be so bloody right?'

I heard Iona's voice again, muffled.

'She's half your age. Just saying.'

'Well, hey. A lot of us don't make the best choices in love, do we.'

How very like Xander, to throw a grenade at Toby before I had the satisfaction of hanging up on him.

~

Later that day, Tess called me about Liv, who had rung the hospital after a panic attack at home. Tess had assessed her over the phone, talked her through her anxiety and suggested a referral for some counselling support, which Liv had agreed to.

I told Tess that she had showed real maturity in how she handled

Liv's distress. I would put a call in to Liv later and make sure she was okay. I felt the cold, wet snowflakes from Liv's dream settle on my shoulders.

In the evening, I went around to Toby's. As he let me into the apartment and pushed the door shut behind me, I could tell he was thinking about having sex against the door, but I extended my arm and put my palm flat against his chest and told him that would be bad for his back.

He smirked. 'You're angry.'

'It was my best friend's birthday. I would have liked you there.'

He took my hand from his chest and kissed it. 'Next time?'

I went and sat on his black leather couch, next to a spiky plant with long green leaves edged with yellow.

Toby followed my gaze. 'Mother-in-law's tongue. Miranda bought it for me, said even I couldn't kill it.'

It did look rugged, the dark green leaves interrupted with small lines of lighter green, like the fretboard of a guitar.

'I need your help with something. It's work-related.'

He grimaced. 'Sure, but – it's the weekend. Can we talk about it tomorrow?'

'Can we talk about it now?'

He came and sat next to me, tracing his fingers up the inside of my arm. I explained the roster problem. 'So, the thing is – Liv has asked if I'll be there, but you're rostered on.' I inched my arm away from his touch. 'Can we swap?'

He screwed up his face. 'She wants *you* there? Does she even know who led her surgery?'

I knew this would be a blow to his ego. 'It's just I've been involved in her care post-op, and she's got to know me –'

'What have you said about me?'

'Nothing!' Now it was me, reaching for his hand. 'I've said nothing about you. You've got to trust me, I wouldn't bury you. I don't do shit like that.'

He thought for a minute. 'Whose list do I get?'

'It's Benson's. Please, Toby.'

He thought for a minute. 'Okay. Will you go down on me?'

'Toby!'

'I'm joking.' He pulled me into his arms and kissed me, and pulled my tee-shirt over my head, and we both knew how this would end.

Remission

a period during which the symptoms of a disease are abated

The morning of Liv's surgery, I jogged to work past a bank of glorious late-flowering jacarandas, the blooms flagrantly purple against the feathery green canopy. The north wind blew through them, and a wave of purple blossom drifted into the air.

The flowers made me hopeful.

I remembered how I'd strutted into Liv's first surgery, full of hubris. I saw my hands over her sternum, with each compression pumping blood out of her heart, and forcing out my fear that we might lose her.

That she would trust me enough for us to operate again was massive. I would not let her down.

As I climbed the stairs to the hospital, I took a call from Toby. 'Hey, Carla,' he said, voice breezy. 'You know the swap you wanted, for theatre today? There's an issue.'

My foot faltered on the step.

'You still there?'

'What – why? Toby, I need you to do this for me.'

'Sorry, but – you know how I've been wanting to do another Nissen. Phil's just offered me one, next Wednesday at Atherton Private. Same time as your list with Benson. I can't turn Phil down – you know that.'

We both had a bucket list of complex surgeries we wanted to do. A wave of jealousy swept over me, that Phil had offered him the fundoplication. But I had a more urgent problem. 'I'll do both lists, then: today's and Benson's.'

He shook his head. 'If Prof found out, that wouldn't be a good look for me.'

'I need to be at Liv's surgery. I promised her.'

'She's a public patient. She doesn't get to dictate her surgeon. That's not how it works.'

I stood frozen on the stairs in front of the main entrance, the hallowed halls ahead of me. I bowed my head. 'Please, Toby. Please help me here.'

'Carla, I'm sorry – I can't, this time. I'll make it up to you. She'll be fine.'

I scraped my teeth over my lower lip, felt my morning espresso repeat on me and climbed the stairs.

~

I sat in the registrars' office at a desk strewn with papers and jumbled power cords. I couldn't deny that Toby was right – any one of the fellows would jump at the chance to scrub in for a Nissen.

But his careless disregard for Liv – his patient, as well as mine. I couldn't help but love him less for it.

Maybe I could see Liv and try to explain. But I saw her frightened face, in the middle of the night. *Are you scared to die?*

I would not leave her there alone.

After staring at the roster for a good ten minutes, I made the call, and Tess met me in the office. She listened to my dilemma and responded without hesitation.

'How awesome that you've kept a good connection with Liv, after everything that happened. That says a lot.'

We concocted a three-way swap that would get me into Liv's surgery and give Toby Tess's list with Will, leaving his Wednesday afternoon free to do the Nissen with Phil, but I felt a pinch of guilt, because it meant Tess would be assisting Benson.

'Have you ever been to theatre with him before?'

She hesitated for a second, and then shook her head.

'You know to wear a tee-shirt under your scrubs.'

Her eyes grew wide and her face grave. 'Oh, right. He's quite – when he's on the ward, I feel like he spends a lot of time staring at my chest.'

Maybe it was unfair to ask her. 'I can look for another solution if you'd prefer –'

'No, it's no issue, I mean – he's a great teacher. Let's face it, I need all the theatre time I can get.'

I thanked her.

'Carla, I've been meaning to ask your advice … about referees? Lachlan told me today he has all of his, and I – I haven't started.'

'Tess! We talked about this.'

She had four weeks to lodge her paperwork with the college. I tried to stifle my irritation – what was she thinking, leaving it this late? I had geared myself up for *months* to have those conversations.

We went through the consultant list and identified who she could reasonably ask, and I told her to map out how and when she would approach each of them.

'You need to set yourself some deadlines, otherwise this isn't going to happen. And this is going to sound calculating, but if you've just done something for a consultant, that's a good time to strike.'

'Maybe I'll talk to Benson about it between cases if I get the chance.'

I nodded. 'And it never hurts to throw in a compliment or two, about how much he's taught you.'

'Carla – thank you so much. It's so good having you ahead of me, I mean – I wouldn't feel able to ask this of any of the guys.'

I told her she'd helped me out of a huge problem, and then I made the call to Toby and locked myself in for Liv's list.

~

I didn't expect nerves, but as I walked to theatre thinking about what I was about to do, my legs felt like jelly. What if memories of the first surgery overran me at the table?

I remembered my first ever surgery, and the wave of terror as I contemplated slicing open unblemished skin. *Primum non nocere* – first, do no harm – was a medical mantra all well and good, except that in surgery it didn't get you very far.

I passed a crowd of nurses in scrubs chatting and laughing as they went to lunch. I imagined their conversation. *Did you hear she nearly killed a patient on the table? And now she's going back for more?*

Liv's chest, a bloodied mess of packs.

Today was a step towards healing, I reminded myself. Liv had told me so when I saw her on the ward earlier. *I'll be beside you all the way,* I had promised.

I willed myself forwards, into the change rooms, into my scrubs, and then to the sink, where I washed my hands to the clock, thirty seconds each side, interlacing fingers to clean the webbing between my digits, scrubbing nails. The ritual reminded me: *I'm a surgeon. I'm more than just one bad day.*

Prof stood opposite me at the table. His masked face, grave with purpose, nodded at me to begin. A few months ago, I would have jumped at this. I planted my feet squarely on the step that brought me level with Prof's height. Beside the scrub nurse lay the tray of instruments neatly arranged on a drape.

I'd prepared meticulously for this – all the hours of assisting, memorising techniques, practising them in my mind and even in my dreams, they didn't dissolve in the bloody mess of that day, did they? I wanted a place in this unit, more than anything. I couldn't let one mistake stop me.

The scrub nurse handed me the scalpel, which rested heavy in my hand. In my head, the scalpel spoke to me: *cut with care*.

Was it even possible? I looked down at Liv's chest, the pink scars stained brown with iodine.

'Carla,' the nurse said. 'Are we right to go?'

The scalpel told me, *Cut with care. She will know.*

I steadied my hand, put the blade to skin, and cut.

~

We worked our way into the operation. Prof's large hands delicately dissected between tissue planes rather than bludgeoning through, as other surgeons did. There was almost no bleeding, no rush and, blessedly, no misstep. Each act seamlessly followed the previous, like a choreographed dance, but one that incorporated improvisation, when the patient's anatomy varied from normal, or the cancer extended beyond its expected boundary. His surgery was a conversation between his hands and the body on the table, one that required presence and careful listening.

I wanted that same sure hand, that exquisite, creative skill.

'Whose requiem do you prefer, Dr di Pieta – Verdi's or Mozart's?' Prof asked.

I hesitated. 'I'm not really into classical music, but I'd have to say Verdi's. My heritage, you know.'

'Ah, yes. Giuseppe.' He mispronounced the name, Ju-sep, and on a reflex I corrected him, earning myself a furrowed frown.

One of the nurses put on the requiem, and the mournful notes of the strings soared into the theatre space.

I swallowed. 'I can see why you choose to operate to this, though. It helps focus.'

'I thought you may need some assistance with that today. Self-doubt can be destructive.'

As we worked, my movements grew surer alongside his. He identified the tumour and its margins, I anticipated with the retractor, giving him a clear view of his field, and he nodded acknowledgement.

The anaesthetist stuck his head over the drape and began chatting with Prof about their plans for golf this weekend. 'Carla,' he said, 'you should join us. Toby will be there.'

'I would have loved to,' I said, trying to sound enthusiastic, startled at the reference to Toby, wondering if it signified he knew. 'But I'm working.'

The anaesthetist shrugged. 'Next time.'

'Suction,' Prof said, his eyes inscrutable.

With the suction catheter, I cleared the wound of fluid, the liquid gurgling down the plastic tube.

The voices of the choir swirled around us as we worked. I remembered the first surgery, pressing on Liv's sternum with the heel of one hand, the other interlocked over the top, my arms straight levers transmitting the force of my body as I willed her back. Liv's voice, piercing the darkness of the night as she asked me, *are you afraid to die*?

It had been the messiest of paths, but she and I were coming out the other side. As I closed up, I took a moment to savour the neat, apposed edges of the wound and Liv's body, minus her primary tumour. I imagined blood vessels constricting, platelets and clotting factors forming a thrombus and securing the area; cytokines rushing to the site like first responders, recruiting white cells to remove damaged tissue, before collagen was laid down in glistening rubies of granulation tissue to knit the scar.

I placed the last suture, and applied a dressing to the incision, and whispered, *Right by your side. Start to finish.*

~

After our list was finished, we went to the ward to review Mrs Greenidge, who had been readmitted. Maggie was adjusting the oxygen prongs in Mrs Greenidge's nose.

Not a coral lipstick day, then.

Mrs Greenidge managed a smile when we walked in. 'Professor! And my dear Carla. You're just in time ...' She took a laboured breath. 'For the life of me I cannot guess today's word.'

I counted her respiratory rate while I scrutinised the nine-letter puzzle on the cut-out square of newspaper by her bedside.

Prof examined her wound, while at the desk my heart sank as I gathered the results of her recent investigations. From the upward drift of her inflammatory markers to the grey, yellow skin near her open wound, everything screamed of dead tissue in Mrs Greenidge's buttock.

Maggie came and stood next to me, folding her flabby arms against her bosom. 'She's tired,' she said in a low voice. 'I don't know how much more of this she can take.'

I shut the file. 'What else can we do?'

'Talk to her. Maybe she wants to stop.'

Stop? This took me aback. 'If we don't resect that dead tissue, she'll die.'

'I know that, Doctor.'

Maggie's Irish lilt didn't hide her annoyance, but I was bewildered now: was Maggie suggesting we give up?

Prof came over. 'Is there an issue, Maggie?'

Maggie opened her mouth and then closed it and shook her head.

Prof returned to the bedside. 'Mrs Greenidge, we need to remove some more tissue.'

Her face fell and she closed her eyes for a long minute. 'Must it be done?'

I felt Maggie's eyes on me.

'We have no choice.'

With a tremble in her chin, Mrs Greenidge nodded. She signed a spidery signature on the paperwork and thanked me as if I were serving her a cup of tea.

We were doing the right thing – it was the only thing. I glanced again at the nine-letter puzzle. 'Conundrum?' I asked her, softly.

Her watery blue eyes lit up. 'Of course!' She gave me a sad smile.

I retreated to the office to call theatre. While I was there, I noticed Prof at the bench, flicking through earlier pages of Mrs Greenidge's file.

Was he looking for evidence of Toby's fabricated visit to Mrs Greenidge the morning of Liv's surgery?

Then he closed the file, and sighed, looking back towards Mrs Greenidge's embattled body. His eyes grew soft and knowing.

~

Emboldened by the success of Liv's repeat surgery, I surprised myself by asking Prof if he wanted to go for a walk, and he surprised me by agreeing.

As we left the refrigerated hospital air, we were hit by a wave of heat. Summer had dried the grass to a stringy yellow, and the concrete path received Prof's heavy steps. The sun slipped towards the horizon in the west sky.

'Prof, I respect how you care for Mrs Greenidge.'

He blinked and frowned. Had I overstepped?

'I mean, it's impossible not to, she's been with us so long.'

He sighed. 'Yes. I confess, I admire her stoicism. One must be careful though, to maintain professional distance.' As we passed the zoo, miner birds called a ping-ping-ping warning.

'The outlook for her is guarded, isn't it.'

The blinking, again. 'We must strive to change the course of her illness.'

I wanted to ask how, when we were doing everything we could, but he spoke first.

'Olivia and her partner were very determined you be in theatre today. You've obviously made quite an impression.'

There was a question in his words. 'I – I tried to build a bridge.'

'Appears that you've done that very well.'

Was he pleased or annoyed? I couldn't tell, and it left me wanting him to know more about what actually happened. I told him about my late-night talk with Anthea and Liv. We were just reaching the hospital door when I thought of something else.

'Actually, Prof, there is something else I wanted to mention. Do you remember that patient, Iain? I didn't remove the drain. One of the registrars did, while I was with Liv.'

He frowned for a minute, and then remembered. 'Ah, that alcoholic with the ischiorectal abscess. I see. Who did it?'

I chewed on my bottom lip.

'All right. A strong – if somewhat misguided – sense of loyalty. I understand.'

'The trainee wants to get on the program. I didn't want to harm their chances.'

'So you damaged your own standing?' His eyebrows rose in unison.

'I – I thought you would trust that I wouldn't make a rookie error like that.'

'I can see your kindness, Carla, your desire to mother the trainees, but they need to work it out on their own.'

Mother the trainees? He caught my expression.

'Well, allowing the trainees to make their own mistakes, then. Part of what you will learn as a consultant is that cream always rises to the top.'

We walked under a row of eucalypts. I wanted to argue the point, but the words *as a consultant* stopped me. Did he have news?

'We can agree on this: after the events of the first surgery, it was no small achievement to establish a strong professional relationship with Olivia. That is the kind of consultant behaviour I'm looking for.'

Rare praise, and I basked in his words, though I imagined he might retract them if he knew what I'd told Liv and Anthea. The sharp scent of eucalyptus filled the air.

He spoke without looking at me. 'Do you remember your first surgery?'

I did. The hospital in Timor, a single-storey building with peeling blue paint, teeming with sick people sleeping on the floor on straw mats; the makeshift, often broken equipment. I had been filled with hopelessness at the poverty, and the only antidote was to learn to operate, the wondrous power of the scalpel in my hand, which brought relief to pain, at least that which we could excise. I came away invigorated, despite the squalor.

'Your surgical skills are exemplary, you've taken every opportunity to learn, and for that, you must be congratulated.' He rubbed at his forehead. 'I cannot say too much, but I am working hard behind the scenes. I hope that a consultant post will be advertised this winter.'

Winter! I wanted to speed through the softened light of autumn to frosts and short days and cold, rainy skies.

'Now is the time to hone your professionalism, in your interactions with patients, and nurses, and colleagues. Be careful not to become over-involved. My advice is to think of yourself as a consultant now – you could model yourself on one of the surgeons you work with – and ask yourself, in any given situation, what would my colleague do?'

His glance at me was deliberate, his eyes intent, and there were barbs in his words – *over-involved, mothering*. I would need to tread carefully.

But he was telling me that in the foreseeable future, there would be a job. My lips pressed tight to suppress a squeal of joy.

Perforation

a hole or break in the walls or membranes of an organ or structure of the body

At breakfast the following week, Tess was an unexpected no-show, and she missed out on Toby and Will arguing over who had done more on-call in the past month (answer: Carla) and Hamish waxing lyrical about the gems he'd discovered on his new favourite website, GomerBlog. I listened, wishing Tess was there to witness that, wondering if Hamish appreciated that it was satire. I held my news from Prof inside and, on my calendar, counted the weeks until winter.

Later in the morning, I messaged her to check in, and she apologised and said she'd meet me as planned at Yarra Bend Golf Club in the afternoon.

Under a bloated purple sky, we teed off. Tess was quiet as she approached her first shot. She set her shoulders at right angles to the tee, breathed deeply and connected with the ball in a sweet strike that propelled it into the middle of the fairway.

When she saw my jaw drop, she shrugged. 'I played with my mother.'

I thought of Gina, rolling pillows of potato and flour into gnocchi at the kitchen bench. *Soft hands, don't be so rough!*

I took a divot from the grass with my first attempt and sliced the ball left into long grass with my second. We hunted for my ball in silence and, after a few minutes, I found it. It seemed possible that I might enjoy hunting for the ball more than hitting it.

We played the course, or at least Tess did, and I battled to keep the ball somewhere approximating the fairway. Tess listened quietly when I told her about Liv's repeat surgery and Prof's discussion about the job, and if I'd expected her usual liberal sprinkling of superlatives, I didn't get them. When she met me near my ball, which was nestled in scrub at the final hole, I noticed that her eyes were rimmed red. Had she been crying?

Awkwardly, I asked if something was wrong.

She put her palm to her cheek and took three slow breaths. 'It's so sad to me that – it's like this, for myself, and for you.'

I wasn't totally sure I understood. 'You know, this – golf habit that the boys have ... don't take it personally. I think they just naturally look for their own. It's not a slight against us.'

'You know something, Carla? You're the reason I went into surgery.'

I coughed out a disbelieving laugh.

'You gave us this tute on suturing, when I was an intern, and the suturing was so clean and neat, the way you did it. It was beautiful. And then you talked about those moments, when you can save a life with surgery, and I got shivers. I thought, well, if she can do this, maybe I can too.' She rotated the silver bangle on her forearm one way and then the other. 'I didn't know if they'd even let me in.'

I remembered talking myself up in front of a bunch of wide-eyed interns, so sure then that I knew my path. I knelt in the long grass to hide my blushing face, pretending I was studying where my ball was placed.

'There's no way I'm going to be able to hit this from here.'

She picked up the ball and walked over to the edge of the fairway, where she dropped it.

We hit our drives, and as we were walking up to find our balls, she blurted out, 'He touched my chest.'

I jerked around to face her. 'What? Who?' But an evil knowing was already seeping through me, and when she sobbed out, 'Benson,' I bowed my head.

We stood in the middle of the open fairway. I put my arm around her and felt her chest heave with her breath.

'He came into theatre and said it was his birthday –'

It's my birthday. Come on, give me a kiss, darling. I felt like I might throw up.

'He asked for a kiss, and so I gave him one on the cheek, but it was embarrassing. I could feel everyone watching me and judging, and I didn't want to, but what could I do? He asked me if I'd ever done a hernia repair, and when I said no, he said, "Oh, so you're a *virgin* where hernia repairs are concerned," and everyone laughed, and I felt so awkward that I started laughing too …

'Then he showed me how to reduce the sac and preserve the testicular artery and the vas, and he let me close up, so I … felt so grateful, you know – some of the other surgeons don't let me do anything, but it was confusing, because I was happy and thankful for the teaching, and at the same time, I was so uncomfortable. Then, in-between cases, he came up to me, and I didn't know what he was going to do. I didn't realise but one of my curls was out of my cap, and he put his finger into the curl and slowly twirled my hair around his finger, and he looked so turned on by it, as if' – her voice rose – 'he were imagining his finger was inside me.'

She looked away and wiped at her cheek. Gently, I asked if she wanted to bail on the last hole, and she hung her head for a minute and said no, let's finish, and we walked slowly towards a sand bunker where my ball sat primly on the surface.

'I'm so sorry,' I said. 'That is an awful thing to happen.' I rubbed at my forehead, wishing I'd never asked her to swap into Benson's session.

She thanked me, breathed deeply and glanced down at my golf ball. 'Do you even know how to use a wedge?'

'Are you kidding?'

With the sand wedge, she showed me how to scoop the ball out of the bunker, and on the third try, the ball became airborne, a spray of sand flying with it over the lip of the bunker and onto the green.

We followed the ball onto the soft, manicured grass. Tess's putt rolled past the hole and out onto the far side of the green. She stood, leaning on her putter.

'After we were finished, I got up the courage to ask him if he'd be one of my referees. And he said we should discuss it in his office.' Her voice was flat. 'And I went, because – I didn't want to be rude. And I need that reference. First, he said he wanted to show me something, and he brought out this simulated laparoscopy kit he'd built and showed me how to use it, and he stood behind me, and then – he put his hand ...' She gestured to her breast.

Getting those words out seemed to have winded Tess, and unexpectedly, she crumpled to her knees. I dropped my useless putter and sat down beside her.

Rain pattered down and, in the distance, the purple sky rumbled thunder. I saw the oily darkness of shame clouding her face, and I wanted to tell her I knew it.

I took her hand and held it.

She looked at me, her lips pressed tight. 'I don't know if I can go back there, I mean – I'd have to operate with him, and what if he tries it again? And I didn't even get the reference. How can I get an accredited job without it?'

Her voice rose to panic.

'No one has the right to do that to you,' I said. 'Listen, we can protect you. I'll do lists with him; we can swap things around –'

'I can't hide from him forever.' She placed her palms flat on the wet grass. 'I think I should tell Prof. He's been so supportive of the Women in Surgery venture; he was the one who suggested I present it at the college meeting next year. I – he should know this is happening on his watch.'

Unease prickled the skin on my forearms. My tongue pushed against my lower incisor as I searched for the words.

'I know you want to go down that path, but you should probably think about this from all angles. You need Benson and Prof as referees, so, whatever you do ... you're going to have to balance that, and make sure you get what you need on both counts.'

Glum, she nodded.

I had another worry. 'Tess – what if Prof backs Benson?'

'How could he do that? Maybe he doesn't know what it's like. I should give him the chance to understand and do the right thing.'

From Prof's vantage point, I didn't think that he could ever understand what it was like, but I remembered Will taking me aside when I started as a resident. *If you can, avoid being alone with Benson.*

I was pretty sure they all knew. They knew, but their response was to not see it, or at most to alert the women who might be at risk, ask them to be on their guard. It dawned on me that it was the women who had to carry the burden of vigilance. Toby never entered a room making sure he took the seat closest to the door.

I told her I wasn't sure how Prof would react, but I didn't want to see her hurt any more than she already was. Her blonde curls grew heavy with rain. I felt frightened for her.

'What if we speak to Edwina? She's known them all a long time, and we can trust her.'

~

I want you tonight

Toby's text came through while I sat on the couch at home as the room darkened. I was thinking about what had happened to Tess. I didn't regret doing the second operation on Liv – that was something I had to see through – but in doing so I had put Tess in harm's way. I didn't know how it was all going to end.

Toby's message on my screen spoke like a demand, and where before I might have thrilled at his passion, now I wanted to know: what about what I wanted?

I left him hanging for a few minutes and then replied,

I can't.

Those words looked harsh on the screen, so I added:

Friends coming for dinner

Cancel

No

Leave early then

Not tonight. Raincheck

Nup. Don't believe in those

I threw the phone down on the couch. I wasn't a service he could summons when he felt horny – there was another name for that, and it wasn't free. A queasy feeling swirled in my stomach, like being spun in a circle on an amusement park ride.

I was making tea when a call came through from Xander.

I frowned. The beautiful man-child. We hadn't spoken since the day after Fleur's party. 'Hey, how are you? Tired from all that running?'

He laughed. 'I'm used to it.' He talked about his gigs along the coast of New South Wales, and I pictured him there with Iona and her hiking boots and her hand on his thigh. I asked about Richard, and he told me that was why he was calling.

'I tried to look after him, but man ... he was hell-bent on getting wasted.' He told me they had fought about it, and Richard left.

'I'm sorry,' he said. 'I thought you would want to know, and maybe ... talk to Fleur?'

Goddamn it, Richard! Fleur was getting back on an even keel. I could imagine her panic when she heard this news.

I said yes, I would talk to Fleur, and I heard him breathe relief on the line.

'Hey, how did things turn out with your patient? The one you told me about at dinner?'

It seemed a lifetime ago when we'd talked about that, and, okay – it was nice that he had remembered. I gave him an edited version of what happened at the M&M, and Liv's late-night visit, and the second surgery.

'Sounds like you took one for the team at the M&M.'

'The head of oncology backed me.'

'Interesting.'

I agreed, thinking about the shift in medical management for metastatic disease.

'Interesting that your support came from outside of surgery.'

My eyes felt gritty and dry, and I blinked a few times. 'They were too busy covering their own arses. I didn't expect anything different.'

He was quiet. 'And Toby? Did he stick up for you?'

I paused. 'Would it be enough to say I can't talk about that right now?'

'I understand.' He was quiet. 'I ended things with Iona. Got a bit messy, unfortunately.'

I didn't see that coming. Why did I even care? I told myself he'd probably already replaced her with someone else, someone even younger, someone who caressed his ego and didn't challenge him.

I asked if he was okay, and he said yes, a bit lonely, but I'm all right, and if I was in the mood for admitting it, I might have told him I felt the same.

Instead I thanked him for the call.

~

Xander's phone call unsettled me. *Toby, did he stick up for you?*

Had he *ever* stuck up for me?

I distracted myself by working on a draft of a case report that Benson and I were writing, and I was on the couch when Fleur came home.

She looked pale and tired, and we made toasted cheese and drank cups of camomile tea. Rubbing hard at her eyes, she told me that Benjy, one of her long-termers, had done a runner. Somehow, he'd got his hands on a set of scrubs and sailed straight out of the ward.

'The guy's been an inpatient for weeks, had five code greys, and this is his third admission, and security think that a man who weighs thirty kilos, has terrible teeth and is covered in ink is a *doctor*? Give me a break.'

I remembered her telling me about Benjy, his childhood spent hopping through foster homes like a frog leaping from lily pad to lily pad until he made it out to the sea that was the street.

'He'll be back when he ODs ... so long as he doesn't die first.'

I felt her helplessness watching that cycle repeat itself.

As we drank our tea, I updated her on Richard. She sat very still, her hands gripping her kneecaps, and then shook her head. 'I can't rescue him. I can't.' She blew air out of her cheeks. 'Most likely he's drying out at his parents'. That's what he did last time. I'll check with his mum; she'll tell me if he's there.'

I asked her if she was okay, and she examined her palms. 'Here's the thing. I can't sit around listening to my break-up playlist anymore.'

That was not the reaction I expected. Fleur the fixer would always have wanted to rescue Richard from himself if she could.

'So, I have some news ... I've signed up to Candour.'

A dating site? 'Wow.'

'Too soon?'

'Well – no, I mean – what would I know?'

'Thing is, I've been waiting for years for him to get his act together. *Years.* I'm doing this for me.' She set her chin. 'I'm going on a date next week.'

'What? Who?'

'Isaac from Moonee Ponds is an insurance broker who loves jazz and walks on the beach. The whole profile thing is ridiculous – everyone sounds like Ryan Gosling.'

'Sounds amazing.'

'I'll let you know if he lives up to the hype.' She chewed at her lip. 'And – don't laugh – I'm trying out for roller derby.'

The image of klutzy Fleur playing contact sport on skates made me smile.

'Cool, I mean – knock yourself out.'

'I probably will!'

'Um ... have you paid your health insurance?'

'Ha.' She stretched her arms overhead and tried to smile.

~

Edwina's house was built on a steep slope in leafy outer Melbourne. As she opened the door, a Jack Russell terrier danced around her feet, barking at Tess and me. We walked down the hall and into the kitchen where a pot of curry simmered on the stove. The air was full of smells of turmeric and coriander and the sinus-clearing sharpness of chilli.

Edwina had suggested we meet at her home. 'Somewhere we can speak frankly,' she'd said, 'other than the female change rooms,' and it made sense. Tess had agreed and it felt wrong for me to keep Valentine's Day free when I hadn't heard from Toby.

It felt a strange intrusion to see Edwina's home. The kitchen bench was cluttered with piles of papers and bills, and on the floor potted plants were arranged in groups, like bacteria colonies clustered together on an agar plate. The far wall was a floor-to-ceiling bookshelf. Two fig plants stood like tall green sentries near the back door. We looked out over her deck onto the last light of the day softening on the treetops.

Tess was brave-faced and pale. In the back of my mind, the closing date for her application loomed: she had three weeks to secure her referees, and her head was not in the right space to have those conversations right now. I knew she would need some time to deal with the whole Benson thing, but she needed to get that application in, somehow.

Edwina's dog was named Lilian, after the first female surgeon in Australia. Surgeon Lilian was tough and tall and swore 'like a man'. In her fifties, she travelled to Serbia to operate on wounded soldiers during World War I. Jack Russell Lilian took an immediate liking to Tess, jumping on her lap once she sat down.

Edwina opened and poured the wine we'd brought. I noticed she was wearing slippers, not the grandma sort, but a pair of black mules embroidered with flowers.

She was magnificently, quirkily, her own woman.

We sat down to eat, and Edwina told us about the Sri Lankan boyfriend she'd had years ago whose mother had taught her how to make curry. 'I think she was terrified that her son might end up with me and starve. It didn't last and he didn't go hungry, but I did learn how to make a wicked spice paste.'

The curry was delicious and wicked enough to need the cucumber raita.

'Emmett Benson,' Edwina said. 'What a contradiction that man is. First thing to say is, I'm sorry that this happened to you, Tess. Second thing is, fuck. Fuck. Fuck. Fuck.' Her head jolted with each utterance, and the force of the word shook her pristine bob. 'Can you tell me a little of what happened?'

Tess talked through the encounter with Benson with tears and pauses and licks under the chin from Lilian.

Edwina's face was grave. 'Stepping away from the incident for just a moment, it would help me to understand more about your long-term plans, because that ... well, it might influence how you handle this. What is your preference, in terms of your career?'

Tess examined her hands and then looked Edwina in the eye. 'I want to be a surgeon.'

'Good. I'm pleased to hear that. Then ... would you consider leaving?'

I blinked, three times. *What?*

Tess looked to the ceiling. 'I love working at PCH, with Carla and everyone. I don't want to leave.'

It sounded like she had thought about it. I knew I hadn't been the most welcoming to Tess when she had started in surgery, but I didn't want her to leave because of Benson. I didn't want PCH to be that kind of place.

'I mean, leaving ... it would set Tess back, right? She wouldn't be able to get the referees for an accredited job, so it would mean another year unaccredited.'

Edwina nodded. 'True. The reason I raise it is that I think you should consider all alternatives here.' She turned to Tess. 'In your mind, what would success look like?'

Tess thought, and swallowed, and spoke. 'I want to be able to go to work and not worry about where he is, or what he will do. That's all I want. Not just for me. I want to know that Carla and all women there are safe.'

Benson's hands on my butt. Inside my shoes, my toes curled.

'I'm okay,' I said. 'You don't need to worry about me.'

Lilian jumped onto my lap and I stiffened. I didn't really know how to handle dogs, or any pets: Gina didn't see the point in keeping animals you weren't planning to eat. I tried to emulate Tess and patted Lilian's head, but she shied away, growling softly.

Edwina smiled. 'Not a dog person, Carla?' She lifted Lilian onto her lap. 'Let's think then about avenues.'

'I want to speak to Prof. He's supported Women in Surgery, all the way. I think he should know that this is going on.'

'Hmm. I understand why you would want to do that. Now, I've never worked with Emmett, but I know he comes with a – reputation. Is there any reason to think that Prof doesn't know already?'

Tess's eyes widened. 'Wouldn't he have done something about it?'

Edwina sighed. 'I would love to think that was the case ... but Emmett and Alister have worked together for a long time. I suspect he may know, and not fully understand the impact it has.'

'Then I can help him see that.'

Tess's voice held conviction I did not feel. 'What other options do you see?' I asked Edwina.

Edwina talked about formal complaints, to HR, or the college or AHPRA. 'Each one would make it official, and as much as I dislike this, it could have consequences for you at some hospitals when you're trying to get a job.' She tilted her head. 'Not at mine, for what that is worth. Not all hospitals are as archaic as PCH. Tell me something – I know it has an excellent reputation, but why do *you* think that trainees are so attracted to working there?'

Tess's eyes were glassy, as though she were somewhere deep inside herself, so I felt obliged to speak, and I did not want to offend Edwina. I chose my words carefully. 'I suppose ... it feels like it is the pinnacle. Like it has the best surgeons, and therefore, it will be the best place to learn.'

Edwina nodded. 'I've heard people say that – being hard to get into increases its appeal. It certainly has prestige and history sewn up. And yet, that very tradition might prevent an openness to different ways of learning, and to trainees from diverse backgrounds. I fear – I don't know your chances of success, pursuing an issue like this, without jeopardising your career.'

We sat for a minute, digesting the reality of Edwina's words.

'If you were prepared to consider it, there might be opportunities elsewhere. It's a shame, actually – I have an accredited registrar going on maternity leave next month, but we've already filled that post. I'm sure other opportunities will arise.'

Imagine a surgical registrar going on maternity leave! They would never get back in after having a baby, surely? It felt like Edwina was describing another universe.

When Tess spoke, her voice was small but sure. 'I don't see why I should have to go somewhere else. It's as if *I've* done something wrong.'

Edwina looked off into the distance and then topped up our glasses. 'It stinks, I understand. Now, what about support for you? It will be crucial to identify people around you who can keep you going, who you trust. And have you thought about seeing someone ... a counsellor, perhaps?'

'Oh, thank you, but – I already have my own therapist,' Tess said. 'Been seeing her for years.'

I marvelled at how easily she spoke about it. Not that I had ever had counselling, but if I had, I would be keeping quiet about it. Tess's preparedness to be vulnerable left me in awe of her, and nervous for her.

'Good that you've got that in place,' Edwina said. She leant forwards, her palms flat on the table. 'You will get through this, in time, I know that. I have every confidence in you.'

The tightness in Tess's face gave way to an anxious, hopeful smile. She turned to me. 'If we could find a way ... moving Benson on would be good for you, too, wouldn't it? Bring about the consultant job. I really want that for you, you so deserve it.'

Of course I had thought of that, but I shook my head. 'I know, right? But I feel as though this has to be about you, and helping you recover some dignity.'

She sat for a moment, and Lilian licked her chin, and Tess decided she wanted to speak with Prof, that she needed to give him that chance.

Across the table, Edwina and I exchanged an uneasy look.

~

I hadn't seen Toby for days. I wanted to tell him about the success of Liv's second surgery, and I wanted him to apologise for reneging on the list swap, but I refused to chase him for something he owed me.

Close to midnight, I was in bed when my phone rang, and I scrabbled for it, hoping it was Toby, hoping it wasn't Toby –

It was Xander, again.

'Xander of the late-night phone call,' I said.

'Were you asleep?'

'Very un-asleep. Why are you calling me so late? Are you drunk?'

He laughed. 'You don't know musos. This is peak hour. The day is just beginning.'

'Forgot how uber-cool you are.'

'I like talking to you, Carla. No one insults me with quite the same passion.'

I could hear the smile in his voice. 'I've barely got started.'

He paused. 'Do you know that Paduan song? The one about outrunning death?'

I didn't, so he sang a few lines, and I settled back down under the covers, listening to the lyrics about running from death and escaping from life. Xander's voice was late-night low and as soon as he stopped, I wanted him to start again.

'I've had that song in my head ever since I came back. Maybe that's what's blocking me from writing, because, man – something is.'

'Maybe it wouldn't be so bad, to stop running.'

'When I think of running, all I can see is my dad, and how he – what he thought of my life. He was so ashamed when I dropped out. He couldn't get it – you know, he'd told all his friends how his son was going to be a doctor. He thought I was mad, to give all that away. For a while there, he wouldn't even speak to me. Then he got sick, and I – well, we didn't get the chance.'

'What about your music – did he like your songs?'

He gave a short laugh. 'I never knew. Music was his language, you know? Only ever needed to hear a tune once. When I was a kid, he'd have his mates over, and they'd jam out in the shed, drinking and smoking and the music would pour out. That was when I caught the bug.

'The thing about my dad – he was better at music than everything else. He fell out with most of his friends, sooner or later, and he stopped playing... I guess music was something he did with them. And then the lymphoma... he got a transplant from my sister, and we thought he would be okay. I wasn't a match, of course. Story of my life.' He gave a bitter laugh.

'So he rejected the transplant?'

'He never got out of hospital.' He sighed. 'That was two years ago, and I can't write a line. I'm starting to think it will never happen.'

'Come on – you did it before, you must be able to again. Like riding a bike, right? What about going back to whatever inspired you, say when you wrote your famous song? Something was going right for you then.'

'That's an interesting idea.' He paused. 'You have a crazy way of making terrifying things sound okay.'

I didn't know what that meant, but he sounded sad. To lighten the mood I told him about my effort in trying and failing to play golf.

'Golf? Geez, you really are determined to wear that surgeon mantle, aren't you?'

I screwed up my face. 'It's the place that deals get done. We have to be at the table. Otherwise, what chance do we have?'

His voice softened. 'That makes sense. I'm sorry, I shouldn't have judged.'

He asked who I played with, and I told him about Tess, her penchant for dangly earrings and her superlative-ridden love for surgery.

'She sounds like she might shake the place up a bit.'

'Maybe. If she can get on the program.'

'You don't think she will?'

I hesitated, and then it spilt out of me, what had happened. No names, of course – I wasn't going to risk that. But it was a burden to hold the awfulness of it, and sharing it eased the load.

Xander's voice, when he spoke, was angry. 'On so many levels, it isn't good enough. The rest of the world is beginning to demand more from men and that place is just pretending, like, "Nothing to see here." I know you feel responsible, Carla – but how about any one of the *men* in your team who could stand up to this man?'

He was right, and I knew it.

'Hey, take care of yourself in there, you know – some of these men are not good people.'

I said I would, and we ended the call.

His comments left me with too much to think about. Why wasn't

PCH cultivating an environment where female surgeons could thrive? I didn't have an answer.

Suction

removal of material through the use of negative pressure, as in suctioning an operative wound during and after surgery to remove exudates

The repeat mastectomy restored my confidence in theatre. The consultants gave me more and more to do – Phil spent a whole hour last week on the phone to his son's school while I led the list, and I held the scalpel with a calm hand. I was ready for this.

Tess was now my biggest concern. She seemed bereft of superlatives, and I was surprised to find work greyer without them.

Late one afternoon, Tess and I left the hospital and walked a small way into the long grass. We sat at a picnic table, away from anyone who could hear, and mapped out the roster for the next week. I swapped into her clinic alongside Benson. Gently, I raised the topic of her job application, and we set goals for her to complete over the next two weeks. I watched her struggle to hold herself together and wondered how long she could last like that.

I walked home, exhausted. I'd never sought to be a support person – to mother the trainees, as Prof put it. I didn't even know if I had it in me – I feared I might be too selfish, or too impatient, unable to have my pace dictated by someone else's distress. Or maybe I would simply not know what to do or say.

When Fleur was an intern, she went through a phase of buying and killing plants, sometimes several at once, each purchase followed by a period of neglect before the plant gave out. Later, I came to realise that the habit was a response to the suffering she witnessed in her job, but at the time it seemed callous, the way she would bring home a lily, or a fern, or even a cactus, and then forget that one needed frequent watering while another turned up its roots if it was left in direct sun. I became an accidental gardener, learning the peculiarities of each plant, finding them a place in our house or courtyard where they could thrive.

Fleur was on the couch when I arrived home, her phone between her knees. I asked if she'd eaten, thinking that over dinner I could get her advice on supporting Tess, but she shook her head, her face drawn. 'I'm going to my parents' for dinner tonight, but I – found something. I need to talk to you.'

I went and sat beside her, thinking, *Richard?*

I asked if she was okay, and she scratched at her neck. 'I – I don't want to do this, but I don't have a choice.' She exhaled, hard. 'Just now, I was on Candour –'

'Isaac from Moonee Ponds didn't deliver?'

She shook her head. 'Keeping my options open.' She looked at me. 'I saw Toby.'

My throat closed over. A noise came, an involuntary utterance, an *oh*, like the sound a cushion made when the dust was punched out of it. Fleur tried to put her arm around me, but my body was stiff, and it felt like she was trying to hug a pane of glass.

'Are you sure? Maybe it's old ...'

'Do you want to see?'

'No.' But of course I held my hand out and, reluctantly, Fleur passed me her phone. In the photo, his legs were splayed, the shape of his pecs visible inside a linen shirt. I knew the shirt. I knew the grin.

I turned my face. He was gone from me.

~

Sleep was out. I couldn't even lie still while my brain and heart slugged it out. My hopes for us screamed like an undressed burn, the pain as real and as humiliating as his picture on Candour. I had wanted a way for us to work. There was no way for us to work. I wanted a way ...

Before dawn, I grew tired of trying to sleep. I dressed and got in my car.

On the freeway, the car hurtled forwards into the dark, and finally I could cry, for me with Toby's body pressing me against the door, and me going down on him on the bridge, me in the M&M, and me lying next to him with the arch of my foot melded into the muscle belly of his calf, our bodies completing one another.

At almost light, I went to the river and sat on a bench near the vacant boathouse. Birdsong chorused like the twinkling of many, many stars.

And in the distance, the pipe bridge. I remembered the cold steel digging into my knees. As daylight tiptoed over treetops, and the birdsong grew boisterous, the warmth of the sun began to spread over the water.

A lone duck swam down the river, a wake of tiny ripples behind it.

AFTER

I'm in the shower, the morning after the gala. The water is on as hot as it goes, and steam drifts from it, occluding my vision, matching the fog in my brain.

I was drunk, it was late, I do not remember.

I have a desire to wash, and wash, and so I soap up an extravagant lather on my skin, cleaning my arms down to my fingers, my legs down to my toes, my torso and back. I open my mouth and let hot water run into it and spit it out. I wash my hair, finding a spot on the vertex of my scalp that is sensitive to my touch. When I rub my hand over my neck, there is a small amount of blood on my fingertips. I trace a circle of broken skin around the nape of my neck. *Abrasion.*

And then my fingers find the necklace, weighted heavy with its diamond, still in place around my neck.

With a force that surprises me, I yank on the chain until it snaps, and the diamond goes flying into the steamed-up bathroom.

I don't know where it lands.

I wash until my skin is red.

BEFORE

Graft

to move tissue from one site of the body to another, without bringing its own blood supply with it

The ache didn't leave as soon as I'd hoped. I thought anger would subsume it, but instead it lost its hardened edge, leaving raw hurt like a wound open to the air.

The pain was less at work, where I was busy, and I had Tess to think about.

On Monday, I sat with her outside Prof's office. It would have been good to get Prof's reference first, maybe even to postpone until Tess had lodged her application, but she said she couldn't stomach the waiting. My tongue pressed against the sharp edge of my canine.

Tess squeezed my hand. 'It's going to be okay. He's a good man. I know he'll listen.'

'I'm here for *you*, remember?' My voice was dry.

Inside Prof's office, we sat down, his massive desk between us. Tess's voice trembled as she explained why we were there, but her eyes did not deviate from Prof's face.

He looked at me, brow furrowed, eyes narrow, and I wanted to say, *yes, you're right – in the ten years I have worked here, I've never come to you like this*. I had played along with the bad-taste jokes, ignored the innuendo, tried to meet the standards to which I was held, knowing they were higher than what was expected of the men. I wanted to tell him, *it should count for something, that I'm here now*.

Would I mention the times Benson had made my toes curl?

'I'm here to support Tess.'

She read from pre-prepared notes, her account factual and understated. She spoke with little emotion and did not describe her humiliation when he groped her breast or touched her hair, and I understood, because that would expose vulnerability, and weren't we exposed enough, sitting here in Prof's office, speaking up?

When did our mentors show their emotional frailties? Almost never and not deliberately.

When Tess finished, Prof stood and walked to the window, looking outwards, hands behind his back. Tess sat with her hands under her thighs, her face tightened into a wince. The muscles in my left shoulder bunched tight.

Eventually he returned to his desk. 'It cannot have been easy to come here today, so firstly, I want to acknowledge that.'

'Yes,' Tess said. 'It's not easy to talk about.'

'Indeed. Nor, unfortunately, is it easy for me. Or – Mr Benson.'

I startled. In what universe was it not easy for Benson?

'I want you to try to understand something. It can be challenging to get the boundaries right, especially when they're constantly moving, and what is acceptable one day is frowned upon the next. You would agree that suggesting you tuck your hair under your cap, given the strict hygiene requirements of theatre, is reasonable – in fact, desirable – would you not?'

Her lips parted and her chin trembled. 'He touched my *breast*.'

'Do you think it is possible that you misunderstood his intention? Mr Benson is one of our best teachers, most generous with trainees. He uses his hands to get a point across. Often the way with surgeons, their hands are their tools of trade, of course. Perhaps it was' – he waved his hands in the air – 'a gesture gone wrong.'

Slowly, Tess shook her head.

'All I'm saying is that it is possible, in the stress of the moment, that you misread him. Perhaps the message was delivered in a tactile way, but – he would only want the best for you. I know that for a fact.

'Now, I would like to give you some advice, and I want you to understand that this comes from a place of care for you, Tess.'

I saw the whites of her eyes.

Prof clasped his hands together and rested them on the desk. 'The reality in any of these situations is that there are two humans involved. Think carefully if you did anything – anything at all – to make this situation more likely, or if there is anything you can do to prevent it happening again. I can assure you, I will give the matter you have described to me careful thought.'

He turned to me. 'Carla, I'm grateful to you for supporting Tess. You can provide valuable mentorship on how you've navigated the world of surgery. I'm heartened to see the women in our team looking after one another, and as you develop your own professionalism, you can impart this to Tess.' He clasped his hands together. 'I am grateful for you bringing this matter to my attention. I would appreciate it if both of you would keep this confidential.'

I heard the gravity of his voice and the warning in his words, but my eyes were on Tess, whose shoulders were shaking.

'You can trust our discretion, Prof – absolutely. And I'd be happy to mentor Tess. I think she is going to be a talented surgeon, and we will want her on our team. She was first operator for an appendicectomy, on Christmas Day, no less. You'd be comfortable, Prof, to act as a referee for her for an accredited position?'

For a split second, Prof looked startled, and then he composed himself. 'Of course, I would be delighted.'

It was almost enough, but I needed to be sure. 'And just for Tess's reassurance, you'd give her the score that would enable her to progress to the interview stage?'

The look Prof gave me was withering. 'I do know how the system works, Carla.'

Tess recovered her ability to speak. 'That is wonderful, Prof. Thank you. I appreciate it.'

'Good,' Prof said. 'Thank you for coming, Tess.' He stood. 'Carla, please wait.'

With a backward glance at me, Tess left the room.

Prof leant his elbows on the desk. 'Do you remember our discussion about professionalism?'

I did.

'Then why did you not come to me alone, first? Such delicate matters as this need very careful handling, and by senior people.'

Bewildered, I looked at the ceiling, and then his desk. 'The incident happened to Tess. I felt she needed to be here.'

'This could jeopardise the business case, and if that fails, my dear, the consultant job goes with it.'

I stared at him, nonplussed. How could a complaint against Benson do anything other than push him out the door?

'I am trying to grow the unit. We need more consultants, that is plain. And if this little concern about Benson reaches the hospital executive, they will hardly be sympathetic to my cause.'

'My job – the new job – isn't Benson's?'

He bristled. 'Mr Benson is a surgeon with decades of experience and a valued member of our team. In your discussions with Tess, bear in mind that it is in everyone's interests if we handle this internally.'

Prof glanced at the door and thanked me for my time. From his desk, the fresh and hopeful faces of his three sons smiled out at me from a black-and-white photo in a silver frame.

~

'Let's walk.' I shepherded Tess down the lift and out of the hospital, where we didn't have to worry who would see us.

We walked under ghostly gums whose leaves danced in the breeze. Myna birds piped a to-and-fro conversation, and a large black crow perched on a fence, watching us.

I tried to compose my face. Prof wasn't planning to move Benson on: he saw him as an *asset*. Where did that leave Tess?

I asked if she wanted to go home for the day and I would deal with her work, and she shook her head. With a few questions I established that she was in clinic this afternoon, as was I. Good, I could keep an eye on her there.

She stopped still on the bitumen under a towering eucalyptus. 'I told him about Benson groping me, and his response is to undermine *me*. How could he? I believed in him.'

'The way I see it, Prof was protecting his turf by turning this on you. There is nothing you did to make this happen. Nothing.'

She nodded, her face serious.

A knot tightened in my shoulder. Prof, my mentor. I remembered standing across the table from him, holding my first appendix aloft, a puce, engorged kind of trophy. He'd known, and I too, that this was where I was meant to be.

Now, I was telling Tess she couldn't rely on him.

Tess stole a sideways look at me, and then cast her gaze at the sky.

'Hey ... at least we got a reference out of him. I wasn't going to leave that room with nothing.'

She exhaled. 'You were amazing. I can't thank you enough.'

'I want you to know, I'm here for you. I believe you, and I will support you every way I can.' I thought of Benson's hands on my butt. 'You're not alone, Tess. For as long as you want to stay in surgery at PCH, I'm going to try to make that possible. We will not let him win.'

My chest hurt watching her force her mouth into a smile. I put my arm around her, and we began the slow walk back into the hospital, where we would put on our professional faces and see patients in pain and try to help, and I would ignore the greasy feeling growing in my gut.

~

I decided I would not think of Toby. I had Tess to worry about, and it felt wrong to steep in my sorrow when she was dealing with something bigger. When my chest ached, I reminded myself, *eyes on the prize*.

Despite Prof's response, Tess remained hell-bent on going to HR. It would be an off-the-record chat, she told me. In a low voice, I reminded her about Simone Gillies, the ortho resident from a few years back who'd complained about culture and was not employed the following year. Tess was bewildered by this and insisted that HR should do their job.

I didn't disagree, but Prof's warning weighed on me. *It's in everyone's interests if we handle this internally.* I couldn't prioritise Prof's needs over Tess's, even if he didn't like it.

The following afternoon we were in outpatients, where the clerks assembled two separate piles of patient files: a smaller one for the consultants, and a taller stack with thick files and a post-it note on the top saying 'registrar'. These were typically the patients the consultants wanted to avoid, usually non–English speaking, or non-compliant, or aggressive personalities with a history of code greys. Some were all three.

Tess and I ploughed through as many of the pile as we could, and then at three pm she went to her scheduled appointment with HR. When she returned, I was with a patient, and it wasn't until six, when the last patient was seen, that we left outpatients.

We climbed the stairs to the ward. The stairwell had a view of a grey-skied city, scattered with rays of glaring white sunlight. Tess paused at the landing, and, staring out at the sky, she told me the woman from HR was sympathetic, but had pointed out all the reasons to walk away: the evidentiary bar was set high for he-said, she-said incidents, and for good reason, according to the woman in HR, given some complaints were found to be false; Tess should remember that Benson was close to retirement and would be gone from her working life soon enough; and she had me as an ally to keep her safe.

When Tess didn't seem satisfied with that, the HR woman offered to transfer her to a role in ED, and initially Tess thought, *what would be the point of that, when I want to become a surgeon?*

The HR woman had also suggested assertiveness training, and when Tess asked why women needed to be trained to avoid being harassed, the woman sniffed and told her these would be useful life skills.

'Like I'll have a lifetime of being around these kinds of men,' Tess said. 'And then she asked me something really strange. She said, "I'm just curious, but why didn't you do gynae?" I was staring at her, like, why would I do gynae? And then I realised: because I'm a woman. She thought I should do gynae because I have a *uterus*. A fucking uterus!'

Her eyes blazed. I hadn't seen Tess angry before, but I had the feeling I was going to enjoy it. 'Don't forget the ovaries.'

'The *fucking* ovaries. The fucking clock-ticking ovaries and their fucking wasting-away eggs. Of course I would want to operate only on the uterus, because in her eyes, that's all I am! A walking fucking uterus!'

She stuck her arms out to the sides and floated them around octopus-style, doing a two-step as she twirled in a circle on the landing, a bleakly hilarious Tess-shaped womb.

Above us, the door opened, and a couple of male residents cast us a look as they descended. Tess wiped at her eyes, and I stifled my laughter. Once they were past us, she grew sombre and said, 'Maybe I should just take the ED role and be done with it.'

'Is that what you want?'

'No. I want to do this job, and I like working with you. But ... I can't see how I can get my application together in time, with all the referees and everything, especially when my head's not straight. I don't know, maybe I'm not cut out for this.'

'Don't make any decisions just now, okay?'

'Okay.'

After she headed off home, I sat on the ward for a while, finishing paperwork. Tess was a good registrar who had the potential to become an excellent surgeon. I had put her in harm's way. If she left surgery altogether, I would feel as though I failed her.

But I needed help. Prof and HR were dead ends here, and somehow I needed to make Tess feel safe and give her the opportunities the male registrars had.

First, we needed to lock in her referees, and we needed to make that happen, fast. Then, I didn't know how, but I had to find some way to make sure Benson was on his way out.

~

It was only Hamish and me at breakfast. Toby was a no-show, and Will was in theatre. When I'd asked, Will had agreed to have Tess join him and, with a bit of luck, she would have his reference by the end of the list.

Hamish ordered a fry-up, and when I asked him, 'What, no granola?', he looked at me with hooded, basset-hound eyes. 'It's an accepted treatment, is it not? For overindulging?'

I took a minute to digest that Hamish needed a recovery fry-up, midweek. 'Everything okay?'

His words tumbled out. 'She wants to take him to Germany. Ursula. Stem cell treatment.'

I pressed my fingertips over my mouth, squashing the skin of my upper lip against my teeth. 'What will you do?'

His fingers combed his bald head as if in search of hair that once was. 'I fear it doesn't matter what I say ... but I don't want her to put something in his body that could harm him. She spends hours online with these families who have had miraculous responses to the treatment and when I question if that is real, she tells me I'm cruel, that I've given up on my son. And she clearly thinks it's my fault.'

Elbows on the table, I cupped my face in my palms, trying to follow. 'Your fault?'

'She says I'm socially awkward, like James. That I can't experience feelings like normal people.'

'I may have misunderstood, Hamish, but aren't James's problems a lot more serious than that?'

'Well, of course – he has severe intellectual disability, along with autism. But his paediatrician told us that when a child has severe autism, often other family members have a hint of it, and Ursula has fixated on that. Not that it changes anything.' He ran his hand over his head.

I swallowed. 'I know, with the M&M and everything, you cared about how I was going. I felt that.'

He inclined his head. 'I'm most grateful for your friendship, Carla. It's the only one I have.'

I sat back in my chair. 'Not Will?'

'Will has me in his circle to guarantee there is someone weaker than him to poke fun at. He's done so since school days. It's a particularly callous form of social inclusion.'

Our breakfasts arrived, and Hamish began dicing his fried eggs, bacon and hash brown into neat squares, and constructing tiny forkful stacks with hash brown on the base, bacon in the middle and egg on the top. He proceeded like this for several minutes before beginning to eat. I was reminded of a mother preparing food for a toddler.

'Hamish, what you're going through ... it must be tough. Do you – need some help? Like, counselling, or something?'

'I don't think it would help.' He smiled a little. 'Hopeless case.'

'You're not.'

'Thank you ... from the bottom of my heart, Carla.'

'If things get hard, you can always call me.' It was one of those offers you had to make.

'I don't find it easy to express how I'm feeling, but I very much appreciate the offer.' He cleared his throat. 'Now, while I think of it, for my sins I am collecting votes for the Casterton this year, which means I must attend the gala. Shall we organise a table?'

The gala was an all-hospital yawn-fest of awards and self-congratulatory CEO speeches. The one time I went, the highlight was the uniquely weird dance action of senior hospital doctors when the DJ played eighties disco. But I wasn't going to leave Hamish stranded, not in his current frame of mind, so I said sure.

'And if you think of any nominations for the Casterton, let me know.'

The winner of the hospital's surgical medal was usually a hospital heavyweight or a surgeon on the way out the door. In my time at PCH, Prof was the only general surgeon awarded it. Eating my poached eggs, I wondered what Benson's chances might be.

Could the Casterton be a way to push Benson off the cliff? Knowing what I knew, I wasn't sure I could stand by and watch him be celebrated like that without losing my dinner. 'Heard any names?'

'Leonard Ellis from neurosurgery was mentioned in passing. Someone will be mustering the numbers, no doubt.'

That was how these things rolled, of course – men sorting shit out for other men.

We finished our breakfast. I wanted to ask his view on what had happened with Tess. Hamish was someone who thought deeply about things. How would he see her predicament? But I couldn't betray her confidence.

'Hypothetically speaking, how do you think PCH would handle a claim of sexual harassment, if it ever had one?'

He startled and blinked, fast. 'Is everything all right?'

'I'm fine. No issue for me. I can't – say too much. But I'm interested in your view.'

Hamish made a face like his fry-up was already repeating on him.

'Honestly, I don't know. I would hope the hospital would demonstrate integrity and care for the victim, but with big organisations, sometimes, the message becomes diluted or, worse, distorted. There's always an element of self-protection when it comes to these things, so anyone who raises a complaint can be marginalised.'

I thought of Tess and her bedraggled, wet curls at golf.

'If there comes a time when you're able to say more, please consider me an ally. It's not the same, but – I know what it's like to be an outsider, of course.'

Warmth filled his basset-hound eyes.

DURING

Hamish and his basset-hound face – downturned corners of the mouth, droopy eyes, unblinking gaze.

At the gala, he sits alone at the table, staring at a half-empty bottle of red in front of him as if his life's meaning might be encrypted in the label. I'm torn, because I am ready to leave, but he looks drunk and lonely.

He sees me hovering near the exit and calls out. *No, no, no. Don't go. Come sit down, here.* His voice is loud and his consonants slur and heads turn and I can't leave him like this. I walk over and sit down, and he pours me wine I don't want.

Drink, he says, and I do.

Did you know, he says, *that humour is sexy? That when you make people laugh, they're attracted to you? Which is wonderful if you're funny, and unfortunate, if, like me, humour eludes you. And if you are the butt of people's jokes, people are repulsed – repulsed – by you.*

He locks his rheumy eyes on me and tells me he is alone. Arabella is staying at her grandmother's, and Ursula has taken James to Germany.

Tears spill on his cheeks. He's weeping, here at the gala, and all I can do is sit with him. When I tell him how sorry I am, unexpectedly he reaches for my hand. *I knew you'd understand. Ursula says I don't do affection but look at me. I should take one of those – you know – selfies.* He stares at our intertwined hands, as bewildered as me. *You're the only one who has stood by me, through all this.*

My throat constricts. Now is not the time for Hamish to lay bare his awkward heart. I suggest he should lay off the wine a bit, and he tells me, a bottle a night, otherwise he can't sleep, that the house is like a mausoleum, all those empty rooms, so terribly lonely, and that's from one who has always felt alone. He rests his glass on a dark red smudge on the tablecloth and asks if he could stay with me.

My stomach plummets. *No* escapes from my lips. He says it would only be a short while, until he gets himself together. My knuckles blanch white beneath his grip.

It's then that I become aware of someone behind us, standing near the pillar in the corner of my vision. A still, silent presence.

I tell Hamish it wouldn't work for him to stay, that I have a flatmate, and maybe he should try counselling, and he says no and leans his head on my shoulder. He tells me he needs me; I am all he has.

His body slumps sideways against me, and I'm wedged into my chair trying to hold him up. I try to sit him upright, but he doesn't cooperate, and his breath deepens and it's possible that he has fallen asleep. I can't see who is behind us or tell if they're close enough to hear Hamish's drunken rambling, but I sense them watching.

BEFORE
Haemostasis

the physiological process that stops bleeding at the site of an injury

Tess and I walked to the ward for our early morning round, making sure everything was in order before the teaching round at eleven.

I sensed a slight uptick in her mood. Will had agreed without hesitation to act as a referee. Phil was next on her list, and I told her how I'd agreed to assist him at Atherton Private for three weekends straight before he signed off on my reference.

'He did ask me once about assisting, but ... I said no, because I had, um, another commitment.' Her face fell. 'That was a mistake, wasn't it?'

I scratched at my neck. 'Maybe.'

She sighed. 'There was a Women's March at the State Library, and one of my friends was speaking.'

'Oh. Well, ask him again? Maybe don't tell him where you were last time.'

She nodded. 'But that still leaves me one referee short, which means I have to go back to Benson. I don't feel like any of the other consultants know me well enough, not to rate me at one hundred per cent.'

I didn't see any other solution, and she only had one more week to sort it. 'Let me know when you're speaking to him, and I'll make sure I'm in the area.'

Oncology had passed on a message that Liv wanted to see us. She had been readmitted with febrile neutropaenia but was due for discharge today, and was already dressed and out of bed when we came past. Over by the window, Anthea stood staring out at the park, while an older Chinese woman packed Liv's things into a bag. I recognised a pair of radioactive-yellow, duck-billed slippers. I felt as though those duck eyes had seen everything that had happened and weren't happy about it.

Liv introduced her mum, Rosy, to Tess and me. Rosy folded her arms and looked me up and down. She raised Liv's arm by the wrist and dropped it so that it slumped to her side. 'Look! No muscle. Weak! No good.'

'We're meant to be thinking positive, Rosy – remember?' Anthea said.

Rosy sniffed. She took two coloured brochures from her bag and gave them to Liv. 'Which one?'

Liv glanced at them. 'Mum's sixtieth,' she explained to me. 'We're trying to decide on a venue.' She handed one back to Rosy. 'This one. More vegetarian options.'

'Ha! Who vegetarian?'

'Anthea. And me, practically.'

'No wonder you're sick.' Rosy snatched back the other brochure. 'This one better. More seafood.'

Anthea coughed. 'I'm going to go and get coffee. Will you bring the consultants past later?'

'Sure, we can do that.' I drew the curtain around Liv and checked her wounds, which were healing nicely. Prof would be pleased to see how well Liv was recovering.

'Mum is excited to meet you,' Liv said. 'She wants you to give me the chemo.'

'Me?'

'She likes the idea of a female doctor, and she knows you've looked after me and I trust you, so in her mind, what else is there? I tried to explain it doesn't work like that.'

'Your mum doesn't know how dangerous that would be. I know nothing about chemo.'

Liv's mouth grew small. 'All doctors are dangerous.'

Tess reeled back at Liv's words. I swallowed, and tried not to sound defensive.

'I can see how much this has taken out of you. Liv – I'm sorry, for what happened.'

'Thank you,' Liv said. 'It means a lot.' She glanced at Tess. 'You've both been so kind to me.'

When I pulled the curtain back, Rosy was standing there with a pineapple. She pushed it towards me and, embarrassed, I thanked her and took it in my hand, its rough skin tinged with green.

'It's good luck,' Liv said.

'You eat it,' Rosy said. She looked me up and down again. 'And meat? You eat meat?'

I nodded.

'You come to my party. June 9th.' She looked at Tess. 'You too. Liv likes you.'

Tess's cheeks coloured.

'Mum –' Liv began.

'Why not? They the good ones. Good doctors.'

I scratched at my neck and looked at Tess, who smiled and shrugged, *okay, I guess?* It felt rude to refuse and wrong to accept, but by June Liv would no longer be our patient, so maybe that made it okay? I nodded uncertainly, and Rosy looked pleased with herself.

As we walked towards the stairs, Tess looked at the pineapple cupped in my hand. 'I've never been to a patient's mother's birthday party before.'

'Me neither.'

We smiled doubtfully at each other, and Tess's musical laugh filled the hallway.

~

Thursday's teaching round was a circus of consultants and junior doctors, med students and nurses. Prof led, and the rest of us traipsed behind as he taught and interrogated and cast a critical eye over how inpatients were being managed. I loved it and hated it – loved those moments when Prof's clear-minded synthesis of a patient's problem paved the path from illness to healing. I hated watching while he interrogated a sweating, squirming medical student.

I found a place in the crowd next to Tess and as far from Toby as I could be. I had been ignoring his texts, and tried hard not to catch his eye.

Prof began the round seeing Mrs Greenidge in ICU. She was conscious, oxygen prongs in her nose. She met my eye and gestured to the newspaper on her bedside table. I stared at the nine-letter puzzle while Prof beckoned Toby to the bedside, which was unexpected. He usually asked one of the students to examine.

Toby took his sweet time perusing the charts. From the other side of the bed, I watched him approach Mrs Greenidge and, as he examined her, I catalogued the muscles under his shirt, those ripples my fingers had thrilled at. I could feel them firm under my fingertips. The soles of my feet proclaimed their aloneness – how they longed to slip into the space where his calves moulded perfectly against the arch, filling it, completing it. I pressed my knuckles to my mouth at the memory of our bodies melded.

Toby finished assessing Mrs Greenidge, put his hands in his pockets and turned to Prof. 'She's doing well. No particular issues.'

'Improved from the last time you saw her?'

His question was asked lightly but delivered with Prof's unblinking gaze. The tips of Toby's ears turned pink. 'Yes, well – um, I would think so. It's been a while.'

'Indeed.' He kept his eyes on Toby, who looked away.

As the ward round moved on, I paused by her bed. 'Prescience,' I said.

'Indeed,' she repeated.

I wondered what she had noticed.

Eventually we climbed the stairs to the oncology ward. I noticed Maggie had joined us, which was unusual. Liv sat on the bed, flanked by Anthea and Rosy, while I summarised her progress.

'All is going well, then?' Prof asked Liv.

'Yes,' Liv said, looking relieved, but before she could say more, Anthea moved so that she stood in the middle of the ward round, oblivious to the startled looks from the team.

Anthea handed a piece of paper to Prof. 'I wanted to give your team some feedback about the care we received, and now seems like a good time.'

Prof grimaced. 'Thank you, we do appreciate feedback. But if there are any concerns you'd like to discuss, we can do that in private –'

'It's exactly that, Professor. Honesty, transparency, telling us what is going on. These are my concerns.'

'Let us make a time –'

'It was a difficult period for us, with Liv being so sick.'

'I understand.'

'I wonder if you do. The nurses were wonderful, and we've very much appreciated the care from the team, but I have to say, there was only one doctor who was straight with us.'

I bowed my head, staring at the floor. My cheeks burnt.

Prof opened his mouth to respond, but Anthea wasn't done.

'As far as I'm concerned, the surgery your team does – it's wonderful.

But without Carla listening to our concerns, Liv would have been too scared to go back for more surgery, which she needed to fight this thing.'

'She's just wonderful, isn't she?' Toby said, and if you didn't know him, you might have thought he was sincere.

Anthea rounded on him. 'What's your name?' It was a simple question, but she held herself very still.

'Toby. Toby Tennyson.' His voice held an edge of defiance.

'Ah, you're the one,' Anthea said. 'Interesting.' She laughed a little to herself but didn't explain the joke.

Toby's shoulders shifted, and his jaw clenched.

Prof thanked Anthea with a thin smile, and as the ward round filed out, Maggie drew Prof to one side to speak with him.

I waved goodbye to Liv, who called out, 'Enjoy the pineapple.'

Toby walked next to me. 'What did you do? Bring them a tray of lasagne?'

'I cared for them, Toby. They didn't even know your name.'

'I wasn't the one who broke her girlfriend's rib.'

'You –' Bile rose in my throat. This was not the place to lose my shit.

Near the nurses' station, Prof paused. 'Maggie would like to share something with you.'

Maggie cleared her throat. 'Well, as far as I can see, it could've gone either way, with Liv, here.'

Toby coughed.

'I meant,' Maggie persisted, 'that communication was difficult and at times quite tense. Carla kept this family on board.'

Maggie, giving me a leg up? This day got weirder and weirder.

'So what I wanted to say was that we should all reflect on that. Why Anthea was so grateful to Dr di Pieta.' Maggie turned and faced me, and bowed slowly, bending from her waist. I felt that she was telling me she was sorry, and she saw me. I wondered if behind the scenes she had encouraged Anthea to deliver her feedback.

'Thank you, Maggie,' Prof said. 'Now, which patient is next?'

Then Tess spoke up. 'Prof, if I may add something...'

Prof opened his mouth to cut her off, and then closed it. Was he remembering Benson's assault?

Tess cleared her throat, her neck blotched pink. 'I think what shone through here was that Carla listened.'

Maggie gave Tess a curt nod and I mouthed thanks to both. Who would ever have imagined that Liv's surgery would ultimately earn me kudos on the ward round?

'Well, it wasn't for her surgical ability.' Toby's voice was deadpan, and he finished with a mirthless laugh, and Prof, who had been growing more and more uncomfortable with the round turning into a debriefing session, turned to him.

They eyeballed each other. Toby's hands fisted by his sides and Prof straightened his shoulders, drawing himself even taller. Neither blinked.

Prof's gravel voice was dangerously soft. 'I presume you would not be demeaning Carla's surgical ability, Toby? Because that would not be wise.'

My shoulders curled inwards. I didn't want my reputation to be defended by Prof, or to be spoken about as though I weren't there. But I would not let that get in the way of what was really happening here. I thought back to Liv's first surgery, and all the trouble that followed, and here she was, with her health on the mend, and my reputation recovering. I had only one thought: *the consultant job.*

Toby wasn't feeling my elation. While the ward round began its trek to the surgical ward, he stood still, in the middle of the hallway, his face brewing a storm, and his eyes locking on me. He held out his palm to me, in a *why* gesture, and I saw him open his mouth to say something, and then falter, and when I saw his lips trembling, I felt a surge of the old feeling for him, a wave of tenderness. Then, even though the ward round wasn't done, and we had more patients to see, he spun on his heels and walked away towards the stairwell, with Prof watching.

DURING

That piercing gaze.

Prof, standing behind me as I try to hold Hamish upright.

I don't want to remember. I want to turn away, shut my eyes on the biggest dip on a roller-coaster, only to learn that the plummet is sickening, eyes closed or open.

My boss, my mentor, a few metres from me, his unblinking eyes on me. My gut squirms.

I know how it looks, how *I* look with Hamish on my shoulder, a red-wine stain on his white shirt, a trail of spittle drooling from his mouth.

Prof comes closer so that he is standing over us and drums two fingers on the table. I shake Hamish by the arm and try again to sit him up, and this time he opens one eye and that is all it takes to register Prof's presence.

With an effort, he sits up, and tells Prof I am a fine woman. Prof says he does not doubt that, and then Hamish says, 'But she won't let me stay with her,' and I try to shut the conversation down, but Hamish waves me away. Magnanimously, he declares that he will endure, and then he closes his eyes and his head slumps back onto me.

This is most unlike him, Prof says, and I explain that he is having a difficult time at home.

Then Prof tells me that I should not put myself in such a

compromised position, in full view of the room.

I want to tell him I was trying to support a friend; isn't that more important than how this looks! Instead, I nod and say nothing, endure the piercing gaze, and wish myself away, somewhere, anywhere but here.

BEFORE

Organisation

the conversion of coagulated blood, exudate or dead tissue into fibrous tissue

I carried the weighty and splendid pineapple home, one hand cupping it at the base. The leaves at the top formed a tall and majestic crown, sharper and spikier than I realised.

I kept the pineapple with me while I sat on the couch, wrestling with what to do.

Today, I had been seen.

It felt unfamiliar, and uncomfortable, and, hell, it felt right.

Was that how men *always* felt, every day they went to work? Seen for the work they do, and rewarded?

As Tess would say, it felt amazing! Incredible!

And yet, and yet –

Toby's eyes, pleading with me. I remembered his face on the ward round as Anthea took him down, his chin quivering. I felt it deep in my pelvis that he was no longer mine, and, yes, it would be my choice to end it, and, no, that did not stop the ache for him in the muscle between my shoulder blades and in the arch of my left foot. His outstretched hand and his trembling lips ... maybe he realised now that he needed me in his life.

I left the pineapple on the kitchen bench and packed a bag, telling myself this was not what I would normally do. I was worried about him; I needed to check he was okay.

So, said a voice in my mind, if this is one friend checking on another, why are you throwing a change of clothes into the bag? Break-up sex is never a good idea.

Thrown on the floor of the passenger seat, the bag mocked me as I drove over to his house.

I let myself imagine our bodies together, like the couple in the MRI machine. I told myself that all the other shit did not take that away. I told myself I needed this moment, and when my mind remembered Toby's misdemeanours, I wrenched it away towards that night we had shared on the bridge.

As I drove up his street, Toby came out of the Thai restaurant. He was talking on his phone, carrying a white plastic bag of takeaway and a bottle of wine.

My eyelids twitched. I parked my car a block away, grabbed my bag and followed him.

He stopped in front of a navy BMW, and, fearful that he somehow knew I was there, I ducked behind a plane tree, hiding behind its thick trunk.

As I watched, the car door opened –

And Phoebe got out.

Long-legged, long-haired, long-suffering Phoebe.

Together, they went into his apartment.

When a neighbour from another apartment walked past, a bearded guy I vaguely recognised, I tailgated him into the foyer, towards Toby's front door.

Which was as far as I got, because inside the echoey stairwell, I could hear them.

Toby's low voice.

Phoebe's groans.

I knew where they were. Against the door, her back hard up against the doorhandle.

When that was me, I'd been excited by his urgency. I'd thought it was a sign of how special I was to him.

Reaching into my bag, I pulled out the diamond necklace and hung it over the handle of his front door. Wanting more, I found the pink satin underpants in my bag and did the same with them.

Then back out to the street, where around me the traffic grunted and hissed and rushed. I stopped only to heave the contents of my stomach into the gutter.

And then I kept walking.

~

I cleaned the kitchen with an unfamiliar fervour. It felt good to be busy, and my busyness stopped me checking my phone or inflicting the peculiar self-torture of replaying in my head the sound of Toby and Phoebe fucking.

I reminded myself that this was the clean and final break I needed, that it was good to have extinguished the very last flames of us, that I could leave it now.

I promised myself I was sure, even when a small voice inside me asked, *Would I ever find someone else I wanted as much as Toby? Someone who made me feel like I belonged?*

I scrubbed the sink until the steel sparkled.

When I'd finished, I decided on a run, and Fleur surprised me by asking if she could join me. Once we were ready, we walked out into light rain on Rathdowne Street.

I started us off on a gentle pace. Drops of rain smattered our faces.

'Since when have you been into jogging?'

She huffed. 'I've realised, now that I'm not holding on so tight to

Richard ... that I can try anything I want to. Even if I'm no good at it. And, well, roller derby has shown me that I'm seriously unfit.'

I grinned.

'Anyway ... he called yesterday.'

Her voice was light, so I kept my response the same.

'Oh yeah?'

'Same-old. He's dried out, he wants to get back together. He doesn't know how he feels about kids.'

'And?'

'I'm done. I love him, but I can't. It's the right thing to do, no matter how much it hurts.'

Her words echoed in my head.

We made it to Princes Park and began a circuit of the running track, the gravel crunching under our feet, my inhalation and exhalation matching the rhythm of my footfall. We ran a lap, and then Fleur slowed, hands on her waist, telling me she was cooked. We agreed that I'd meet her at home, and I ran on, taking the bitumen path under Royal Parade, the tunnel covered in graffiti and littered with spray cans and flattened cardboard boxes indented by the shapes of the homeless bodies who slept there.

I ran up the hill, feeling the strain in my calves as they fought the rising path. Birds sang and I ran until there was no more aching for Toby, until all my energy was spent.

At home, I showered and changed and was fixing some lunch when the doorbell rang, and I opened the door to Xander.

The New South Wales coast had left him with a golden tan, and his hair had grown longer, and a few strands looked like they'd bleached a toffee brown, almost like they held the sun's light.

He stood, holding his guitar case by the handle, an uncertain look on his face. 'Can I come in?'

'Do you ever call first?'

'Not if I think I'll get a knock-back.'

Inside, I made us tea and we sat on the couch.

'I guess you're wondering why I'm here.'

'I thought you had another week of gigs?' I raised my eyebrows and waited.

'I – did, but … I was thinking a lot about our last conversation, and what has been going on at work for you, with the behaviour from that surgeon, and I realised I'd blame myself if I didn't tell you this … but, I have to be honest, it'll make things complicated, because … it's about Toby.'

I held up my hand. 'Xander, you don't need to –'

'Hear me out. I've come all the way from Byron to tell you this.' He cleared his throat. 'Actually, would you like to walk?'

'I've just made us tea.'

'Please? It will be easier.' There was something intent and almost desperate in his voice, so I said okay, and we went outside. The rain had stopped but the humidity remained. The heat stuck to my skin.

We walked in the grass next to the cemetery, under a row of palm trees.

'This is difficult, because I know you care about him, and I want to protect the girl involved, but I also want you to be safe.' Xander cleared his throat. 'When we were at uni, there was a lot of blokeish behaviour, right, no surprise. You know the kind of thing, how many girls you could be with, all of that. So, the summer at the end of fourth year, I went to a party at Toby's beach house. I don't think you were there, but a lot of people from our year were.'

I would have been on my trip to Timor, I remembered.

'Anyway, it was pretty wild, and one of the girls got absolutely wasted. Couldn't stand up. I found her in one of the bedrooms … a few guys were taking turns, having sex with her.' His voice caught. 'I know you care about him, Carla, but … he was one of them.'

I drew short, shallow breaths. It hurt to breathe. 'Are you sure?'

He ran a hand through his hair. 'I saw him. And I should have told you earlier, but I ... the whole thing was fucked. The girl was really messed up by it, but she didn't want to do anything, or tell anyone, and I ... I was already on my way out of medicine, and so I buried it. I'm sorry.'

'What happened? To the girl?' I didn't want to know who it was.

He winced. 'I'm not sure. She deferred a year, and I lost contact with her.'

The air drew close around my face. 'Xander, the incident at work – it wasn't Toby. And I'm not seeing him anymore, so you don't have to worry about me.'

He looked taken aback. 'You're *not* seeing him?'

'No.'

'Oh, oh, good ... that's good.' The words came out with a rush of air. 'You still need to be careful around him, Carla.'

'Okay. I hear you ... thank you for telling me, though. I'm glad I know.'

Two birds called to each other, and it wasn't the I-told-you-so cockatoos, but it may as well have been. Saliva pooled in my mouth as though I'd forgotten how to swallow.

It was a long time ago. It was different, then. Maybe he was drunk.

But what he did was wrong then and wrong now, and I had no proof that he'd changed. The M&M, Candour, Phoebe ... *Toby has always found the easy way.* What would it take for me to stop believing in him?

We crossed the road over wet, shiny tramlines, parallel lines of steel that extended left and right, as far as I could see.

~

After Xander left, I sat on the edge of my bed.

I wondered where the girl was now. I wondered if she'd ever

confronted Toby. I hoped that what they did to her did not define her, though I feared it might have.

I remembered one year in the lead-up to Christmas when my mother was on the phone, and Luca showed me the boxes of gifts high up in Gina's wardrobe. I stood on a chair and rummaged through, finding the toolkit I had begged for, and two dresses Gina would force me to wear. It was shocking, the discovery that those taunts from the older kids in the playground were true: my parents had lied. Santa wasn't real, and it wasn't just my parents in on it but the entire world, participating in a massive deceit driven by a misguided but romantic notion of childhood.

My body felt hollowed out by all the ways I had been wrong. I thought I had Toby's measure: I thought I understood his drive and his passion. I remembered, earlier in the relationship, being excited to realise Toby had no limits. Now I was just ashamed, and terrified at the choices I had made.

I would not love him anymore.

I dismantled every tender memory – I found that there weren't many.

Now, I needed to act to protect myself.

I took out my phone.

> I know what you did to that girl
> In 4th year
> At the beach house
> Stay away from me and my job or I promise you I will
> use it

I turned off my phone before he could respond.

~

Tess had one week to finalise her application, which meant it was crunch time. Over coffee at Bea's, she and I went over her application and CV. Her responses were impossibly honest and self-deprecating, and in this endeavour I was one hundred per cent sure she needed to channel a few more superlatives.

'It's good, but ... you're selling yourself short. You haven't listed the appendix you did!'

'Well, I wasn't sure, I mean – I didn't do *all* of it.'

'Tess. Listen to yourself. You led the surgery – give yourself a break! You're very generous when you're judging other people, you know – this person is amazing, that person is incredible. How about giving yourself some of that?'

Her eyes grew wistful.

'We have to beef this up. Imagine you're talking about someone else.'

'I could pretend it's you,' she said.

That wasn't what I was expecting, but sure.

We edited the text to sell her achievements more, and she told me about the assertiveness training that HR had arranged.

'Once I got past feeling irritated about it, it was actually quite good. I find it hard, to ask for things, you know?'

I knew.

'So, I tried it.' She twisted her bangle in one direction and then the other. She told me that Prof had altered her roster, so that there were no more sessions with Benson, but that they had been replaced with ward work and outpatients, meaning she hardly ever got to go to theatre. She would have no chance to practise her skills or learn new ones.

Prof had told her this as if he'd done her a favour, but it left her less and less likely to get the case numbers she'd need to compete for an accredited job. Unease grew in my gut.

'Did you speak to him about it?'

She sat up tall and looked pleased with herself. 'I did. I told him I would prefer to be treated like anyone else, and could he please reverse those changes, and he said he would. He told me it was good that I had recovered.' She smiled, but a shudder went through her body. 'What I wanted to ask was ... would you come along, just to the first case with Benson? If you're free, of course. I think if you're there, he will probably behave better. Once I'm over that hurdle, then hopefully I can get on with the work.'

'Of course.'

She smiled. 'Awesome!'

'Keep it coming.'

'Amazing! Incredible!'

I smiled back at her. That was more like it.

~

I drove home very late on Friday, after an emergency laparotomy for a woman in a motor vehicle accident who had lacerated her liver.

The house was dark, and I crept in so as not to disturb Fleur. I made myself a cup of spearmint tea, noticing Rosy's pineapple sitting upright on the kitchen bench. I thought about the many small flowers that coalesced to form the fruit, the wind cooling its skin and singing to it as it shifted through the leaves, the plant sacrificing nutrients and water to form the sweet acidic flesh and growing the thick, callused hide to protect it.

I remembered the day Rosy gave it to me, and Anthea's speech to Prof, heard by everyone – Prof, Tess, Maggie ... Toby. I remembered sitting next to it on the couch, the night I drove to Toby's.

No more.

Offering a silent prayer of thanks, I beheaded the pineapple.

I placed its crown on the bench, the tough leaves sprouting skywards from the skin, and cut through the golden flesh, the fibres resisting the force of the knife, less at the ripe edges and more at the fibrous heart. At the kitchen table, I ate a few pieces, tasting sweet, acidic sunshine, and leaves, shifting in the wind.

The sweet, acidic feeling spread through my body to my toes. I had done good, and it felt all the more intense for having faced the real possibility of losing Liv.

I stared at the beheaded crown of the pineapple. The job now was surely well within reach. Even filled with Friday-night fatigue, my muscles held a small tension, poised to jump.

Toby, Benson? You'd better be ready. Because I am coming.

Compression

pressure on a vital structure by external forces

It was Monday, after nine pm, when my phone rang while I was in the change rooms in my underwear.

I'd had a long, satisfying day in theatre – a list with Will and then Prof, where to the background of Verdi's Requiem I had done most of a Nissen fundoplication.

The Nissen was another box ticked. I imagined the path taken by an inchworm, a minuscule easing across concrete to reach the vegetable patch. If I had to scrape my belly over concrete to get there, I would.

Standing in the change room, I was happy, tired and ready for home. I took off my theatre cap and threw it in the bin, removed my clogs, took my phone and badge from my scrubs pocket, and put them on the wooden bench. Then I peeled off my scrubs, tossing them in the white laundry bag in the corner of the change room. I opened my locker, and was pulling out my day clothes when my phone rang.

'Carla di Pieta.'

'Dr di Pieta?' I recognised the bored nasal twang of Chen on switchboard. 'External call.' She hung up, and I heard a click as the calls were connected.

'Dr di Pieta,' I said, hoping this was not some random nut job calling to ask about a buried stitch or wanting to describe in detail the precise consistency of their post-op bowel actions.

At first, I heard nothing, and I wondered if Chen had stuffed up the connection. But then, there was something, a deep inhalation, followed by an out breath.

'Hello?' I said.

All I could hear was breathing. I leant in and listened hard. Who was this? Who are you? I heard the scrape of the exhalation as the air passed through trachea and larynx. I imagined it sighing over tonsils and palate before exiting through moist lips.

'Toby?' I whispered, my throat dry.

The only response was another breath. It could be anyone, right? Some patient, probably wasted or disturbed.

'Who is this?' I asked. My voice shook.

And then, two short coughs, a clearing of a throat, moving on whatever dust or mucus had gathered there, and I tried to read the pitch and cadence, but they were gone too fast.

In between the breaths, I tried to interpret the silence, and it bothered me that whoever was on the line could be reading mine, hearing the short gap between my shallow breaths. And I caught a glimpse of myself standing in my underwear, and I covered my chest with one arm, and it made no difference that the caller couldn't see me, because it felt as though they could.

I ended the call, and once I was dressed, I rang switch. One of the men answered. I asked to speak to Chen, and he told me she'd finished for the night.

I sat down on the wooden bench, the palings hard beneath me. 'She put a call through to me, around nine-thirty. Do you know who it was?'

The guy on switch gave a humourless laugh. 'Do you know how many calls we get every hour? Hundreds, love.'

Through gritted teeth I thanked him, knowing that an off-side switch guy could make my life hell, and hung up.

~

My thoughts spun in useless circles. It had to be Toby, didn't it? After my message about the beach party, he'd sent a volley of abusive texts. Although crank calls seemed a little indirect for him – he was more likely to call and abuse me *and* demand a hook-up.

Only, he had Phoebe for that now.

That night, I set my alarm to maximum volume and took a temazepam. Sleep was blissfully dreamless and weightless, but as soon as I woke, I remembered the crank call and my abdomen drew tight. Who the hell was it?

I decided it was the uncanny timing, the caller catching me semi-naked in the change rooms, which had left me spooked. Maybe it was Iain, still angry at the days he'd spent with his bare arse draining pus when he could have been sinking beers.

I would never find out, and it was fruitless to waste time on it. I got ready for work and buried the memory.

With five days to go before Tess's application was due, I arranged for her to join me on a list with Phil, and while he chatted to his stockbroker in the tearoom, I guided her through her second hernia repair.

I saw the tremor in her hand as the nurse handed her the scalpel.

You're a virgin, where hernias are concerned.

I imagined the ghost of Benson in the theatre, but I kept her busy, and her tremor dissipated as she worked her way into the case.

At the end of the list, I overheard her tentatively ask Phil to keep her in mind for any weekend assisting, and he offered her this Saturday and the next, and then, as they walked to the tearoom, she asked about him being a referee, and he agreed.

Ka-ching!

After theatre, we went to Bea's and put the finishing touches to her application, which was now as assured as any male's.

Her CV was still a bit thin on publications. We brainstormed other papers she could write, and she told me she had thought about writing up her experience with Women in Surgery.

'Yes, you should. I can help you, if you want. For your application, you can cite it as "manuscript in preparation". And definitely include Prof as an author – that will help get it published.' Nothing like authorship for minimal effort to please a consultant.

She sipped at whatever hideous perversion of a coffee she was drinking, something enormous and milky with caramel and a layer of cream on the top. I asked her how she was feeling about the list with Benson on Monday, the same day her application was due, and her curls shook with nervous laughter. 'Cutting it so fine. You know what I fantasise about? Finding a way to move him on.'

'Just curious ... how violent do these fantasies get?'

'Well, there's always a scalpel involved. Thing is, I don't want to go to prison ...'

'Well, get the reference before you knife him.'

She laughed. 'Sometimes I do wonder ... why he picked on me.'

Sweat prickled my armpits, and inside my shoes, my toes curled. 'I wouldn't spend any time inside his head, if I could avoid it.'

She smiled. 'Right, good point. I need to focus on me, not him. One more reference and I'm there.' She held up her drink. 'Have you tried this caramel frappuccino Bea makes? It's amazing.'

'You know you're insulting my ancestors.'

She startled, and then realised I was joking. Her laugh climbed a scale of notes, and I joined her.

~

More calls, always from a blocked number, always at night. Unless I was on-call, I didn't take them. I told myself I didn't want to give this person oxygen. I could still hear their breathing in my head, and my stomach lurched at the sound.

But I didn't like the missed calls either, because they spawned questions – were they all the same person and, if so, who was it, and what the hell did they want? Each time my phone rang, it was as if the caller was in my bedroom, breathing, watching, waiting. Sleep deserted me then.

I didn't tell anyone. What would I say: I'd got myself a crank caller? Best to ignore it, and whoever it was would lose interest.

When my phone rang one Friday, I flung it on the couch and growled at the dusk.

If it was Toby ... how dirty could this fight get?

I knew shit, remember.

I told myself that at least now I could go for the job with no compromise. Now that we were done, I was glad that we had kept it quiet. I would prefer that Prof never found out. Best if I stayed single in the run-up to the job, too. Easier that way.

I no longer missed Toby but, in the almost-dark, I felt my aloneness. I hugged my arms around me.

When the doorbell rang, I jumped up and went to the hall. Through the glass window beside the door, I could see the silhouette of a man. Toby? Or whoever had been calling me?

Uneasy, I went to the laundry and grabbed a broom and walked down the hall. It wasn't Toby; I could tell by the angular shoulders. He was holding something ...

'Who is it?' I called. My hand gripped the broom, tight.

'Xander,' came the voice through the door.

I sank against the wall and let out a heavy exhale. When I opened the door, he was standing there with two bags of food. He was wearing a black tee-shirt emblazoned with a bass clef, and below the seam of the sleeve, I could see the curl of his bicep.

He stared at me – breathing hard, broom in hand. 'You okay?'

I made a feeble attempt at a sweeping motion, and then abandoned it. We both knew I didn't *clean*.

'Have you eaten?'

When I said no, he asked if he could cook me dinner.

The crank calls had left me feeling paranoid. 'Why?'

'Does there have to be a reason?'

'I guess not. What are you cooking?'

'Will that determine whether you let me in or not?'

I was surprised to discover that I was glad to see him. I let him in, and we went to the kitchen, where I found a bottle of pinot and poured us two glasses.

He unpacked the shopping, put a pot on to boil and began dicing onion and eggplant, only his method was chaos. Random hacks with the knife, generating pieces of all sizes. With a start, I realised that the guy standing in my kitchen butchering the onion was beautiful. I could not stop staring at the way each muscle in his forearm rippled as he chopped. And his slender fingers clasping the knife – it was compelling, and it irritated the hell out of me, because hadn't I just minutes earlier decided I would stay single?

'Give me that.' I took the knife from him, marshalled the onion slices into rows and diced them into tiny, symmetrical pieces.

'Very neat,' he said. 'But we reach the same end.'

'I don't think so. Tastes better this way.'

'I didn't think you cooked.'

'I wouldn't say this is cooking!'

'Right,' he agreed. 'It is not.'

While he put the pasta into the boiling water and then finished preparing the sauce, he talked to me about his tour. It had gone well, and his manager was furious that he had cut it short, but he had no regrets.

'Performing, you know – it's like eating fast food. Fun at the time, but you feel a bit sick after. Sometimes I feel as though the crowd is in this massive fish tank, and I'm feeding the fish with pieces of me.'

He drained the pasta into a colander in the sink and I watched him. Those forearms ...

Steam rose from the sink.

When he had finished cooking, we carried our dinner upstairs and ate on the balcony. The tagliatelle with eggplant and sugo tasted smoky, sharp and delicious.

'How is your colleague going? The one who ...'

I knew who he meant. 'She's all right. I'm trying to support her, but we're not getting much traction from above.'

'You're a strong person, to take on that system.' He raised his glass, and I drank to that, unsure that I was who he thought.

I looked down at my empty plate. 'This sauce is nearly as good as my mum's.'

'I'd like to meet her.'

'You sure about that? She's a dragon.'

'Family trait?' He raised an eyebrow, and – oh, his eyes were like goddamn velvet, and his lips, so full and kissable –

I flung my serviette at him.

Later, as darkness stole over us and a band of rain swept in, we retreated downstairs. He insisted on cleaning the kitchen, and afterwards we went to the lounge room where he pulled out his guitar. 'Mind if I play?'

I did not.

As he got his guitar out, he asked me, 'Do you hear music, in this house?'

'Uh ... no?'

He frowned. 'Each time I've been here, I've heard it. You know that I've had trouble writing? Here, I wonder if it could be possible ... and maybe I should try, because I feel like Dad took my music to his grave and won't give it back.'

'That's one malicious ghost.'

'Even now, it's like he's standing over me, listening to anything I come up with, shaking his head ... nooooo.'

I thought of Gina and our prickly love. 'I guess it must be complicated to grieve someone who hurt you.'

He drank some wine. 'If I'm honest – I don't think I have.'

'Could be a song in that.'

He flashed me a grin tinged with fear, and I found it hard to look back, or look away. The pull of him, it was intense.

Ridiculous.

I told him my grandparents used to have parties here that sometimes involved late-night singing, so maybe there were echoes of that in the walls, and I meant it as a joke, but he listened intently.

He began a tender song I hadn't heard before, and I rested my head on a cushion and floated away to the sound of his voice, rough and rich as charcoal.

Rain pattered on the roof, and it sounded like music.

~

Benson was likely to ask why I had randomly joined his list with Tess, so when he arrived in theatre his customary five minutes late, I spun a line about mentoring Tess in preparation for an accredited job next year.

He frowned, and where Phil had shrugged and told me to go for my life, Benson said he would still scrub in. I could tell from the stiffness in his shoulders that we'd offended him – or maybe just interrupted his birthday-kiss routine. He invited me to scrub in as well, which wasn't necessary, but I didn't want to upset him more, so the three of us gowned and gloved.

Benson loitered while we gowned, insisting on tying our gowns for us, grasping the tie and holding it while we spun on the spot so that the gown wrapped around us, and I'd done this a thousand times but with Benson it felt like a sleazy dance-floor move.

Tess and I stood opposite him at the table while he quizzed her about the approach for thyroidectomy and revised the neck anatomy with her. She blinked repeatedly but got through the questions. I watched from a respectful distance, and soon they were murmuring over the neck wound. They seemed to be having some trouble, and eventually Benson looked up at me.

'The anatomy is atypical in this patient. Carla, come and see if you can identify the recurrent laryngeal nerve,' he said.

He gestured to his side of the table, and I moved around to stand next to him, but I couldn't quite see, so I edged nearer. The table was too tall for my height, so one of the nurses brought my step, and I climbed onto it.

'Here, here,' Benson said, gesturing to the space between him and the table.

I didn't want to stand so close to him, but I had no chance of seeing from where I stood. This patient needed the nerve identified so Benson didn't accidentally sever it, leaving them with a hoarse voice. And I was practically a consultant. I could do this and keep things professional.

In a few minutes of careful searching I found the pale thread of the nerve, which had split into anterior and posterior divisions outside of the ligamentous attachment of Berry. 'There,' I said, gesturing with my forceps to show Tess.

And I felt Benson's body nudging against my back, as his arms encircled me. He was tall enough to see over my head. As he spoke, I felt his breath behind my ear.

'Kudos, Doctor di Pieta. Very nice.'

The flirty smile in his voice churned my stomach. His body was pressed into my back. Was that an erection I could feel? My face grew hot, the gown over my scrubs suddenly felt heavy and airless, and my mask clung tight to my nose and jaw. Was I going to throw up? That would be such a first-year thing to do, Will would be gunning to buy me a bucket as his next bad-taste gift.

From the other side of the table, Tess watched, her eyes wide. I was here to support her, goddammit, not be the subject of Benson's attentions.

Sweat prickled on my forehead. I had to do something, or I would vomit into this patient's neck wound, which might be career-ending.

'Mr Benson,' I said. 'Could you – take a step back, please?'

There was a click of steel as the scrub nurse laid a pair of forceps on her tray, and then the entire theatre was still. A monitor beeped a regular rhythm, and the anaesthetic machine sucked air in and out.

'I – beg your pardon?'

'Could you move back a little? You're in my space.'

For a moment, he didn't speak and when he did, his voice was loud. 'I do believe, in fact, this is my case, and you are in *my* theatre?'

I needed air. I stepped down from the stool, peeled off my gloves and gown and moved towards the door. 'I understand. I'll wait outside.'

I felt eyes on me as I disrobed and left the theatre.

~

No surprise that I lost my breakfast, but once I did the queasy feeling subsided, and as I stepped through the day, an awareness grew: I had done it. Told him to back off. When he called me to his office later that day, I was nervous about what it might have cost, but the moment when Benson was forced to actually do as I asked and step away? Fuck, it had felt good.

Tess was similarly effusive, though I realised that she had never picked up my habit of swearing. She thought it was *awesome, amazing*. In her view, I was professional, courteous and got what I wanted. She was *inspired* by me, she said, to ask Benson for the reference, and he had obliged.

Now that Tess had made a successful return to theatre with him, it crossed my mind that maybe that was enough. But then I remembered him pressing himself against me at the table.

In the late afternoon, I took a seat in his office across the desk from him, leaving the door ajar.

He stood and closed the door. Damn.

'Did you know,' he said to me, 'that I have trained more surgeons than anyone else at this hospital? Even more than Bill himself.' He gestured at the wall to his right, where a portrait of Bill Casterton hung.

I glanced at the painting. This time Bill sat with his fists on his knees, and I was reminded of photographs of football teams, the players posed with their torsos leaning towards the camera. Must have been hard for Bill to find time to get to theatre, with all the portrait-sitting forced upon him.

I wondered what portrait-Bill had seen go on in this office, over the years.

'You're widely known as an excellent teacher, Mr Benson,' I said, wondering how much ego-stroking I would have to do to get out of here.

'So, then ... what was the little exercise about, this morning? I'm quite capable of supervising Tess myself. I've done it many times over the years, and many times more than you.' He looked down his nose at me.

I noticed tufts of hair growing out of his ear canals. Didn't his wife trim those?

'Tess has – lacked a little in confidence recently and asked for my help.'

'Hmm. I see, I suppose. Tell me, Carla. Would you say I have assisted you in the development of your career?'

'You have been a wonderful teacher,' I said, and that was true. He had taught me many of the basics when I started at PCH, and I had lapped up any morsel of teaching I could find, even if it came with his close attention.

'I would think that I've had a seminal influence upon you. Not that anyone around here would have noticed, especially, but I have come to realise that if you wait for the accolades which you rightly deserve, well ... one could die waiting. Especially if you are alongside others who more naturally gravitate to the spotlight.'

I gave a nervous smile. I didn't really want to listen to Benson dish the dirt on his colleagues.

'I have spent so many years under his shadow, of course, that no one even notices anymore. University chair, hospital prizes. And recognition, for me? Oh, Emmett, you can go and do an extra list with one of the trainees. He needs me, of course – who else is going to cover his lists while he's at yet another international conference junket?' He pointed a finger at his own chest.

'And then you young women – you come in here at the eleventh hour, as if this place is yours and you own it and you have rights and expect everyone to work around how you would like it to be – do you think anyone ever afforded me that privilege? You could not imagine what I endured as a trainee, the hundreds of hours I worked with no sleep.

'Do you think that my boss was a gentle, encouraging mentor? He once threw a scalpel across the theatre when I wasn't holding the retractor precisely where he wanted! And of course there was Alister, like the favourite child who always starts the fight and never gets punished.'

He leant forward, and my toes curled tight inside my shoes.

'Surgery is a physical profession. At times, there will be physical proximity, and my belief is that if that is in the best interests of the patient – as it was today – then so be it.'

He brought his fingertips together, à la Casterton of the meeting-room portrait, and bounced the tips off each other, in a slow rhythm.

'You may have made your own judgements about me – the young are, of course, notoriously quick to do so. But have you stopped to consider – even for just a minute – what I have done for you? I don't believe you have. I have the sincere hope that someone, some day, will pay me the respect I'm due. And do not confuse my mild manners for someone who can be walked over, Carla. In your situation, hoping for a consultant job, it would not be a good time to make enemies, especially of the people who have supported you the most.'

'I – I did not mean to offend you, Mr Benson.'

He waited, lips parted.

'I'm very grateful for all that you have taught me.'

'There is still a lot I could teach you. You have a lot to learn. And in your situation, you need all the allies you can get.'

A nerve twitched an irregular beat in my cheek. What, exactly, was my situation?

'I gather you've been frequenting the MRI recently.'

I startled, wondering at his meaning. Very slowly, his tongue traced a path from left to right over his lower lip. He breathed through his mouth as he did so, and his pupils were dilated. His hands were under the desk, and I didn't want to know what they were doing.

Toby's face, at breakfast. *Want to do it in the MRI?* My stomach plummeted. I tried to breathe, and tried again. No air. My abdominal muscles tightened, the deep sheets of muscle and fascia drawing upwards over my abdomen. Was I going to shame-spew twice in one day?

'Mr Benson, some of the things you might have heard about me ... they're not true.'

'Oh, I'm sure. Hospitals run on salacious gossip, don't they? It can be quite cruel. Remember, I'm here for you. I'm in *your* corner.'

'I didn't intend to make you feel disrespected,' I said. I stopped short of apologising.

'Ah, well – you will make amends, I'm sure.'

The queasy feeling rose from my pelvis through my stomach into my chest. I stood, forced myself to return his smile, knowing I didn't have much time. 'Thank you for your time today.'

'I enjoyed our chat. Let's do this again. The better we understand each other, the more we can help one another. One needs allies, in a place like this. Oh, and just so you know – I'm not planning on going anywhere.'

As I left, I glanced at Bill Casterton, hands on his knees, poised to spring into action, his blue eyes focusing on me.

Toilets are the third door on the left, his eyes said. You're not the first, and you won't be the last.

DURING

I'm in the registrar's office, having escaped the gala.

The floor sways.

Stupid, stupid, to drink this much.

Home calls to me like a welcome light on a porch.

I switch on the light and even though I've been in this office for hours on end, I'm struck afresh at the ugly faux-wood panelling in a tiny room with no windows. It feels like a sleazy Scandinavian sauna from the eighties.

This room is one of those neglected hospital spaces inhabited by transients, with its cheap acrylic carpet, four desks crammed in, piled with paper, and a scramble of wires connected to tired PCs and two grimy landline phones.

Working in here had only fuelled my ambition to get out.

A sound, then, of footsteps. Is someone on this floor?

My thoughts fuzz. Why am I here?

My things. I need to collect my things. I find my satchel under a chair and swing it onto my shoulder, only my keys are not in there, and it's while I'm searching for them that I see him, walking towards the open doorway of the office, watching me.

That understated strut, leading with his shoulders.

He comes into the room and closes the door behind him, and greets me, a smirk on his face.

Avert my eyes from this memory. I cannot face this – no.

I will not endure it.

The hot and cold creeps into me like the feeling at the peak of a fever, simultaneous cold in your bones that chatters your teeth and goosebumps your skin while your cheeks flush and your head burns.

I know this feeling.

It is the hot and cold of shame.

How did I end up here?

BEFORE
Division of adhesions

removal of scar tissue that is causing discomfort and pain

Benson was going nowhere. I had always attached the idea of my job to him leaving, and I discovered that the lustre of the job faded if he was still around, especially with the impact that it would have on Tess. What's more, Benson knew. At least, he *thought* he did. Toby must have spread lies about me, and what if those lies had gone all the way to the top? What if my job chances were shot?

The unfairness of it ate at me. Most of the dirt I had on Toby could implicate me. And my heart sank as I realised I couldn't use the story of the girl at the beach house. Even without her name, there would be people in the system who knew. It wasn't my story to tell, and if she had wanted to go public, she would have.

I was changing into pyjamas when my phone buzzed.

Not a phone call this time, but a message, from a blocked number, with a link to a song.

Billy Joel.

I couldn't help myself ... I clicked on the link. Music streamed out of my phone, and I recognised the piano chords of 'She's Always a Woman', and I'd always thought of that song as a love song on the cheesy side of romantic, its rolling piano notes a kind of a lullaby, but now I heard the menace in the lyrics – killing with smiles, laughing while Billy bleeds – and the careless, patronising description of the woman changing her mind. Even the humming as he finished the song sounded like someone who *knew things*, a keeper of secrets.

I remembered 'Ring a Ring o' Roses' and the way I felt when I heard the theory that *all fall down* depicted the deaths of children from the plague.

Always a woman. It couldn't be a coincidence. Whatever I did at work, I was always a woman. Was it someone who knew about me and Toby, playing a sick prank? If Benson had ideas about the MRI, then who else might?

It could have been *anyone.* Would Xander do something like this? Billy Joel wasn't really his schtick, but who knew …

I replayed the song, and felt as though the caller was listening too, their heavy breathing matching the cadence of the song lines, no comfort in the lullaby.

~

I dreamt, not of Benson, but of Bill Casterton, watching me as I went through a hospital day – getting dressed, brushing my teeth, emptying my bladder. Eyes on me, fingertips touching in the midline. Watching, judging.

When I woke, I tasted bile.

I remembered something about the Casterton portrait – a hospital medal, golden and glinting, hung around his neck.

The Casterton.

The idea of getting Benson the Casterton returned, stronger now. It still repulsed me, but … what if the outcome justified the means? Maybe I could stomach him getting an award if it meant he would go.

Before Tess told me what had happened to her, I knew only one way to handle Benson, and that was to convince myself that his behaviour didn't bother me. Then, when he groped Tess, I wanted to protect her, and to prove that PCH was a safe place for women to train. And now, I could see that Benson was more than a harmless old pervert. It did bother me when his hands tucked in my top inside my scrubs or his erection pressed into my back in theatre.

It bothered me, too, that my sex life was the titillating topic of the week.

I wanted a workplace where I was able to be myself without fear or discomfort, and I didn't know how, but I needed to make it happen – not just for Tess.

For myself.

~

I started with Hamish, who sounded morose and withdrawn when I called. The situation with Ursula had worsened, he told me. They were barely speaking. He was still drinking. I begged him to get some help.

When I explained I was nominating Benson, in a deadpan voice he agreed and said he would do what he could, and then I heard commotion in the background, a child crying and Ursula's raised voice, and he ended the call.

I moved on to Will, remembering his warning about Benson when I first started at PCH. I messaged him suggesting lunch away from the hospital, and he agreed.

He chose a new cafe in a dead-end lane near the uni with blond wooden tables arranged along a white wall. I walked past a middle-aged woman tapping away at her Mac, a bearded guy jiggling a pram with his foot, and three long-haired, bed-haired girls yawning over brunch.

I sat down opposite Will, the weight of what I wanted to make happen sitting like a stone in my gut. He smiled.

'I haven't seen you at breakfast.'

'No. Fair bit going on.'

He glanced at the menu. 'Guess they don't do dim sims here.' He ordered zucchini flowers, the only fried food on the menu, and I chose a cauliflower salad.

'Well, breakfasts haven't been what they used to be. Hamish has been hit-and-miss too. And as for Toby, he's not his normal self.' His eyes flicked a glance at me, and then away.

Our meals arrived. I loved eating in cafes – during my shifts I often skipped meals, and at home I was usually too tired to cook. I loaded my fork with some of the quinoa, coriander and roasted cauliflower, the scattered pickled daikon packing a salty acid punch.

While Will crunched his way through his zucchini flowers, I brought up the Casterton. 'Any nominations from gen surg this year, that you're aware of?'

His eyes crinkled into a smile. 'You're not going to put *me* forward yet, are you?'

I returned the smile. It was always about Will. 'Not you. I thought it was for old crusty types.'

'Indeed.'

'What do you think about ... Benson?'

With his serviette, he wiped away traces of parsley and ricotta from the corner of his mouth. 'Tell me more.'

'Well, he's always the first one to volunteer for teaching, and he takes the juniors for all their tutorials.'

'Well, sure ... I'd be happy to vote for him.' His eyes narrowed. 'You wouldn't be trying to move him along or anything, would you, Carla?'

I protested my innocence, and he laughed and sipped his coffee.

'Carla, may I give you some advice?' When I nodded, he continued. 'This would be a tricky road for you to navigate. Especially ... just now. I think you should focus on keeping yourself squeaky clean and let events take care of themselves. It's not a good look at this stage of your career.'

Grains of quinoa caught in my throat. I swallowed some water. 'What do you mean?'

'You must know ... your own reputation isn't pristine.'

I laid my fork on my plate and stared at him.

'People know, Carla. Half the hospital does. You must realise that.'

My breath turned shallow and shaky.

Will sighed. 'Someone saw you go into the quiet room with Toby, that morning of the mastectomy that went belly up.'

Out the window, a gaggle of uni students walked past, talking and laughing.

I remembered the moment in the M&M, when Will and Lachlan sniggered, and I hadn't known why. And I saw Lachlan, standing bleary-eyed next to Toby and me in the lift, the morning of Liv's surgery. I had felt sorry for him then, working nights.

'Sex in the quiet room ... you have to be more careful.'

'We didn't –'

'That's not what Toby's been saying.'

'And you believe him?'

'You were seeing him, everyone knows that. You went into the room together. What do you want us to believe?'

'We did *not* have sex in the quiet room! For God's sake, Will.'

He twisted his mouth to one side. 'Toby's been telling stories. I've had a word to him about it, but ... that's Toby. He's hard to stop when he's in that kind of a mood. I don't know if that gossip has made it all the way to Prof, but ... you need to take care.'

'And Toby? Do they think he slept his way to the top?'

'Come, C.' Will's voice was gentle, concern in his eyes. 'I'm not pretending it's fair. But Toby didn't need to, you know – Geoffrey and all. Anyway, everyone knows Toby's dick rules his head.'

I sucked in a breath and it felt as heavy as water. 'And that's okay?'

'I'm only telling you how people will judge you. It's a sad reality, I'm afraid. I still think you're in with a chance for the job, though, so long as you play your cards right.' He drained his coffee.

'I'm surprised you're prepared to be seen with me in public. Me and my smutty reputation.'

'Oh, Carla – I didn't mean to offend you. You're a good surgeon, you have my respect, you know that. It's a tough old world out there, and I want things to go well for you.' He patted me on the arm. 'You're a trailblazer, no doubt about it.'

I wanted to tell him where he could shove his advice. Instead, I sat in a spiral of shame while Will called for the bill.

~

I walked up the narrow street where my parents lived, towards the single-fronted terrace with a lemon tree encased in concrete in the front garden.

My steps were heavy, and it took all my effort to deaden the endless internal voices of Will, Toby, Lachlan, Benson – everyone talking about my kinky sex life. Even dead Bill Casterton, watching, fingertips touching.

'Always a Woman' played on repeat in my head.

I wished I could do what Billy said I could, and kill with my eyes. If I could, I'd start with Toby. Next, Benson. And I wouldn't stop there.

Nino greeted me at the door. In the kitchen, Gina stood in front of an enormous pot on the stove and skewered one of the unpeeled potatoes in the simmering water. I thought of trays lined with neat white pillows of potato gnocchi, and remembered an argument Gina and I had had when I was about eight, and she discovered me and Luca playing a grotesquely fabulous game where we dismembered the doll collection sitting unloved in my bedroom and randomly reapplied limbs to different torsos. Furious, Gina dragged me to the kitchen, insisting I help her make gnocchi, but I refused. Luca was still busy amputating doll legs: how come he didn't need a cooking lesson? While we fought, Nino sat at the kitchen table reading *Il Globo*. When I said I didn't want to learn, there was no way I would waste my time on this stuff, Nino stood, shoulders shaking, and shouted, 'This is your heritage – of course you must learn! Do not disobey your mother!' Intimidated by the rare, purple rage suffusing his face, I followed Gina's instructions but learnt nothing, except that my father saw my future with a different lens from mine, and it did not do to speak up.

Now, on an impulse, I asked her to show me how to make them.

'*You* want to learn?'

'If you'll teach me.'

Gina gave me a measured look, like she too remembered the events more than twenty years earlier, then she passed me the potato ricer. When the potatoes had cooled, I got into the task, enjoying the melding of potato and flour under my fingertips, ignoring Gina's sniff of superiority as she looked at the tray of gnocchi in front of me. 'Make them smaller. And you need more flour.'

'Okay, Ma.'

Luca arrived with a bottle of red, and he poured us all a glass and began telling us about his new job.

'Dean, the manager, he's got some moods on him – especially when all the ladies pile in after Pilates. I don't get it, you know – five lattes or fifty, we'll make them eventually, just keep the wheels spinning with a bit of banter and she'll be right – but old boy Deano, he looks like he wants to exterminate the next person in athletic wear who orders a decaf long mac. Not exactly welcoming for the customers, is it?'

I smiled.

Luca turned to me. 'What about you, superhero – saved any lives lately?'

'Every day – you should know that.'

'Ha. Hey, got any new rocks from your lover boy?'

I saw the diamond, hanging on its chain on Toby's door, and then Will's expression when he told me my reputation was shot.

Luca read my face. 'What, don't tell me you've broken up?'

'Luca, just – leave it.'

'C'mon, those surgeons, they'd be out for a good time –'

'Stop!'

Luca startled. 'O-kay.' When he spoke again, his voice was softer. 'Sorry, I was just – goofing around. You okay?'

I rubbed at the knot in my shoulder. 'Stressful time at work, that's all.'

'Okay. If there's anything I can do – you name it. Hitman, barista – your own personal St Jude ...'

I smiled and protested, 'I do *not* need a patron saint, and I'm not a lost cause!'

Gina served me a massive bowl of gnocchi. 'You lose weight.' She pinched my arm.

'Ma, take it easy,' Luca said. 'She's been working hard, is all.'

Gina's jaw dropped. Luca was usually sticking the knife in, not standing in my corner.

The gnocchi were light and fluffy, the sugo salty and rich, and to sit around the table and share a meal with my family quietened my angsty thoughts.

'Any news on the big job?' Nino asked me. 'When will you know?'

'Waiting for an old guy to retire,' I said, which was no longer true.

'When will that be?' Gina asked, and I told her I didn't know.

'Knife the bastard,' Luca said, and we laughed, and I didn't tell him I'd been thinking exactly that.

Afterwards, Luca made coffee and had us laughing trying to guess the coffee order of his customers. 'Okay, so Ray. Beady eyes, lotsa ink, looks like he could have murdered three people before breakfast.'

'Espresso?' Gina asked.

'Milky decaf. Can you believe it?'

Gina sniffed. 'What is that? That's not a coffee.'

Luca grinned. 'Next one. Chelsea – she's got a thing going on, perfect bob, fake nails.'

'Almond-milk latte?' I said.

'Decaf-no-foam-almond-milk double shot.'

Nino drank his espresso, shaking his head.

'Okay, so you'll love this. Peter, he's built like a jockey, the opposite of tall, know what I'm saying?' He pinched his fingers to a centimetre apart. 'You gotta think!'

'Piccolo,' Nino said, and Gina guffawed in disgust, and Nino and I laughed, which delighted Luca. I looked around the table, at my goofy brother with the big smile, and Nino, who was as constant as a heartbeat, and even Gina, with her bossy, cross love.

I was glad these people were my own.

~

But Will's words festered. He knew that Toby and I had messed around in the quiet room when Toby should have been seeing Liv pre-op. He thought I had slept my way up, and who knew how many people might think the same?

I felt so stupid. Stupid, for thinking Toby was important enough to risk harm to Liv and damage to my reputation.

Stupid, for thinking Will was my friend.

Stupid, for falling in stupid love.

And that fucking awful song, a hideous, impossible riddle now. *Always a woman.* Who sent it and what did they mean? Should I call Toby and confront him? But if it wasn't him, would I be giving him precious information about where my head was at? I didn't want to grant him any more advantage than he already had.

When I couldn't think of anything else to do, I thought of the comfort of making the gnocchi, and I decided to make a batch of sugo. I remembered how Gina did it – finely dicing the onion, sautéing it with the garlic in olive oil and then adding the passata, and the familiar smell made me feel better until I saw myself standing at the stove, stirring the pot.

While the men laughed and joked about what I was prepared to do with Toby in the quiet room, *this* was what I was choosing to do?

Gripping the wooden spoon tight, I flung it at the wall, and it splintered on its long axis. Fingers of wood flew off in pieces, and splattered sauce bled lines of red down the tiles.

Amputation

the severing of a limb or other body part

Three soft knocks on my front door.

From the couch, I told the world to go away. I was on a roll, listing all the ways I had been wronged, and I didn't want to be interrupted.

Here was my list: told to be more professional when simply caring for my team; subjected to some creep crank calling and sending Billy Joel songs; patronised that I was mothering trainees; rostered on for Christmas, *again*; judged by a completely different standard to Toby's; judged for having sex in the MRI, which was blatantly untrue; judged for sleeping my way up when that was simply unfair ...

'Carla?' Xander's voice came through the door. 'I've shopped. Want to eat?'

I hesitated. I was a mess right now ... but I had a feeling Xander would understand.

I let him in. He was carrying a wicker basket laden with food, a baguette and a bottle of wine poking out the top. He took stock of me standing there barefoot in a hoodie and trackpants, hair unwashed, and set the basket down.

'I was thinking ... a picnic?'

I gestured towards my general appearance. 'Not in the best headspace.'

He shrugged and smiled, and I said, 'Okay, give me five.' I changed into jeans and a shirt, ran a brush through my hair, and we left the house and walked to the park. The light was forgiving, and the grass a soothing green.

We found a spot near a Moreton Bay fig, and Xander laid out a blanket and small plates of mezze – baby beetroot with goat's cheese, freekeh with lentils, red pepper in olive oil and flat bread.

He told me how, when he'd visited last time, he'd written the first part of the song to his father.

'I imagined your grandparents and all their friends around me and when Dad told me the song was shit, they shoved pasta in his mouth and told him to shut the fuck up.'

'Did it work?'

'Kinda. I'm beginning to think I'm always going to carry shit from my dad.'

We sat in a comfortable silence.

'So ... would I be right in thinking something is up?'

'Psychic.'

'Okay. I'm not going to ask you to tell me – used to drive me nuts if I was upset and Mum tried to drill it out of me. All I can say is if you want to talk – go for it.'

First, I needed to check something. 'Do you like Billy Joel?'

He frowned. 'Well ... I think he's a clever songwriter. But do I listen to his music? No.'

Okay. Not Xander, then. I gulped some mineral water and told him about Toby spreading smut about me, and how I felt the cards were stacked against me in the fight against him, that perhaps I could never win, no matter what I did, because I was judged on a different standard.

'So when you were with Toby, he was a stud, and you were a slut ... is that it? What a fucked system of losers. They don't deserve you, that's how I see it.'

Shy, I lowered my gaze to the grass. *More, please.*

He asked about Tess and her battle to brave the handsy Benson, and I told him that Edwina had suggested we should look elsewhere for work.

'Hmm.'

'It's more complicated than that.'

I told him about Anthea's speech to the ward round, and the pineapple, and in the retelling, I grew animated. 'That is what I want. A hospital where I can do my job, my way.'

'With humanity.'

'Is that nuts?'

He smiled at me and said no. 'But is PCH the place?'

I scrunched my nose. 'I don't see why not.'

We finished eating, and he stretched his arms above his head. 'You feel like a walk?'

'Where?'

He shrugged. 'Anywhere. Just a walk.'

We packed up the picnic and walked on lush grass under the figs, the canopies fanning out from their trunks like massive organza skirts.

'I know you're a PCH fan from way back, but – is there somewhere else you could go? Seems like you deserve better.'

I kicked at the ground and said maybe.

'You've done so much to get this far.' He smiled. 'You were always going to be a surgeon.'

I remembered that night, years ago, outside the pub, cold air on my cheeks, his warm kiss. When I looked across, I knew he was remembering it, too.

His hand gently brushed my arm and my skin goose-bumped.

I wondered if I could.

The paint was still wet on my break-up with Toby. I didn't know how I would feel or react if someone else got close.

Part of me wanted to try.

He fidgeted with his sleeve and massaged his chin and under a massive Moreton Bay fig he stopped and faced me.

'I hate seeing you hurting. You're the most amazing, gutsy woman I've ever met, Carla.' He took my hand. 'Don't let them steal your dream, hey?'

He leant forward and touched my cheek.

On a whim, I kissed his lips, and yes – it was as good as I remembered: his stubble soft, his lips warm. He smelt of lime and honey.

The kiss deepened, our breathing lengthened, and he put his arms around my back. I gave myself up to it, and ran my hands through his hair, and we kissed and kissed.

At some point, I was no longer there, under the tree. I was falling through the air, not knowing or caring if there was soft ground beneath, the falling so delicious that it was worth a broken femur or a heart that could be mended.

Tumbling now, air whooshing around me, I was a meteor, splitting a dark sky on my course to earth, picking up speed as I went, faster, faster, and there was a new feeling – fear, now – where was I going, how could I stop; I needed to right myself, get back on track, and I saw a pink G-string and an ugly big diamond, and the great gaping hole of the MRI machine, like a massive mouth shaped as an O –

'What – is something wrong?'

The tree branches closed in. I stepped out into the light.

'I shouldn't have ... this was a mistake.'

We walked slowly home, and the trees, the traffic, the very sky pressed in on me, leaving no air to breathe.

~

Overnight, I reviewed the situation.

It was the right thing to do, no question. The job, for one. I couldn't afford any more rumours about me. It was unfair and unnecessary but better that I had zero action in my love life until that was done.

I allowed myself to feel it, again – the falling, the delicious not knowing. Yes, it was good. No, it was not for me. Could not be. This feeling that Xander was impossible ... it wasn't just that I'd been scalded by Toby. There was another sensation, an ugly one, that sat at the back of my throat.

He had dropped out of med school. I knew that it shouldn't matter, and I knew that it did.

When I was a resident, I worked with a male nurse in urology. He had curly dark hair and what might have once been a lisp before speech therapy taught him to push his tongue back between his straight white teeth. One afternoon, he paged me to the ward and asked me out, and I said yes, but when we went on our coffee date, I realised that it didn't matter how cute his curls and his lisp were. I told myself it was because there was no chemistry, but tonight it occurred to me ... was it because he was a *nurse*?

I squirmed. Must have been something else – too awkward to date someone from work, or maybe I was studying for exams at the time. Will's advice – *easier to be single, in this job*. Except, I had countered, you have a wife, and he laughed and said, yeah, well, we *all* need a wife, right?

In the morning, Xander called. He asked if I was okay, and I said yes, and sorry, and he said no, I'm sorry, it was the wrong thing. I knew you were still getting over Toby. Wrong time, obviously.

'I'm just – going through some stuff, is all.'

'Understood. Sorry if I made it worse.'

'I kissed you, you moron. Don't take all the credit.'

'Yeah.' In the silence, I imagined him smiling as he remembered. 'So ... we're okay, then? Wrong place, wrong time kinda thing?'

His voice was light but laced with sadness, and I said, 'Yeah, well ... if you weren't so damn argumentative ...' It had nothing to do with anything, but I wanted us to go back to that funny sparring stage where

I didn't feel like I was losing something.

There was a pause, and then he said, 'Take care of yourself,' and I didn't know if it was a farewell, but it felt like it might be.

~

Sleep was a battle of sheets, unanswerable questions and that damn song, often only possible with a small, white tablet. I went into work early on Thursday for a morning list, and when I opened the door to the registrar's office, Toby was sitting on the edge of one of the desks. Sitting on the seat below him, her back pressed into the chair and hands gripping the seat, was Tess, and in the careless splaying of his legs and the forward lean of his torso, I felt his ease and his oblivion to her discomfort, and it infuriated me.

I thought about the phone calls with no caller ID, me standing in the change rooms hugging my arms across my half-dressed body.

I imagined plunging a scalpel deep into his groin.

Tess jumped up when she saw me and hugged me, and this was not our usual businesslike greeting at work, but as her body exhaled relief against mine, I understood. She excused herself, saying that she had to get to theatre.

Now it was just Toby and me, and the wood-panelled walls closed in around us.

'I'm glad you're here.'

A surprised smile crossed his face.

I faced him. 'I need you to stop spreading rumours about me.'

He laughed. 'Bothering you much? Don't be shy now, we live in a liberated society, nothing to be ashamed about.'

'You lied about the MRI –'

'I told a few people about Hamish's study, that's all. I can't help it if people have dirty minds.' He smirked.

'Just leave me alone at work, okay? You do your thing and I'll do mine. And if you think creeping me out with phone calls is going to throw me off my game, you're wrong.'

'What?'

'Always a Woman?'

He looked bewildered. 'You know what? I think you're losing it. First you want to get it on in public, then you act as though you've never had sex in your life, and when people find out you're not a virgin, somehow I'm the bad guy? You're accusing me of shit that never happened.' He leant towards me and his voice was low and mean. 'Losing. It.'

I stood and faced him. 'I'm nominating Benson for the Casterton.'

He raised an eyebrow and grinned. 'Nice.'

'You should do the same. And when the job does come up, at least grant me a fair run at it, Toby. We can both promise each other that. Then whoever gets it, fair and square –'

He fronted up to me, thrusting his chest into the space between us, and I could smell his cologne, mixed with sweat. I had to steel myself not to step away.

'You really want to compete for this?' he said, his voice incredulous.

'I want this job.'

'Okay, then,' he said, squaring his shoulders. His cheeks were slightly flushed. 'Game. On.'

DURING

I'm in the registrar's office, searching for my keys among the tangle of cords from desktops and printers. I find them hidden under swathes of paper next to a mug that says 'You're the greatest, Dad', its insides marked with concentric rings of milky coffee stains. They remind me of the rings used to determine a tree's age.

This cup is ancient, obviously. Which dad did it belong to? Why was it here, forgotten, and had it ever been washed?

I sense someone at the door, and I hear Toby's voice. *I was looking for you.*

I swing my satchel over my shoulder.

His words slurred and quiet, he tells me he has forgiven me, even though I don't deserve it. He says that we have something worth fighting for, and I wouldn't know he is upset except for two small blotches of pink over his cheekbones.

He holds his arms out wide and tells me we can put all this behind us, that we're good together and we both know it. He tells me he loves me. That he doesn't love anyone else. Then he moves towards me, and I shake my head and step back, but I lose my balance and stumble, and he steadies me with his arm.

He kisses me. He tastes of beer.

No. No. NO.

I pull away. I tell Toby I don't want this. I don't love you.

His lip shapes into an ugly curl. *This another game?*
I tell him no. I say I want to go home.
He kicks the door shut behind him.

BEFORE
Proliferative phase

when a wound is rebuilt with collagen and extracellular matrix

The queue for coffee was long, but Tess and I were desperate. It was the morning lull after early rounds, when we could skip the ward for a break before Maggie or another nurse started hounding us about discharge paperwork, or the calls from ED ramped up.

Other units were here, too – ahead of us I spied rheumatology, wearing plaid jackets and perplexed faces, perhaps pondering which monoclonal antibody they would use for their patient with the complex auto-immune disorder in ICU, and gastroenterology behind them in sharp suits.

While we waited, Tess and I discussed her Women in Surgery manuscript.

'It's impressive,' I said. 'Insightful, well written.'

'You sound surprised,' she said.

I was. Possibly the hyperbole had blinded me to Tess's sharp intellect, but her manuscript laid it out.

'There's one issue. You sound too – human. You need to go for a more objective tone.'

'Dry and boring, got it,' she said. 'But I want to keep "transformative". That is the actual truth.'

'Okay. But not "transformative" *and* "emancipatory". Too much.'

When the cardiology round arrived, they doubled the queue with their residents and registrars and consultants. Above the hubbub I could hear the baritone voice of Harry Oltis-Jones delivering a monologue about something no doubt fascinating to Harry. There was laughter from his entourage, and then I heard a female voice ask, 'But how did they even get into the MRI?'

I pressed my eyes shut, but the conversation continued. I wished myself away. Maybe I didn't need coffee after all.

Curiosity got the better of me. I turned to see who had spoken – most likely the female resident in a tailored pink dress with a navy blazer standing next to Harry. She was almost on tiptoes trying to get his attention.

I faced back to the front of the queue. With the gastro team between us, I was invisible to them. I thought about the resident in the pink dress, and I caught myself clenching my forearm, wishing I could slap her, which brought me up short. Shouldn't I be reserving my worst judgement for Harry?

I thought of my silence at all of Will's jokes, the time when he described detouring the entire ward round to see if the oncology nurse with the incredible legs was working an early shift. I didn't laugh ... but I didn't say anything, either. How could I expect another trainee not to play the game?

We collected our coffees, and as we walked back past the queue, I paused. I locked eyes with Harry, taking in the handkerchief in his suit pocket, his second chin and the fat filling the spaces between his fingers. I imagined the cholesterol from too many French pastries lining his coronary arteries, lying in wait for him, and it made me smile as I spoke.

'Harry, I wanted to ask: do you have a sister? Or a mother?'

Harry looked startled. 'Well, yes ...'

'Good. Maybe think about them next time, before you open your mouth.'

With a condescending smile, Harry tilted his head and patted me on the back. 'It was only a –'

'A joke. I know, how funny.'

I felt their eyes on my back as I walked away.

~

Over coffee, I pitched Tess my idea about the Casterton, and she stared at me like I had lost my mind. 'How would that help? We're trying to show the man is a pervert, not stroke his ego!'

'I know, but here's the thing: it's often awarded to a surgeon near retirement.'

Tess scratched at her cheek. 'Are you saying we try to get him the medal, hoping he'll retire? What if he doesn't? I have to say, I don't like the idea of rewarding his disgusting behaviour.'

'True,' I said. 'But ... what if we give him an ultimatum? Take the medal and get out. Or else we'll go to the college.'

Tess bit at her lip. 'I don't know if I can see that through. Not just my story against his.'

His hands on my butt. My toes curling in my clogs. No doubt it would help Tess to know she wasn't alone, but at the idea of talking about it, an oily feeling seeped into my pelvis. I would have to talk about my body in front of Prof, about how I was vulnerable to a man who couldn't keep his hands to himself. I'd have to admit that I lied when I said I had no problem with Benson. I'd spent ten years trying to prove I was *not* vulnerable, that I was as tough as any male. No – tougher.

'I don't plan for us to have to actually go to the college, just – make him think we might. Anyway, don't worry about that just yet.'

She chewed her lip as she thought. 'Surely Prof is looking for a way to move Benson on. Maybe if he gets the medal, Prof will make it happen. We could talk to him ... only, I guess we know what he's going to say.'

I watched her face fall as she remembered Prof's response to the assault. 'I don't think Prof would appreciate it, coming from us.'

'Well, it isn't a lie, I suppose ... Benson *is* the best teacher. I've learnt a lot from him. I have to give it to you, Carla, this idea – it's out of left field. I didn't know you were in touch with your creative side.'

Even as she smiled at me, I frowned. 'I can be creative! Don't you think surgery needs innovation at times?'

'That's true.' She twisted the bangle on her wrist. 'How are we going to get all the nominations we need? And how will we convince Benson to bow out?'

'You are going to finish your paper,' I said, 'and leave that to me.'

~

I borrowed the Women in Surgery contact list and, starting with Yasmin and Liane, began making calls to solicit votes for Benson. I wanted the other women in training to understand that this was an act in support of Tess. I was upfront about the fact that I was not doing this for my own gain, though if our plan worked, I would undoubtedly benefit.

I didn't need to tell them too much about what Benson had done. Several of them knew him, and when I said that Tess and other women wanted Benson moved on, they guessed the rest. The response was unanimous: residents and registrars from ortho, vascular and neuro were all on board, and agreed to speak to as many members of their team as they could. Even if they hadn't had any direct interaction with Benson themselves, they were prepared to nominate him out of solidarity with Tess.

Emboldened by so much support, I wondered if there might be another way. I asked the trainees who knew Benson if, hypothetically, they would put their name to a letter about him. They responded no, using terms like *job suicide*, *boys' club* and *are you fucking crazy?* and I didn't push.

Next, I perused the list of all surgical consultants. I talked briefly again with Hamish, who was busy in outpatients but promised to add his vote to the mix. I tried to read the tone in his voice, but he was in work mode. I made a mental note to call him later. I phoned a few other consultants from other departments and, finally, I made a time to see Geoffrey.

Without warning on Tuesday, Lachlan brought me coffee in the registrar's office, carrying the two cups in one hand, one cup stacked on the other, his notebook in the other hand. His eyes focused on the cups as he walked careful steps, and I almost laughed. He hadn't paid his uni fees waiting tables, that much was clear.

And what was he doing bringing me coffee anyway? The guy was on the golf course with Prof, what else did he need? Help with a project, maybe, something not important enough to bother the men with.

He handed me the cup and stuck his tongue out very slightly against his lip.

'There's something I want to ... well, I want to apologise, actually.'

He exhaled a heavy breath, and paused. 'It's to do with that difficult case – Liv. I know that with the first surgery and everything – this is sensitive and maybe I shouldn't go there, but – I saw you, that morning, with Toby. And I – I told Will. In the M&M.'

My fingers gripped the cup, and my body grew still. So it *was* Lachlan.

'I thought he was your friend. I didn't realise he would spread it, and I didn't know how nasty it was going to get. And now, with Toby talking, I wanted you to know I'm sorry. It was a dumb thing to do.'

'Thanks,' I said, a little wearily. I was glad that he had spoken up – I didn't want to punish him for it. But I added, 'It would be good, next time, to not be part of the problem.'

He winced. 'I know. I *do* want to do better. Anything you need –'

'There are two things, actually.' I asked him to vote for Benson and ask his friends to do the same. 'He has to get more votes than Leonard Ellis.'

'My friend in neurosurg says Leonard's a prick,' Lachlan said.

'Then they should be easy to convince,' I said. 'Second, you're a member at Hawthorn Dales, right? I want you to book a round for Tess and me. And Benson.'

'O-kay. I'd be happy to take you around if you wanted.'

'That won't be necessary.'

'It's members only ...'

'Can't you make it happen?'

'I guess.' A guilty smile curled over his mouth. 'Tess and I – we're going for the same job, you know that.'

I shrugged. I guessed he thought that this was a strategy to improve Tess's job chances. 'Do you mean what you say about doing better?'

'You know, I'd hate to get on your wrong side.'

The comment was careless, but I wasn't in the mood.

'One thing I've noticed around here. When women are assertive, they're labelled pushy. When men do the same? They're decisive. Have a think about what you just said to me, and if you'd ever say that to a male colleague. Would you?'

He stroked his baby cheeks with his thumb and forefinger, opened his mouth to speak and then thought better of it. I nodded, grimly, and took my coffee with me to finish on the ward, leaving him alone.

DURING

I'm on six. Away from the noise, and from people.

Blissful quiet.

But I have an urgent need to pee.

I walk the corridor and my head is badly fuzzed from the wine. If I don't find a toilet soon, I could wet my pants.

I reach the men's, and that's when I realise I'm at the wrong end of the hallway. The women's is right down the other end, an afterthought of a toilet near the store room and the stairs.

I open the door, grimacing at the stench of ammonia from the urinal, and find a cubicle, enjoying the relief as I pee.

Then the hinges of a door squeak, and there are footsteps outside the cubicle.

Someone is in here.

I wait. Gives me a minute to steady my head, anyway. They will pee, and leave.

I hear the stream of urine hitting the urinal and amuse myself trying to guess who it is. Good stream, so unlikely to be Prof or Benson or anyone else over fifty-five. It goes for quite a while, so someone who has been on the beers. Will, maybe?

I do not want to see Will with his penis hanging out of his pants. Or any of them, for that matter.

I wait for the creak of the door to signal the person's departure, but none comes. I peek under the door and see a fine, pointed pair of dress shoes ... and bare ankles. No socks, and the trousers finish just short of his shoes.

Lachlan?

What is he doing up here when the party is six floors down?

He's finished urinating but is still in here. But he'd understand that I needed an emergency pee. I unlock the door and open it.

He is bent over the bench next to the sink, sniffing white powder through a rolled up twenty-dollar bill.

He startles, his soft cheeks flushed bright red, and he swears. Then, as if he momentarily forgets about me, his eyes dart to the bench, and he finishes the line, which tells me he was already wasted, and not prepared to lose a gram.

Once he is done, he sniffs, and stays with his back to me, looking at me in the mirror through bloodshot eyes.

He says, *Jesus, are you everywhere? Everywhere, with eyes.*

I can see that I interrupted his fix. I say sorry, I needed to pee. And you might want to do that somewhere more private. People around here talk.

Why do you think I came up here? Did you follow me? I watch as the cogs turn in his brain. *Are you going to tell them? It's just a bit of fun, you know – takes the edge off.*

Needing a line to get through a midweek work dinner seems like more than a bit of fun, but I am not going there.

He turns and steps towards me.

Lachlan, can you – get out of my way?

I'm fucking sick of being told what to fucking do! Get the coffee, Lachlan – wipe my arse, Lachlan – Jesus! He spits a little as he speaks.

His body is rigid. His soft baby cheeks are flushed and furious.

BEFORE

Dehisce

to gape or burst open, as in the separation of the edges of a sutured wound

On Friday night, I drove Tess to a Chinese restaurant in Doncaster for Rosy's sixtieth. My beat-up Alfa took gentle corners as if they were F1 turns, and Tess laughed when I told her this was the only way to drive this car.

Things were shaping up for Tess. She had done another appendix with Will, and Prof had given her positive feedback on her manuscript.

As we arrived at the restaurant, I grazed my teeth over my lip. All the surgeons I knew would judge that transgressing doctor–patient boundaries was for flaky doctors who didn't know better. Tess felt it too, and we shared a nervous smile as we went inside. It occurred to me that, for the first time ever in surgery, I had a true ally at work. I hadn't known how much I needed one, or that they would arrive with a camellia tucked behind one ear.

Rosy greeted us excitedly and seated us at a table with Anthea and Liv, who wore a cherry red wig. We were fed platters of braised pork, whole steamed snapper and Chinese broccoli.

Liv gave a speech for her mum, full of love and funny stories. I drifted back to the moment I stood over her pulseless body on the operating table, to the moment I told her and Anthea the truth. And here she was, at least for now, living the life she wanted.

It was in no way a fairytale, but it was the kind of happy ending I could live with.

~

In theatre on Tuesday, I took a call from Tess about Mrs Greenidge. I was scrubbed, so one of the nurses brought the phone to my ear.

Tess gave me Mrs Greenidge's vitals. 'I'm worried about her. I've never seen her this sick.'

I instructed Tess to work her up as we'd done so many times before, sending bloods for culture and markers of sepsis.

'And call ID and ask about her antibiotic cover.'

I went to the ward once my list was done. Mrs Greenidge lay propped up on pillows, gasping shallow breaths, nasal prongs delivering her oxygen.

'Not good?' I asked her and she shook her head.

Beneath the dressing on her wound was more affected tissue, some inflamed and some already dead, and I could feel that the bacteria were winning, invading tissue before my eyes, seeping into her bloodstream. They would trigger the release of cytokines designed to fight the bug, but also make her blood pressure plummet and accelerate her heart rate – stressors that Mrs Greenidge's eighty-year-old body might not survive.

'The infection has spread. We'll need to operate.'

She sank back into her pillows, her face abject despair. Her eyes pleaded with me. *Must I?*

I looked out the window. What other choice did we have? Let her slip into a sepsis-induced coma and slide away?

When I looked back, she had composed herself.

'Do you think you can manage one more?'

'I'm tired, so tired,' she said.

I took her hand, held her clammy palm.

'Last one. I promise.'

~

Maggie and I stood around the nurses' station while Tess got on the phone to plastics to coordinate a theatre time.

'What do you think we should do?' I asked Maggie.

I couldn't remember ever asking Maggie's advice on anything before.

'I'm worried about her. I don't know how much more she can stand. I don't know if we're being fair to her.'

'There's nothing fair about necrotising fasciitis.'

She sighed. 'That's true.'

'She consented.' Phil would back me, I was sure. No one wanted Prof's favourite patient to die on their watch. 'I told her this would be the last time.'

Maggie raised an eyebrow. We both knew that Mrs Greenidge would consent to anything we asked of her.

'All right, then,' Maggie said, but she stayed standing next to me without speaking for long enough that I felt awkward.

Thinking she wanted to push me on it, I waited. I was trying to learn the new rules with Maggie, and I knew we'd shifted from outright hostility to something more civil, but I wasn't sure yet how she wanted to play it.

She fiddled with the fob watch on her dress, and then spoke.

'Can I speak with you in private?'

I tried to read her face, but it was closed. 'Sure,' I said. 'What if I buy you a coffee? In, say, half an hour?'

She sniffed. '*Someone* has to look after all these patients you refuse to discharge, Doctor. Let's make it three-thirty instead.'

~

Maggie leant her forearms on the table, and then frowned, dusting grains of sugar from both elbows. Her hair rose almost vertically from her forehead until it went into a curl, which gave her a perpetually quizzical look. I wondered if anyone had ever told her how intimidating her glare could be, and I decided if they had, they wouldn't have lived to share it.

'Before we begin, would you mind taking that off?' she asked a little briskly.

I followed her gaze to my neck, where my stethoscope was hung.

'I find it easier to talk to you, person to person, without that – *there*.'

Bewildered, I stared at her. I didn't feel any different with the stethoscope on my shoulders ... or did I? Its black tubing resting on my shoulder proclaimed me a doctor, and I both knew it and liked it. I had never thought about it getting in the way of communication before.

Ironic, for a listening device.

I pulled the stethoscope off my shoulders and rested it on the table, feeling a little bare.

'Good, now we're just one person speaking to another.' She cupped her latte with two hands. 'There's been quite a lot of talk going around, and it's made me rather uncomfortable. I wanted to – check in on you, Carla.'

I blinked, and stared down at the Formica table, feeling heat rise in my face.

She rested her cup on the table.

'You know, Carla, when our nursing students start, I give them a talk about safety, and I tell them most of the doctors will respect your physical boundaries, but there are one or two ... I warn them, never let yourself be in the room alone with them. And if you are forced to help them, say, with a catheter or an IV on the ward, carry your scissors in one hand at all times.'

She pulled her scissors from her pocket and showed me how she gripped them like a weapon.

'Toby is one of them. And I, for one, don't believe much that comes out of *that* mouth.'

I blinked and breathed. How had I been so blind to this side of Toby? 'Jesus,' I said. 'And – thank you.'

'I've seen a lot, over the years. Enough to know it is not pleasant being the subject of all that innuendo. I hope that you're being supported.'

'You and I both know support around here can be hard to come by.'

'Which is why I'm here.'

Maggie, offering me her support. I did not think this day would come. I thanked her, and then hesitated. 'Um, Maggie? Who are the other doctors? The ones you warn the nurses about?'

Her eyebrows raised so high, they almost met her hairline. 'You really need to ask me that?'

I drank my coffee. Could I trust her, with our plan? She stared at me with her fierce, inquisitive eyes.

'Have you put in a vote for the Casterton, this year?'

'Did you know that nurses have only been allowed to cast a vote in the last two years? Before then, we couldn't. Just like the suffragettes.'

'I hadn't appreciated.'

'You wouldn't.'

'I'm not – all that different to you, Maggie. There's a lot that we both put up with, more than you think.'

'Oh yes, I know. But you are in a position of privilege I will never have.'

She looked at me, a little exasperated for not catching on.

'I can never forget who sits in the seat of power. *Never.* No matter what happens, no matter how many decades I work here, I will always have to defer to the doctor, even if I know what they want to do with a patient is blatantly wrong and not in the patient's best interests. Always have to hold my own counsel, even when they behave like *pigs*.'

In a quiet voice, I told her about what happened to Tess, and our unsuccessful efforts to seek redress.

'The system doesn't want to know when men cross the line with us, either. So Tess and I have been thinking about ways to shift Benson out.' I told her about our plan with the Casterton, genuinely curious to see what she would think.

Her lips pursed. 'It absolutely galls me. The only way to ensure a safe workplace for women is to laud an old man's pathetically fragile ego! I mean, where is the justice?'

'I would have thought you were used to it by now.'

'You never get used to oppression. You just get worn down by it.'

'Do you think you could? Vote for Benson?'

She scowled. 'Through gritted teeth ... but, yes, I will. And, I might add, I have a mighty network of nurses who could help.'

'Would any of them be willing to tell their stories about him? We're going to need to front up to him about this, and the more evidence we have, the better.'

She pondered this. 'Well, that would be a lot to ask of them ... You'd already have more than enough between yourself and Tess, though, wouldn't you?'

I agreed and thanked her, trying not to think of Benson's breath on my cheek.

~

Later that day I wrote up the surgery notes for Mrs Greenidge, documenting the invasion of her body by the bacteria, and the futile resistance from the team of surgeons – Phil, Geoffrey and Alan, a plastics registrar.

'Pissing in the wind,' Phil had muttered under his breath, and Geoffrey nodded his agreement. The two of them exchanged notes on the best conferences in the US to combine surgery and a golf tour, and debated the best single malt whisky on the market, and Alan contributed from time to time.

I worked silently alongside them, noting the finesse and precision of Geoffrey's work. We debrided dead tissue until we could see twitching muscle, glistening fat and bleeding around fascia – signs of life.

At the end of the session, Geoffrey thanked me and told me he would see me next Monday. I felt his eyes on my back as I left theatre.

I wondered what he had heard. I wondered what he knew.

Debridement

the removal of necrotic or infected tissue to help a wound heal

On Monday, I hustled my way through the ward, organising discharge plans with Tess and Maggie, and promising them I would come back to finish. At three, I went to the sixth floor for my appointment with Geoffrey.

As I walked the hallway of the sixth floor, I wondered where Geoffrey's loyalty lay, and as I passed the registrar's office, the door opened and Toby came out.

I said hello in a cool and civil voice, and he grunted a response. We stood there for a moment, with everything and nothing to say. Above me, the clock ticked closer to three.

'Sorry, I have to keep moving. Got an appointment to keep.'
'Yeah? Who with?'
'Gotta go.'

I paused when I reached the closed door, which was a pale varnished wood that looked like it had been there since the seventies. I could feel Toby, down the hall, watching, feel the anger in his stillness, hear his voice inside my head: *what the fuck do you think you're doing?*

I knocked.

Geoffrey's office had a large desk overlooking the park and a round table to one side, which was where he and I sat, side by side. The effect was different from my interactions with Prof, where we were separated by a massive desk.

He smiled at me. 'Don't tell me – you loved the graft we did at Christmas so much you want to transfer to plastics.'

I was fairly sure he was teasing me. 'I did love it.'

'Of course you did. Plastics is the most sought-after specialty.' I noticed the fine cotton of his shirt, and his solid silver cufflinks, the tanned dorsum of his hands. 'All right, I'll stop trying to poach you. Alister would have my guts for garters if I did.'

I paused, realising that now was the time to come to the point of the meeting. 'I – wanted your advice about something. I was wondering if you would support nominating Benson for the Casterton.'

He removed his glasses and leant back in his chair. 'He would be a – very suitable nomination, absolutely.' He paused. 'Your goal is to celebrate a fine surgeon who has given years of service to the hospital?'

I hesitated. 'He is a very generous teacher, especially of the junior medical staff ...'

'Ye-es.' His tone conveyed that he knew there was more. 'Is there a problem?'

'Not – exactly, but ... it might help the, um, general environment if he was moved along towards ... retirement.'

'Do you find him difficult?'

'I wonder ... could this conversation be confidential?'

'Of course.'

'I'm fine,' I said. 'But for some of the more junior staff ...' I didn't want to use Tess's name. 'He can be hands-on, I guess, and they find that challenging to deal with. There are – social mores – which have changed over the past thirty years.'

He asked what Prof knew, and I admitted that I hadn't approached him.

'Well ... it's a most interesting angle, Carla, I have to give you that.

And, between you and me, I would have to agree that Benson's time has come. But you're going to need Prof on side to make anything happen – you know that, don't you?'

'I wondered – I thought I would sound you out first. I thought you might understand that this is more a question of the culture needing to change.'

'Yes, and I do, don't get me wrong. However, Alister and Emmett have been colleagues for more than thirty years. It does make it difficult to be impartial, with so much history there. I will need to think about the best approach with Alister, but I can tell you now I'd be happy to support Emmett's nomination, and I will do so when the heads of department meet to discuss the matter.'

'Thank you.'

He looked sideways at me. 'I suppose, in addition to improving the environment, it would free up another consultant post.'

'Sure, but – my focus right now is supporting the junior staff.'

He nodded. 'Laudable too, if I might say.'

As I left the office, I glanced down the hall.

Toby was gone.

~

On Monday, I left the hospital at about eleven, after seeing the last of the patients in ED. My Alfa was parked in the multi-level car park, which was now nearly empty.

The car park was greasy and grimy with oil spills and fumes. My head was full of the events of the day, and I couldn't remember where I'd parked. I cast my mind back to arriving that morning, but all I remembered was the lemony sky, the cool air of early morning and my nerves at the prospect of meeting with Geoffrey. Under fluorescent light, I dragged my heavy bones along seemingly endless orange painted lines, searching for my Alfa.

When my phone buzzed with a text, I scrambled for it in my bag, hoping it wasn't ED, ready to give them a serve if it was.

    I like how your arse looks in that skirt

I gasped and spun around. No one. The fumes made me queasy. It *must* be Toby. It sounded like him, but why was there no name?

And where was my fucking car?

In my head, the Billy Joel song looped its sick lullaby.

I saw a sign saying P2, and my heart sank as I realised: I was on the wrong floor.

I walked to the narrow concrete stairwell and entered it. Descending the steps, I remembered a story that did the rounds when I was a resident, about a registrar who came in one night to see a psychotic patient in ED. When she left to go home, the patient followed her to her car.

I never heard if she recovered enough to make it back to work.

My footsteps echoed upwards and downwards in the stairwell, and I heard a noise, a shifting of weight, a shuffle of a shoe on a step. I paused – nothing. And then I was running, hustling down the stairs as fast as I could, I wouldn't stop now, and I made it to P3 and opened the door back into the car park, and my car was there, where it always was, and I'd never been so happy to see my little Alfa, its black duco spattered with dust from recent rain, hardened white blobs of bird shit sculpted on the bonnet.

I unlocked the car and got in. I locked the doors, rested my head against the steering wheel and waited for the trembling to settle.

~

It was midnight when I made it home.

I wandered the rooms, checking the windows and doors, wishing

Fleur was here. I did not like the feel of the empty house. I did not like its quiet. I wished I could hear music here, like Xander could.

With last night's mee goreng in a takeaway container on my lap, I sat on the third-highest step of the stairs, where I used to sit as a kid after I was meant to be in bed, my knees tucked up under my chin, listening to the laughter and arguing and drunken singing, the men demanding late-night pasta aglio e olio, and the smell of garlic frying in oil as the women made it.

The mee goreng was better the night before. My thoughts drifted back to Xander and the feeling when I kissed him – *falling, falling* – and the sour realisation that when faced with a beautiful man I had feelings for, I had walked away.

Was it because he dropped out of medicine more than ten years ago?

Sour again, at the back of my throat. Power had been a turn-on, initially, with Toby ... and the memory made me press my fingers into my eye sockets until I saw stars. I couldn't bear how meekly I'd submitted, the resigned knowing in my marrow when he let me down and I put up with it, like the grumbling women in the kitchen cooking their drunken husbands a second dinner.

I dropped my hands from my eyes and told the quiet, empty house, no more.

Xander answered on the third ring. I must have sounded different, because he asked if I was okay, and I told him about the phone calls and the texts. We talked about what I could do – I had nothing concrete to report to the police, or the hospital. And who was it, doing this? Toby had denied everything.

'I'd come over if I could,' Xander said. 'I hate the idea of you being alone with this.' He had played the Lorne pub tonight, he told me, and was doing another show tomorrow before travelling further west.

'Sorry, I've probably interrupted something ...'

'Nothing doing here, I can promise you that. Listen, I'm glad you told me about the calls. Be careful, right? Can security walk you to your car?'

'I guess ... if I need to do that, I'd be letting them win.'

'Sure, but they're not important here ... you are.'

I closed my eyes, undone by his kindness.

He asked when Fleur arrived home, and I told him she was at a conference in Sydney.

'Okay. What about your brother, would he come around?'

'Yeah, maybe.'

'Will you do that? Please?'

The worried tone in his voice reached me. It wasn't okay, some creep following me in the car park at night. Around me, I felt the dark and its shadows. The cool air prickled my bare forearms.

'I'll call Luca.'

'Good, good.' Relief, in his voice. 'Hey, I wanted you to know ... I've been writing.'

'That's great. So good. Maybe the house unlocked something?'

Quiet, for a minute, and I thought I had said something wrong – what would I know about creativity? – until he spoke.

'Actually, I think it was you.'

'*Me*?' I gave a short laugh, set the empty takeaway container on the stair and drew my forearm around my knees. 'What have I got to do with your writing?'

'Carla ... you know what "Cobblestones" is about, don't you?'

I cast my mind back to the lyrics. 'Can you sing me some?'

His voice in my ear sang the words in a whisper, like he was singing me a secret. 'Beer on her breath, chill on her cheeks, ambition in her eyes ... She picks the lock, casts me a kiss and keeps on walking.'

I frowned, trying to solve the puzzle. 'An angel?'

His turn to laugh. 'Yeah, well – I wouldn't call you that, now.'

'Cobblestones' was about me? A tingling feeling filled my chest.

'I can't believe you haven't worked it out by now.'

'I guess, I thought – you had a lot of women to choose from.' I couldn't help grinning. 'And it's not all complimentary, you know – beer breath? Singing in the wrong key? I don't remember tripping.'

'You did, when you were leaving.'

'No way – you added that in for dramatic effect.'

He cleared his throat. 'You know – this tour? I'm travelling alone. I've taken my very own vow of celibacy.'

I laughed, a little disbelieving.

'It's true.'

'Why?'

'I wanted – to prove to myself that I could, I guess.'

'And? Can you?'

'Yeah ... I can.'

Sitting on the third-highest step, I hugged my knees to my chest as we said goodbye.

DURING

My heels click on the sixth-floor lino. Click, click, click.

I'm in the dimness of the corridor, walking towards Prof's office. The door is ajar, and a triangle of light spills through the crack.

Tonight has been too much, but still, the light draws me. Let me try, I tell myself. I want Prof to understand me. Let me try to make good.

Inside my heels, my pinched toes beg for freedom. I pause, lean a hand on the wall and wriggle my toes free for a few sweet minutes. Then I slip my shoes back on and resume walking. Click ... click ... click.

A fluorescent light buzzes on above me, and I blink at harsh white rays cast over the hall, and then it buzzes off again.

Now the dimness seems darker, closer to black. I focus on the light coming from Prof's office. I realise I've never told him his significance in shaping my career. It feels like he should know that. I remember how I felt when Tess explained the same to me. Perhaps, if I put that on the table, we could reach a deeper respect for each other.

Am I trying to butter up my boss? I wonder, and decide no. There's no sugar-coating our differences. I simply want him to know what he means to me.

As I near the door, I hear a rolling sound and some kind of rummaging. Then a drawer slams.

I lurch back at the noise. Prof's temper isn't easy to be around. Maybe this is a mistake?

Standing at the doorway, I tell myself I'm practically a consultant. I want Prof to understand. This might just be a turning point for us.

I step into the room.

BEFORE
Rigor mortis

the stiffening of the body after death

Two weeks out from the gala and I heard that Hamish was on sick leave. He wasn't picking up his phone, and I didn't think I could call Ursula, even if I knew her number. I left a couple of messages, asking him to call me and promising I would visit him soon. *After the gala*, I told myself. Once all this was done.

I had spoken to everyone I could think of about the Casterton – except Prof. I needed to do it, but I baulked at every opportunity. I was too busy, now was not the right time.

But I only had two weeks, and he needed to know.

It had been a while since Mrs Greenidge had last worn coral lipstick. I reviewed her on the ward at Maggie's request, and her skin was alabaster, her eyes closed. On the monitor, her heart rate climbed and her blood pressure dipped.

Drawing back the bedsheets, which were elevated over Mrs Greenidge's wound by a plastic stand, Maggie showed me a red finger tracking down the left leg.

My abdominal wall tightened. The only option would be amputation. Would she even survive that kind of surgery?

On the table next to her bed, I wrote up analgesia and fluids. Next to her chart was a square of newspaper with today's nine-letter puzzle. Words were written in spindly letters in pencil in the margin, but none nine letters long.

Maggie whispered, 'She doesn't want this anymore.'

I knew she was right. And I'd promised Mrs Greenidge before the last surgery that we wouldn't go back.

As I drew a chair to the bedside and sat down, I imagined Prof's furrowed, furious brow. I hadn't had the right to make promises – and he would let me know it.

Mrs Greenidge opened her eyes, and I took her hand. Her skin was as crisp and dry as baking paper. Her fingertips were white.

'Are you in any pain, Mrs Greenidge?'

'Yes.' One quiet, rasping word.

I asked Maggie to increase her analgesia.

'Mrs Greenidge –'

'Esther.' She gave me a small smile.

I hesitated. She had been Mrs Greenidge to me for so long. 'Esther, if we operate, it would be a big undertaking. We may have to remove your leg.'

Her eyes on me, not wavering. Slowly, she shook her head. She whispered, 'Tired.'

I heard her.

She asked after her nieces, and I told her we would call them in. Her head sank back into her pillows then.

'Wonderful doctor. Best of the lot.' She took a laboured breath. 'My friends call me Essie.'

I swallowed against a dry mouth.

'I've enjoyed caring for you ... Essie.'

Her eyes drifted over to the nine-letter puzzle. I picked it up, and while Maggie administered the morphine, I stared at the letters.

When I looked up, Mrs Greenidge was sleeping.

'Chrysalis,' I said softly.

A tiny smile fluttered across her lips.

~

By the time Mrs Greenidge's nieces arrived at the hospital, she was unconscious.

Prof came by the ward, and his eyes narrowed when he saw her leg. I told him she was in renal failure and hypotensive.

'Consent for theatre?'

I hesitated and motioned for us to leave the room, and Maggie followed us into the corridor. I explained that she had declined surgery.

'She's exhausted, Prof – she didn't even want the last debridement we did. She's been in hospital for months, and she's had enough.'

'No question,' Maggie said. 'She wants to die.'

Prof's mouth set in a line. 'This is a treatable condition.'

'Yes, but the treatment is awful for this woman,' Maggie said. 'What kind of a life is this?'

He stroked his chin. 'I cannot make a decision like this on hearsay. I'll speak to her relatives.'

After he left us and returned to the room, Maggie bowed her head. I wondered how many of these battles she had fought and lost with Prof over the years.

'Maggie, I don't want this to go ahead.'

She nodded, folded her arms and told me to call orthopaedics and get the paperwork ready.

'We have no choice. He can't let go.'

~

Sixteen hours of surgery, seven units of blood, one limb lost and one wish to die ignored. Mrs Greenidge may have given up, but her body fought on in ICU. I had assisted Prof, and even as I wrestled with myself, I marvelled at his skill and innovation in excising the diseased tissue. Most surgeons would have admitted defeat.

I saw her pallid face before the previous surgery, when I had asked her, do you think you can manage one more? The smallness of her voice with its ever-dignified vowels in reply, 'I'm so very tired.' And me, telling her, 'Last one, I promise.'

As I shifted the retractor so Prof had the best view, I whispered, 'I'm sorry. I'm sorry for letting you down.'

After she was wheeled out to recovery, he turned to me. 'Difficult job, well done. Her family will be well pleased.'

Her great-nieces rarely visited. Something hard like cement lodged in my gut.

Dawn broke over the parklands as I left the hospital and walked down an asphalt bike path, and then onto the gravel path beside the zoo. Sunshine glittered from a buttery sky. Over the red brick fence, parrots squawked, a lyrebird sounded a warning call and a pair of cockatoos screeched *I-told-you-so*.

~

Mrs Greenidge spent several days in ICU ventilated, all markers of sepsis trending upwards. Late on Friday, while finishing a list in theatre, I got a call from ICU. They'd had the chat with the family and extubated her.

Off the vent, as often happened, she took a few spontaneous breaths, the pre-morbid rasping excoriations of the airway that Cheyne and Stokes had first described. Imagine your legacy in medicine being the death rattle.

I handed some jobs over to Lachlan and went to ICU. Maggie and the nieces were sitting by the bed. When she saw me, Maggie stood.

'It's time. Will you?'

I swallowed and nodded.

Mrs Greenidge's face was a white mask. I hoped she would be buried with a fine application of coral lipstick. I was sure Maggie would see to it.

I took her hand, her palm dry and cracked. Taking stock of her still body, I felt that she had already left this weight of lumpen humanness, ridden with infection, and I was glad.

Chrysalis.

I put my stethoscope to her chest and watched the second-hand traverse a full sixty seconds on my watch, and I listened for nothingness, for what I knew wouldn't come. Her nieces watched me, as though somehow I might be able to bring her back, and I wanted to tell them that I couldn't, because she had already gone.

I remembered a nine-letter word we did together. Mrs Greenidge had guessed this one, and I'd recalled the prayer from church. *Beatitude.* Blessings.

When the time was up, I withdrew the stethoscope, noting the time of death, and bowed my head.

Beatitude, Essie. Beatitude.

~

Stethoscope in my hands, I watched as Prof passed on condolences to the Greenidge family, and around the time that Maggie took a cloth and warm water and began to wash Mrs Greenidge's body, I stopped believing.

In these hallowed halls, and this vaunted unit, and in the man in the room who cared for Mrs Greenidge but ignored her last wishes.

Before Prof entered the room, he and I had spoken briefly. She was a wonderful woman, he had said, and I knew that she was *his* kind of woman – obedient, deferential. Only, she *did* have her own mind, and she spoke it to me.

I chose my words deliberately. 'I liked her a great deal,' I said, 'but I'm glad for her. She was ready.'

His face twitched and then composed itself, and he murmured, 'Rest in Peace.'

Now, I ran my fingers over my stethoscope, from the smaller bell and the larger diaphragm, along the thick black tubing to the earpieces. Some surgeons dissed the stethoscope – not their instrument of choice – but not me. I traced the curve in the tubing where my stethoscope had moulded itself to my neck, and I remembered, as an intern, the first, proud day I wore it.

I thought about how my stethoscope had moulded to me, and I to it.

I tapped on the diaphragm, the widest part of the stethoscope head, an old habit to determine the flow of sound within the tubes. This diaphragm had lain flat against the sweaty skin of a terrified septic woman and transmitted the skittish rhythm of her tachycardia. It had heard the surprising syncopation of an arrhythmia telling a thick-throated bloke who was really the boss, and the crepitations and laboured respirations of emphysematous lungs too worn out to exchange more oxygen.

The *beat, beat, beat* to which we all marched, and the absolute, eerie silence when it was no more.

I heard the tremor in Mrs Greenidge's voice as she told me she'd had enough.

I couldn't choose not to hear it anymore.

Survival curve

graph of chance of death over time

I waited for Prof outside Mrs Greenidge's room and asked if I could speak to him.

'Could we walk?'

I was no longer afraid, but it would be easier to speak outside these walls.

He suggested we take coffee with us, and we called past Bea's on the way out.

It was late afternoon, and darkness was already creeping at the edges of the day. I was cold, and the coffee was terrible.

'Prof,' I began, my mouth sickly with the shoddy coffee. 'I'm not sure if you've heard, but we've been gathering a few votes for the Casterton.'

'Oh, yes?' His voice was hard to read. 'And who might these votes be for?'

I took a sip of the bitter, tepid coffee. 'Mr Benson.'

For a few minutes he was quiet. Birds called a nightfall warning and our steps crunched gravel. I drank more bad coffee.

'First of all, Casterton nominations are generally a matter for the *consultant* group. We select an individual with strengths across the board: clinical, education and research. Emmett's research record is not quite of the calibre we would associate with the Casterton. Having said that, he has been generous leading the training program, and he does many thankless tasks. My point is, you should have talked to me before you acted on this. There are many facts to which you are not privy. This – this is *not* the way things are done.'

I took the dressing-down in silence. The light faded further, the day escaping.

'And what exactly are you hoping to achieve – his retirement, I assume?'

'I want PCH to be a place where women can thrive.'

'Let me explain a few things. Firstly, Emmett lives for his work. He doesn't have outside interests. It won't be a simple matter to give him this award and move him along. It could even paradoxically make him feel more attached to the hospital. Had you considered that?'

I had not.

'Second, even if he does decide to go, it's no forgone conclusion that the hospital will continue to fund his post. They might argue that we don't need to replace him. Do you know how many meetings I attend where the bean counters carry on about the perilous state of the hospital finances, that we need to cut this per cent or that from our bottom line? As if we can wave a wand and make that happen. And I'm yet to hear an outcome on my business case.'

He stopped walking and drew himself tall, his voice harsh and loud. 'There may not even *be* a job, at the end of all of this.'

My shoulders caved and I felt myself shrivel. 'It wasn't about the job ...'

He stood tall. 'I will not have the tail wagging the dog in my department. Do you understand? This is not your place.'

My place. Where was my place – in the kitchen, making sugo? All these years, all I had wanted was to make PCH my place.

'I was trying to do the right thing.' I thought of Tess.

'So, these nominations, they've been lodged already. Is that correct?'

'Yes.'

He breathed heavily. 'I will need to speak to Geoffrey.'

After all of Prof's ranting, I didn't feel able to tell him that Geoffrey already knew. I could only hope that Geoffrey had my back.

We turned back, walking towards the pointed finger of the main hospital building, its bricks turned to sullen rust in the dusk. Cockatoos screeched, and my footsteps were heavy with the question I was too intimidated to ask: would he support the nomination? And what would happen if he didn't?

~

Late at night, I parked Prof and his eye-bulging fury, and filled my head with nine-letter words. I had to work hard to erase the pallid mask that death had bestowed upon Mrs Greenidge's face and picture her alive, coral-lipsticked, frowning over the square of newspaper with its edges folded, her pencil in her hand. The look of delight when she or I would solve it.

I thought about what kind of doctor I had tried to be for her. I had done my best and failed her, and she had known, and forgiven me.

Beatitude.

The blessing she'd left me was a glimpse, when all was said and done, of what really mattered to me. Holding true to what I believed in, even when it meant head-on collisions, with Prof, or Benson, or any of them.

Despite Prof's anger, I was glad I had spoken up.

Next was the golf game with Benson. *Fortitude* was the nine-letter word I needed.

It was big, what we planned to do. Audacious, certainly. If Benson and Prof and Geoffrey compared notes, it could end badly for Tess and me.

Foreboding churned in my gut. I did not want to be alone with this feeling.

I reached for my phone and called Xander.

'Not asleep?'

'Nope.'

'How is celibacy treating you?'

He laughed. 'Pretty good, actually.'

I told him about Mrs Greenidge, and Prof, and Benson, and the golf game.

'Jesus,' he said. 'You are the gutsiest. No other word for it.'

'Stupid, maybe?'

'No. No way. Not a chance.'

'I don't know if it's going to work.'

'No. No, you don't.'

I sat with that, the darkness drawing around me. 'You know ... when we – kissed? I didn't realise it then, but I had all these ideas in my head, of the kind of guy I would be with.'

'Yeah? What kind of guy was that?'

I hesitated. 'It's embarrassing ... I think I was a looking for a man who was more powerful than me, as if they were better, or more attractive, or something. Like somewhere in my brain, I was replicating the same bullshit bias I'm exposed to every single day. Seriously fucked up, hey.'

'No way I'm judging you for that. You're surrounded by power structures led by men.'

I thought of Prof, and Geoffrey ... and even Nino, who could silence Gina with a look. 'Well, it's wrong, on a whole lot of levels.' I paused. 'Anyway, next time you're in Melbourne ... could we catch up?'

He didn't respond immediately, and I buried my face in my pillow. *Catch up*? I sounded like a silver-haired woman inviting him for a hand of bridge. I tried again. 'I'd love to see you, Xander. And – thank you for writing "Cobblestones".'

'O-kay.' I heard a tentative smile in his voice. 'Maybe I can play you my new song.'

'Can I hear it now?' *Was it about me?*

'Not quite. When it's ready.'

'Something else, then? I feel like I'll never fall asleep tonight.'

He began a slow song that I didn't know, and I closed my eyes and let the song take the edge off my jittery, jangly mind.

~

On the day we met Benson for golf, the sky held heavy clusters of grape-like clouds.

Tess wore a tight-fitting cap and checked knickerbockers, and I stared at her for a minute, knowing something was different.

Wait – there were no curls under that cap.

'You've ... have you?'

Slowly, she removed her cap, revealing a close-cropped shave of her head. Her scalp was pale white, and her golden curls were gone. She straightened her shoulders and faced me, and I felt the loss of her wild mane of hair, but it was also as if she had removed the dust sheet from a beautiful painting. Her face was the feature now, and the open generosity in her eyes shone.

'Wow. You look – amazing.'

'Incredible?'

We smiled at each other. 'Awesome.'

'I decided that whatever happens today, he will never put his finger into one of my curls again. I made sure of it.'

'Well, it's magnificent. It really is.'

She lowered her eyes, shy.

'Thank you.'

We waited out on the practice green, lost in our thoughts, laced with doubt, of how we would make today work. I had updated Tess on Prof's reaction, and we were steeling ourselves for another difficult conversation.

Benson did a double-take when he saw Tess, and a look of dismay crossed his face before he composed himself. 'My goodness, Tess, that is a dramatic change. I imagine it will be a very – practical haircut.'

'Yes,' she said.

We walked out to the first tee, and Benson ushered us ahead of him towards the women's tee, but we shook our heads. Even though the shorter course would have helped my cause, today was not a day for our shots to be dictated by men.

I approached the tee and placed my ball, remembered the tips that Tess had given me.

'Square those hips,' Benson said, approaching me from behind and reaching his arms over my shoulders to grip his hands over mine.

Tess and I had planned for this. I stopped, straightened up, and our bodies were still too close, but I resisted the urge to step back and instead I smiled up at him.

'Mr Benson, you've taught me a lot over the years. But today, I'm going to ask you to let me make my own mistakes. We are on the golf course after all. Not a matter of life and death here – just how many shots over I go. And just think how good I will make you look.'

Benson's jaw dropped.

I waited, but he didn't move. 'I'm going to take my shot now.'

He took a faltering step backwards, and I stepped back up to the tee. For the first time ever, my club connected sweetly with the golf ball, hitting a respectable shot down the fairway.

Maybe I could grow to like this game.

Tess took her shot and hit a solid drive, and Benson's first shot was skied off to the right, and I made a mental note to make sure I fudged the next shot. I thought the chances of that were high. We couldn't afford a bruised golf ego.

We took a leisurely walk down the fairway against a backdrop of gum trees and oaks. Tess asked Benson about how long he had been training junior doctors, and this launched a monologue that lasted for several holes, about how hard he had worked to train each generation, to impart his knowledge, and how unappreciated he was. We listened, made sympathetic murmuring noises and made sure he was winning the game.

When we reached the final hole, a par four, Tess and Benson hit their tee shots down the middle, and I sliced mine to the right. I felt the weight of what I was about to do and my second shot was no better.

Tess gave me a nervous smile.

'Mr Benson, your contribution to training – we wanted you to know that this *has* been noticed, at least by us,' I said.

He looked surprised and smiled. Tess hit her next shot and it landed short of the hole, and I took a divot of grass out of the turf with my attempt. I looked at the divot of dislodged dirt. I straightened up.

'We think you deserve a more formal recognition, especially at this stage of your career. Which is why we have nominated you for the Casterton.'

Benson stopped walking and then leant forward so he was standing in a crouched position, hands on his knees, like a runner at the end of a marathon. His knuckles were knobbly and the joints in his fingers swollen and arthritic. How did he even manage a scalpel?

'You have done this, for me?'

'Yes. Mr Benson. You deserve it.'

He blinked a few times and cleared his throat. His eyes were watery.

'Regardless of the outcome, I must say, I feel quite overwhelmed by this gesture. Thank you, ladies. It means a great deal to me.'

We took our shots and walked up to the green, Benson's steps slow and dogged. Tess and I exchanged wide-eyed looks. Seeing Benson so moved by the nomination made the next steps harder, and it was a struggle to remember that this man with arthritic hands and a feeble gait was the one who groped women while they worked.

We examined the lie of each ball. Tess's and Benson's had made it onto the green, while mine sat lodged in the rough that sloped down to a bunker. Tess took a slow walk around her ball, examining it from every angle. She looked up at me and nodded. Yes.

I went and stood beside Benson, who leant hands on his knees while assessing his shot.

'If we can make it happen, Mr Benson – receiving the Casterton would be a fitting way to bring your career to a gratifying end.'

He slowly straightened up next to me. 'I'm – unsure what you're suggesting, Carla.'

I squinted up at his face. 'It would be a very honourable note on which to retire. An appropriate recognition of everything you've achieved.'

Tess came and stood next to us. 'It would be so wonderful, for your legacy in training to be passed on. And Carla here, if she were appointed, she could build on the program you have developed –'

Benson listened and frowned. 'And what would happen if I don't?'

There was a pause then, and I waited. Tess moistened her lips and swallowed.

'Mr Benson? I have seen today how much this recognition would mean to you, and I understand that. But I need you to understand something else. When you cross the boundaries at work: ask for a kiss, touch me when I didn't ask you to –'.

His jaw fell open. 'Is *that* what this is about?'

'Please. Let me finish. When you did that, I felt really uncomfortable. And unsafe, worrying about what was going to happen to me next time we were in theatre, or in your office. I deserve to feel safe at work, Mr Benson.'

'Are you seriously suggesting I make you feel unsafe? *Me?*'

Tess did not falter. 'Yes.'

'Have you ever considered why it is only you who seems to have this problem? No other women have ever raised this with me. They seem to understand friendly banter when they come across it.'

I stepped forward. 'Each year, when the new batch of nursing students start their rotations, Maggie warns them about you.'

Benson exhaled a derisive laugh. 'Maggie? She has a chip on her shoulder the size of Uluru. Of course she would say something like that.'

I walked over to where my ball had decided to rest, on the gentle slope running down from the green to a bunker. On a similar shot earlier in the round, I had been tentative with the chip and my ball had run up to the edge of the green and down again into the bunker. This time, I chipped the ball, and it ran onto the green, coming to a stop a metre from the pin.

Walking up onto the green, I breathed deeply, and planted my feet squarely opposite Benson. He looked down at me, defiance and doubt in his eyes. Above me, heavy cloud promised rain.

'Mr Benson, we have worked together for a long time, and you have taught me a great deal. But you've assumed that I'm okay with the liberties you take around me.'

I heard a sharp intake of breath from Tess. 'And ... that's wrong. When you do things like tuck in my scrubs, or put your hand on my back, I don't like it. And I believe that you are aware that it's inappropriate, because it only ever seems to happen in private. So, no, it's not just Tess. You can't write this off. This is about you. We want to see you get the Casterton, and take that opportunity to retire. And if that doesn't happen, we would have no choice but to lodge a complaint with the college about your behaviour.'

Benson's mouth turned sour, and his eyes grew small. He walked around the green and took his time setting up his putt. The ball rolled down the slope, lipped into the hole and then out again, and the missed shot seemed to enrage him.

'I see what this is about. This is a set-up. What makes you think you have the right to do this? You are trainees, you should know your place.'

'You had no right to do what you did,' Tess said. 'You made me feel – violated.'

He shook his head. 'You're living in the wrong universe if you think *that* is a violation. After everything I've done, for both of you.'

He went and tapped his ball into the hole, and fished it out, and as haughtily as his doddery legs would allow, he stalked off the green.

~

On the night of the gala, Tess and I stood in the foyer area outside the dining room. She wore a jade full-length dress with a camellia pinned to her bust. Her cropped hair looked amazing.

We clinked glasses and drank.

'Do you think Mr Ellis has a chance?'

I had to admit I didn't know. We had spoken to everyone we could think of and encouraged nominations, but who knew how many of Maggie's staff and the men on our team actually followed through? And what if Prof had blocked it?

We drained our glasses, and a waiter brought us more champagne. Tess told me that Prof had asked to be removed from the Women in Surgery manuscript.

'Well, I guess that saves us from having to work out how to get him off the paper.'

She laughed nervously. 'Whatever happens, Carla – I will never forget what you've done for me.'

'Actually, I – I needed this, for myself.'

'I didn't realise what you'd been through.'

'Tucking in my scrubs, ugh. I would try to prevent it, but the scrubs are so oversized that they always end up untucked. And that ridiculous line, "It's my birthday, give me a kiss", when everyone in theatre knew. It was gross, but I put up with it. I – didn't know what else I could do.' I bowed my head. 'I wasn't as brave as you.'

'I don't believe that. You spoke up when it really mattered.' She hugged me, and I let the warmth in, and it floated on top of the waves of dread and what-ifs and hope.

DURING
Evisceration

the process whereby tissue or organs that usually reside within a body cavity are displaced outside that cavity

I have been writing sideways to this place, a crabwalk into a storm.

The memory constantly shifts its shape. It is like trying to grab a fog in a fist. The room is packed, I remember that, and it vibrates with loud conversations, and it feels as though many people are talking but no one is listening.

We are in the corporate suite of the hospital, the folding doors of several meeting rooms opened up to make a ballroom of sorts. A dance floor of temporary parquetry has been laid over the hardworking, teal-coloured carpet, and from the windows along the west wall, we get to watch the sun go down over roofs and treetops. The view is only partially obscured by large rectangular rooftop generators – we can pretend that they're not there.

I am seated between Will and Hamish, with Tess on Will's left. I scan the room, but I don't see Toby, and I'm glad.

Near the main table, Geoffrey is standing talking with Leonard Ellis. Leonard has his back to me, so I try to read Geoffrey's face: is this a pre-award discussion? A commiseration? It ends with Geoffrey patting him on the back, and I can't tell if that is a consolatory or congratulatory gesture and the not-knowing is killing me.

As Geoffrey moves on from that conversation, he catches my eye.

We have a moment: bold, unblinking eye contact, which feels loaded in some way, and I can't tell what it means, but I hope that it's a good sign.

The waiters buzz around, serving mains, and somebody places a hefty steak in front of me. Will stares in disgust at the plate a young pimply waitress has laid down before him, a piece of white meat swimming in a buttery sauce.

This is a choreographed dance we both know well, only tonight I baulk at my role. Tonight is a steak night. I tell him no.

Will looks surprised. He tops up my glass, and Hamish demands the bottle. Will obliges and leans forward, his voice a drunkenly loud whisper. 'Do you think it will actually happen?'

I shrug. I don't even want to name it, lest I put a curse on the plan.

The hospital CEO begins formalities, delivering a superlative-laden speech of which Tess would be proud. Then they award the physicians' medal to one of the senior gastroenterologists I barely know.

'They only have one because we had the Casterton,' Will says. 'Joneses.'

After that, Geoffrey comes to the podium, delivering a short speech about the year in surgery, referencing notes on his phone. Quite tech-savvy for his age, I decide. When he comes to the Casterton, I press one thumbnail into the other, blanching the nailbed until it hurts.

He speaks about the winner's teamwork ethos and commitment to research, and I throw Tess an alarmed look. Prof had said Benson's research wasn't up to it.

And then he switches gear, talking about teaching, and when he makes a joke about always being late to theatre, Will looks at me, his eyebrows dancing up and down.

'The winner of the Casterton for 2015 is ... Emmett Benson.'

Our table roars, already three sheets to the wind, and I see Maggie clapping heartily from a table of nursing staff on the other side of the room.

Okay, Benson – over to you.

Benson stands and gives a speech that meanders left foot then right through memories of weekends on-call which started on the Friday morning and ended several appendixes and gallbladders and trauma surgeries later on the Monday night. You wanted to have your car accident on the Friday, believe me, Benson says. I lean forward, listening for the words, but he keeps on with the stories.

The room grows a little restless and there are murmurings when our table runs out of wine. Hamish gestures to the waiter, and our glasses are topped up.

Benson's tone turns plaintive, and he talks about how much he is going to miss surgery. I hold my breath ... *is he? Will he?* When he says, 'I wish my successor as long and happy a career as I have enjoyed,' I exhale a long-held, wine-scented breath. Across the table, Tess blinks back tears.

She reaches for me and we grip each other's hands in the kind of fierce upright handshake usually reserved for rugby players. We did it. Prof didn't sabotage the plan, and neurosurg didn't have their way. Who knows what Geoffrey did behind the scenes? I'm in the moment, full of gratitude to Tess and Maggie, when I notice Toby, standing near the entrance and nursing a glass of wine. He claps his free hand languidly against his wine glass and, when he sees me, tips his glass towards me.

Jubilant, I raise my glass back at him, and then at Benson as Prof proposes a toast. Once formalities are over, we return to our seats.

'Well, my, my,' Will says to me. 'Aren't you the mover and the shaker, eh?'

'She is,' Tess says. 'She's going to be the next consultant in your team.'

'Wahey!' Will smiles. 'We'd be honoured to have you, Carla.'

I give Will a steely smile. I haven't forgotten his rumour-mongering.

'Carla is magnificent,' Hamish says. 'And we need more wine.' His lips are stained ruby red.

Soon after, the band starts, and Maggie finds us.

'Shall we mark this moment?' she asks. When we say yes, she leads the way, through the dining room, picking up glasses and a bottle of champagne along the way, and down the hall, to where there is a small concrete balcony outside the hospital offices.

We walk out into the night air, carrying our champagne glasses.

'We did it! We FUCKING did it!' Tess yells, and a wide smile breaks her face open.

'Awesome! Amazing! Incredible!' I yell, shaking my fists at Benson, and Prof, and those men who dared to think they could stop us. We are a force, an unstoppable force.

'Women will work as surgeons and nurses and whatever they fucking well want to at PCH, and they will do it safely. Carla, I am so, so grateful.'

I hold up my palm and shake my head. We did this together, I tell her.

I will never forget this night, she says.

Maggie drinks her champagne, looks out at the city lights winking at us. 'I would love it if this spelled the end of all the sexism women endure here. But that bastard is only one of them.' She nudges at me with her elbow. 'I'm looking forward to seeing what you get up to next.'

'Benson's job! It belongs to Carla.'

'Cheers to that.'

We clink our glasses, and the relief, the booze and the sense of warmth between us go right to my head. For the first time I think I know what sisterhood feels like.

~

Back in the dining room, a six-man band is playing jazz and people are already dancing – older couples, and younger people, mostly women, in large circles. Maggie returns to her nurses' table, and two residents come over to Tess and drag her onto the dance floor, and she waves at me and is gone. I take a moment to listen to the band. I recognise the smooth chorus of 'Bye, Bye, Blackbird'.

The band plays a laid-back version, trumpet and voice alternately taking the melody, with piano providing the chords. A deep sense of satisfaction washes over me. I feel like escaping the dinner already and going home to spruce up my CV, as if doing so would bring the job ad closer.

The band changes gears, and I'm watching the dance floor, so I don't see him coming.

My knees buckle. I'm swung around, and the room whizzes and I'm thrown, and I see faces leering and cheering – *cheering* – and my dress rides up, and are my boobs covered? I don't know.

And then I'm righted, and I tug at the top seam of my dress as Will's shiny, grinning face comes into view. 'Don't you love Miles Davis?! Do you know this song? Bye, Bye fucking Blackbird! How perfect is that?!'

And before I can tell him not to, he's swinging me again, and I am thrown around, stiff as plasterboard.

Finally, he sets me down. I push his hands off me and yell, 'I'm not a fucking doll!'

He makes a mock sad face at what a bad sport I am and holds out his hand for another dance. 'Peace offering? No stunts this time.'

I back away, mouthing 'no', and the crowd parts as I leave the dance floor.

~

I take a minute to sort myself out in the toilets. As I stand in front of the mirror, my teeth clenched at Will's effort on the dance floor, I straighten my dress, reapply my lipstick and declare that I won't let this night be wrecked by the stupid actions of one male.

I am not a fucking doll!

In the time it takes me to distinguish between the cubicle doors, a locked cupboard and the exit, I realise I am seriously wasted.

I don't want people to see me drunk. I should get out of here. I walk back into the dining room, planning to leave early, but standing a few metres in front of me are Benson and Prof.

They meet my eye, and I have no option but to join them.

Benson is holding a cup of tea on a saucer. He speaks with his eyes on my chest, and for the second time tonight, I'm regretting the strapless dress. 'Here we have it,' he says. 'The future of surgery. And what excellent hands it is in.'

He is not looking at my hands.

Prof coughs and nods and says, 'Yes', and I don't feel the conviction behind the word.

I congratulate Benson on the award, and he tips his glass at me. 'Surgery is my life,' he says. 'I cannot think how I will fill my days. But the surgical world is moving past me, it seems … I'm no longer needed.'

'Emmett, you know that's not true,' says Prof, but Benson silences him with his hand.

'No longer needed,' he repeats.

Before I can speak, he walks off in search of an extra chair. Prof sits down and I stand, unable to look him in the eye. When Benson returns and slides a chair in behind me, I feel his hand on the curve of my butt, his voice in my ear.

'You must be pleased with yourself.'

I feel as though I might be sick, and I will him to move away. I shift my weight forwards and pull the chair in towards the table.

He leans down, and I smell Darjeeling tea as he tells me I have a most lovely behind, just as he remembered.

As soon as someone comes to congratulate Benson, I make my escape. I want to be anywhere but here. I am on my way to the exit when Hamish calls my name across the room, loudly, twice.

'No, no, no,' he yells. 'You can't go home, not yet. Come, sit down here.'

Heads turn, and I can't leave him like this. I walk over to the table and sit down and he pours me wine I don't want.

'Drink,' he says, and I do.

He leans forward and places his forearms on the table, beginning a monologue about the awful state of his life. When he begins to cry, I don't know what to do. I tell him how sorry I am and, unexpectedly, he reaches for my hand.

'I knew you'd understand,' he says, and I stare, bewildered, at our intertwined hands.

He tells me I'm the only one supporting him and asks if he could stay with me, gripping my hand white-knuckled.

And he hums a few lilting lullaby notes, just like Billy Joel does at the end of 'Always a Woman'.

'Was that you? *You* sent me that song?'

His face shapes into a smile, and then as he sees my horror, the smile morphs into an anxious grimace. 'It reminded me of you. Don't you like Billy Joel?'

'You scared me. It was seriously creepy, Hamish. Don't do shit like that.'

He looks hurt, and sheepishly tells me then that he sometimes rang my phone to hear my voice on the voicemail, that it comforted him, and my body shivers and I want to be away.

'Did you follow me in the car park? Was that you as well?'

'I would never do something like that!'

How did I not realise? Like most doctors, he had his number blocked on his phone. But I'd been imagining a predator, not a troubled soul.

I tell him he has to stop calling me, he needs to get some professional help. I can't be the only one in his corner. I'm not sure I ever asked to be.

I sense it then, the shape of a person standing near us, a still and silent presence in the corner of my vision.

Hamish leans on my shoulder and says, 'But I need you,' and his body slumps against me, and I feel eyes are on us, watching.

And then Prof appears, standing next to us as spit dribbles from Hamish's mouth.

I try to push Hamish upright, and it is impossible.

Prof tells me not to put myself in these kinds of positions, not with everyone watching. He leans forward and in his low, gravelly voice he says, 'I know what you did. You might think that these little games you're playing are acceptable, but I *won't* have it.'

I'm wedged in next to a semi-conscious Hamish, and Prof's face is closer than I would like, his skin an unhealthy shade of purple. There is so much I want to explain, but in the corner of my eye, I see Geoffrey and Will watching on. I don't want to be the centre of attention here.

I wish myself far, far away.

~

Once I extricate myself from Hamish, I farewell Tess, who is dancing with joyous abandon on the dance floor, and climb the stairs to six to collect my things. I pass Maggie on the stairs, who offers to take me home, but I refuse – I'm old enough to take care of myself.

When my bladder announces it urgently needs emptying, I stop by the toilets on six. Is it a measure of how wasted I am that I don't care whether I choose to pee in the men's?

If I'm honest, there is an element of fuck you about the gesture, which only I am meant to know about, except that Lachlan chooses that moment to find a quiet spot for his fix. And he does not appreciate me witnessing it, not one bit.

I leave him, smouldering with indignation, and go to the registrar's office, where I find my satchel under the desk. I take a while to locate my keys, and when I've finally found them and am ready to leave, I see Toby in the doorway.

I can tell from his dilated pupils and the blotch of pink on his cheeks that he is drunk, or turned on, or angry, perhaps all three. He tells me he was looking for me, and that he has heard what I did. 'Ballsy,' he says, 'to try to push Benson out like that.'

He says, 'Your arse looks good in that dress too,' and my hazy head connects the dots.

'It *was* you.'

He grins, feigning confusion. 'Who else would it be?'

He holds out his palm, the diamond necklace cupped within it.

He comes close.

His kiss tastes of beer.

It is almost out of habit that I let him kiss me – our bodies haven't forgotten each other, but when his hands circle my throat as he fastens the necklace, a fog clears in my head. I am branded now, like cattle. I am his.

No. I draw away. I tell him I saw him with Phoebe, and an ugly curl shapes his upper lip as he accuses me of playing games.

He is standing between me and the door.

I tell him, again, that we are done. I say that it is for the best, that with Benson going, there will be a job up for grabs, and he says, 'And you'll keep flaunting that arse of yours until you get what you want.'

I kick him, hard, and his reflexes are slow, so I strike him flush in the balls. The soft tissue of his penis and testes gives easily under the pointed toe of my stiletto, and he keels over and exhales a groan, like air seeping out of a punctured tyre.

I imagine the inflammatory factors streaming to the injured area, fluid swelling his scrotal sac, pain fibres transmitting emergency signals to his brain. Soon, a haematoma will spread through this skin, colouring it a brazen purple.

I step around his doubled-up body and leave.

~

In the hallway, I take a minute to lean against the wall, my hands on my thighs, and breathe. I've never been violent with anyone before, and I'm surprised how good it felt to see him gasping for breath.

Above me, a fluorescent light buzzes on, and then abruptly switches off. Down the hall, I notice that the door to Prof's office is ajar, and the light is on inside the office.

He must have come up here to escape the gala. I knew the feeling, of wanting away from the noise and the need to be nice.

As my breath returns to normal, I remember our angry words earlier in the night. He accused me of playing games. I wonder if I can set things straight. How would Prof feel if he knew that just now, Toby tried to trap me in the registrar's office? Might be in my interests for him to know that before the job is appointed.

More than that – and notwithstanding everything that has happened – I want Prof to know that setting up Benson was an act of desperation.

The light in his office draws me towards it. My steps click, click down the empty hall.

I call out, 'Prof?'

No answer, but I hear a noise, like the shuffling of papers, and a drawer slam.

What if he doesn't want to be interrupted?

Or maybe someone else is in there? Has Toby, somehow, made it into Prof's office? I tell myself that is ridiculous, I left him writhing on the carpet in the registrar's office.

I stand at the threshold, hesitating.

Slowly I push the door open.

Standing at the filing cabinet, rifling through papers, is Geoffrey.

A jolt of surprise runs through me, and when he turns and sees me, he startles too, as though an electric impulse has travelled from me through him. What is he doing in Prof's office?

He composes himself, but his jaw clenches.

'Why, Carla,' he says, taking a manila folder from the cabinet and closing the drawer. 'What are you doing up here late at night?'

I stammer a response and tell him I'm looking for Prof, and he laughs.

'Oh, I don't think you want to be seeking him out right now. Give him time to calm down first.'

The bravado I felt in the hall evaporates. 'Is he angry with me?'

'You – *could* say that. Nothing you can't handle, of course. I have to say, your effort with Benson – it was most impressive.'

'Not in Prof's eyes.'

I see the interview looming, hear the bitterness of his voice saying *I know what you did*. And my body begins to shake uncontrollably. I've done all that work, and if Toby swoops in now and takes the job ...

Geoffrey sits against the edge of Prof's desk.

'Well, perhaps I can help you,' he says. 'You're a very talented surgeon, Carla. I take the view that the organisation needs to foster talent like yours.'

His eyes are locked on me.

I press my trembling hands against my thighs. 'I'd be really grateful for your support.'

'Of course,' he says easily, taking a step towards me. 'It won't be difficult for us to bring Prof around.'

'You'd do that for me? Even if it meant Toby missed out on the job?'

'It's time that Toby fended for himself. I can't keep saving his bacon if he's going to squander every chance he gets.'

He moves towards the door and closes it, and I hear an extra click.

My eyes zero in on the door handle – brushed silver, mounted on a metal plate. Above the lever is a snib turned to forty-five degrees. He picks up my hand and kisses it.

I can't swallow, or speak. As the clock on the wall ticks each passing second, he guides my hand to his groin. Slowly, the world tilts off its axis.

Prof's sons smile out at me from the frame on his desk – three of them, arranged in height order – and they watch as Geoffrey guides my hand up and down his penis until he's hard.

'Geoffrey, I – I need to go. I'm sorry.'

'I don't think you need to go at all.'

An oily dread seeps through my pelvis.

'Do you think your little scheme was successful all on its own? Are you that naive?' He lets go of my hand, and unbuttons his trousers. I see his penis, pink and erect, and his greying pubic hair.

'You do know I made it all happen, for you ... don't you? Now.'

He reaches for the upper edge of my strapless dress and draws it down to my waist, exposing my breasts, touching them. I push his hand away and draw my arm over my chest, shaking. I want to make myself small.

When he grabs my head and shoves it downwards, I shake my head, *no*, and try to push him away, but he grabs a fistful of my hair and pushes me down, onto my knees. 'Nothing in this world comes free, Carla. You need to show some appreciation.'

I find my voice then. 'No!'

He pulls harder on my hair and pins me with his leg.

'Geoffrey, you're hurting me!' I push against his leg with all my force, but he is stronger. He grabs the necklace and yanks it tight like a tourniquet around my throat.

I open my mouth to yell, but all that I can summon is a raspy exhalation. I look around the room for something I can use as a weapon. Nothing but a pile of files on the desk, and the glint of silver from the photo frame of Prof's sons, who watch and smile.

The eldest shares Prof's hazel eyes.

'Come now, Carla. This won't be the last time we have this conversation if you want to make it up the ranks here.'

My jaw drops open. Air is sucked from my chest.

He shoves his penis into my mouth.

Move.

Scream.

I see only one way out.

As Prof's sons watch, I begin to weep, for me, and for them, and for the way this world is for anyone who doesn't have a voice.

When Geoffrey comes, tears spill on my cheeks.

AFTER
Simulation

any activity that replicates medical scenarios

At home in bed, I hide in a cocoon of doona, sitting up to stop my head from spinning.

All my thoughts, willed away.

I can't think about it. I can't think. When sleep eludes me, I take two temazepam and wait for the comfort of white.

~

I catalogued the next day in shifting shadows on the wall. The hard top-hat of the lamp shade, and the lumpy mountain-range curves of my body under the doona.

I turned off my phone and stayed away from Fleur. I wasn't ready to talk to anyone who could sniff out trouble.

I was drunk. My memories were shifting fragments that fuddled my head – the moment of goose-bump triumph on the balcony with Tess and Maggie, and the instant where the point of my stiletto impacted Toby's groin.

And, then –

No. I would not think of it.

I streamed something on Netflix but couldn't tell you what I watched. I tried to eat, but the nausea wouldn't let me.

I took Panadol for my head, water for my dry mouth, temazepam to sleep. And whenever the oily feeling spread through me, I stood beneath a scalding shower, willing the feeling to wash itself down the drain. Towelling myself dry, I found that I was still wearing Toby's necklace. My fingers found the jagged edge of a graze around the nape of my neck.

I stared at the necklace, the chain broken, the diamond flung away onto the floor.

In the mirror I saw the line of red around my neck like a collar. A trickle of blood oozed onto my wet skin. Why couldn't I feel it?

~

On Sunday evening, I packed my bag for work, finding my pager, my lanyard, my stethoscope and the leather-bound diary that still had Friday's to-do list pinned to the front with a bulldog clip.

Normally I would fling these objects into my satchel on my way out the door in the morning, but today each task demanded care and concentration. I crept out into the kitchen and filled my water bottle, placing it in the fridge to collect in the morning.

I needed to be ready, because if Benson was leaving soon, then the job interview could be anytime, and that was all I could see.

I would bury the oily feeling: it would not serve me now.

I turned my phone on, and it beeped with missed calls and messages, one from Xander.

I let out a small gasp when I heard his voice.

'Hey, I know that you're out partying, but it's two a.m. now and I've tried to call a few times, so, anyway – I found this song that I thought you might know. Thought it might help you sleep.' He began singing, 'Fa la nanna bambina', and I was taken back to early childhood, lying in bed and Nino singing into the darkness until my eyelids grew heavy.

I swallowed more temazepam, wiped at wet cheeks and climbed under my doona, playing the message on repeat.

~

I didn't know how I was going to manage at work, but with a phone call to Geoffrey's secretary, and through scouring the theatre and outpatient booking lists, I learnt his schedule in public and in private, and it helped me feel calmer being on the ward.

It turned out Benson was making a swift departure, and Prof magnanimously told me he had convinced the hospital exec to fund a replacement. Interviews would be in two weeks. Toby's application at least meant Geoffrey could not be on the panel.

I worked, and prepared for the interview, and in the rare moments when the memories of the gala threatened to move from the edges of my mind towards the centre, I washed my hands in scalding water until my breath calmed and my abdominal muscles relaxed. I took tablets to sleep, and the abrasion on my neck healed and faded.

Prof's secretary called and booked in the interview, and after I heard the words, I closed my eyes and exhaled, a moment of blessed relief. I'd been shortlisted, but even before my next breath, the questions began: who else was being interviewed? Who would be on the panel? Olive or charcoal?

Tess and Maggie were ebullient that the job ad had been posted, and I tried to match their enthusiasm, knowing that excitement would have been my reaction if I wasn't expending so much energy keeping my focus on the here and now. Inside, I limped and ground out those last days, meting out meagre atoms of energy for each task: one more outpatient clinic, one session in theatre, always with an itinerary in my head.

Wherever he was, I was not. I checked the lists a dozen times a day.

I visualised the meeting room where all previous interviews had been held: the lime green chairs, the pastel abstract artworks on the wall. I made a mental note to go with my charcoal suit, which would look smart against the green. I answered questions in my mind, my voice confident, articulate, professional.

I visited my parents more than I ever had, Gina's cooking the only thing I could stomach. She tut-tutted at the red, cracking skin on my fingers and offered me a half-empty tube, creased and wrinkled where she had already pressed out the white anti-fungal cream onto the tinea between her toes.

I wanted to tell her then. *Something happened to me, Ma.* I wanted her to fold me into her chest and smooth my hair, and tell me no one could ever hurt me again. I wanted her to turn her big, big anger onto Geoffrey and make the Chief of Surgery scared to be alive.

I took the useless half-empty tube, and on an impulse, kissed her cheek.

After that, Gina or Luca dropped off ice-cream containers of chicken brodo every few days; it was all my untrustworthy stomach would take.

~

The sharp blue sky made me squint as I left the house, and I was surprised by a flowering daphne from the neighbour's garden, the tiny pink and white flowers sending forth their sweet scent and signalling they'd had enough of winter.

The blossom was an omen, a new beginning.

I walked to work in my charcoal skirt. I tried not to scratch at the skin on my hands.

Morning clinic passed, with too many patients and not enough doctors, and I had one eye on tender abdomens and breast lumps and one on the clock. Each stuttering shift of its hands brought me closer to three pm.

I finished clinic at two and had time to grab a coffee, which I drank on the ground floor. Too much time on six was a risk.

In the bathroom, I brushed my teeth, puzzled by my hollow cheeks.

This was my day, I reminded myself.

With ten minutes to spare, I climbed the stairs and walked left towards the meeting room, but there were drop sheets and scaffolding everywhere. The lime green chairs were stacked four-high against a wall and covered in dust.

A guy in a hardhat walked past me, and I remembered some memo about renovations – had I read something about that?

I spun on my feet and walked the other way, swallowing against a dry throat, trying to recall the instructions from Prof's secretary. Where was I meant to be? I cursed myself for not triple-checking, but I still had seven minutes. Plenty of time.

Only – now I was walking north, towards Prof's office.

I forced my feet forwards, my head dizzyingly light.

Should have had lunch.

I pushed onwards, until I reached Prof's secretary in her alcove outside his office. Her long fingernails pecked at her keyboard.

I asked her where I was meant to be, and she chided me for not checking my messages. She tilted her head towards Prof's office. 'They're all in there.'

I stared at the silver handle on the closed door. My stomach tightened and threatened. I sat on a seat outside, my hands beneath my thighs. The skin on my palms stung in the cracks.

I'd rehearsed answers to every imaginable question, but I'd seen myself in the meeting room, not here, where the fluorescent light buzzed above me. And there, by my shoulder, the light switch.

My fingers, feeling for the wall, and on the wall is a switch.

Finding the light.
Realising I am in the hallway.

A door opened, and I heard voices joking and laughing, and I saw Toby, shaking hands with Prof and Will and two other navy suits. Toby walked towards me with his familiar strut, and as he stopped by my chair, I smelt his aftershave –

'Good luck,' he said, one eyebrow flicking upwards. 'Don't kick anyone in there, will you?'

I thanked him with a mouth-only smile.

Prof spoke to me then. 'Carla, will you be joining us?'

I stood, and through the open door, I saw myself, sitting on the carpet, Geoffrey on the desk, holding me by the hair.

I walked into the room, my gut churning, feeling the burn of eyes from the navy suits on me, while I looked at the floor. Charcoal carpet, my clenched fingers gripping its plush pile. The *tick, tick, tick* of the clock. Behind the desk, Prof's medical degrees mounted on the wall. And the photos of his sons, smiling out at me, while I stared back, knowing –

My clothes, bedraggled. The smell of cologne and sweat on me, the milky taste of his come in my mouth, while in the corner, he dresses, buttoning his cuffs, taking care that the knot in his tie is symmetrical, perfectly positioned in the midline.

I sucked in a breath, but I couldn't get air, and the grimy nausea rose and rose –

'Excuse me, I have to –'

I ran in search of a toilet.

Excision

surgical removal

I lay on my side in the cubicle, my knees curled up to my chest, vomit on my breath.

Some violent tremor invaded my legs, and I had to press my hands on my thighs to stop them shaking.

When I walked back in, Prof's face set in a frown, which deepened when he started with a question about my application. I stumbled over my words, my voice halting and drying up –

There was silence, and a throat clearing.

Mine.

Someone asked me a question, but the meaning was hard to grasp.

Prof's three sons smiled out at me from the photo frame on his desk.

They saw everything.

'I'm sorry,' I said. Every word cost me an effort. 'Could you repeat the question?'

Two navy suits exchanged a look.

~

In the morning, Fleur found me sitting at the kitchen table in the semi-dark, eating Gina's brodo. Outside, rain pelted the window. Fleur turned a light on, took in the patch of red skin I was worrying at on my left knuckle. She spoke to me, but I was somewhere deep within myself, and conversation was out of reach.

'Carla – is something going on?'

Some*thing*?

I repeated the word 'thing' in my head, the harsh 'th' colliding with the finality of the 'ing'. I touched the vertex of my scalp where the hair was growing back.

Th-ing.

Th-ing.

It was, definitely, a th-ing.

But what?

A jittery laugh started deep inside. Once I began, it was hard to stop.

The doorbell rang, and Fleur went to answer it. I swirled my spoon in the bowl and watched the tiny tubes of ditalini swimming in the brodo.

When I looked up, Xander was standing next to Fleur. Sweet, impossible Xander – what was he doing here? He crouched down on his haunches next to me.

'Carla ... what's wrong? Do you think that you could tell me?'

The rain intensified, hammering and knocking on the windows. The fridge hiccuped and resumed its hum.

I pushed away the bowl of half-eaten brodo and felt for the scar on my neck. I held out my hands in front of me on the table and catalogued the state of them – generalised redness, the surface beaded with inflamed skin, rough like cheap toilet paper. Around the joints were the points of weakness, the bending and straightening of my fingers a constant strain on the damaged skin. Here were the cracks, linear breaks that revealed the pink underbelly of connective tissue.

Through the cracks in my fingers, my truth seeped out.

~

'Fuck.'

From Edwina's mouth, spat out with venom. We sat around her lounge room, Maggie and Tess and me, Tess with the adoring dog upon her lap.

I heard my voice, flat and factual: *Geoffrey locked the door to Prof's office and forced me to give him a blow job,* and I was reminded of the emotionless delivery of the medical students on the ward round: *fifty-year-old male, homeless alcoholic, stage four rectal cancer.*

Edwina's vehement *fuck* released a valve and broke the silence, and all three of them spoke at once then, filling the emotional void with their fury, and I watched them and listened and it was nice that they felt that way, but I felt as if I were underground, buried in dirt, like when Luca would bury me in the sand at the beach, my entire body covered, and I would have to lie perfectly still lest I disrupt the damp, gritty cast encasing my body.

Maggie looked at me in concern.

'Do you have somebody taking care of you?'

Practical Maggie – always the nurse. I told her that my housemate Fleur had organised counselling.

She didn't look entirely satisfied. 'And work?'

I shrugged. I had a theatre list with Prof tomorrow, and I hadn't thought past that.

It was Tess who asked about the job, and then the wet, dense sand around me began to crack.

'The interview was in Prof's office. I – I couldn't. It's over.'

In quiet voices they spoke to each other about ways to ensure other female staff were aware of the risk of being alone with Geoffrey, and I sat with my head in my hands as their words washed over me.

Maggie turned to me. 'Would you consider making a complaint?'

Across my chest, the sand cracked and split in two.

'There's no point now, is there? The job's gone.'

'Fuck,' said Edwina, again.

~

A subtotal gastrectomy with Prof would have been a bucket-list moment – a complex surgery, an opportunity to learn from the master – but after the interview, the only way I could front up to the hospital was to shut down so completely that my lips felt numb.

I wanted to wash my hands, feel the scalding water sting the cracks in my skin, and know I was alive. I had trouble following conversations, distracted by the dread in my gut.

I hadn't seen or heard from Prof after the interview. What was there to say? It was a train wreck. I only wondered how all my years of competence and capability weighed up against it.

It took all my effort to quiet the inner thoughts and focus on the gastrectomy. I stared at the white, white walls and let myself be soothed by the low-pitched beep and flow of the anaesthetic machines. I tuned in to Prof's precise movements, and by listening to the conversation between his hands and the body on the table, I was able to anticipate where he needed the retractor and when to be ready with the diathermy.

Afterwards, I was writing up my notes when he came and stood next to me, pushing his glasses up his nose.

'The ... er ... consultant position.'

I looked up at his face and saw the grim set of his mouth. I bowed my head, waiting for the guillotine. My breath drew in, and out.

I looked up again. His mouth was moving but no words came out. He rubbed a hand across the back of his neck. He didn't seem able to say it.

'I didn't get it, did I?'

His face eased then. 'We've made the decision to appoint Toby.'

With a clean strike, my head rolled off, onto the floor, and I stared at it, the hint of a smile still on my face from the moment before all hope was ripped away.

'I know you will be disappointed, but your performance in the interview left us no choice. I imagine it was a bad case of nerves?'

Nerves. Neuroses. The afflictions of women. I stood up.

'No, actually, it was not nerves. Something bad happened to me, Prof – at the gala, and it impacted my performance at the interview.'

'I'm sorry to hear,' he said, in a distant voice that was not sorry at all. 'You seemed to rather enjoy the gala, as best I could tell.'

I rubbed at the scar on my neck.

'Well, there will be other opportunities, of course. We can extend your fellows' position.'

A flat road, dry and dusty, stretched out in front of me: Toby as a consultant, Geoffrey the most powerful surgeon in the hospital, and Prof, preserver of the status quo. I saw myself climbing the stairs, day after day, trudging feet, my calves braced for just one more flight, my lungs hustling air in and out of my chest, hoping I was getting close. Not understanding that no matter how many futile acts of service I fulfilled, or stairs I climbed, I could never reach the peak.

After he left, I traced my steps back into theatre and searched for answers in the empty space. So many times before, I had found what I needed here. But not today.

I walked over to the operating table and put my palms flat on the surface, breathing in the disinfectant. In the corner, I saw my metal step, which brought me to the height of the men. I hated that smug, squat little step.

I thought about standing over Liv at her first surgery, the horror at discovering the flecks of cancer dotting her chest wall; her snowstorm dream, and my triumph at getting her back to theatre. I remembered the hours toiling over Mrs Greenidge, and the relief when she was finally allowed to die.

I went to the change rooms and emptied my locker, unwilling to undress and change. On my way out, I souvenired a scalpel-holder and blade, which I slipped into the pocket of my scrubs.

~

The battle of kids versus a piñata was never a fair contest. Destruction by force, each blindfolded kid wanting to be the one, bashing in turn at the gummy glue of papier-mâché.

Toby's appointment split me open, and once the hole was rent, it grew bigger than any patch could mend.

All I had spent holding myself together I had spent freely. So many tiny moments when all my energy went into preserving myself – Benson touching my butt; Will's humiliating jokes; Prof's put-downs. Even when Geoffrey shoved his putrid old cock in my mouth, I soldiered on, spinning like a battered piñata, still believing I could absorb the blows.

But Toby's appointment proved that it had all been for nothing.

Everything spilt out of me in a rain of chaos then.

~

On the third day after Toby's appointment, I woke up angry. I couldn't traipse around the ward after Toby's smug smile, checking behind me in case Geoffrey lurked in a hallway.

In the bathroom, I applied make-up to the dark circles around my eyes. I glanced down at the space between the bath and the toilet and remembered sucking on the orange lolly, Nonno's heaviness and my own inability to speak.

That would not serve me today.

I needed to finish what I'd started, but I would need help getting back. It made me vomit just imagining the hospital steps – the cold concrete, the steep ascent to the pointed finger of the main building. I called Maggie and Tess, and they agreed to meet me there.

The clouded sky gave off a diffused, soft light as I walked the familiar path to work. I couldn't see the sun. A cluster of cyclists hustled past in lycra, and miner birds screeched a conversation as I passed the zoo.

I searched the eucalypts for the know-it-all cockatoos, but their branches were empty.

My satchel was light on my shoulder, containing only my stethoscope, a half-empty water bottle, my phone.

My dogged steps drew me towards the hospital. On the steps, Tess and Maggie waited with funereal faces, and we walked, one on each side of me, to the stairwell, where we fell into single file and climbed to the sixth floor. Once in the hallway that led to Prof's office, Tess squeezed my arm and whispered, 'We are right here, we've got your back,' and Maggie gave me a fierce nod.

While Tess and Maggie stood near the stairwell trying not to watch, I paced the hall, my lips rehearsing the words. When I got close to the door, my breath was snatched away and my body froze, and I had to gather myself, and try again. I felt like a kid trying to muster the courage to jump into the water from a height. On my fourth attempt, I muttered *my truth, my truth,* and my feet marched to the beat, and I ignored Prof's secretary telling me I couldn't go in. Without knocking, I opened the door.

I was hoping Prof would be on his own, but the room was as full as it had been for the interview. Shoulders ensconced in navy suits turned at the disruption. Eyes, framed by furrowed brows, zeroed on me.

And in one corner was Geoffrey, in the best cut suit, straightening his torso in his seat, his tie perfectly tied. He smiled lazily when he saw me.

My breath caught and my stomach turned, and the room swooned as if gravity had lost her hold.

I steadied myself against the wall, remembering Tess and Maggie outside. *We've got your back.*

'Carla – is this urgent?' Prof asked. 'We're in the middle of a meeting.'

It was too late to go back now, and even if I did retreat, where would I go? I was barely able to hold down a coffee, let alone see patients and open them up. I had no future beyond this moment, and if I did not speak, then everything I had worked for meant nothing.

I focused on the framed degrees on Prof's wall.

'I have something ... I need to say.' My tongue moistened my parched lips. 'I love surgery. It is my life's dream to work in this hospital. I gave everything I could to work here.'

A cough. Someone shifted in their chair.

'But I can't anymore.'

I breathed in, and with the exhale, I pushed out the words.

'I was assaulted, here – in this hospital. By a staff member.' I did not look at Geoffrey, but I felt his eyes on me.

Looking down at me sprawled on the carpet, smelling of sweat and come, while he zipped up his trousers, knotted his tie.

I pressed my palms to my thighs to stop the shaking, and I tunnelled myself deep inside my body. He could not hurt me now.

Prof rose, his face alarmed. He held up his palm, but I shook my head.

'Please, let me finish ... it won't take long. The thing I want you to know is that this place is made for men. For men, by men. If you want women to thrive here, *you* must change that.

'Each of you here has stood by and done nothing. Where were you? You might not have committed sexual assault, but you built a hospital where women watch their backs. When we speak up, we're told to be more professional. Less bossy. Less emotional. Less maternal. What you're really saying is, be more like *me*. Which is no solution for a woman.

'I'm a surgeon, and I'm leaving. And you should think about why it is that a surgeon can't work in this place, and what you can do about it.'

Then I took my time to eyeball each man in the room, starting with Prof and working my way right, ignoring whether they returned the look, or squirmed, or even smirked. I finished with Geoffrey. Tiny beads of sweat formed where his hairline met his forehead.

And then I walked.

AFTERMATH
Vasovagal syncope

a sudden drop in heart rate and blood pressure leading to fainting, often in reaction to a stressful trigger

The furthest star of the Southern Cross is Delta Crucis, a mere 364 light years away. In the year I was fallow, light from Delta Crucis 364 years prior traversed the vast expanses of space to reach my overtired, underslept, burnt-out retina through the window of my room when I was meant to be sleeping. I spent many nights that year staring at the starlight through the open window. I thought about the path of that light, and the lives that began and ended while it travelled the skies.

The 364 days I was fallow were accompanied by La Niña, and the rain seemed to follow me, soaking the grass until it was sodden underfoot, pattering the window and sliding down the glass.

It took what felt like 364 hours of therapy to feel safe enough to cry, but once I started, I couldn't stop. I was my own private weather system, tears sliding down my cheeks and into my ears, and my nose running snot into my mouth and on and on. I asked my therapist, Nate, when it would stop, fearing the answer might be never, and he promised me I wouldn't always feel like this, but added he didn't know when, and I told him that as a weatherman, he was pretty shit.

In the time I did not go to work, billions of ants scurried the earth, making up for my inaction with their busyness. Hundreds of new surgical residents woke before dawn and went to bed dreaming of tying the perfect suture under their consultant's watchful eye, and woke with their fingers looping imaginary thread around an invisible needle before securing the knot, tight.

I had to learn to eat again. Gina made litres of brodo, and that was my safe place to start, but anything eggy or milky reminded me of the taste of him and then I was back there, on the carpet, feeling small, and my stomach was the first part of me to say no.

All kinds of things took me back there – the ripping sound of a zip being undone, the buzzing of a fly that echoed the *zzzz* noise from the fluorescent light in the hospital hallway.

Nate convinced me to keep a diary and write down what was causing the panic. Memories of the night came in short, disconnected snatches, and I wrote them, and they began to come together like a jumper knitted by a beginner – many dropped stitches and a few gaping holes.

It was always possible to report the crime, Nate told me, but too late to collect any meaningful evidence. If we ended up in court, I would have to trudge through the mud that was he-said, she-said. He didn't spell it out, but I could imagine how a jury would view my evidence against a respected Chief of Surgery, when I'd just missed out on a job that was awarded to his son – who happened to be my ex. I could see the knowing smirks of a jury when they heard about the places where Toby and I had fucked.

I stifled my growing resentment and kept writing.

The week after I burst into his office, Prof telephoned me. He told me he was in the presence of someone from HR, and he asked me if I planned to make a formal complaint. Stunned by the sound of his gravelly voice, I concentrated on holding the phone to my ear without dropping it.

Some days I almost didn't get out of bed, saved only by a full bladder, which drove me to the bathroom. Some days I almost caved, deciding surgery wasn't for me, but my hands itched and burnt in protest. Some days I wished Saint Jude would step in, as I was sure I met criteria for lost causes, but that would require me to buy into the whole God thing, and I couldn't. Some days I wished I hadn't spoken up, but if I were unpicking stitches, where would I stop – standing up for Tess? Liv's surgery? No regrets, I decided – more a wish that the outcome was different, and over that, I had no control.

A few months after the gala, I sat at the kitchen table with Luca, Gina and Nino, and, over a plate of pasta, I told them.

Gina flew into a frenzy and ran to the kitchen, dumping flour and water onto the bench and, even though we were in the middle of dinner, began working them into a dough. I could hear her muttering to herself about *sacrifice* and *no place for a woman* and *they treat her like this, after everything she's done*. Luca hugged me hard, and Nino's breath grew shallow as he held his face together.

Later, I went to Gina and offered to help her, and she told me I was useless with the dough and rested her head on me.

A few weeks later, Nino cajoled me into visiting him at work and led me to the cool room and gave me simple jobs to do. I found pleasure in hacking and splitting and chopping and finessing the carcasses into cuts of meat. As the blade divided the muscle fibres, I saw the fascia and connective tissue and tendons, and I traced the veins coursing through the muscle. The technical challenge was enough for a time and Nino's presence soothed me, but I yearned to feel the pulse of a patient under my fingertips and the fire in my belly when I knew what to do to restore them to health.

One day I was changing after a run, and I found a set of scrubs scrunched into a ball in the bottom of my wardrobe, and, in the pocket, a scalpel, the blade still wrapped in its plastic packet from when I souvenired it after my last list. I slipped the scalpel into a pen box and took to carrying her with me, and when I needed a reminder of where I was heading, opened the pen box, feeling the hinge give way to reveal her silver blade sharpened to a point.

Every few weeks, Tess and Maggie and I met at a quiet pub in North Carlton, with red patterned carpet and sticky brown Laminex tables. They didn't labour the point, but not much changed after I left. Benson had finished up, Toby was installed as a consultant and Geoffrey continued on his merry way.

Regrettably, Maggie told me, my departure speech had not precipitated any male soul-searching. As she complained about her latest batch of nursing students who wore fake eyelashes and didn't want to change a bed pan in case it damaged their acrylic nails, I wondered if soul-searching was even possible for those men.

Lachlan had asked after me, Tess said, and expressed concern that I had left, the same day that he invited Tess to play golf with him and Will.

I told her she had to go, that she had to beat them and show me the scorecard.

I told them how I missed leading the pack of doctors and nurses on the round, being the one who knew the pulse of the ward – which patient was ready for home, and which was not. I missed the rhythm of theatre, the busyness of a case and the lull in between. The moment when you placed the final suture and stood back from the table.

Tess spoke then. 'Carla? I want you to know something ... I've been offered an accredited place, for next year.'

I smiled, and tried to speak, and goddammit if the tears didn't take over, and I promised her they were happy ones. Tess getting on the program was an achievement after what she'd been through, and I told her I was proud.

She reached for her hair, her fingers making a twirling motion in the air, and I wondered if they were searching for her long-lost curls.

'I'm not sure yet, if I'll accept.'

I stared at her. Was she mad?

'It doesn't feel right ... without you there.'

At that the tears began to flow. I sat and waited for them to slow, and then I spoke.

'Tess, you *have* to take it.'

'I just don't know if I can survive there, the way it is.'

She sighed and stretched her arms overhead, triceps elongating, palms facing upwards, and then fanning out and down to her sides.

'I just – I want to be somewhere that is patient-centred, first and foremost. Somewhere there would be just punishment for men who assaulted women.'

'And for the men who protect other men,' Maggie said. 'Take them out and stone them.'

We laughed, and then worried she might be serious.

I asked Tess to promise me she would take the job, and she promised me she would think about it.

~

The next month, Edwina offered me sessions at Spotswood Private every Thursday. I accepted, biting the inside of my cheek, feeling for the scalpel in my bag.

I didn't know how I would feel returning to operating, but turned out my body remembered the moves, and it was a relief to have my hands busy and get outside my own head. To do something knowing that no one would ask about my *feelings*. Edwina let me do as much as I felt able, and I got a deep, melancholy joy from seeing an incision neatly sutured, edges apposed, dressing applied, white cells already migrating to the wound, martialling the troops, healing already begun.

I was good at this, I remembered, and it made me happy.

I talked with Nate about how I could return to work. Edwina had sessions for me in private for as long as I wanted, but I craved the bustle of a team. Nate asked, what about another hospital? I twisted my mouth while I thought about this.

He listened, and waited, and in a small voice, I told him.

'I want justice.'

He told me that a workplace complaint was worth considering – less confrontational than the courts, an investigation which would typically take weeks rather than months or years. It was still my word against Geoffrey's, of course, but the idea stayed with me, a nervous friend at my shoulder as I wrote in my diary and assisted Edwina and met with Tess and Maggie and had dinner with my family.

On the 365th day, I jogged around the zoo, ignoring the raucous laugh of the cheeky sulphur-crested cockatoo, whose yellow comb fanned out splendidly. As the jagged pointing finger of the tallest PCH building came into view, my nervous friend whispered, *you know you're not done with them. Not yet.*

~

A week later, I perched on a stool in a cafe looking out on a quiet Brunswick side street, with Anthea next to me.

Was it okay, to ask for her help? She was my patient's partner. But Liv was no longer my patient, and Anthea knew the world I worked in.

And I had questions.

'I'm glad you suggested meeting outside the hospital,' she said, twisting her legs around each other like strands of spaghetti.

I explained that I wasn't working there anymore, and she tilted her head, waiting. I asked her if I could get her legal opinion on something, and she said of course. I handed her my written account and she read it. The cracked skin on my fingers itched and burnt.

'Was this the night that – I saw you? In the lift?'

I nodded. *Next to the steel doors of the lift was a tall woman, texting furiously on her phone.*

'I knew something wasn't right. I should have – intervened.'

I shook my head. Too late, at that point.

'Not to stop what happened – although I would have loved to – but to help you as a witness. Now it's his word against yours.'

'I'm going to lodge a complaint. At PCH.'

'Okay.' She spoke for a bit about the process, how Geoffrey would likely be suspended, at least until the investigation was complete.

I pursed my lips into a smile. Okay, that did feel good.

'One thing to consider is that it might become public knowledge. Once he's suspended, people will ask questions. And be prepared for your private life to become public – old relationships, that kind of thing.' She unwound her legs and planted her feet on the lower bar of the stool. 'You sure you're up for this?'

I drank my coffee and told her about Toby, and she winced.

'They will use that; I have no doubt.' She shook her head. 'Collect any dirt on him you can find. On both of them.'

Between Maggie and Tess, I was pretty sure we'd be able to dig up something.

~

In the summer, Xander sang to me, and he kept singing even when the leaves changed colour. By the time June frosts were upon us, and the trees were bare-limbed, I couldn't imagine being without his music. He sang songs of comfort, and his voice felt like a shawl draped gently over my shoulders, holding me. I still recoiled from touch, but it made me feel held nonetheless.

I had bad days, when I believed everything I had worked for was for nothing, and then we would jump in the car and seek out waves.

One such Sunday, he drove us south until we reached Gunnamatta, where the beach stretched wide and long. Above me was a vast, crisp sky. Stripping down to my bathers, I slapped at a sand-fly loitering on my leg and put on my wetsuit. At the water's edge, I dug my toes into the coarse sand as cold water rushed over my feet. Next to me, seagulls danced on dainty legs. A teenager lolled around on his belly in the shallow water, lazy as a seal.

We swam, and the cold stole my breath and the water stung my cracked fingers. I dived under dumping waves, the water pummelling my back. My ears filled with water and the cold emptied my head.

Sometimes, when a wave curled up in front of me, threatening to break, I would turn and paddle furiously and then shape myself into a torpedo, coasting on the crest of water, a few blissful seconds of effortless motion as the wave carried me and deposited me on the shore.

I did it over and over.

We were like two kids playing alongside each other in the sand, sharing the shovel and passing a cup of sand this way and that, and even running down to the water's edge to fill a bucket for the other, but never actually talking about *us*.

When I could no longer feel fingers and toes, I sat on the sand wrapped in a towel staring out at the hazy horizon. Beneath it, over and over, a glacial swell rose and crested and broke before the tide sucked the water back. The ocean's breath.

Xander paddled out for another wave, his hair slicked back in long, wet curls and his body sleek in his wetsuit. He joined the other surfers dotting the swell like pinpoints of black and then he had to wait, because the sea glistened flat for a few minutes. When a wave appeared that he liked, he paddled fast, then turned his board into it, getting to his feet and riding the wave close to its highest point, twisting with it as it closed in on him, and as the foam crashed down, he gave himself up to it.

I watched him, feeling the pounding of my heart, and the warm, familiar desire in my chest, and, for a moment, I let myself back into my body. I longed for his hands, which held on to his board, his strong musician fingers, to cup my face. For his eyes to lose their doubt and not look away. I longed to feel his skin under my fingertips, his forearms, his shoulders, his back.

I waited for the oily slick of shame that spread through me whenever I felt something for Xander. It had kept me stuck here, longing for the day when the damage done to me was less important than living my life. I dug my toes deep into the sand and held myself still, fearing that the stench of Geoffrey would always be with me, sullying any chance of happiness.

A wave crashed to the shore and receded, the water glassy on the sand. And another. Crash, recede. Crash, recede. Here, perched at the edge of the ocean, I didn't smell or taste Geoffrey.

I knew he wasn't gone, that perhaps he would always be with me.

But I wondered ... had the sea returned me to myself?

~

The next day, late in the afternoon, when I could no longer pace the house and rehearse the words, I asked Xander to come with me for a walk. We strolled in parkland through long grass. My thoughts jumbled and jostled for space. The sun cast long shadows with her horizontal rays. Our shadows stretched out ahead of us, two people walking close but not touching, side by side.

A massive Moreton Bay fig tree had branches fanning up, and out, and down almost to the ground, covered in an enormous ballooning skirt of leaves. I led us to the space under the tree and stopped there. Xander watched me, a question in his eyes.

'Here's the thing,' I said, and then I stopped, because what was the thing? I didn't know how to name my long list of doubts, but I wanted him to know how I longed for him. 'I don't know – when I'll be okay.'

He waited, calm and still.

I fidgeted with my sleeve. 'So, it's probably crazy to do this, but – I want you to know that if you – well, if you still wanted to try *us*, then – I want to ... only, I can't promise how I'll be –'

My voice cracked. He took my hand and held it, and the warmth of his skin reminded me, *this*.

'I want you in my life. I want to try – us. If you do, that is.'

Under our tree umbrella, my words hung in the air.

'Us?'

He looked down at his feet, and I wished my words back. Then he looked at me and his eyes were smiling. 'You do know I'm not your type?'

A smile snuck through my pressed lips. 'I've evolved.'

'I'm impressed.'

'Just – I don't know ... we may need to be patient.'

'Carla ... I've been waiting ever since that night on the cobblestones.'

With dappled light scattered over us, under a glorious umbrella of olive leaves, I kissed him.

Healing by secondary intention

the healing of a wound in which the edges cannot be apposed

Jamie from HR was a twenty-something woman with a suspiciously expressionless forehead. When I explained my complaint, she used all the right phrases, but her mechanical delivery left me wondering if she was reading from a script. She spoke reverently about the process, and I listened, trying not to focus on whether her forehead would move.

The complaint precipitated an investigation, and a few days later, a card arrived from Hamish.

> Dear Carla,
> I truly am sorry for my behaviour at the gala. I was mortified afterwards that I had embarrassed you. And now, knowing everything you were subject to — I'm so sorry. For everything. It is not the standard I expect from myself, and I should not have subjected you to that. The fact that I was in something of a bad way is not an excuse, but it did prevent me from seeing the impact of my behaviour on you.
>
> I should have contacted you earlier, but I have been on extended leave. In fact, I went to Germany, which was an olive branch of sorts with Ursula. It opened my eyes to what she endured every day with James. We're on the mend, I believe. James's diagnosis — well, it

has taken quite some adjustment, but I'm learning how to show that I care for him. I want him to grow up knowing that.

If you will accept it, I would like to support you any way I can. I know you well enough to believe that an injustice has been done. I don't want to stand by and allow it to happen.

Yours,

Hamish

I sat with his card in my hands for some time. The apology would have been enough to let me move on from his behaviour at the gala, but the line that tore at me was this: *I know you well enough to believe an injustice has been done.* In a strange way, it had always been Hamish who had seen me.

Tess delighted in telling me that Geoffrey had indeed been stood down. No small thing, for the Chief of Surgery. I waited, then, but no other women came forward. I hoped it was because he hadn't hurt anybody else. Deep down I knew that being a lone voice had left me vulnerable.

Tess also let me know that Lachlan had approached her, offering me support. Was I okay with that? I remembered my conversation with Lachlan and assured her that I was.

~

Two weeks later, Jamie sat opposite me in her office. She told me that due process had been followed, and I braced myself then, because I had started bad-news conversations with patients with the same kind of nothing statement.

Jamie's forehead stayed still as she said, 'The investigation found no evidence to substantiate your allegation. Several of your team mentioned you had been under a lot of strain. You know, the Doctors Wellbeing Program could be of assistance –'

'I was under strain,' I said, my voice tight in my throat, 'because I was assaulted.'

'One of your colleagues mentioned the consultant job, which I can imagine must have been very stressful for you. And another said something about a surgery that went wrong?'

The room began to spin. I gripped the sides of the chair, feeling as though I might fall.

They were using Liv against me.

'And no one could independently verify that Geoffrey was ever on the sixth floor that night. His colleagues said he was at the dinner for the entire evening.'

The plastic chair frame could no longer keep me steady, and I reached for the edge of Jamie's desk. 'He was in Prof's office.'

'He disputes this. And Mr Benson says he never found you a chair, or touched you, inappropriately or otherwise. As you're aware, he has retired now, so he would have no reason to lie.'

That's when I knew the stitch-up was complete.

~

Tess and Maggie organised to meet the next Sunday afternoon at the Rainbow Hotel. As I entered the courtyard, a band played lazy jazz in one corner. I found Tess and Maggie at a table, and stopped dead when I saw Fleur and Xander sitting next to them. Across the table, I saw Edwina and her auburn bob, Anthea armed with a folder of notes, Hamish in a buttoned collar shirt and fine woollen jumper, and Lachlan, the only one who looked remotely at home in jeans and a striped tee.

'Come and meet your war council,' Tess said, pursing her lips into a pleased smile. She pinned a felt brooch to my shirt. 'I made these so we could show our solidarity.'

The brooch had a black background, and embroidered on it were gum leaves and the downward spray of petals of a red flowering gum. I ran my fingers over the embroidered surface of the brooch. I thought about all those breakfasts when Toby and Will had parried and parroted and poked fun at Hamish and sometimes me, and how strongly I had believed that they were my clan, my surgical brothers.

I took a second look around the table, and everyone – even Hamish – wore a brooch. These people were here for *me*. They wanted something different for me.

My breath caught in my larynx, and I sipped water before speaking.

'I want to start by thanking you all for coming. I'm overwhelmed by it, actually. I'm weighing up my options for what to do next, but I want you to know that I am not finished at PCH. I'm not letting that decision be the last of me – hell, no.'

Edwina inclined her queenly bob at me and nodded into her beer.

'I want to be able to go back there and hold my head high.'

A flurry of voices spoke then, one calling for action at the college and another asking about legal options. I let the buzz of conversation wash over me, like a baptising tide. Inside my handbag, the steel of my scalpel burnt.

~

I hadn't believed Edwina when she warned me that college committees worked at a glacial pace. How could they sit on a compelling submission, authored by Anthea with contributions from the war council, which detailed multiple threads of evidence of systemic failure at PCH?

It took the long months passing for me to realise she was right.

I took her advice and enrolled in a short course in simulation training, and when I had completed that, I began a certificate in medical education. My previous training as a teacher had consisted of the medical mantra *see one, do one, teach one*. I enjoyed discovering a complex theoretical system underpinning medical teaching, and once I had disentangled what I had learnt from Benson and Prof from my sense of the men themselves, I was able to integrate the best of my training into that.

And as days rolled into weeks and months, I reminded myself that whatever the outcome, I had done what I set out to do: stand up. What the college chose to do with that information was out of my control and, most likely, within Prof and Geoffrey's sphere of influence.

~

One Wednesday in April, I found the broken necklace when I was cleaning the bathroom, hidden under the curved drainpipe between the toilet and the wall. The chain had snapped, and the diamond was coated in dust.

I sat in the tiny square of space between the toilet and the bath with my back against the wall and my knees tucked under my chin. I remembered sitting there next to Nonno's still body, sucking on the orange lolly and feeling scared.

I cupped the diamond in my hand, feeling its bevelled edges against my palm, picturing the carbon atoms held tight in their covalent bonds. I imagined what it would feel like to crunch it under my heel, my weight grinding it into the dirt, the splintering sound as the stone shattered, the sparkle of the fragments on the tiles.

Instead, I put it in my satchel.

I might need it, and anyway, as I knew from experience, diamond was tougher than skin.

The following week, an unmarked A4 envelope arrived for me in the post and, before opening it, I scrutinised the handwriting – long, slanted, cursive letters, unfamiliar to me.

Inside was a manila folder and a piece of letterhead embossed with the Tennysons' address.

I spent my childhood watching him size up and proposition the most attractive woman in the room, who was never his wife. For years, I witnessed him take what he wanted with no regard for the hurt he caused — and watched my brother follow in his footsteps. Consider this my contribution to your cause but, in truth, I am doing this for me, and for my mother, and for all women. Enclosed is a folder found in Geoffrey's home office. Please protect my identity if you're able.
Miranda

I sat down at the kitchen table and placed Miranda's note next to the folder, my hands trembling. Inside the manila folder were multiple loose-leafed papers, all dated in Prof's hand. I saw his heavy ballpoint pen poised over Anthea's letter itemising their concerns about Toby's care. There were other complaints too, one from a nurse about a late-night interaction with Toby, which was subsequently withdrawn, and a letter from a patient who felt belittled by Toby scrolling on his phone while she described her struggle with anxiety.

I had never stopped to wonder what Geoffrey was looking for in Prof's office that night; why he seemed so relieved that it wasn't Prof who found him rummaging through those files. I guessed these complaints never made it through the formal channels and so this file was the key. At some point, Geoffrey must have stopped trusting that Prof would protect Toby.

I read and reread Miranda's letter, until the long, cursive letters were imprinted on my brain.

Miranda had delivered us a critical piece of evidence, Anthea told me later, and we submitted a second report to the college. When we had still heard nothing by June, we launched a media campaign, run by Tess and Lachlan from an anonymous Twitter account, questioning why the college was sitting on evidence of systematic misogyny at one of Melbourne's largest hospitals.

In the first week of July, the college announced an inquiry into surgery at PCH, leaving Anthea to mutter that Twitter was the new judge and jury.

I visited Liv in day oncology, because I wanted to see her, and I was ready to test myself, and I wanted to deliver a massive *fuck you, I'm still here* to Prof and Geoffrey and anyone else who might hear I was in the building. As I walked through the hospital halls, I had a disorientating sense of familiarity and difference. I couldn't place what had changed, until I realised that the difference was me.

Liv was knitting what she called her survival shawl with oversized wooden needles and burnt orange wool.

'I decided it was time I learnt to knit,' she said, and in her grave brown eyes I glimpsed her awareness of the uncertainty of her future. We talked about her treatment, and she told me she'd had a good response to the trial drug and would stay on it as long as she could.

'Guess it's not placebo, then?'

With every cell in my body, I hoped not.

'I set myself little goals,' she said. 'Rosy's sixtieth, and Christmas. And now, I want to be around to see you back here as a doctor.'

'I'm not sure that that will happen.'

'So, a good goal for a cancer patient, right?'

She told me Anthea was determined to screw those men over, and *hard*, and I remembered Anthea's ferocity when Liv was in ICU.

'Those men do *not* know what they're taking on,' I said, and we shared a quiet laugh.

Fleur was looking ahead, too. One evening, we stood out on the balcony among the bare winter branches of the plane trees. She had exhausted every possibility on Candour, she told me. She was not going back to Richard and his angst. She confided that she'd had an initial assessment with an IVF specialist to explore her options.

'Turns out, I'm all in order, where fertility is concerned.' She leant on the wooden balcony and looked sideways at me. 'I'm going with a sperm donor.'

I took a minute to digest her news.

'You're going to have a baby?' I asked, smiling hard, and she grinned.

'Yep.'

'I'm going to be so, so proud to be an aunty.'

She crossed the fingers of both hands, and we looked at each other and laughed, tears in her eyes and in mine.

~

In August, winter dragged its heels like a tired toddler, and I worked with Edwina, studied medical education and spent more time with Xander. I had days where I didn't think about PCH and my career-that-was, and nights where I couldn't think about anything else. Tess rang me one evening, her voice breathless.

'Prof's gone,' she said.

I had to ask her to repeat herself.

'Gone. Retired. No one knows why, or what's coming next.'

I felt myself fold inwards. I heard his gravelly voice calling me down to dissect when I was a medical student and saw his exquisite surgical skill. I heard his gaslighting of Tess, and the day he informed me that he'd appointed Toby, despite everything he knew was in Toby's file.

After I hung up from Tess, I danced and hollered around the living room, before coming to a halt. Why Prof, and not Geoffrey?

Two hours later, the war council gathered at my house, everyone except Edwina, who sent a cryptic message advising we gather at five and keep the news channel on. Everyone had a theory as to what had happened.

On the news, we watched a joint press conference held by the head of the College of Surgeons, the CEO of PCH and the head of the

Australian Health Practitioner Registration Authority, announcing that they had found evidence of a sexist culture and workplace in the department of surgery at PCH. They named Benson and Geoffrey as two of the alleged perpetrators.

Then the camera panned out, and sitting next to the head of the College and AHPRA was Edwina, her bob immaculate. The hospital CEO announced Edwina as the next Chair of Surgery, and as we hollered and cheered, Edwina calmly fielded questions about how she planned to clean up the hospital culture.

'I will be asking people to commit to a new culture of respect,' Edwina said, 'and if they are unable to do that, we will be bringing in new blood.'

She looked down the barrel of the camera then, and I knew she was speaking to me.

Two months later

There was only one skirt I would wear on 16 October 2017. I walked the path by the zoo in my olive pencil skirt, the high-pitched pinging call of the bell miner heralding my return. As I ascended the hill, I smelt the stench of elephant shit, and I got in first with the cockatoos.

I told you I could do this, I said to them, and they squawked back, *not the way you planned*, before fanning their yellow combs at me, spreading their wings and taking flight.

I breathed in eucalyptus and smiled. A frost left a faint dew on the grass, droplets of water like tiny pearls on the tips of each blade. Ahead of me lay the higgledy-piggledy sprawl of the hospital buildings, the pointed finger of the main block, the red bricks and cream mortar, still steeped in heritage and oozing prestige. But these buildings no longer housed Benson, or Prof, or Geoffrey. Edwina was in charge, and it changed everything. My steps quickened, and caffeine buzzed in my veins. I was hungry for this.

At the top of the hill, I took a call from Tess, who was already in at the hospital.

'Two things,' she said, her voice breathless. 'No, three! First – welcome back, Carla! Your first day as a consultant! You're officially a PCH surgeon.'

Her words reverberated around my head, through my bones down to the marrow. A PCH surgeon. *I am a PCH surgeon.*

Tess kept talking. 'You've waited for this day for so long – I'm that excited, I can barely talk. Now, do you think you could do an extra list this afternoon? We're down one surgeon.'

'No problem! Awesome! Amazing!'

Truth was, if someone rostered me onto theatre for three days straight, I would have agreed. Edwina had warned me to expect some instability, as they weeded out the dead wood. For now, Will and Toby were staying on. I wished I didn't have to deal with Toby, but he existed now in a universe where his every action would be scrutinised.

'So ... do you want to know what happened?' Tess barely stopped to hear my answer. 'Over the weekend, one of the nurses on the ward was helping Toby with a catheter, and afterwards he came on to her in the quiet room, and she stabbed him in the hand!'

I froze at the foot of the hospital steps, and for a moment I was back there in the quiet room with the vinyl chairs and Toby's hard-on, ignoring the plaintive beep of his pager. A wave of shame. It would pass.

I remembered Maggie's strategy to protect nurses against *certain* surgeons. 'Scissors?'

'Yep. Right hand. Severed two tendons.'

I closed my eyes and inhaled deeply through my nose, exhaling out a massive exultant roar, which started from my gut and filled my chest with grunt and grandeur, and I kept going until my breath was spent. It was loud enough to startle the early morning smokers leaning against the brick wall of the hospital, who were not used to expressions of emotion from medical staff.

Still on the phone, Tess laughed. 'I know, right? I don't wish ill on the guy, but, man – he deserved it. At the very least he'll watch where he puts his hands next time.'

I laughed.

'So ... one more thing. Have you seen what has happened in the US overnight? Some actresses have come out publicly about sexual assault in their industry, and it has gone nuts – millions of posts from other women, calling it out. You're part of something bigger, Carla. The whole world is waking up to this shit.

'Anyway, we can talk later. See you in theatre, Ms di Pieta!'

I looked online and my breath caught as I saw post after post, tagged #metoo.

~

Under my feet, the concrete was worn smooth, indented by years of foot traffic, and I imagined the trudging steps of generations of women who had been here before, heavy with what they had to endure to survive a shift – women who were nurses and theatre techs and doctors, compromising and fitting in, ignoring their skin crawling and pretending it didn't bother them to be touched, to be other, to be less.

I pulled my stethoscope from my bag and slung it around my neck, and the weight of it helped anchor me to the here and now. There would be patients who needed me today. I thought of Prof and Benson and Geoffrey, and I deposited them on these concrete steps, alongside the bird shit and discarded cigarette butts. I paid homage to Liv and Mrs Greenidge and all my patients, for retaining their humanity, for refusing to be complacent and compliant.

I took a last look skywards at the pointed finger of the main building above. Slowly, with deliberate steps, with the women who came before and the women who said, *no more*, I walked into the hospital, scalpel in my pocket.

Acknowledgements

In my years of working on *Cut*, I sought the essence of the story like a dog turning circles on its mat, trying to find *the* place to rest. I'm grateful to all the people whose belief sustained me while I tried to figure out what this book wanted to be: Olga Lorenzo and Toni Jordan, the RMIT lecturers who nourished me as an early writer; my circle of first readers, Samarra Hyde, Kate Goldsworthy, Tina Gamble and Lauren Draper, all talented writers who read and reread with generous honesty and supported me always. Thank you to Sarah Sentilles, who encouraged me to write words my soul knew to be true. Many of my favourite passages in this book were written in Sarah's amazing workshops.

Perhaps the day I truly began to believe in myself as a writer was when *Cut* was shortlisted for the *Kill Your Darlings* Unpublished Manuscript Award, and I'm grateful to Rebecca Starford and the KYD team for this recognition and for investing time and energy in unpublished writers.

And then, to the magnificent team at Affirm, whose passion for my book helped me realise its potential. Special thanks to Kelly Doust, who taught me so much and was a complete joy to work with. Huge appreciation to Sandy Cull for the edgy, atmospheric cover, which I love. I'm grateful for the expert editing of Jessica Friedmann and Kevin O'Brien, the astute marketing and publicity work of Bonnie Tai van Dorp and Rosanna Hunt, and the wise leadership of Martin Hughes and Keiran Rogers.

I was especially fortunate to draw upon the expertise of health-professional friends and family when I reached the limits of my knowledge. Thanks to Michelle White, Tyron Crofts, Jasmina Kevric, Liz McLeod, Renee Fitzpatrick, Hannah Matthiesson and Ian Summers, and several other doctors who gave me advice but would prefer not to be named. Any errors of fact are mine.

Writing about misogyny in medicine while working as a doctor has at times challenged me, and I'm so grateful to family and friends for their counsel. To Carolyn Worth from the Centre for Sexual Assault, your generous advice helped me enormously – thank you.

My heart holds huge gratitude and love to my family: my mum, who fed my reading habit with regular library trips; my dad, who is no longer with us in body but whose determination and zest to get shit done is with me each day when I get up at dawn to write; my sister and brothers, who tolerated incessant book chatter and kept an eye out for hazards while I read on our walk to and from school, in church, at the dinner table and any other time I could get away with it; my daughter Amy and son Eddy, who bring me so much joy; and to my husband, Ivan, for his support, belief, patience and love.

To all women in health care, my wish is that somewhere in the pages of this novel you will know that you are seen, valued and understood. May we strive for a system and culture that bring the best of humanity to the care for our patients, and for each other.

Reading Group Questions

1. In *Cut*, Carla wrestles with how to manage the bond she develops with Liv and her family. She knows her colleagues would disapprove. How do you think doctors should deal with their boundaries around patients? Should they show vulnerability? What is the cost if they do or don't?
2. Is Carla a feminist? Why or why not?
3. Carla experiences a sexual assault in a system that tacitly condones misogyny. Do you believe the system played a role in her assault, or should be held responsible in any way? How?
4. Carla and Tess conceive a plot to nominate Benson for the Casterton as a way to get rid of him, even though they know that, if successful, they will be celebrating a man who gropes women at work. What do you think of that? Do the ends justify the means?
5. In medical school, the intake of students is 50:50 male and female, and yet, many public hospital hierarchies remain dominated by males. How might that influence the culture?
6. How does unconscious bias shape Carla's views of the men in her life?
7. Respecting a patient's wish to die can be confronting for health professionals. How do Prof's beliefs influence the care of Mrs Greenidge? Was her final surgery justified?

8. When Liv arrests on the operating table, Carla thinks, 'this train wreck of a mastectomy could jeopardise my job'. Should doctors be thinking of themselves when a patient's life is at risk?
9. Xander knew about Toby's history of rape from uni days, and yet elected to initially say nothing, at least in part out of respect for the woman involved. Should he have spoken up earlier?
10. How does generational change influence the different responses of Maggie, Tess and Carla to misogyny? How might the newer generation of men and women respond?